Warrior Class Taming the Wind

Other Books by S. L. Kassidy

Warrior Class
Sky Cutter

Please Baby

Scarred Series
Scarred for Life - Book 1
New Cuts, Old Wounds – Book 2
Bandages – Book 3
First Degree Burns - Book 4
Learning to Walk Again – Book 5

Warrior Class Taming the Wind

S.L. Kassidy

Desert Palm Press

Taming The Wind
Warrior Class – Book 2

By S. L. Kassidy

©2019 S.L. Kassidy

ISBN (trade) 9781948327503
ISBN (epub) 9781948327527
SBN (pdf) 9781948327527

Desert Palm Press
1961 Main Street, Suite 220
Watsonville, California 95076
www.desertpalmpress.com

Editor: Kellie Doherty
Cover Design: Jamani Hawkins-El (http://www.maddrandom.com)

Printed in the United States of America
First Edition December 2019

Dedication

This book is dedicated to my family, who supported my writing long before I thought it was worth anything, and to my friends, who helped me believe in myself and my work. Thank you all.

.

Chapter One

IT HAD BEEN DAYS since Nakia Lysand returned home to Phyllida after months overseas in the East. She had been confined to her room since then, yet the air still smelled strange to her. She couldn't put her finger on it, but even now as she sat on her balcony on a stool she couldn't find comfort on, the smell of the air was off. The scent made her stomach roil and burned her nose and throat. Even the taste seemed different. The way it lingered on her tongue left an almost ginger-like aftertaste.

The aroma was different from Khenshu, which was expected, but it troubled her in a way she couldn't put into words. It upset her in ways air shouldn't. It made every part of her tremble, her nerves twitch, and had her long for a desert with hot, honeyed air, full of barbarians, led by their insane, irksome queen, Ashni Akshay.

The thought of Ashni made Nakia's stomach settle, but it never untied itself from the tense knot it had been in since she stood before her father a couple of days ago. Her discomfort went beyond the fact that she felt like a pawn in her father's machinations and that her father wanted to marry her off to some random nobleman. She always expected that to happen. It happened with her sisters.

But, there were a few key differences. Her father never sent her sisters off to barbarians as a goodwill hostage. Her sisters had never lived in a new culture and been treated as a servant, as a clown. They had never had a warrior queen pay them all the attention in the world and not realize what that meant. They had not been embraced by not only the queen but those closest to her. They had not laid in the arms of a queen, felt safety and love for the first time, and then had all of that ripped from them to the point where it felt like her skin had been removed. She was the only one with that mark seared into her soul.

Worse yet, the wound throbbed and itched in the absence of Ashni. Nakia did not know how to handle it. Tearing away from her seat, she tried to shake off thoughts of that place, that woman, but it did nothing except cause her tunic to rustle and her bracelets to ring out in

1

the silent space. Somehow, even her traditional clothing felt different, heavier than usual, the reds and yellows glared at her and irritated her skin. She wanted to peel herself out of herself.

She paced her rooms, weaving around polished dark wood furniture, a maze of couches and tables. The mosaics on the walls watched her, accused her somehow. The eyes of her ancestors made her chest burn. The columns lining each space, bedroom, sitting room, and study seemed like prison bars and she felt caged, imprisoned in a way she had not in Khenshu, even when she had literally been in golden bonds.

The sound of her light steps against the tiled floor hammered into her, pounding against her bones. Birds sang outside and the sound carried through her open windows like thunder. Each noise threatened to shatter her.

Taking a deep breath, she released it through her nose, trying to ease the pressure crushing her ribs. Rolling her shoulders, she tried to keep the sounds and feelings at bay, but to no avail. Going back to the balcony, she stared out into her city, a sea of orange tiled roofs, cream buildings, and movement like ants from her view. Her gaze went even beyond that, passed the thick wall and the open grasslands parted by stone roads. Part of her wished to see the armies of the Roshan Empire, but that was a fantasy.

She wouldn't come for you, risking everything for you. Even if Ashni wanted her back, it would take longer to mobilize her troops to storm the city for Nakia. Ashni wouldn't risk her father's dream of conquering the West. Nakia would never think she was that important to Ashni, but she believed she meant something to the queen.

"No, I know I meant something to you." Nakia had to say it aloud, had to say it like she spoke to a person and not the empty room, as that made it truer than she already knew it to be. "But, what does that mean now?" Nakia wasn't sure. *Would Ashni consider my return home an acceptable loss? Was Ashni going to come to my rescue? Do I need to be rescued?* She shouldn't feel that way while at home, but she did. She'd be married soon to a stranger.

Anger shot through her at the thought. Anger tended to be her first emotion and she liked that. It made it feel like she could do something. But, as she considered her situation more, she couldn't do anything about it. *You will need to be rescued because you're too weak to do it on your own, just like you were too weak to stop Father sending you across the sea. You're weak.*

Before she realized it, tears slid down her cheeks. She wiped them away, even as she felt her eyes sting with more. Ashni wouldn't like to see her crying. *It doesn't matter. She's never going to see you again. You'll be married and moved like a piece of furniture, never to see Ashni or the East.* Nakia needed to accept that part of her life was over.

Approaching footsteps shook her from her thoughts. She wasn't surprised to see her father joining her on the balcony. He had been by to see her twice since her return. The first was to inform her of her fate, the marriage to his ally. The second was to seek information about the Roshan, and he probably wanted more. She wouldn't give any. *Why make things easy for him? He never made things easy for me.*

"Taking in the view? Glad to be home, I'm sure," her father said, his barrel chest puffing out as if he made the view.

Nakia bit her tongue to keep from snapping at him. She missed that about Khenshu. She had been able to speak her mind with little fear, especially to Ashni. Her father wouldn't be as amused or forgiving with her as Ashni had been. Here she wasn't allowed to be equal to any man, but especially her father, the King. She wasn't allowed to give him her opinion and even if she did, he wouldn't listen. Her opinion didn't matter, and neither did her wants or needs.

She wanted to ignore him, pretend he wasn't there or she was somewhere else, but that wouldn't do her any good. She watched him out of the corner of her eye. His expression didn't change, like he didn't notice her discomfort.

"Shall we sit?" He motioned to a bench by the railing with his large hand.

It was posed as a question, but it wasn't a request. She sat at one end, uncomfortable once again on the seat. At first, she blamed getting accustomed to the Khenshu pillows and she'd have to adjust to couches at home. Now, she knew it had to do with her father as he sat at the opposite end. Along with the odd smell of the air, there was thick tension too. She did her best to breathe normally, but being in her father's presence was overwhelming in a way it didn't use to be and strangled her.

"How are you feeling? Your servants reported you haven't been eating."

She shook her head. "I am not quite so hungry." The most ironic thing she learned about her appetite was that she found her food too bland now. *I never would've believed that when I first arrived in Khenshu.* Now, she longed for the spices to flavor her meats or sweeten her cereals.

"You should try to eat something. I'm sure living with those monsters couldn't have been easy, but you're safe now." His voice was soft, but the emotion didn't meet his eyes. He had learned how to sound concerned, but he couldn't look it. It wasn't in his nature.

"I know. I can't force myself to eat, Father." *Will he try to force me to eat?*

He frowned. "We don't want you to waste away before King Caligo arrives. You're rather thin as it is." He looked her up and down with a slight curl to his top lip.

Nakia swallowed heated words to prevent her from biting back at her father and they burned all the way through her chest to her stomach. She was out of practice in eating her rage, but she needed to keep her composure to avoid serious trouble. The feeling only added to the tension inside of her from the forced marriage already.

She had yet to meet Caligo Mor, her future husband. He was on his way to Phyllida from his home, Nex, a land up north. Supposedly anything beyond the great River Reve was savage territory, and she suspected Nex was beyond the river because she hadn't heard of it. Sold from one set of barbarians to the next. She doubted her luck would hold and these barbarians would be as welcoming as the last.

Considering the future made Nakia's throat tighten. *Don't think about it. Ashni will come for you.* Or so she hoped. Prayed really, as she couldn't think of any way out of it.

"Is there something, Father? Beyond checking on my physical form," she said, making a serious effort to keep her words calm rather than curt. She wanted him out of her space as soon as possible. His presence never failed to make her day worse, but actually having to interact with him now was like being raked across hot coals. Every moment he pretended to be concerned for her was like having her skin peeled back.

"I wanted to find out if you remembered more about the Roshan and their demon queen that might help us in the upcoming war."

Of course that was what he desired. She hadn't given him much to work with the last time he attempted to debrief her. She didn't want to outright lie to him, not like he did. She didn't want to be like him, but she wasn't a spy. *Besides, at this point, what does it matter?* A lie by omission was still a lie, a betrayal. And he had betrayed her first. A father was meant to protect a daughter, and he hadn't. He had used her in so many different ways.

Ashni's father never would have done so from what Nakia learned while in Khenshu. Ashni's father had allowed her to become a warrior, go on campaign with him, and had inspired her to the point she insisted on carrying his dream as her own. Nakia barely wanted to think about her father existing. *How could a so-called barbarian be a better father than mine? Why was I cursed with this man?* She couldn't even imagine having a father who inspired her.

"There's not much to tell. I was kept in rooms, away from anything important. From the way things sounded outside, I feel as if they party constantly. Loud, drunken parties, as you would expect of a barbarian. There was always thumping drumming music and bellowing laughter. Rooms hazy with thick, white smoke like I've never seen before. I believe even the Queen played dice games." Let her father get cocky and underestimate Ashni.

He made a noise deep in his throat and nodded. "Did they have a lot of guards around you?"

"No. I assume since the city is in a desert and I was so far from home, they didn't think it was necessary. Where would I run away to, after all? Not to mention, I knew if I left, they'd destroy this city. I would never risk that and they knew."

He slapped his knees, knocking his royal violet sash off of his thigh. "Well, we don't have to worry about that anymore. With Caligo Mor, we should be able to wipe those filthy wretches off the face of the planet."

Nakia held her breath to keep in a snarl over the mention of the man she would be given to. The light in her father's eyes didn't help endear Caligo to Nakia. He was nothing more than a pirate, as far as she was concerned, looting her from where she wanted to be. And, pirates weren't to be trusted. *How could he help my father, help our city? What makes him trustworthy? What makes it better to strike an alliance with him than with the Roshan?* Maybe she could get answers from him. *I can't help myself, can I?*

"Where did you meet this king, Father? I have never heard of him," Nakia said. She wasn't owed an explanation by her culture, but it wasn't something she agreed with. She should be worth some words of comfort from her father. *But, you're not and you know it.* The thought made her teeth itch. *So, why bother?*

"There are many things you haven't heard of, but he'll treat you right, Nakia. I'll make sure of it." He threw back his shoulders.

She had to hold in a scoff. *You don't care how I'm treated. You're throwing me to barbarians again.* It was like he didn't think she had been traumatized by any of this. Not once had he asked about her wellbeing or if the Roshan had done anything to her. *No, just moving onto his next scheme and how I might factor into his game.* It shouldn't bother her. She should be used to it, but she couldn't help thinking of Ashni with her father, her following behind him, being accepted for who she was. *Who am I to Father?*

I'm a pawn and that's possibly all he'll ever consider me. That was all he considered my sisters before me. Because I'm female? Is that why this war with the Roshan, who were led by a woman, drove him to such extremes as to partner with barbarians to the north and give me away to one of them?

Her father continued, slamming a fist onto the bench. "With his backing, we can get the surrounding cities to join with us and outnumber those Eastern barbarians and send them back to Hell."

"Have the other cities agreed to this?" Nakia felt like her father planned too far ahead with many unknown variables still in play.

He narrowed his gaze, as if he didn't know who she was, and she held in a yelp. *I can't do that here. I can't show signs of intelligence or question the leadership.* Her father didn't want her opinion, thoughts, or questions. It burned her up inside. *How dare he judge my ability to think based on my gender.* Especially when so-called barbarians took her words under consideration when she was little more than a goodwill hostage. *To Hell with him!*

The burning in Nakia's stomach felt like it erupted and it took every ounce of her self-control to keep it in, but she could feel it destroy bits of her. Her will and hope could've been casualties and she didn't want to risk that. She needed to get him out of her rooms now before he obliterated every piece of her.

"Father, I'm a little tired," she said, feigning a delicate yawn. She covered her mouth with the back of her hand.

"I assume so. Your ordeal has been great. Be sure to eat. If you remember anything else about the barbarians, tell me." He rose to his feet.

Nakia nodded and breathed easier when he was gone, a weight lifting from her shoulders, the tension in her chest eased. Yet other things still pressed against her. Her upcoming marriage would haunt her until the moment it happened.

She wasn't sure what to do. *Should I resign myself to my fate? Or should I try to escape?* She scoffed. *Escape where? I didn't even understand the concept of money before going to Khenshu and befriending Bashira. How would I make it on my own?* She wouldn't make it. Simple as that. Her stomach felt shredded and she felt the fire inside of her dim more than she had ever felt in her life. Her heart fell into her feet. She'd always be a tool, a pawn.

***

Queen Ashni Akshay slumped on her throne, wishing the soft, silky pillow beneath her could offer some comfort. It had been too many days since she lost her hellcat and she could feel the absence in places that didn't have names, places she didn't know existed. She felt cold from the loss, like there was a chill just under her skin, cutting deeper into her with each passing moment. Her mood was rather down for someone who got a fortune in gold and she couldn't change that, even though she understood it. Worse, she was about to have all her hard work come together, about to make her dreams come true, about to do something even the son of a god hadn't done, yet none of it mattered.

I've never missed someone like this before. Granted, Ashni hadn't lost many close people in her life to feel this way. She considered it might be normal, but it felt more like mourning than missing. She was intimately familiar with mourning thanks to the passing of her father, and she refused to accept that eternal ache. Mourning meant her hellcat was gone forever, never to be at her side, never to be in her arms. There had to be something she could do to rid herself of this malaise. There had to be some way to get Nakia back to her.

Ashni sighed, weariness in her bones. "Princess, I don't have time for you." *Or the patience.* Her sister slid down from a line on the ceiling next to her.

"But, I have a plan," Layla replied, still hanging from her line.

"You have a plan?" Ashni was beyond skeptical, but couldn't be bothered to roll her eyes. "Does it involve us going to the training ground to spar?" It was a request her sister made daily and she wasn't interested. If a person wasn't presenting her with a proposal to return Nakia to her side, she didn't want to hear it.

"My idea involves consulting an oracle to know the proper method for us to approach this problem. We have way too many ideas. We should find out which ones the gods favor and then we'll know what to do. It's not like your father would steer us wrong, right?"

Ashni hadn't considered an oracle. Honestly, she hadn't come up with many plans either. She couldn't keep her thoughts together long

7

enough. Without her hellcat by her side, she couldn't focus and she knew it was driving Layla and Adira mad with worry.

"You just want to go to an oracle to find out if I'm fit enough to lead us to victory," Ashni grumbled. *What would the gods have to say about any of this? What would Dad have to say?* For a long moment, she had been ready to throw it all away for her hellcat. *Am I fit to lead, fit to chase my father's dream?* Part of her thought, yes. After all, her father had done something similar for her mother. But, her father didn't have the dreams of hundreds of thousands on his shoulders. Surely, the gods would frown on her selfishness.

Layla shrugged. "Not me. You know I'd follow you into the dark, cold depths of Hell and enjoy the ride there. But, it's getting around that you're sulking over your lost kitten."

Ashni growled and made a fist. "I'm not sulking."

Layla arched an eyebrow. "No? Then what are you doing?"

"Brooding."

Layla sucked her teeth. "Oh, yeah, that's a big difference. Look, we have to see an oracle anyway. You know the troops like it when the oracle gives us the blessed words of the gods. We can get that and the blessing on a plan to get your spouse back."

"She's not my spouse." Not that Ashni didn't want that. She'd enjoy having Nakia by her side in any way, but she'd prefer spouse. Then, Nakia's bastard of a father couldn't take her back.

"No, she's just the person you're brooding over and willing to do anything for. Again, big difference. You can't just sit on the throne until the day we leave. Let's go talk to an oracle. What could it hurt?"

Ashni didn't respond. It could hurt a lot. She might have fallen out of the gods' favor and they'd have the oracle let her know. She'd find out that losing her kitten was only the beginning or it was a personal punishment from some failing she didn't even know she had. *How else can I explain having someone so precious ripped right from my grasp without even a farewell?*

"You're brooding again," Layla said. "You've got to get up. You've got a date with destiny." Layla punched her fist into her palm. When that failed to ignite Ashni, Layla scowled. "Don't make me get Adira in here. She will nag you off this throne."

Ashni had no doubt about that and groaned, falling back as much as she could without lying down. She didn't want to get up, but more than that she didn't want to hear Adira's voice. She didn't want to hear Adira reprimanding her over neglecting her duties or complaining about how she was the only one working.

"I should probably get off my ass," Ashni said. If only to save whatever sanity she had left.

"Right. The West isn't going to conquer itself. Besides, if we storm into the West, you could always steal your kitten back. I mean, come on." Layla blew a raspberry.

Ashni wasn't sure that was the right way to get back to Nakia. She planned to take over her Nakia's homeland. *Would Nakia come with me after she wades through a river of blood from her own countrymen? Would Nakia even be able to look at me after I personally snatched everything King Dorian built and reshaped it to my own liking?* Maybe their time together had been a fantasy, something that couldn't live when she continued her destiny. Perhaps the oracle would have an answer. And perhaps Nakia had actually been the punishment from the gods. Talking to the gods would be the only way to find out.

Ashni sighed and pushed off of the throne. "Let's go. I can find out if I lost favor with the gods when Nakia was taken or when she arrived." *Why would they allow her to affect me as she has if she wasn't going to be in my life? Well, if she was a punishment then, that's your answer.*

"Yes! I win." Layla pumped her fist in the air.

"You and Adira had a bet, didn't you?"

Layla followed her out of the throne room. "No, Adira was too pissed to bet me, but Naren did. He thought you'd sulk for at least another week or so."

"I am not sulking!"

Layla smirked. Ashni suspected Layla was purposely getting on her nerves but knowing that didn't make it less irksome. It didn't make her forget the hole inside of her, the void, oozing and messy, gaping all the same. It didn't thaw the frost in her veins, nipping at her soul.

"Maybe we should make a sacrifice before we go see the oracle. I mean, it couldn't hurt, right?" Layla asked.

"We make an offering to the oracle. I'm not sacrificing anything beforehand and accidentally pissing the gods off further." Ashni wasn't sure what she had done to upset the gods to be punished so harshly, but she didn't want to chance doing something wrong and making matters worse. So, there would be no grand sacrifice to the gods beforehand. *That'd be too out of the ordinary.*

Layla shrugged. "Fair enough. Don't want the gods to think we've lost our minds here, making huge gestures for the answer to a question that we have to make an offering for anyway."

Ashni wasn't sure if Layla actually agreed with her or was humoring her. It didn't matter. They'd do everything above board and proper. Maybe then the gods would see fit to return her hellcat to her. Or at the very least not impede her invasion plans. No need to ruin her and her father, and the hopes and dreams of everyone following her.

"Do you want to make a trip or should we just visit the oracle here?" Layla asked.

"Let's start small. Making a trip involves making a trip." She didn't have it in her to go on a journey for answers that would come in riddles just yet. Also, it could eventually involve her mother who Ashni wasn't in the right mind to deal with. Not that she was ever in the right mind to deal with her mother. Going to the greatest oracle in the Empire would attract her mother's attention, and she didn't want to have to explain to her mother what was going on in her life.

"We can get some food on the way and see a show," Layla said.

Ashni scoffed. *No, too much right now.* She needed the gods' assurance she wasn't damned, as she froze from the inside out, lost to the divine light of the Sun. Exiting the palace and needing to shield her eyes from the brightness didn't help. She felt so cold.

Khenshu was busy, as always, and Ashni was both disappointed and proud that it continued on, even as she hardly functioned. Somehow, the world still moved while she felt like it crumbled around her. The urban din surrounded her, loud voices, barking dogs, and the creak of cartwheels felt like an assault on her soul rather than her ears. The nerve of these people to still have lives while she had nothing. Rainbows of fabric moved around her as people rushed by. Some tried to engage with her but neither she nor Layla paused. There were times when she'd talk to her people and there were times she was on a mission and they'd have to wait.

The oracle temple was near one of the busiest markets of Khenshu, and the crowd from the market spilled over to the crowd of the temple. Animals braying, birds singing, and whatever other sounds they made mingled, some for sale and others for sacrifice. The smell of fire, smoke, and incense battled with food, perfumes, and sweat.

"This is more people than I expected," Layla said. There was a line well beyond the temple doors. It was possible people were merely cooling off by the large reflecting pool outside of the temple or on their way to the market, but there were more people around than usual.

Typically, Ashni didn't care about lines. She was the queen, divine, and about to conquer the West. Now, being so pushy seemed like tempting fate. Skipping the line could anger a god, and then that god kept her from the West or from Nakia. It could be the tipping point where the gods decided to go from simply pushing her to punishing everyone under her command and rule.

"Come on!" Layla yanked her by the elbow, managing to get hold of her body proper even in yards of light teal fabric. Layla didn't believe in lines but more because no one would stop her. If jumping the line was an issue, surely the gods would be just and hold it against Layla.

"Your Highness." A priest bowed to them as they walked to the white gates painted with lions, bears, wolves, and leopards. Painted statues of the gods covered in jewels and precious metals lined the tall walls as if holding the temple up. *Do they still hold me up, though?*

"We need to see the oracle. It's about our destiny!" Layla bounced on the balls of her feet, eager to get to the conquest, to the glory.

The priest smiled. "Of course. Danish!" He waved over a short young man in golden robes and feathers braided into his curly black hair, who hurried over.

Danish bowed, lowering his lightly made up face. Kohl underlined his dark eyes and yellow powder splashed against his lips, showing his mouth was blessed should the gods ever decide to speak through him, like many of the priests and priestesses of this temple. *Maybe I should get my whole body blessed. It might be a little difficult to lead my troops into battle covered in powder, though.*

Ashni and Layla were quite familiar with Danish. He often accompanied them when they visited this temple. They both waved the bow off, used to his hustle and bustle, like this was his way of being a part of their conquest. He'd get them on their way as fast as he could, so they could live their destinies. Danish led them down the smooth, polished stone walkway by more statues of the gods, lush trees, and holy pools.

They came to a teal and gold door with a detailed carving of Khurshid, the Sun and chief god, on one end and Dima, the Sky, on the other, both decorated with the finest jewels the Empire had to offer. Dima might be the god she upset, a harsh mistress with whims no one could understand or calculate. One day she was clear and beautiful and the next, ugly and cruel. She'd stay clear until Khurshid burned them all, destroying the shade by killing the trees, and taking what little water they might save. And, then the next she could call in her daughter to bring bountiful rain and make everything good again.

"Can I waste my question to the oracle on which of these two you pissed off?" Layla pointed to the doors as if she could read her sister's mind, which she almost could.

"There's no way I pissed off Khurshid. I mean, come on, my dad would vouch for me," Ashni replied. Surely the Sun God would take her circumstances under consideration, as her father was also derailed for want of a woman. *How could the Sun deny me what my father was granted? Perhaps I have to prove myself as he did. But, what more would I have to do?*

Layla shrugged. "Unless this is to teach you a lesson, like leave your sister's spouse alone or we'll take yours from you."

"There are so many things wrong with that statement." Ashni turned her attention to the priest. "Danish, can we go in? I can't stand out here and not strangle my sister in this holy place."

Danish bowed his head. "I'm sorry, Your Majesty. Someone's in with the oracle at this moment, but they should be done soon. We weren't expecting you."

"I don't think she was expecting her either," Layla said and even though it didn't make sense. The stupid smile on her face made Ashni want to body slam her.

Ashni took a calming breath and reminded herself why it wouldn't be the best idea to fight her sister here. First off, it was disrespectful to the gods, the King and Queen of the gods most importantly. Second, punishing her sister for telling the truth was beyond a sin. Third, possibly injuring an important part of Roshan destiny was an offense to her people and their shared dream. She might actually get struck by lightning in the temple if she touched Layla right now. And despite being the Sky Cutter, she was certain divine lightning could at least wound her.

They waited until a noble Ashni recognized, but wasn't very familiar with, stepped out with another priest escort. Both the noble and the priest bowed their heads to Ashni and continued on their way. Danish held the door open for them and motioned for them to go inside. The small room was bathed in blue light from the ceiling, walls, and floor. The oracle was on her throne, sitting high at the back of the room. A thin veil covered her face, draping from a silver circlet dotted with pearls and emeralds.

"Your Highness." She bowed to Ashni, beads in her hair clacking together as she moved. "Your Highness." Layla was given a respectful nod.

"Before we get started, can I ask a question and not have it count as my question?" Layla asked. Her first time visiting the oracle, Layla blew her only question by asking if she could ask a question. The answer had been, "Well, not now." Ashni and the oracle had a good laugh over that one. The gods had funny moments.

"It is all the will of the gods, Highness. You know that," the oracle replied. Her voice was soft, like a bird's song. "I am only their vessel."

"Okay, we didn't map out how we want to do this," Layla said to Ashni. "What if there's only one question for each of us? You want to ask about your spouse and I ask about you cursing our conquest?"

Ashni rubbed her face. "You have to be a punishment from the gods." Layla's presence, usually a comfort, felt like a mockery of her whole existence. *How could Layla, who had given herself to an unworthy clod, have her relationship and union blessed by the gods while I'm shunned for taking an intelligent, fierce equal?*

Layla offered an impish smile. "It's possible. Your people did originally think us demons, if you remember. What were we called again?" She tapped her chin.

"You're Roshan now." Ashni didn't like to think about a conquest of years ago, even if it gave her Layla. Sometimes, her brothers still whispered about her "shadow beast." Ashni had never uttered the term, even back then, as her father always respected the Shadow Walkers, their abilities, and their culture. *Different doesn't mean wrong and conquest doesn't mean right*, he used to tell her.

"Right. So, you ask about your spouse and I got the conquest." Layla patted herself on the chest.

Ashni shook her head and stepped forward. "Will the gods speak with us today?" she asked the oracle. There were days when the gods refused, as was their will. She never minded, certain she had their favor. Now, she wasn't so sure.

The oracle tipped her hand toward Ashni. "Your Highness first."

"Will I fulfill my destiny?" It was all Ashni needed to know. Everything else she could claw out herself, regardless of how the gods felt about her.

The oracle nodded. Danish poured a dark liquid into the fountain of water by the oracle's chair. There was a flash, and smoke flowed over the rim of the fountain. Danish prayed over it and then filled a chalice. The oracle muttered long prayers while rocking back and forth. When she stopped, Danish placed the cup to her painted lips and she drank deep. Ashni waited, hoping the gods wouldn't keep her there for the day, as they sometimes did. The oracle inhaled deeply, her body shook, and then a deep gurgle escaped her, a sign of a god's arrival.

"Daughter of the Son of the Sun, why trouble us with such a question? Your destiny can only be fulfilled. That's why it's called a destiny," the oracle replied, her voice now scratchy, raw, and ancient.

Layla laughed. "You're so out of favor with the gods."

Ashni's nerves popped with the desire to tear her sister apart. For a long moment, the world fell away, sound ceased, and all she could think about was laying waste to everything before her. She wasn't even sure how she managed to hold back. *Why have the gods forsaken me now?* "You think this is funny? We could lose everything!" The sound of thunder boomed outside. *I could lose everything!*

"Stay your hand, Golden One. This child of the Moon is of yourself," the oracle told her, voice still rough.

Layla cackled. "And you got scolded by the gods! Think that was the Amir? I bet that was him. Your dad liked me." She puffed out her chest.

Ashni bit her lip to the point of blood. *How did I get to this point? Why didn't the gods tell me so I could make amends?* She wasn't so arrogant she'd ignore their words. Their refusal made the trip a waste of time.

Fury rushed through Ashni and she felt like it ripped her in half. There were two of her inside her now. There was one who wanted to do everything in her power to regain the gods' love and attention. But, the other one, a louder one, was ready to get things done without worrying over the gods or her hellcat or anything else that kept her sidelined. She didn't need the gods' favor. *You have a warrior spirit inside of you and beside you.* Her father would never abandon her. She had him, she had Layla, she had Adira, and she had her own two hands. She'd get back Nakia and take the West by her own will. *You are the Sky Cutter. You control lightning, just like the gods, and you get things done with or without the gods.*

"Do well to remember yourself, Golden One. Do well," the oracle said and then slumped in her chair. Her voice of the gods gone.

For what? What have the gods done for you lately? What have they done for you that you can't do for yourself? What have they given you that you couldn't get for yourself? A part of her felt like it was wrong to think that way, but she ignored it. She was capable. She was a demigod. She could handle herself, and whatever the gods decided to put in her path, she'd demolish with her strength. *Because I am strong.* Her other half couldn't be silent at that. *Strong enough to defy the gods? No one was. But, I'm not no one. I'm the daughter of the Great Amir. I am*

Queen Ashni, the Sky Cutter.

"Do you have something?" Ashni asked Layla to take her mind off of the fact that the gods seemed to know she felt like she could do this on her own. They had made her strong and capable, so they should be proud of her doing things on her own.

"I feel like I can leave here satisfied, knowing the gods themselves scolded you for your treatment of me. In fact, I might actually be able to die happy right after I tell Adira this happened," Layla replied with her chin in the air.

Ashni groaned, gave her offerings of her favorite sweet fruits by the oracle's throne, and rushed out of the room before she committed unspeakable acts in the holy place. The sound of bare feet on the floor chased after her, letting her know Layla was right behind her. Danish wasn't far behind, murmuring what might have been excuses or prayers for them. Ashni didn't care. She was about to grab destiny by the balls.

Chapter Two

ASHNI FELT CERTAIN LAYLA told Adira about their visit to the oracle even though Adira didn't say anything. There was just something in her eye, a glint that made it sparkle like a brown diamond. Ashni resisted the urge to pluck out said eye. Saniyah would never forgive her for blinding Adira, even if Adira deserved it, and she needed to keep Saniyah happy because the woman was a genius war engineer. Still, there had to be some way to get Adira to stop looking at her with something like amusement and pity.

"Are we going to get ready for the march?" Adira asked, standing at the bottom of the dais. Ashni sat on the throne, back straight, shoulders squared, gazing down at her as if that somehow made up for the expression on Adira's face. Adira could have been a hundred feet beneath her and she was certain her friend would still be the victorious one.

"Isn't that your job?" Ashni replied.

"You're usually more hands on with this. What's wrong now?" Adira groaned, as if just asking pained her.

Ashni growled. She refused to say it aloud. Everyone knew what was wrong, though. She heard the servants whispering. The only reason she hadn't slaughtered all of them was that Layla kept her occupied, but she wasn't sure how long that would hold. It was easier to slay gossipy servants than a princess with a tight control over shadows and darkness.

Ashni pointed out of the throne room. "Go do your job."

"I am," Adira replied, arms folded across her stomach.

Ashni narrowed her gaze on her general. Adira was supposed to be preparing their armies to storm the West in a much more permanent fashion rather than dancing over Ashni's raw nerves.

"I have an idea."

"About?" She doubted she wanted to know.

Adira looked at her like she was the idiot. "About your problem."

"I don't have a problem." She'd be better when Nakia was by her side, but until then, she could function. She could lead. She could fulfill her destiny. The gods said so. Yes, it was in a snide way that only further proved she had done something to fall from grace, but she could fix that. She could. *I am strong enough to do what I need to do without the gods holding my hand.*

"Okay, you don't have a problem. But, if you did, I have a solution that's just crazy enough to work," Adira said.

Ashni scowled. "What's your idea?" Her tone was sharper than she meant, but it didn't matter.

"We propose an alliance between us and Phyllida. For this alliance, you'd marry Nakia. It would offer them protection none of their neighbors could offer. Hell, even privileges none of their neighbors will enjoy once they're part of the Empire."

Ashni scoffed. *I expected so much better of Adira on ideas.* And then she expected better of herself as she dared to imagine Nakia dressed in teal, gold, and red robes with pearls in her hair as they bonded together at their wedding. *Do you want things to go that far with her?* She didn't have an answer. *I do know I want her back.* "That would never work. You know how the West feels about women being together. Even Nakia thought it was impossible and this was after we were together."

"I think the confusion might work in our favor. They won't understand what you mean and I'm sure the King will think he can fool us. He won't ask questions. He knows he can't beat us on the battlefield. This would be the best way for him to avoid a fight," Adira said.

Ashni rolled her eyes, more for show than anything else. At least Adira thought this out more than it seemed. "He won't go for it." Any other people might, but the West was set in its thoughts of what women could and couldn't do.

Adira curled her lip in a sneer. "Can we at least try? You don't usually give up this easily."

"You usually have better ideas."

Adira ground her teeth together. There were undoubtedly endless insults on her tongue, but she swallowed them, which surprised Ashni. Adira wasn't one to be bashful.

"Say it," Ashni ordered with a motion of her hand.

"I have nothing to say. Why would I? You're not listening. I don't know who you are and I don't know how to approach you anymore. I get losing someone you're close to, but what do you want to do with this? Do you want to sit here and pout for the rest of your life? Did it ever occur to you that's why the gods were so snippy with you? You've forgotten yourself."

"I know who I am!" Ashni pounded her armrest. "I am the Chosen One, the Sky Cutter. I command a divine power and stand by the greatness that was my father, our great Amir. I know who I am." *I am strong and I need to do something about this.*

Adira blew out a breath. "The person you just described wouldn't be sitting here, pouting."

Ashni shifted in her chair and rubbed her palms together. She wanted to say she wasn't pouting, but that would be a lie. Something was wrong inside of her, broken possibly, and she was all too aware what it was. She could feel it spreading, slowly, but surely and soon it would conquer the whole of her. If she didn't do something about it, she'd lose herself and lose sight of the greatness she'd been chasing her entire life. *Is this feeling part of falling from grace? I lose the gods' favor, fall away from the light of Khurshid, and end up frozen in a dark pit of despair and inaction.* She couldn't live this way.

You don't have to live this way. You decided you could do this without the gods. It felt like she was at war with herself. One part mourning, not just losing Nakia, but losing the gods, and the other part fired up to prove she didn't need the gods. *You can do this. You have the best people with you. Go take what's yours. Command what's yours.*

"Do you think the marriage proposal would work?" Ashni found herself asking. It seemed like such a stupid idea. *But what the hell else do I have?* She could take her army and raze Phyllida to the ground. *Would Nakia still want me then? Does Nakia want me now?*

The question sparked up the other her. *Why wouldn't she want you?* Her brain tripped over itself to provide more than enough reasons and the frost under her skin nipped at her nerves.

Adira shrugged. "Doesn't hurt to try."

Ashni grunted. "I suppose."

"I'll write it up. For all I know, you'll offer the whole empire to Dorian for Nakia." Adira smirked.

Ashni wished she could dispute that, but she felt like she'd lost her mind and she'd definitely give her right arm for Nakia. "Show me when you're done."

"Of course. While I work on that, do you think you could go make yourself known to the army?" Adira asked.

Ashni glared at her, even though she took the point. Adira made the point, Ashni took her point. Adira had neglected her duty long enough. Nakia wouldn't approve of her behavior. She took care of military duties for the rest of the day. Her soldiers all seemed quite pleased, and maybe even a little relieved to see her. *Step one to showing you're strong will be appearing before your troops more often.* She returned to the palace for the evening meal. Adira joined her.

"I have a first draft of the alliance proposal," Adira said. She passed a scroll across the table to Ashni and set about finding some sustenance, wasting no time mixing chicken and rice on a piece of flatbread before covering them with gravy.

"Is that what we're going to call it?" Ashni asked. She was more interested in this than eating right now. Eating had been hard since Nakia was taken. Her stomach refused her beloved sweets, especially apples, as the taste reminded her of her hellcat.

Adira took a delicate bite of her food. "I think it'll go more smoothly than saying marriage proposal to people who don't think women can marry each other. Where they get that from, I don't understand."

Ashni waved the comment off. "These are the same people who think women are inferior."

"I wish we could just drop your mother off there and come back in a month. I'm sure those attitudes would change."

"Right. Just leave my mother and Princess' mother. They'd properly train the West."

Adira chuckled. "I wonder why they don't understand spirit bonding. I mean, my people believed in that before the Roshan Empire came in."

Ashni nodded. "My mother's people didn't believe in spirit bonding in a romantic sense, but it's because they believe marriage is about children. You go elsewhere for romantic involvement."

"Your mother's people also believed your mother could defeat your father, so I'm not counting on what they know." She smacked her lips together as she took a much bigger bite from her food.

Ashni rubbed her chin. "Were they wrong, though?" Her father had been ready to do anything for her mother, including defying his own father. He willingly gave her mother power well beyond what anyone thought an outsider from the hills deserved. *And you are his child, ready to give up everything for an outsider from across the sea and make her your equal if she'd let you.*

"A marriage should be about balance. If your spouse doesn't balance you, what good would your children be? How could you ever raise children who were greater than you?" Adira's face scrunched up.

"You're speaking from the perspective of someone who plans to raise her own children. You have to remember, not everyone does that."

Adira curled her lip. "And those that don't are disgusting." She finished off her chicken, rice, and bread and started on a bowl of stew.

Ashni didn't argue that. Her parents had raised her and her brothers, even as they were conquering and governing. The Roshan believed it was a parent's duty to rear their own children, to grow them into the best versions of themselves. A child was a seed and needed to be cultivated as such, treasured as a precious crop, and tended by those who needed them the most to make sure legacies carried on.

"We're off track," Ashni said. She didn't want to think of children, not while her kitten was so far from her. *Would Nakia want to bear children? Does the West believe in adoption?* She quickly shook the curiosity away, certain that path led to madness.

"Yes, we are. It's very simple so far. In exchange for Princess Nakia, we'd leave Phyllida to Dorian and wouldn't even need a dowry from him, even though I never specify we'd be taking her for you to marry her. A simple alliance. We get her, and he gets this illusion of governing Phyllida."

"You think he'd go for that? He'd be a figurehead at best." Dorian would see that. "He's not the type to give up power so easily."

"He has to know we can devour his darling city from the inside and out. I don't care what type of army he fields against us or whoever he begs to come to his aid. We've got more soldiers now than when we went the first time. We have new weapons and better tactics. That was a taste. This is the meal," Adira replied.

"Include the old numbers of our ranks. I'd like to scare him a bit, but tell him those numbers wouldn't be used against him. They'd be with him, as we'd be his allies."

Adira nodded. "See what happens when you start thinking clear? We're going to get her back."

Ashni didn't say anything. She couldn't understand why losing Nakia affected her so much. All she could think about was getting Nakia back, but she couldn't think of any way to make that possible. *What has that slip of a girl done to me?*

Adira chuckled as she grabbed some bread to dip into her stew. "It's all right, you know?"

"No, you're going to tell me, though." Ashni sighed. She was sick of

Adira and Layla acting like they knew her so well.

"It's all right to miss her and be miserable without her. I voluntarily leave Saniyah to go with you and I miss her every day, think about her every spare moment I have when we're not on the battlefield, and use thoughts of seeing her again to motivate me. You had Nakia ripped from you and I don't think either of you ever considered what you were doing together. You didn't get a chance to understand what you had. That's why it feels this way."

Ashni cracked her knuckles for lack of a better thing to do. "This makes no sense."

"I don't think you've realized it yet."

With a scowl so tense Ashni feared her mouth would splinter from her face, she glared at Adira. "What? What the hell don't I realize?"

"That you're in love."

Ashni narrowed her gaze on Adira. "What's this idiocy you're speaking?" She knew what being in love looked like and was quite sure she wouldn't dare do such a thing.

"You're in love. I've seen it on you before."

Ashni blinked, certain Adira lost her mind. *And they think something's wrong with me.* "You've seen me in love before? With who?" She had never come close to being in love.

Adira had the nerve to wag her finger. "Not with a person. Never with a person, but an idea, a dream. The spark in your eyes when you talked about our great conquest, the hitch in your voice as you discussed your father's dream. The way you waxed poetic about how we'd be remembered forever when we became the masters of an empire the gods would envy. You're in love with this lofty notion of the world being Roshan and I've always respected that."

Ashni kept a stony facade. *Is that being in love?* She held her father's goals in high esteem, but she never thought of it as a love affair like Adira described. "And now?" *Have I lost Adira's respect? Just like I lost Nakia and the gods?* Her stomach dropped. *How can I do this without Adira? How far have I fallen if I've lost Adira?*

A small smile settled on Adira's rough face. "I respect you even more when I see the same look because of the princess. I know what it's like to love a difficult, free-spirited woman with a mind of her own. I know what it's like to want to do everything in your power for her. I want you to know we don't think less of you for this. Well, unless you let it stand in the way of our collective dream."

"Never," Ashni vowed, feeling the cracks in her soul heal a little.

She had to keep it together for Adira, for Layla, and every other person who followed her. The West would be theirs, even if she had to do it without grace.

Can you do something like this without the gods? Do not dismiss them so easily, especially if this is a test. The voice inside of her trying to hold onto her religion sounded suspiciously like her mother. She wouldn't let the gods down any more than she had already. She'd just have to figure out how to remain in Nakia's favor, if she was even still there, as they flooded the West.

"Then this isn't a problem. We'll get Nakia back. As I know you'd never rest if I lost Saniyah," Adira said.

Ashni nodded. "I would never."

"And as much as I would act like I didn't need your help, I know you'd still help and I'd be pissed about it, just like you are now. This is why you're not getting rid of me. Princess, on the other hand, just wants to see her sister happy. The little weirdo."

"Leave my sister alone." But, Ashni felt a smile on her face for the first time in a long time. She had people who would do anything for her, as she would for them. So, she needed to get herself together and let them help. *Kitten, I'll have you back...if you'll have me as well.*

***

Nakia lost track of how long she had been home already. The days ran together worse than they used to as she tried to find ways to keep herself occupied. She didn't like being home. It didn't feel like home anymore. Or maybe it never did and she didn't know until she left and returned. *But, if this isn't home, what is?* Her heart knew the answer and her brain feared it, so she buried it under the strange smell of Phyllida and dreams of freedom.

More and more often, she stared at the horizon, waiting for signs of the invasion. The sting in her eyes came from the crisp autumn wind as she sat on her balcony, not the fact that she wanted to cry over her captivity. She wasn't sure what would happen if Ashni did invade, but part of her still hoped for rescue. It was a miserable thing to be home and waiting for a rescue. *Would I feel the same if Father listened to me and acknowledged me?* She doubted she'd find out.

"Highness, your father calls for you," a servant reported from behind her.

"Where does he want me?" Nakia did not bother turning around.

23

She had grown weary of her father long ago. His questions about the Roshan were tiresome and he refused to tell her more of the man he promised her to.

"He's in the throne room, your Highness."

Nakia nodded, but didn't leave her balcony, didn't stop staring out where the sky met the land, green trees pushing up to clear blue. Never before had she wanted to be outside of the city walls. Now, it was all she could think about. Beyond those city walls weren't only freedom and respect, but Ashni. Her heart fluttered at the mere thought of the warrior queen. *When did she affect me so?*

"Highness," the servant said again.

"Coming." Nakia sighed, putting her longings away. She turned, following the servant out of the room to her father.

Her father was on his throne, scrolls piled up high front of him as he read through one. The maroon and gold at his back seemed to mock her. For her whole life, she stared at those colors and never dreamed she could sit on a throne, could rule anyone, and then she met Ashni. A queen, a woman who beat her father at every turn, except for this moment. Ashni hadn't fought him for her, but she didn't fault Ashni. The Queen respected her decision to honor the agreement, just as Ashni honored the agreement. Her father never would do such a thing. Even now, as he worked, she knew it was some underhanded dealing to cut down the Roshan and manage to control more of Kairon than he already did.

Something to screw me over again, somehow. Or something to lie to the Roshan again and try to outsmart Ashni. It was all the same.

"Father," Nakia said.

"Nakia, your future husband will arrive shortly. I expect you here to greet him."

"Of course." She knew the protocol. She watched her sisters go through it, and there had been a childish curiosity to it all then. Now, as contempt weighed her belly and chipped away at her spine, it felt like a sentencing. Her father had doomed her sisters, sold them as part of some grander scheme, and now her turn had arrived.

"The servants will prepare you."

Nakia gritted her teeth together. "Of course."

He waved her away, dismissed much as he would do a slave. It was hard to deal with after being somewhere that her words, her presence carried so much weight, even when she didn't realize it.

Walking away, her stomach felt like it tore in half and it took all of her willpower not to throw up. Something must have shown in her demeanor, though, as a servant fell to her side to help her. She pulled away, but once she made it to her rooms, she allowed them to bathe her, listening to the servants drone on about her future husband. It wasn't the chatter she expected, like when her sisters went through this. They didn't speak of rumors of how handsome he was or how wealthy.

They whispered about him, about his dark magic, and about his power. Each word sent shivers down her spine and twisted her guts into tiny, pinching knots. None of the servants said anything good to her, none of them giggled over him, and none of them spoke about how beautiful the wedding would be. She dared think some of them even pitied her as they watched her with glistening gazes. Later, when they thought she wasn't listening, they spoke about how she was passed from one barbarian to the next and how cruel her father was to her. She agreed.

After her bath, she was oiled and perfumed before being wrapped in her finest robes, red and yellow for her royal status. A purple sash draped around her, also to proclaim her royalty. Her hair was done, tied back with precious jewels and golden lace, and a golden headband on her forehead with a single ruby dangling between her eyebrows. None of the servants looked at her, so set in their tasks. Their motions were slow, deliberate, almost ritualized, and she had never seen this before. *Is this how a lamb feels before being given to the gods?*

Nakia's throat tightened as time ticked by, drawing her closer and closer to her doom. This frightened her more than when her father sold her to the Roshan. She had hoped for a rescue then or even plotted an escape, but all she had to do was wait. Marriage was permanent. This was forever her new life.

The servants walked her into the banquet hall. Each step she took felt dense, dragging, like she might collapse under the heft of her robes. The sounds of a gathering in the hall cut through her like jagged blades and it took all of her willpower to remain standing, to at least look like a princess. A mass of nobles had already gathered, murmuring. Her father reclined on a couch sat atop a platform, allowing him to look down on everyone. With him was a nobleman Nakia was vaguely familiar with, but she couldn't recall his name. Then, there was a man she didn't recognize...probably her future husband.

That now familiar burning sensation caught in her lungs and Nakia found it impossible to breathe. *Escape! Escape!* Her eyes darted around for an exit that didn't exist. *Escape where, fool? This is your life now.* Her chest remained tight. A cold sweat gathered on her brow and her insides were in impossible knots.

"Your Majesty. We present you Princess Nakia," a servant announced.

The men all turned to her and Nakia bowed, feeling yards of fabric flow around her, but it was like being in shackles. Her father motioned for her to join them. She nodded and moved up the platform, wishing it would swallow her whole. There was an empty lounge next to the stranger, which she assumed was for her. She settled and tried to calm her heart, but it felt like it wanted to escape her tense chest. Her throat burned with bile from her upset stomach and she found herself scanning the room for an exit yet again, even though she wouldn't be allowed to leave. *This is your life now. Accept it.* But, her body rebelled against the thought, nerves itching and skin ready to peel away to get out of this mess. *Why should I accept this? But, what can I do to fight it?* She had no answers.

"King Caligo, this is my daughter, Nakia. Isn't she lovely?" Dorian asked with an oddly proud smile. It wasn't so much that he was proud of Nakia, but proud of something he made.

The stranger turned to her, giving her a good look at him. She had never seen anyone so sickeningly pale. He seemed like the color of spoiled milk. Shaggy brown curls fell in his face, making it hard to tell how old he was. His face was clean of hair, but there were bags under his dark eyes, like he never slept. There was something crooked about him, even as he lay on the chaise. His dark robes suited the aura surrounding him.

"She is a beauty. Your description of her didn't do her justice," Caligo replied. His voice was a low whisper and seemed to slither out of his throat.

"Then we have a deal?" Dorian asked.

"Of course. I wouldn't have come all this way if we didn't. We need to work together to stop this Eastern scum from spreading," Caligo said.

"Then why marry me at all?" Nakia found herself asking before she could stop herself. All eyes went to her, and she bit the inside of her cheek to keep herself from flinching. She managed a quiet swallow as unease crushed her chest. *You just can't help yourself.* There were only so many times she could hold back. That fire in her might diminish, but it would never go all the way out. *You're already in enough trouble and you don't know how your future husband might react to this. Don't be reckless.*

Caligo grunted. "You didn't mention she had such a free spirit."

Dorian scratched his chin. "I think she might have been corrupted from her time with the savages. Who knows what she needed to do to keep her sanity while she was there. It's taken her some time to settle back into appropriate behavior and decorum."

Caligo turned to her with an unnatural stiffness and jerky manner like the bones in his neck were cogs. She wouldn't have been surprised if he creaked. A smile twisted his mouth, like it was broken, cut at the wrong angles. She took a breath, as best she could, trying to convince herself her mind was playing tricks on her.

"Tell us how you managed to survive those animals," Caligo said.

Something in his eyes made Nakia's skin crawl. If anything almost flickered out the dim flame of her personality, it was those unending voids. He focused on her like she was an insect he could squash at any time and for the first time in her life she believed that look. She resisted the urge to fiddle with her fingers under his intense attention, but she'd show more restraint with her words now.

"There's not much to tell. I was there as a guest and treated as such," she replied, truthfully with hopes Caligo would turn away. Having his full attention made every hair on her body stand on end.

"But, what does guest mean to those people?" the nobleman she couldn't quite remember inquired, leaning forward. His gaze wasn't chilly, but intrigued.

Nakia couldn't believe she had their undivided attention. Once upon a time, this would've delighted her. It would've made her feel important, valuable. Now, all she wanted to do was retreat to her room and hide. This felt like more of a prison than even that, like she was a toy on display. Yes, she was valuable, but only because she could spin tales of demons and how these men could be great heroes when they defeated those demons. *Wasn't that what made you valuable before?* She had always been important in the sense of how her father could use her. Yet it had never disgusted her more than now. Maybe because she never felt it quite so sharply, like being stabbed with shards of pottery.

Nakia shook her head and tried to breathe easy. "I was given everything I needed and invited to all events at the palace."

"I think what Owen means to say is what sort of events were there. How did they behave?" her father asked.

Owen. That was the nobleman's name. *Why is he here?* Last she recalled; her father had no love for this young upstart. He always thought Owen had more gall than sense. *What changed?* She glanced at Caligo and figured whatever changed had something to do with her upcoming marriage. *Does this make Owen another player in this game?*

"Wild," Nakia replied. She thought the Roshan were wild when they were allowed to let go. Ashni's parties were decadent and lavish beyond anything she had seen at home.

"Of course. They're animals," Caligo said.

"We'll sacrifice them to the gods like animals as well," Dorian said.

Caligo grabbed his golden chalice and tipped it to Dorian in agreement. Her father laughed and took a drink himself. *How are they expected to beat the Roshan with only their two kingdoms? Does my father plan to have others rally with them?* They didn't rally the first time the Roshan showed up and now the West knew what the Roshan were capable of. She didn't ask, knowing they wouldn't answer.

They went on to speak as if she wasn't there. There were plans on how they'd defeat the Roshan, but nothing seemed solid. They thought the surrounding people would join in once they saw the strength of "this great alliance." She pretended to scan the food as her father clapped Owen on the back.

"It's good you managed to bring us together," Dorian said to Owen. "How'd you know King Caligo?"

Owen shook his head. "I am not well acquainted with the good king."

"He's heard of my reputation, I'm sure," Caligo said.

"I did and I knew you lacked an heir. Why not have a child with fine Phyllidan stock?" Owen motioned to Nakia with an oyster shell in his hand. Her father had gone all out, bringing in seafood for this feast. He wanted to show their wealth, how they could afford such finery when the sea was days away. Of course, in reality, they couldn't afford this at all. Most of their valuables went to the Roshan to keep Ashni at bay for a little while longer.

Caligo glanced at Nakia, who wanted to shrink into the couch. He leaned over and touched her, completely breaking decorum in front of her father, who said nothing. He ran a callused finger across her hand, and she felt like she was touched by death. Cold and clammy. A complete contrast to when Ashni made it seem like fire danced through her veins.

Nakia pulled away on instinct and didn't care how rude it might seem. Caligo's eyes shot to her. Something malevolent shimmered in his dark gaze. She glanced at her father, and found him silent and frowning.

Apparently, his betrayal of the Roshan, continuing a war instead of paying tribute like he agreed, was more important than a man taking liberties with his daughter. A servant rushed in.

"King Dorian, I come with a missive from Queen Ashni," the servant reported, bowing at the foot of the royal platform.

Nakia's heart jumped in her throat. *Ashni has contacted my father?* Part of her dared hope it was to get her back, but she doubted she was that important. *Why should I be precious to Ashni?* Another small voice whispered back, *because she told you that you were precious to her.* Nakia wanted to believe those words were the truth. Ashni's word was truth.

Dorian turned to the servant. "Give it here." He snatched the scroll from the servant and broke the Roshan royal seal. His eyes scanned the document, but he didn't share what was in it. He started laughing.

"What does it say? Did the bitch realize she can't win, no matter how many dirty curs she has with her?" Caligo inquired.

"She's offering an alliance. She wants Nakia, but it seems like she wants to marry Nakia, saying this alliance would join our nations. How backwards are these people?" Dorian cackled as he summarized the note.

Nakia could hardly breathe and it wasn't because she felt a crushing weight on her. Her mind spun with possibility while her heart filled with raw joy. She meant more than something to Ashni. *Ashni wants to marry me?* It was possible in the Roshan Empire. *Am I so important to her she'd embarrass herself in this way?* Surely Ashni knew Dorian would never agree to an alliance, would never think Nakia could marry a woman.

"We'll be doing the world a favor when we get rid of them." Caligo smirked at Nakia. "I'll give you that miserable woman's head for even mentioning you in such a distasteful letter." He grabbed her hand and held on tight. The contact was more than enough to halt her thoughts of Ashni. A swell of dread flooded her. She would've vomited, if she had eaten anything lately. *Is this a test from the gods?*

If it was a test, she wasn't sure she'd pass. But, then again, if it was and she failed, she wasn't worthy of Ashni, the daughter of a god. She had to be worthy of someone who was a demigod, who clearly saw her as worthwhile and enough. She had to be strong. The fire inside of her, the fire that first drew Ashni to her, grew a little bigger.

Chapter Three

NAKIA EXCUSED HERSELF FROM the feast, unable to take her father and future husband any longer. They only wanted to discuss how they'd bring ruin to the Roshan and what they'd do to Ashni when they had her. Their fantasies scared her more than the Roshan's Bloody Orchard.

"Forgive us for conversing about such things in your presence, Princess," Caligo said, standing to see her off.

Nakia waved his words off. "It's fine. It's not my place to interrupt." Of course, it was their place to know what was polite conversation to have in front of women. It didn't seem to matter to them. She didn't seem to matter to them. *But, so what? You matter to Ashni.*

"I'll have servants see you to your rooms," her father said.

She objected, but it meant nothing. Servants were to come with her, but she wasn't going to her rooms first. She needed to clear her head and make sense of what was going on. Ashni wanted to marry her. Her father thought it was a joke, but was willing to marry her to this stranger from the north. She needed advice. For however long she had been home, she felt like surrendering, like it was all over, but clearly it wasn't. Ashni still wanted her. Ashni wanted her enough to propose marriage.

Nakia wanted to consult the gods as best she could. There weren't temples in the palace like in Khenshu, but halls and tunnels led to temples outside. There were plenty of altars she could've gone to, but she needed something more personal. She needed the god to be there, not just listening to her. She wished to consult the only god she thought would help her—Felicio, the god of happiness and luck.

The luck was usually on the part of the person praying to him. He wasn't an easy god to grab the attention of, hence why there was so much unhappiness and misery in the world. She'd give all her worldly possessions for a simple sign from the god to let her know there was some respite coming soon.

"Highness, we're supposed to return to your rooms," a servant said, breaking her from her thoughts.

"I will. I'd like to pray first. We're about to go through life changing events. I'd like the gods' blessings."

The servant bowed and was silent from there on, even though Nakia had never gone to a temple on her own before. The walk took long minutes, but Nakia soon got to the end of the corridor, which opened up to the veranda of the temple. There was the expected bustle of people going in and out of the large marble building. Some moved about with bottles of wine or oil or even tiny goats on leashes, and all of those aromas mixed with smoke and fire inside the temple. *How do I get offerings?* Scanning the temple, eyes roaming by thick, grooved columns, she noticed a booth by the wall. It reminded her of the marketplace in Khenshu, so she took a chance and went to it.

"Offerings for the gods?" The seller motioned to his wares—fruits, jars of oil, nuts, berries, milk, and wine. There were even sheep and goats in a nearby pen.

"Whatever this'll get me." Nakia pulled a golden pin from her hair and placed it on a scale in front of him.

He nodded. "You could get a goat with this." He motioned to the full-sized goat.

She laughed, not expecting that. *Surely a large sacrifice would get the god's attention, right?* The fact that Felicio granted her happiness in Khenshu should mean something as well. He was already aware of her. She should at least thank him for those months in Khenshu, for the time she finally knew what it meant to be content, and then ask for guidance here. *How can I regain the blessing the god saw fit to give me?*

"I'll take a goat," Nakia said. *I'd like to sacrifice a bull, but that takes too much ceremony and space.*

"You can pick. A priest will come to properly slaughter the animal for you."

Nakia nodded and picked an all black goat with mighty horns and amused golden eyes. For a reason she couldn't place, it reminded her of Ashni and seemed appropriate as a gift for the god. A priest wearing a golden cloth draped over his long, white tunic, came for the beast. He led Nakia away to a room that gave her a good view of the statue of Felicio, but also some privacy. She halted her servants at the entrance, not wanting them to glimpse her prayers. The priest tied the goat to an intricately carved post before moving to a table by the wall.

"Write your prayers here." The priest motioned to strips of papers.

Nakia nodded and picked up a reed to begin her prayers. *What do I want to say?* A thanks was priority, for giving her happiness in what could've been a miserable situation and for blessing her with kindness in Khenshu rather than the harshness and cruelty she expected.

Beyond that, she entreated a sign for her happiness to continue. *Should I fight? Should I obey my father, as the gods often preached was the right thing to do?* She couldn't sit back and do nothing, though. Not anymore. Not when Ashni tried to regain her, not when there was a fire inside of her. It was the first thing Ashni noticed about her.

Ashni noticed something worthwhile in me. She should remember that. Her father didn't have anything to do with it, didn't want anything to do with it. *So why should he have control of me?* Her life was her life. *She'd encourage you to do this, to take control, to do what you could.* Ashni loved her fire. She wouldn't let it go out.

Nakia handed over several strips of paper to the priest. He walked over to the sacred fire and said prayers before he took a bowl to the goat. She flinched as the goat cried out when the priest slit his throat. The priest caught some bright-red blood in a small bowl and dipped her prayers in the blood, finally throwing the paper in the fire. With luck, the message would make it to the heavens and Felicio would care about her wellbeing again.

"If you pass your fingers through the sacred flame, the gods are more likely to acknowledge you," the priest told her.

Nakia knew that, as the priests said that anytime someone came to pray, but she had never done it before. The thought of touching her finger to a fire so hot it burned blue never appealed to her. Yes, she wanted the gods to hear her, but she didn't understand why she'd hurt herself for that to happen. Today, she didn't hesitate. She shoved two fingers into the fire, expecting it to bring her great agony. Instead, she felt nothing.

"You should feel the gods touch you and a light come into your heart. That light is love and hope," the priest said.

Nakia wished she could confirm that. There was nothing there, though. She didn't feel anything, no better, no different, not even worse. It was like the gods had turned their backs on her. She wasn't even worth their wrath. It made her feel beyond tiny, not even insignificant. Something even smaller than that. *Why should I have thought otherwise? When have the gods been on my side? They gave me to a worthless father, who doesn't even care for me as a protector like he should.* Her time in Khenshu, with Ashni, and even meeting Bashira had been a mockery from the gods, a taste at a life that would never be hers. They turned to see her long enough to have a prank at her expense.

Oddly enough, what should have been more than enough to snuff out her fire, didn't. Maybe some gods had laughed at her expense. Maybe Felicio was even one of them, pretending to give her happiness, but she had impressed someone divine. *I can do it for the rest of the gods. I'll show them that I have value.*

"Thank you," Nakia said to the priest.

The priest didn't respond. She left, her servants picking up with her as she began her journey back to the palace. *This isn't home. What makes some place home, though? Had Ashni made Khenshu home for me?* Ashni seemed to think so if she truly did propose marriage.

Ashni wants to marry me. Why? Nakia felt like she should be able to answer that, but didn't, couldn't accept what her mind offered. Her body felt it. Her heart fluttered. It was like she could float off into the sky, but the feeling was short lived as she reached her rooms.

Her father waited for her, and Nakia's heart sank into an abyss. She watched him with caution, but she wouldn't let him intimidate her anymore. He didn't care about her, only what she could gain for him. Ashni cared. Ashni would come for her.

"Where did you go?" her father said, eyeing her with a narrowed gaze.

"To pray to Felicio for happiness." There was nothing suspicious about this. *What bride wouldn't want her marriage to be happy?* Still, she watched her father, waiting to see if he believed her or if she needed to try something else.

"Having children will make you happy. Being a mother will make you happy."

She didn't respond. She never thought of being a mother, of having children. It was odd. She should've imagined that as her future, as that tended to be the future of all Kairon women. But, it never felt like *her* future. She didn't think there was anything wrong with being a mother though she never imagined herself as such. She didn't know how she thought she'd exist in Kairon society without having children or getting married, but now she had seen the alternative. None of the women she met in the Roshan Empire were mothers. They chased other dreams. Hell, they had other dreams. Maybe she could actually dream a dream before she got to chase it.

"I was wondering why you think the barbarian queen would propose a marriage alliance," he said.

Nakia shrugged. "Why would I know?" She brushed imaginary dust from her sleeve and maintained eye contact for a moment longer than was proper.

Dorian's jaw clenched, like he chewed on that answer. "You've spent the most time with them. You should know how they think."

Nakia arched an eyebrow. "Should I?" He was suddenly giving her a lot of credit, like he believed she could observe matters and piece together what was going on. Quite unlike him.

"We both know how observant you are, how you get into places you shouldn't, watch things you shouldn't. I know you did that there. So, tell me what you saw. Tell me why the barbarian queen would do this."

Nakia took a breath. "The Roshan…" She shook her head. "Women marry women there. So, I suppose she's decided just as you did with Caligo, an alliance. She's not breaking her word."

Dorian grunted and glared at her with such fierceness it was easy to forget he was her father. "You dare suggest she's better than I am? I'm trying to save our people!"

"You've betrayed the agreement you made with them." She had learned from the Roshan, from Ashni, how important a promise was.

"To save our people. Besides, what does an agreement mean to animals? You said it yourself, women marry women there. Even female animals don't pair up. Do you think they even understand what it means to be allies?"

Nakia tilted her head. "Do you really want my opinion?"

He waved the question off. "Of course not. My point is I'm not breaking my word. I don't know what that bitch thinks she'd do with you, but I wouldn't let them defile you like that."

No, you'd just let this creep you want me to marry defile me. He reached out and took her hands in his. His hands seemed to swallow hers, like he seemed to swallow her. She felt covered by him, shaded from the world. An unbearable cold overcame her, and she feared if he held her long enough, she'd die from the gelid numbness annihilating her very being.

"And what will you do after you defeat the Roshan?" Nakia found herself asking. The idea itself made her stomach twist.

Dorian frowned and stepped away from her. He studied her for a while, like a specimen in a jar, like he was trying to decide who she was or what happened to her, but she wasn't sure why. *It's not like he ever really knew me in the first place.*

It was a bit disappointing to realize her father didn't know her because he didn't want to know her. But, that meant he could fill in whatever blanks he desired and had no problem treating her any way he wanted. She relaxed, needing to come off as docile as she had been lately. She didn't want him to come up with some new way to use her for angering him. *Do not tempt him or the gods.*

Dorian patted her on the shoulder, the motion impersonal and heavy. "It's nothing for you to worry over. Focus on keeping your husband happy. His army, his power is a key to victory."

"And how do you know he won't turn that power on you after?" Nakia didn't understand why her father got into bed with this man.

"Because we've agreed you'll send your first son here to learn how to govern. He'll be my heir."

Nakia blinked. First off, the thought of bearing the child of Caligo made her skin crawl. If a simple gesture like him touching her hand felt like touching death, she could hardly imagine what it would be like to be intimate with him.

Beyond that, Nakia couldn't believe how worthless her father's word was. She never remembered him being such a liar, but he seemed ready to go to any lengths to win against the Roshan. *And he has the nerve to think lowly of other people? Has the nerve to think basically nothing of me?* She ground her teeth for a second, swallowing down both disappointment and fury. "Father, you've already agreed that Saffi's first-born son would be your heir."

He shook his head. "And Saffi has done nothing to help the process along. Barren undoubtedly. Useless to the end."

Nakia held in a flinch as best she could, but felt her neck jump. This was frightening to her, for someone's entire existence boiled down to having children. Saffi was her older sister, Dorian's middle daughter, and while she was practically a stranger, it was infuriating to hear their father dub her "useless" for not bearing children. She recalled her sister was well-read and elegant. Saffi had also been considered "unruly," for arguing with noblemen over matters she always seemed quite knowledgeable about. If she were a man, their father would probably praise Saffi's intellect and standing.

Instead, Saffi had been sold to people considered barbarians by Dorian and Phyllida and maybe even all of Kairon. Some tribe from even further west who wore animal pelts and painted their skin. Their king seemed to think marrying Saffi would give them legitimacy and her father bowed to that in exchange for a military alliance, as well as a claim to Saffi's first-born son since Dorian had no heirs. Saffi seemed to get the last laugh there. *I'm on that level and I doubt I'll have even the smallest laugh.* There went her stomach again. She winced from the pain.

Dorian gave her a hard look. "Don't question my methods. If all goes well, our family will rule this land. I'll unite the cities under me and drive out the Roshan."

Nakia held her tongue, but it seemed like he needed Caligo for this to work. *What would stop Caligo from taking all the credit? What would stop Caligo from turning on him?* Phyllida was powerful, but it seemed like Caligo was even more so.

"Do your part, daughter." Dorian took her by the shoulders and gave her a rough squeeze. She wasn't sure if he was trying to be affectionate and botching it or if he was threatening her. Neither worked.

With those words he was gone, and she was left to mull everything over. She understood her father's agenda, and she knew Ashni's agenda. Caligo was a mystery. *And what about Owen?* He had found his way into her father's inner circle, so there had to be more to him. She'd have to think on it, piece together what she knew, and see if the knowledge could help her in any way.

***

Ashni sat at her evening meal alone, eyes focused on nothing. Her closest companions were preparing for war and, yes, she had been more involved with that lately, but she was preoccupied with worry over the reply to her alliance proposal. When Adira entered with Layla, she knew the news was bad, could simply feel it from them. Gritting her teeth, she waited for them to report. Layla helped herself to food while Adira wrung her hands together, probably thinking of the best way to approach the subject.

"Dorian said no," Ashni said.

"Beyond that. Spies report he saw through the wording and laughed," Adira replied.

Ashni clutched the table, almost crushing it beneath her grip. Her anger spiked. "Laughed at me?"

Layla sucked her teeth. "What a fool."

"Do they not call me the Daughter of Death?" Ashni said. Now, she was a joke to him for simply wanting to marry his daughter. *Is this also from the gods? They've turned you from the Chosen One to something*

37

even a flea would snicker at? I'll show them all.

"He has an ally whom he seems to think will tip the scales against us. We haven't found out much about this new player, except he's from some land north, which may or may not be part of Kairon, as it's across a great river. A barren piece of rock we wouldn't care to think about, but somehow Dorian's interested in him. He also has the husbands of his other two daughters and their kingdoms. So..." Adira shrugged.

Layla leaned forward, elbows on the table, a dark smile curled onto her impish face. "I could so easily enter the palace and slit his throat for you, sister. I could bring you his head even. While your kitten is annoying as hell, I can't stand for us to be disrespected like this. How dare he turn you down for some..." She looked to Adira.

"Walking corpse at this point if he plans to oppose us." Adira rubbed her palms together, as if in deep thought.

"Do you think Nakia had a part in turning down the proposal?" Ashni asked. The notion caused an ache in her heart.

Layla scoffed. "Why? She's lucky you want someone as troublesome as she is."

"Nakia doesn't seem to have a say in who she can marry, so she didn't turn you down. None of the spies say she reacted. I have one person shadowing her, and she went to pray after she heard the news. I think she's waiting for you," Adira replied.

"I've learned you're a romantic," Ashni said. Still, the ache in her heart eased and strengthened her. Her nerves jumped, lightning buzzing through her. She wouldn't let her hellcat wait for long.

Adira snickered and squared her shoulders, like she was proud. "I am, but I'm also practical. She can't turn you down. She doesn't have the right. Dorian turned you down. He thinks he's going to get the better of us." She grabbed a handful of grapes and ate them one by one.

"Well, we can't let that sit." Ashni couldn't stand by and let a fool halt their goals. She wouldn't let him stand in the way of her happiness either. "Do we know anything about the man Dorian's forcing on my hellcat?"

"His name's Caligo Mor. I've already ordered scouts to his desolate piece of nothing called Nex. We'll have more information before we reach the shores of the West. It'll all come together," Adira said.

Ashni scratched her chin with her thumb. She wanted to know as much as possible about Caligo Mor. She wasn't sure if it was based on him being an enemy or a romantic rival of sorts. There was no way he was worthy of her hellcat or any danger Nakia would want him, but that didn't matter. He'd have Nakia, whether she wanted it or not. Nakia, a person so precious she might have been divine herself. Ashni couldn't stand the thought of it. The frost that had been devouring her since Nakia left spread to the point it infected her spirit.

Phyllida would be a reminder to the West because of Dorian and this Caligo Mor's actions. They needed to remember what the Roshan were capable of. *I'll remind them who we are and what we do.* The thought stoked fire in her veins. Now, she had a purpose beyond her dream and beyond retrieving Nakia. *Thanks, Dorian.* The gods might have placed him in her path, maybe even gave him the courage to think her a joke, but in the end, she was still the Daughter of the Amir Khalid. Her father had given her every tool imaginable to march as far as the burning gates of Jaha and storm the heavens themselves. *I may be out of your favor, but I will not be stopped.*

"I need everything. As soon as possible," Ashni said.

Adira snapped her finger and soldiers came in with satchels of scrolls. Adira was probably waiting for this moment, waiting for her fire. The wait was over. She'd crush the West just for taking her hellcat from her. The disrespect and breaking their word, they could have those things. She'd destroy everything in her way until her kitten was in her arms again. And should Nakia decide she didn't want Ashni or she didn't care about her homeland anymore, gods save them all.

"There might be a change in plans soon," Ashni said.

Layla scoffed. "We've been expecting that from the moment Nakia was dragged from the marketplace."

Ashni nodded. "You guys are smart. I guess I'll keep you for now."

"If you didn't keep us, you'd have died a long time ago," Adira replied.

Ashni rolled her eyes, but fought down the urge to argue. She had reading to do, strategies to study, and punishments to imagine. Dormant energy from weeks without Nakia was back. If the West thought she was the Daughter of Death before, they were about to see what that really meant.

***

Nakia had to fight down the urge to throw up as she was packaged into her wedding clothes, her servants tugging at her as they tried to make everything perfect. There were servants down in a hall somewhere, doing the same to the wedding space. This was all happening so fast. It seemed like Caligo had only just arrived, like she had only just gotten news of getting married, but maybe it had been days. A week even, maybe. She wasn't sure. Her mind couldn't keep track. Everything was tilted and wrong.

The white linen of her wedding garb felt heavy, like it cut into her bones, weighed down with the might of circumstances and lack of choice. *Has Felicio forsaken me or is this a test?* She didn't have the answers, and it didn't matter. The Roshan weren't on the horizon and her wedding feast was made and ready. Maybe Ashni didn't want her.

Her stomach rolled at the thought. Ashni had to want her. Ashni proposed a marriage for her. There was no way Ashni would leave her to this horrible, terrible fate. *Right?* The bile rising in Nakia's throat seemed to think so.

"Your Highness," a familiar male voice said, drawing her out of her thoughts. Her servants paused, shocked by the new presence.

Nakia turned. No man should be in her rooms right now, except maybe her father. Instead, she was face to face with Owen. There was a glint in his light eyes, and Nakia fought hard to keep her face passive. She wouldn't give anything away to him.

"You shouldn't be here, sir," Nakia said, waving away her servants. The dress was fine at this point. She didn't care. None of this was for her anyway.

"I thought I could come with a proposal for you," Owen said with a smirk. He brushed off his velvet red sash, as if showing how nonchalant he was. She glared at him, but it didn't have any effect.

"You've picked a poor time for it." Her voice sounded harder than she meant it to be. He didn't seem bothered by that either.

He continued to smile, a smug twinkle in his eyes. "I think this might be the perfect time for it. I mean you no disrespect by being here. I merely wish to talk to you for a moment." He took a step back, hands up in surrender, even though he was barely in the room.

She wanted to scream for him to leave, but she buried that, too curious about his attempt to be non-threatening. *What's he trying to pull?* "Of course." *Does he consider me a pawn, too? No, you're not a pawn. You've been taught how to predict moves, how to win. Do your best to play the game and win.* She wasn't sure how she could win, but if her father could see an outcome where he won, *then why not me?* She needed to take a moment and think rather than react to each moment that happened around her.

"I'm sure you know King Caligo is little better than being in bed with the Roshan," Owen said.

"And yet you're the one who brought this idea to my father." Her father was gone enough for it to seem like a good idea, but then again, he thought he could manipulate the Roshan when he sent her to them as well.

"It takes a savage to beat a savage. He's not to be trusted." Owen's face twisted like he tasted something sour.

She smirked. "And you are?" She was surrounded by people who betrayed each other at every turn. *I'm not so stupid.*

"We only need him through the marriage. He has no kin, only you and your father after you're married. He could have a little accident."

Nakia's jaw flexed and she swallowed down her disgust. The backstabbing never ended. No one kept his word on anything. She could only wonder what betrayal Caligo had planned, unless this was a sickness only her father and those around him held. *You would be free of him.* She didn't want it that way, though. "Is this your suggestion or my father's?" Probably Owen's. Her father would need Caligo a little longer than the marriage. Someone had to command his army after all.

He smirked, but a strange twinkle lingered in his eyes. "Let's say it's your father's suggestion. We could have everything we need after you marry Caligo, and he's not necessary. And we both know you don't want to be married to that thing." His lips curled in a sneer.

"Thing?"

Owen wagged his finger. "Thing is as accurate as I could call it. Some say he's a demon. There are tales his father was a dragon who raped his mother and his soul never fully formed. There's talk that he's actually dead already, but he's not allowed in the Underworld for the gods find his existence too distasteful. Do you want to lay with that? Have children by that?"

Nakia shuddered, remembering his cold, clammy touch. He could be a walking corpse for all she knew. She wasn't sure dragons existed anymore, having only seen images in painting, mosaics, and other art, but his cold, dark eyes could've been the eyes of a dragon, the ultimate predator.

"What do you suggest?" She had a feeling she was about to be handed poison for the second time to kill a reigning monarch in only a few months. *How the hell did I manage to go my whole life without handling poison until this year?*

"I have wedding gifts for you," Owen replied with a smile. He held up a small purse and opened it to reveal several small vials with dark red liquid in them. "Use it whenever you see fit, but I would do it before he wants to start on an heir."

Nakia nodded and accepted the bag, unsure if she would use it. It felt heavy in her hand, like the weight of the world was in the bag. She hadn't killed anyone and wasn't sure if she could, no matter how horrible her circumstances might get. Her throat burned at the thought. *What if things do get that bad?* She held out some hope the Roshan would invade, as planned, and Ashni would show up. A glimmer in her heavy heart.

She went through with the wedding ceremony but wasn't really present for it. She could hear flute music, but it sounded more like a dull hum than music to her ears. She didn't know many of the nobles there, except from seeing them at a distance over the years. It didn't matter, knowing people wouldn't make a difference.

She barely took in the bridegroom, beyond to imagine him being the dead son of a dragon. The more she looked at him, the more she could believe it. Under his pale skin, there seemed to be little lines, perhaps cracks, but it gave his flesh the appearance of being scales. The chill she felt wafting from his body held true to him being a corpse. His wedding clothing only supported the notion, a striking black tunic, even though she had always been told black was the color of mourning. *Is he mourning, too?* She doubted it.

Black seemed to be his color. Somehow, he seemed even more bent as they stood before the crowd, her swearing herself to him and his pledging to take care of her. Two lies to the gods in under thirty seconds. *Well, it's not like the gods held any love for me before the lie.*

At the wedding feast, she could've poured one of the vials into Caligo's wine, but couldn't bring herself to do it. Not just because she hadn't killed anyone before, but it seemed incredibly stupid. She'd be the prime suspect if her husband died at the wedding feast with her so visibly unhappy. She didn't want to think about how her father would react. Owen watched her the whole night, as if trying to force her hand. *What would he gain? Does he think I'd view him as my savior and then marry him?* It would give him access to the throne of Phyllida and possibly Nex if Caligo didn't have any family.

At one point during the festival, Nakia locked eyes with Owen. She took a vial from the pouch and watched his face light up. Then, she watched him crumble as she poured the dark liquid onto the floor. *I am no one's pawn, not anymore.*

Chapter Four

ASHNI STOOD AT THE bow of her ship, eyes focused ahead on the West. The mist of the ocean and the warmth of the sun danced on her face. The sea air never failed to invigorate her, and it stoked the fire in her belly. With each inhale she felt more like herself, like pieces of her slid back into place.

But, beyond the magic of the salty air, this was really it. The final moment. They wouldn't turn back in the winter. They wouldn't see Khenshu again until they'd taken over all of Kairon and the rest of the West. Khenshu would be the capital city of the Western end of the Roshan Empire. Eventually, the world would be Roshan, like her father dreamed. That was the big plan, but there had been some tweaks on what would happen when they touched down, so she could have peace of mind as she conquered whatever was in front of her.

A surge of seawater crested the ship's hull and splashed onto her face, pulling her out of her thoughts. Spitting, she wiped strands of sienna hair from her eyes. At least her braids saved her from having a full mop of curly hair in her face. *You too, Narayan?* To have the God of the Sea practically spit in her face did nothing to her confidence as far as taking the West but reinforced what happened with Nakia was a punishment of some kind. *I didn't think all the gods stuck together like this, but whatever. As long as the fleet lands, I'm still on track to do what needs to be done.* She'd be fine as long as the sea god didn't decide to sink her fleet and that didn't seem to be on the god's list of things to do. She toweled off and stared down her destiny.

"Changing the plan?" Adira asked as she stepped next to Ashni.

"The plan has already been changed," Ashni replied. Adira knew that, but was probably hoping for a change to the change. No, everything was done. "Aren't you pleased to be letting your best lieutenant try his hand?"

"It's not that. I trust Hafiz to do all that I taught him and more. Besides, he has his mother there to direct him if anything should go wrong."

"That he does. So, the plan is the plan." Ashni wasn't as confident in Hafiz as Adira was, but he was her protégé. It was time to see what Adira taught the young warrior about leading the most important battle he'd ever be involved in. He could either sink or swim, and Ashni was certain anyone who caught Adira's attention in battle would swim to the point of making fish envious.

Adira ground her teeth. "Are you sure you don't want me to go to Phyllida? You could take Princess with you."

Ashni glanced at Adira. *What would life be like if Adira didn't worry over matters that were already settled?* In the past, Ashni would've made a sex joke, but she wasn't in the mood. Right now, she needed Adira to understand why she set things up the way she did.

"Will Princess stop me if I go too far? Who's going to remind me that we're here to take the West and not for me to burn the whole accursed thing to the ground?"

Adira nodded. "You make a point. But, you really think Naren's ready to watch the Princess as she leads an attack?"

"He has her back." As much as she loathed to admit it. Naren would never be her favorite person and she'd never pick him to be her sister's spouse. He wasn't on Layla's level as a warrior, he lacked her ambition and drive, he wasn't that smart, he was lazy and a glutton, and sometimes seemed to think his wealth made him better than others, even though he hadn't always been so high on the social ladder. But, he'd do everything in his power to keep Layla safe and on task.

Naren chased Layla when her recklessness got the better of her and put his body on the line to make sure she wasn't touched. Ashni had seen him do the impossible when he thought Layla needed him, reacting faster to situations than he ever did on his own, like following her over an enemy wall before Ashni even knew what happened. He had saved Layla's life that night, shoving her to the side and inhaling poisonous powder. Ashni believed the only reason he didn't die from it was because Layla needed him alive. Most thought she should respect him from that, but he hadn't done it enough. Layla did the impossible on a regular basis, and Ashni saved her dozens of times.

Adira nodded. "But, he can't stop her like we can." Sometimes, they felt like Layla acted the way she did, reacting rather than thinking, because they were there and she trusted them to pull her back.

"He'll have to learn. He can stop her from getting killed, but he needs to stop her from killing the wrong person, stop her from rushing through it all, and learn sometimes you need to be subtle. I'd like for him to prove to me he deserves my sister. He should complement her, make her better, and walk alongside her at the same pace rather than letting her drag him along. How dare he marry someone who should live among the stars and not be able to keep up with her?"

Adira arched an eyebrow. "You really want to do that now?"

"We don't have a choice. I can already feel what I'm going to do when I lay eyes on Caligo. There's no way my kitten wants him and there's no reason he should have her. So, I'll get her and teach him why he shouldn't touch what's mine." Ashni made a fist so tight her nails bit into her flesh. This was why she needed Adira with her. She wouldn't be able to control herself once she saw that rotter.

They hadn't gotten many reports on Caligo or Nakia's marriage, but some wise soul made sure to mention the marriage wasn't Nakia's choice. It seemed to be part of the scheme of some Phyllidan noble called Owen. He was the one who brought Caligo to Dorian. Her spies sought more information on Owen.

She was also made aware Nakia would be taken back to Caligo's land when the wedding was over. It was Kairon tradition, so Ashni planned for it and split their forces. Layla would replace her and lead their original planned attack while Ashni went to retrieve Nakia.

"I doubt she'd like you claiming her like that," Adira said.

"Why not? In her culture, isn't that what husbands do? Claim their wives as property?" The words tasted funny on Ashni's tongue. There were no such things as a "husband" or "wife" in Roshan culture. Married people had a spouse, or several spouses, but no words existed to let a person know the gender of the spouse.

Adira scoffed. "Yeah, and why do you think she fit in so well with us? Her culture is bullshit in that regard. She doesn't want to belong to anyone. I'm not even sure she accepts most of her culture at this point. She just didn't know any different until us. So, try to remember that when you go rescue her. The last thing we need is for you two to have another stupid misunderstanding."

Ashni scowled, but Adira had a point. She had already caused two rifts between her and Nakia from acting like she was in control. Nakia was unpredictable and didn't want to be forced into anything. *I'll respect her.* Actually, it was one of the things she loved about Nakia. She'd go to Nakia, but she had to give Nakia a choice. She wasn't entitled to Nakia in any way, shape, or form.

"Let's go over the plan once more with Princess, if only to be sure. After that, we'll work through it again with Hafiz and the other generals," Ashni said.

Adira nodded, and they moved away from the edge of the ship. Layla was with Naren, near the bow of the ship. Naren was eating, which wasn't a surprise, and they were playing a game of mancala, which also wasn't surprising. Layla felt like the game helped keep her mind sharp and she liked playing before battles. The game was moved as Ashni and Adira sat down.

"Guys, we're fine with the plan," Layla said before anyone could speak.

"We've got this." Naren had the nerve to put his chin in the air, like he wasn't one step away from being totally incompetent.

Ashni couldn't be more skeptical if she tried and even Adira gave him a deadpan look. Layla scowled at them both.

"I'm not an idiot, guys. I've led attacks before," Layla said.

"Never without us," Ashni replied.

"How hard could it be?" Naren asked with a shrug.

Ashni flinched, hand balling into a fist for a quick moment. But, she caught herself before she hit him. He was serious. This person who probably wouldn't get out of bed before noon if he wasn't married to someone who had to keep moving had the nerve to think what they did was easy. Naren barely did anything that didn't involve following Layla when the fighting began.

"I love that you think planning and executing an attack is easy. Why haven't we been letting you lead us into battle all this time?" Adira inquired, properly insulted if her sneer meant anything.

"Because we like to win," Ashni replied.

Naren scoffed. "How do you know I couldn't win? Obviously the gods like me more than they do you right now."

Anger flaring as fast as lightning, Ashni grabbed Naren by the throat. How dare he throw her fall from grace in her face like that! *Calm down, you don't need the gods. You said so yourself.* Yes, she might have said so, but no one had the right to point out the gods had abandoned her. *And how could the gods just abandon me? What have I done to deserve this?* She didn't have any answers and swallowed the pain of knowing the gods weren't with her. She had to be tougher, for Nakia and for not just her father's dreams, but the dreams of their people.

Layla and Adira jumped, pulling her away. She was tempted to take Naren's windpipe with her, but she decided to let him live. Surely the gods wouldn't be happy with her should she murder her sister's spouse, even if he deserved it. *But, the gods aren't with you, anyway.* The sky darkened and the ship rocked, but everything cleared up once Layla and Adira glared at her.

"And this is why you're coming with me," Ashni said, nostrils flaring as she pointed between her and Naren. Layla crawled over to Naren and cradled him to her chest.

"I can see your point," Adira replied.

"That wasn't right," Layla said, petting Naren's head.

"Why? She'd taunt you if you lost me," he replied.

Layla locked eyes with her sister. "No, she wouldn't."

Ashni shrugged. She probably would, but she'd also help Layla get back her irksome spouse with all her power, even if the ass was dead. She would walk into the Underworld by Layla's side, right up to the flaming gates of Jaha, and rip his soul back from any creature that tried to stop them. It had nothing to do with him and everything to do with her caring about her sister. Maybe one day when he did something worthwhile she'd change her mind, but at the moment, the only reason he mattered was because Layla loved him. *Ugh.*

"First off, Ashni didn't lose Nakia. Nakia was noble enough to honor her father's agreement. Which is good, as it seems she was the only one who had honor at that moment," Adira said, cutting a hard glance at Ashni.

"You tell a group 'keep the gold' once and you never live it down," Ashni grumbled.

"Because who in their right mind tells someone to keep gold that's about to finance the dreams of hundreds of thousands of people, especially when you can easily get back the person you want?" Adira gave her a smug look.

"I think we've established I wasn't in my right mind," Ashni replied.

"And you never will be again, such is the nature of our ailment." Adira patted her on the shoulder.

Ashni groaned. "Great, something else to look forward to. Have the gods actually forsaken me?" She looked to the sky. "What did I ever do to you, Dad? I just rode with you from the time you allowed it, learned all I could, and put your lifelong goal into action. This is the thanks I get?" Even as she made this joke, she could feel deep in her heart, she longed to be back in the gods' favor. *You can do this on your own.*

"Isn't it the same thanks he got? After all, he ran into Chandra. Your hellcat isn't nearly that," Layla said.

Ashni never thought of that. Her mother had been an obstacle placed in front of her father. She wasn't sure if he conquered the obstacle or what the gods intended when her parents met. But, Nakia wasn't her mother. *Or is she?* Nakia was the only person to give her pause and rethink something she had done. Anyone else outside of Adira and her sister, she bowled over and went about her business. And even Adira and Layla had to earn her respect to get her to pause.

What if Nakia's appearing or disappearing isn't about being abandoned by the gods...but being tested instead? Oh, damn. I've never been tested before. What the hell am I supposed to do? What do tests from the gods look like? Nakia? My mother? It seemed so. The thought of being tested was better than the notion of being abandoned, but she didn't understand how these tests worked. *Is my treatment part of the test, part of my failing, or simply the gods forsaking me?* She didn't know the answers and didn't want to think on it right now. *I don't need the distraction.* Another gush of ocean water splashed onto her face. Maybe that answered those questions.

***

Nakia found herself traveling more in the past year than she had in her entire life. Now, she was on her way to Nex, her new homeland. She and her husband shared a carriage. The inside wasn't glamorous, barely comfortable, and she couldn't help comparing it to when the Roshan had transported her a few months ago or when her countrymen took her home. There was hardly any cushion on her seat and no back support. Bits of wood cracked and splintered around her. She felt every single imperfection in the road. Not the transport one would expect of a king. The only saving grace was Caligo had to sit across from her as there wasn't enough space for them to sit side by side.

In the small space, Nakia was certain she knew what death smelled like, and it had to be Caligo. There was a hint of rot and smoke to him that never seemed to go away. *Betraying his dragon heritage, perhaps?* It scratched at her insides, threatening to choke the life from her and possibly transfer it to him, like some sort of incubus. The more she sat with him, the more she felt like he was a creature who had stolen the skin of a corpse and put it on its own twisted form to stroll among the living.

"Should you be returning home, my Lord?" she asked. She wasn't sure what Caligo wanted her to call him, so she went as formal as possible without simply referring to him as "your majesty."

"It won't do to have my new wife go to my palace on her own.

After all, you haven't seen the place. You don't know what to expect, Princess," he replied. He used her title with a hiss, like it was an insult. He glanced at her, and then dismissed her with a look outside the carriage.

She nodded. It seemed polite, but she had learned in the few short days she knew him, he didn't have manners. Tradition didn't seem to mean anything to him, either. He hadn't seemed interested in her after their marriage ceremony, and he hadn't tried to consummate their marriage, not that she'd dare complain. *So, why accompany me to his home?* There was something more. There was a reason he needed to go home with her.

"What if you miss the battle?" she asked. He didn't strike her as a coward, so she didn't think he was running from the war. He boasted to her father and other Phyllida nobles about his vast, mighty armies.

He shook his head. "The battle will come to me and then I'll show the Roshan true power."

She furrowed her brow and worried over how deep it might run. "Why do you think the battle will come to you?"

He looked her up and down. "How do you think?"

I'm the bait to get the Roshan to come to him? Why would he go through the trouble? How did he know that would work?

"Wouldn't it have been easier to just wait for them at Phyllida?" Nakia asked. *This seems more complicated and risky than waiting where he knows the Roshan will show up.*

"Easier if I wanted to be in a melee battle, which I don't. I only want the barbarian queen and I think we both know she'll come for you."

"What makes you think that?" This was a huge gamble on his part, especially since he made this agreement before he heard Ashni's proposal letter.

He scoffed. "You don't have to play coy with me like with your father. It's obvious you enthralled her. The Queen of the Roshan proposed marriage to you in an effort to get you back."

"So? You proposed marriage for an alliance. Why can't they do the same?" *Maybe you should stop asking so many questions before something happens.* But, Nakia couldn't stop herself. He seemed open to speaking to her, not at her. Sure, he still seemed to think she was of low intelligence, but more because he was condescending than because she was a woman.

"Because I know this queen. She doesn't make alliances in that manner. She wanted *you* back. She'll come for you. I've been told by those who know."

She held in a gasp. "Like who?" *How did he get such information? Has a Roshan betrayed their own? How much does he know? Does he have even more information, enough to defeat Ashni? Is that why he wanted to break away? He could take all of the glory for himself?* Her father wouldn't see that coming.

"I have my ways. She'll come for you." He smirked, folding his arms across his chest. He was the picture of confidence.

Nakia nibbled the corner of her mouth. "And you'll what? Fight her one-on-one for my honor?" If he wanted to fight Ashni, that was on him. She'd eat him alive, smiling all the way through.

Caligo's eyes sparked with something like a dreadful amusement. "I'll fight her for my entertainment and to prove I'm stronger than she is. I'll trade you for what I really want, though."

Nakia arched an eyebrow. "And what's that? And what makes you think Ashni would give it to you?" He might be gambling on her being worth more than she was. *Beyond that, what could he possibly want from the Roshan? What did a king from the North want from perceived barbarians from the East?*

The smile that spread across his face was downright predatory. "The fact that you call her by name says a lot. And again, she proposed marriage to you. For Roshan royals, marriage is a huge deal. She sees you as an equal. She sees you as part of her. She needs you back."

Nakia didn't have a response for that. She didn't know anything about Roshan marriages, except they seemed to be love matches. Bashira told her the story of how Ashni's parents met, married, and had grown more than attached to each other, even though Ashni's mother didn't have a choice in the matter at first. The few couples she knew in person chose each other. She remembered Bashira trying to tell her about Roshan believing in different sorts of bonds, connecting them to people on different levels. She assumed marriage was connected to those bonds, but she didn't know.

"You seem to know quite a bit about the Roshan Empire," Nakia decided to say. He seemed to enjoy talking, so he might let her in on the secret.

"You lived with them for months." Caligo leaned forward, licking his lips. "Did you get a chance to see their libraries? Read any of their books? See their war manuals?"

Nakia shook her head. She didn't even know there were libraries.

Of course, for half of her stay, she didn't think the Roshan knew how to read or didn't think they'd want to record information. But, now that he brought it up, she was curious about the stories they wrote. She knew they loved the tale of Amir Khalid and his wife Chandra. *What other stories are cherished and told? What knowledge do they have?* She knew they weren't mindless brutes, after all. Ashni probably had a vast library and now she wished she bothered to see it.

"Why do you want their war manuals?" Nakia asked. Before she knew anything else about the Roshan, she was aware they knew matters of war as that was all her father and the nobles at home spoke about when it came to the Roshan.

Caligo's eyes actually twinkled and looked alive for the first time. "Not just their war manuals. There's also magic, science, and martial arts. Centuries of knowledge locked away. Thousands of techniques kept from us."

"And what good would it do you?" Nakia wasn't sure the Roshan had all of these things. *If they're as advanced as Caligo made them seem, why didn't they use that knowledge to destroy the West the first time? And if the Roshan kept it from people, how does he know in the first place?*

He shrugged and sat back again. "I'd merely like to educate myself."

"For what purposes? And where am I in all this? You'd really just give me to the Roshan?" Nakia inquired.

"No, I'd give you to your beloved Ashni," he dragged out the name.

"She's not my beloved anything," Nakia sneered.

He watched her as if he could see through her. "We both know the truth."

"Why aren't you disgusted by the idea of a woman trying to marry me?"

"I know all about the Roshan and their unnatural matches. It's even more so in Ashni's territory. But, I don't care about that. I care about the mountain of tomes she has. What she does with her personal matters are on her."

"She won't betray her people and give you anything for me."

He chuckled. The sound came from deep in his chest like it scratched its way out of an abyss, but sort of rattled, too. It crawled through her and settled in her belly, making her stomach tremble and her blood feel like it fled her body. His eyes seemed to blacken. Their carriage creaked and groaned, the most noise she heard since they crossed the River Reve, but he didn't seem to notice, refusing to look away from her. He was probably used to the eerie silence of the land.

"I think she'll give me everything for you. The way she put it on the line for you, sending that proposal to your father, knowing he wouldn't accept, knowing he wouldn't even understand, knowing he'd mock her as a barbarian. She'd do anything for you, little one. And I'll make sure she gives me everything."

Nakia swallowed. She didn't know how to respond. It was one thing to be a pawn, but it was something entirely different to be bait. To be bait and find out how much she might mean to someone. To mean everything. *Was that what Ashni meant when she told me I was precious? Would she give up everything for me?* Almost every part of her told her no, but there was a small piece of her that considered otherwise. *What if he's wrong? What if he's right?*

It was far scarier to consider Ashni would come for her. Her heart sped up to the point she feared it might explode with a terrible hope. She couldn't imagine how she could mean more than Ashni's dream, her father's legacy. She couldn't imagine Ashni betraying her culture. *How could I live up to something like that?* It wasn't realistic, which meant eventually Ashni would realize it and abandon her.

Mind spinning, Nakia turned her attention to the outside. She wasn't sure if they crossed into his country yet, but they were in the north and the scenery looked bleak. While the land leading to Khenshu had been bathed in red rock and a sea of fine sand, this territory looked like someone set it ablaze and it never healed. *Perhaps it was the dragon who raped Caligo's mother.*

Dark, even though the sun was high. The sunlight crackled through dense, but bare, bent branches of the crooked, thin, leaning trees. Even the grass was somehow the color of charcoal. Maybe it was from the way the light cut through the woods, but everything looked charred. There was little noise, like no life existed in this forest. It was otherworldly in the sense that she feared she might have died and passed into some haunted afterlife.

The chill in the air supported that frightening thought. She felt the cold down to her bones and no matter how tightly she pulled her cloak around her, it cut through her protection and herself. It felt unholy, a different type of cool than the approach of winter, like frost gathering under her skin.

"Do you like my country?" he asked, his twisted smile back in place. It was like he knew the place was a horror, but he was proud of it.

"It's odd. Cold. Quiet." *Like a grave.*

His eyes drifted to the window, seemingly at peace with this desolate woods. "Yes, that's how I like it. I need the silence to read and practice. Keep that in mind when we get to my home."

Nakia understood the threat. "How do you keep everything so quiet?"

"Nothing lives here."

She could believe that. "Why?"

"Because I don't want anything to."

Nakia bit the inside of her cheek to keep a squeak from escaping her throat. This only supported the idea he was some kind of demon wearing human skin. Maybe he was an incubus and he stole the life-force from every single thing in his land. "What's the point of ruling a country of nothing?"

"It gives me time to study."

She was afraid to know the answer, but she had to ask. "Study what?"

"The mystical and martial arts."

Nakia nodded, even though that answer didn't make much sense to her. Martial arts, she mostly experienced from watching Ashni and her annoying sister spar. She hadn't had a lot of experience with mystical arts, even after hearing how Ashni was part-god, so she wasn't sure what those arts entailed. What she did know was she didn't want to witness them through him. He seemed to know her struggle, eyeing her with a devilish smirk.

Her heart raced and she felt sweat pricking at her palms. *Don't squirm. Keep your cool and keep him talking.* She took a breath to calm her heart and maintained eye contact with him.

"Your father doesn't know much about me, which is why I have to assume he was fine with marrying you to me. He's an intelligent man, but too full of himself," Caligo said.

"And you're not?"

His smirk grew. "I have reason to be."

"And my father doesn't?" While she wasn't a fan of her father, he was doing something right, at least from his point of view and from Caligo's point of view. After all, Phyllida should've been conquered territory for the Roshan already, but her father held them off. Yes, it involved lying, cheating, and perhaps some luck, but he did it.

Caligo shook his head. "Your father thinks he knows everything. He's about to learn differently. He's not prepared for what the barbarian queen will bring down on him. He doesn't know he didn't even see a percentage of the true power of the Roshan."

She tilted her head, taking in not just his words, but his demeanor and the light in his eyes as he spoke. "You sound like you admire them."

He frowned. "Never. They've managed to steal most of their great manuscripts. I'm convinced they don't even understand their full power."

"And you plan to let my father witness this power as you wait for the queen?" *Is he trying to teach my father a lesson? Why would he do that?* Caligo shouldn't have interacted with her father enough to dislike him. Maybe Caligo was insane, a madman of some kind. Something had to be wrong with him to think the Roshan were both some kind of magical beings and also barbarians.

He dismissed the question with a flick of his fingers. "Don't worry. I don't plan to leave him wanting or waiting. I just want to take on the queen on my own terms."

"So, you won't betray him?" Unless he said he'd betray her father, Nakia wouldn't believe the answer.

"I'll honor my end of the alliance."

That certainly didn't answer her question. She was used to double-talk and backstabbing at this point. *But, what good would it do to betray my father other than for entertainment purposes?* Frustrated, she felt like she didn't have the tools to put the puzzle together. *How do I get out of this?* She'd like to do so without compromising her morals, but that might not be possible. If push came to shove, she could always use the poison Owen left her.

She wanted to wait for Ashni, as her husband planned, but she doubted that would work. A thought struck her like a bolt of lightning. *I'm married now. Married.* Ashni might not want her simply because of that. Nakia curled into herself. *Being abandoned by Ashni would be worse than being rejected by her.* She couldn't see a reason for Ashni to desire her like before. She was married to Caligo, tainted by his name, by his vow, even if he didn't mean it. Ashni might leave her to him.

"What if she doesn't come? What will you do to me?" Nakia asked, trying her best to sound normal, but her voice sounded small.

"She'll come and if not, you'll do your duty." He shrugged as if it didn't matter to him.

The thought made her stomach flip, like she was seasick, and she swallowed down the urge to vomit. She'd have to lie with him. His simple touch made her skin crawl, and she'd have to be with him. She couldn't imagine what that would be like, but there wouldn't be any pleasure for her. Being with him would be an invasion and her body would be poisoned, even to herself. No one in her country would want her after that, much less Ashni. She'd belong to Caligo.

No. If that's the case, I belong to Ashni. She didn't want to possess me. Not that it mattered. The gods had abandoned her, and Ashni might do the same.

She was silent the rest of the trip. Partially for him to think she wanted to please him, but, also because she wanted to think of a way out of this. She couldn't afford to be passive anymore. Her fearlessness had impressed Ashni, and she needed to hold onto that. It would help her survive here, just as it helped her in Khenshu.

Chapter Five

THE LARGEST ARMY THE Roshan had ever put together landed on the shores of the West and Ashni could only think of one thing—Nakia. She was on the cusp of being the greatest conqueror known among her people. She was about to surpass her father. She was about to achieve her place in heaven. None of that mattered. Nakia mattered. She needed her hellcat.

Adira put her hand on Ashni's shoulder. "We'll get her back."

"I know. I'm more concerned with that." Ashni motioned to Naren, who got seasick the second they got off the ships. Layla rubbed his back as he vomited into a bush. A warrior who couldn't even make the short voyage across the sea was supposed to keep an eye on her sister and help conquer the West. It was like a bad joke.

Adira pinched the bridge of her nose, looking away. "Yeah, I can understand that. It's not too late to put me in charge."

"I'll do just that if you truly believe that's the best course of action."

Adira seemed to think on it, staring off to the horizon. "No, I'll come with you. You were right about why I should go."

Ashni nodded. She'd need Adira by her side to talk sense into her if she lost herself, especially depending on what Nakia would want. *Will Nakia want to come with me?* She could only hope. If that hope was misplaced, she had no idea how she might react. Adira would ground her as best anyone could, get her back on track, and help her do the right thing.

"Do you have any new reports?" Ashni asked as their military moved around them, collecting items off the ships and getting ready to move out.

"They're coming in now that we've landed. We'll find out where your kitten is momentarily," Adira replied.

"I'd rather spend more time preparing the Princess. I want to make sure she understands she's in charge. She's holding the dream of many in her hands." Ashni was certain Layla understood that, but she needed to be sure.

Adira glanced over at Layla and then back at Ashni, quiet for a long moment. "It's time for her, just as it's time for Hafiz," Adira finally said. "If we're going to carry on from sea to sea, we have to be able to let them loose to do what they do."

Ashni nodded. Her father's death taught them all, no one lived forever. She didn't have an heir yet, but her dream could live on through Layla should anything happen to her. The same could be said for Adira. They needed to let the younger ones learn to lead. Now would be the best time, mostly because Ashni wasn't in the right mindset to lead the conquest.

"Do you want to find Hafiz and speak with him again? Make sure he understands he's now you?" Ashni asked.

"He understands. He claims to be ready. I think he is. I only worry about him being imaginative enough should the battle call for it. His thinking is quite strict. Good for learning, not the best for creating," Adira replied.

Ashni sought Hafiz Vivek in the crowd of their military, finding him quite easily, a broad shouldered lad with long white feathers in his dark brown hair. Tattoos on his face stood out, marking him of the Bear Clan, stood out, but they weren't why he was easy to find. Hafiz rode an alphyn. It was the closest thing to a dragon or a griffin many of them had ever seen. Once, when they were more abundant, there were tales the creatures were used to hunt dragons. Hafiz's alphyn, Yata, was massive, the size of a giant workhorse, but with the body and face of a lion, scales on its thick front legs that met dark brown fur at the thigh, and long talons. Yata's dark crimson mane ran the length of his back, down his tapered, dragon-like tail and ended with a tuft of fur. Hafiz had a saddle made especially for Yata but held his mane rather than using reins.

The soldiers liked to gossip over Hafiz and Yata, telling tall tales of how he faced the alphyn down and roared so loudly in Yata's face, Yata had to bow to him. He told Adira the truth one night, and she told Ashni. He found the creature some years back and nurtured it from a hatchling to a best friend. Somehow, that impressed Ashni more than the idea of him beating the beast in battle, and she was certain Adira would say the same.

The army marched to the nearest town, a place they had conquered their first time in the West. The town, which had changed its name to Ashi to show its loyalty to Ashni, welcomed them. Several of their soldiers had stayed behind and the town was the first of the West to understand what they could gain from being part of the Roshan Empire. They already enjoyed new products from the East. Ashni and her closest comrades were given a posh villa with a lush garden, open spaces, and large rooms to stay for the time. Once they were settled in one of the sitting rooms, they received reports on what happened during their water crossing.

"It's been confirmed that Nakia married Caligo Mor and they've headed north to his country of Nex," Adira said as she pushed a scroll to the side. A pile of paperwork lay stacked on a low table between her, Ashni, Layla, and Naren. They sat on pillows on the floor.

"Then that's where we'll go. Did it say how many men he had?" Ashni asked.

Adira scanned parchment after parchment, her face scrunching. "There are no numbers on his army."

Layla scowled. "How are there no numbers? What are your spies doing?"

Adira glared at Layla from across the short table. "Their job. What have you done? Your Shadow Walkers. Where are they?"

"With me, ready to take this miserable piece of dirt if we could get some accurate information." Layla rapped her fist on the table.

"Adira, this is a little weird. Your people have held everything together here. Why don't we have numbers on Caligo?" Ashni inquired with a tilt of her head. This lack of information wasn't usually something Adira accepted.

"No one ever got a look and he never said anything. He arrived at Phyllida with a handful of servants, but nothing more. Even the servants weren't actually his but on loan from Dorian. From conversations they picked up, he's a master of dark magic," Adira replied.

Layla shrugged. "It doesn't take much to be a master of dark magic."

"Yeah, isn't he one?" Ashni motioned to Naren. The fact that he was a Shadow Walker always made her second-guess her knowledge of Shadow Walkers, even though she saw them in battle. Not to mention, she saw them when her father first conquered their people.

"I'm good at my craft." Naren thrust his chin in the air and held his fist up. Shining, obsidian smoke glinted from his hand and the heat was sucked from the room.

Adira waved a scroll at him. "Can you stop before we freeze to death?"

"I'm just saying..." Naren waved his fingers and the smoke vanished. The temperature returned to normal.

"My point being it can't be hard to do it if you're considered a master." Ashni resisted the urge to call him an idiot and turned to Adira. "Do we have any reports on what type of magic?"

Adira shook her head. "Caligo's a mystery still. He didn't use any magic on his visit and didn't really discuss his craft style. Everything they have is hearsay. Caligo's not the type of king to shout his glories to the mountains."

"Where did he find this man?" Ashni wondered aloud than genuinely asked. It had been a long time since they came across an enemy like him, a mystery man.

"Spies confirm a nobleman by the name of Owen Acheros first brought the idea to Dorian. They're not entirely sure how Owen knows the man. There were no hints Owen traveled to the north," Adira answered.

"He has to know Caligo from somewhere. He didn't just pull a king from thin air," Layla said.

"We'll take a small force then. Not much they'd be able to do against magic anyway, especially dark magic," Ashni said.

"You take less men because they can't stop magic?" Layla frowned.

"You need all the men we have for this conquest." The conquest was everything for everyone else and Ashni couldn't take away from that, even for Nakia. Also, deep down, she wanted to be the one to free Nakia from Caligo. It felt like her responsibility and she needed to do it, for herself and for Nakia.

"You're going to rejoin us, though. It's not like I'm marching on without you. I'm taking Phyllida and possibly any town or city after that, but nothing more. Phyllida's practically conquered already," Layla replied.

"I know, but Dorian is slippery. He has allies. We have to be careful," Ashni said. She wouldn't count Phyllida as conquered until she tore the city walls down. Until then, the city was still in play and Dorian was probably watching her people as closely as they watched him.

Layla pursed her lips. "You going into the unknown with limited forces isn't careful."

"But, this is a detour. It's a taste, a nibble. You're on the main course. We have to focus on that," Ashni said. As much as she wanted her hellcat back, they couldn't lose sight of the main objective. She might not like it, but she understood it.

"We got it," Naren said.

"Make sure you watch her." Ashni pointed to Layla. She'd tell Hafiz the same. She didn't think he'd do the best job, but more eyes were always good. Layla was more than a force of nature, and there were times when even Ashni felt like she had to simply get out of Layla's way. Of course, she never actually did, but others might.

"I don't need him to watch me." Layla folded her arms across her chest.

"I think we all know that's not the case," Adira said. "All right, let's focus on the main attack. Dorian's prepared for us, but we can work your command style and Hafiz's command style. You're almost opposites, so it'll be difficult to counter you the same way. We just need for both of you to stick to the plan unless necessary." Ashni believed this was the biggest problem for both of her stand-in commanders. Layla often went off script while Hafiz couldn't fathom there was a way to change a plan.

"What's going on with our people on the inside?" Layla asked.

"They're waiting on word from you. As soon as you give the order, they'll do what they do," Adira replied.

"Why didn't Dorian lock them all up?" Naren scratched his hairless chin.

"He's locked up some, but he doesn't know everyone involved. Beyond that, he probably didn't want to draw too much attention to his plans. If he locked up enough of our people, someone would send word. Remember, Dorian wants us to believe he's still on our side since he gave us our tribute. He wants us to believe he's still honoring our agreement," Adira replied.

"He's an idiot if he thinks we still believe that," Layla said.

"You knew he was a snake the moment you met him," Ashni said.

Layla leaned her elbow on the table and rested her chin in her hand. "Right about that."

"Glad we agreed on something. Now, how about we actually go over this battle plan and get something done? Get Hafiz and the other generals in here." Ashni tapped the table, rustling some of the documents.

Servants moved to make things happen. Ashni needed to have faith in her sister. It was just so damn hard to do considering the things she saw Layla do and the many times she watched Layla almost die from her own impulses.

***

Nakia found herself in disbelief. Somehow her husband's country got more and more depressing as they traveled through it. There was a constant chill, but it still wasn't a winter cold. It remained a crawling shiver under her skin, scratching at her bones. There was darkness always, like the place was under the shadow of a giant even during the day. Nighttime seemed like a vapor of tar covered the country. She could make out jagged cracks in the ground, as if the land itself was crying for help. Nakia could relate.

When they came to Caligo's stronghold—as that was the only word for it—she was stunned. Sitting atop barbed black stones, every bit of it seemed sharp, pointed, and dangerous. It loomed with dusty, grey stones, glaring down on them as they approached. Smoke wafted from it as if it was breathing. *Why would anyone choose to live here?*

"This is home?" Nakia asked. The stronghold left a feeling like there were ants under her skin.

"For now," he replied.

She held in a frown. "And what does that mean?"

"You won't be here for long. I promise. We know Ashni will come for you." He gave her a wicked smile.

Nakia frowned. He didn't plan to keep her, but he planned to defeat Ashni. *Soon, will I be part of his dead things?* "And what of me?"

"If all goes to plan, the Roshan will take you off of my hands. I have no use for you." He dismissed her with a flick of his thick wrist.

Yes! For once, it worked in her favor to be seen as useless. "What about heirs?" Not that she cared, but she wanted to be certain he didn't have other plans for her. He had claimed if Ashni didn't come, she'd have to do her wifely duties. It seemed like something that mattered to him since he brought it up and she wanted to be sure he was willing to let that go. She'd very much like to get out of this without having to touch him. *So far so good.* With luck, that would hold, but she didn't want to get her hopes up.

He tilted his head. "Do you know the Roshan have a secret to immortality?"

It took all of Nakia's self-control to not laugh. "What makes you believe that?" *If the Roshan had the key to immortality, why not use it to save their beloved Amir?* She was certain if Ashni could've saved her father, she'd have done it through any means possible.

"I've seen some of their books. I even practice some of their magic.

I know what they're capable of."

"Hard to believe when we've all agreed they're savages." His faith in the Roshan and their magical knowledge didn't sound like someone who thought the Roshan were blood-thirsty barbarians.

"Oh, but they are. They have all of this stolen knowledge, and they don't know how to use it. Do you think they know they have the secret to immortality?" Caligo scoffed.

That seemed possible for the Roshan to have stolen knowledge since they conquered so many people and so much territory. Still, she doubted they had the secret to immortality. She doubted they had knowledge they didn't know about as well. "So, how will they know what to give you?"

"I know the exact books I'll exchange for you, the titles, which libraries they're in, and all. I'll get everything I deserve, and they'll get you. I think I'm getting the better end of the deal."

"Which is why it most likely won't work. They won't exchange me for such valuable and useful information."

He smiled. "Won't they?"

She wished she was as confident in Ashni as he was. Yes, she made a fool of herself for Nakia with the marriage proposal, but that didn't mean she was willing to part with her nation's treasures.

"You plan to fight the queen. If you defeat her, the Roshan wouldn't want me," Nakia said.

His nostrils flared briefly and he sat back. It didn't seem like he considered that, didn't think about the possibility of his plan not working. She wouldn't care, but his reactions to things would dictate her life until she figured out a means of escape.

"Ashni would make this deal before she comes to save you. I'd release you once she arrived. She should see a true master before I crush her."

Nakia arched an eyebrow. "But, why does it matter to defeat her in battle?"

"So she knows, so *they* know they're not worthy of any of the knowledge they've stolen. Beyond that, she thinks she's a top warrior. The Roshan worship her like a god. I will show them a true god." His eyes glinted as he made a fist.

It was a little funny to see so many men chasing after Ashni's back, trying to outsmart her. For all their talk of being the superior sex, Nakia didn't see it anymore. Her father's every move now revolved around the idea of defeating a woman. Caligo was almost the same.

As they came to the dour walls of the citadel, the gates creaked open. Someone had to be there, but she couldn't see anyone. *Does he do everything with magic?* She hadn't witnessed any magic beyond parlor tricks done at banquets. The carriage groaned to a stop.

"We're here," he said, knocking on the carriage door. It opened. He stepped out and then put a hand out for her. She waved him off. His mouth curled downward for a second, but he got out of the way, so she could get out on her own. Her sandals touched down on hard, grey stone and the cold went through the leather to the sole of her foot immediately. She squared her shoulders against the gloomy atmosphere.

"Welcome home," Caligo said with his crooked smile.

Nakia scanned the area, trying to assess the situation. She was surrounded by dark wood and what looked like black marble making up the construction of the manor. It was like being swallowed by a blank spot in the night sky. The courtyard itself was empty, no plants, no fountain, nothing to make a person feel at ease.

Caligo cleared his throat. "Come along. I'll show you to your room." He moved toward the main house and she followed, their footsteps somehow silenced like every other thing in Nex. *His magic?*

"No servants?" Nakia asked. *How could a wealthy man, a king no less, not have servants?*

He chuckled. "I could have my servants show you, but I don't think you'd like meeting them."

The shadows gave an unholy growl for a brief second, enough to make her heart skitter, and Nakia decided to take his word on it. He knew his land and people better than she did. They entered the main hall of the manor. Even with white lights running atop the wall, the place still seemed morose and shady. She wondered what sort of light it was after seeing the Roshan had bioluminescent creatures for light and her own country used insects. The light wasn't from candles or fire. *Are there other ways to make light and somehow still have the house seem covered in shadows?*

"Don't fall behind if you value your life."

Nakia hadn't realized he was so far ahead of her in the hallway. She hurried after him as the darkness seemed to move, shift, and even lean in for a closer look. For a moment, she was certain a shadow crept off the wall to touch her shoulder. Caligo gave the wall a sharp glare. *Is this my imagination or his power?*

Even with his stare, she could have sworn the darkness was

breathing on her, casting icy exhales on the back of her neck. It stalked her as they moved through the halls, wiggled near her, as if getting a feel for her.

"This'll be your room." Caligo led their way upstairs. He motioned to a door. "If you know what's good for you, you'll stay in there."

Nakia opened her mouth to ask a question, but it died on her lips as a gaping, fang-tooth maw appeared on the wall. The shadow-mouth shot out toward her. Rooted to the ground and her mind completely blank, Nakia expected her demise. Caligo waved his hand. The maw disappeared like black smoke. *What the hell was that?* Nakia's heart pounded through her chest, and a cold bead of sweat cut a chilly path down her cheek.

"You control the shadows?" Her teeth chattered, even though she tried her best not to show fear. This was beyond anything she had ever seen, almost more than she could take. He could murder her with his home if he felt like it, and she doubted anyone would ever know. She didn't know how to make sense of that.

Caligo smirked. "Just some of the things I've learned from Roshan texts."

Nakia's brow furrowed. He didn't seem to have the best control over these shadows. Unless he did that on purpose to frighten her and give her a taste of what he capable of.

"Stay in here until I say so. Eventually, the barbarian queen will send for you and I'll let you go."

Something pushed her into the room. The door slammed behind her and she was alone, but she didn't feel alone. There was motion all around her, subtle but there. She swallowed her fear.

The room looked plain, nothing like what she was used to. A slim bed sat in the corner with a desk in the opposite corner and nothing more. No frescos like at home or even tapestries she had gotten accustomed to in Khenshu. No windows, either. The walls were painted black. The only light was from the top of the wall, running in along the lines where the wall met the ceiling, possibly there from magic as she couldn't see a source. If Caligo could control the light, he could leave her in total darkness whenever he desired.

"There has to be a way out of here," Nakia muttered, exploring the walls, running her fingertips along the cold stone. It was like touching water, but only the surface. Somehow, the shadows rippled and rolled under her hand. It didn't stop her from feeling for an exit, but nothing on the wall stood out.

She went to the door to see if she could open it, but found it as steady as the wall, as if she had been sealed in. She couldn't even make out a sliver in the wall for the door's edge. After checking the floor for any sort of crack or crease she could exploit and finding none, she didn't know what else to do. There didn't seem to be a way to finesse herself out of the room. *What else can I do?* She tried brute force. Rushing the door, she hit it with her shoulder. It hurt. A lot. Set to try it again, she moved to the back wall, ready to push off, but the door opened and she was yanked back. Darkness wrapped around her like cold spider legs, and she screamed.

"Careful, dear. Wouldn't want your queen to think I broke you," Caligo said.

Nakia grunted and did her best to pack her fear away. She wouldn't let him see her shake. "Let me go." She was proud that her voice didn't waver, and she gave him her best glare.

"I've got dinner for you. When you finish, I'll bring you water for a bath if you'd like." He put the food down on the desk and left without another word. The shadows released her as soon as the door was closed. She dropped to the floor, the thudding impact echoing through the small room, and an ache throbbed through her thigh.

Nakia picked herself up, wincing. She rushed the door, hoping it would move. She wasn't sure why, but she thought the door would open now since it had just been open. It didn't budge. *It was silly to think it would when you just rammed it and got nothing for your troubles, but a hurt shoulder.* With a growl, she scanned the room once more for some way out, but settled on the food, her stomach rumbling. It had been a long time since she had any food, and she needed to keep her energy up. *Food might help your thought process a bit more and you won't throw yourself at the door again.*

It was a simple meal. Bread, cheese, a couple of hard-boiled eggs, and a small jug of wine with no cup. The food of a prisoner. Someone who didn't deserve meat or fruit or flavor or variety of any kind. *I'll live my life going from prison to prison.* No, she'd think of a way out of here after she ate.

***

Ashni rode Midnight Thunder through some of the bleakest landscapes she had ever seen, and she had seen much in her twenty-plus years of life. The crooked branches of the twisted trees seemed to reach for Midnight Thunder's muscled form. Typically, with his size, her horse barreled through everything, but here he avoided the branches as best he could. Ashni could understand, not wanting to feel their scratch either, like they might curse her. She and Adira had separated from Layla and Naren after they had their meeting with Hafiz and the other generals, going off to Nex. They had with them only a few units, accompanying them into what might be the ends of the world.

Now, Ashni and Adira marched for Nakia while Layla, Naren, and Hafiz marched to show Dorian why it was never a good idea to cross her. Adira rode by, a frown etched on her face. They had a handful of light infantry with them, who never stopped scanning the area. Topnotch soldiers and handpicked for this mission, they were quite pleased with the assignment. Helping the queen meant glory and that was more than enough for them. Well, glory and bonuses.

"This is unnatural," Adira said, coming a little closer to Ashni, so their voices wouldn't carry.

"We've seen it before," Ashni replied. *Well, something like it.*

Adira shook her head. "No, we've never seen anything this desolate. This is death."

"No, I am Death. This is when you fool with matters you don't understand on so many different levels," Ashni replied. She could feel magic humming through the environment, but just as the terrain was dark and twisted, the magic was as well. It made her itch like there were tiny bugs crawling on her. The death around them, creeping closer, was all misuse, mismanagement, and mistakes.

Adira chuckled. "How much of this man are you planning to leave behind?"

"None if he touched my hellcat. If one hair is out of place, there won't even be ashes left to blow in this poisonous wind." Ashni growled, and energy popped throughout her body, causing a crackle in the distance. Midnight Thunder snorted and stood a little taller, bracing himself.

"Calm down. It's bad enough we're riding horses into this country, but do you want to let the whole place know we're here?" Adira glared at her.

"You see the shadows as well as I do. He has eyes everywhere." They were robbed of their element of surprise, but it didn't bother Ashni. If a fool wanted to challenge her, she wouldn't deprive him of the death he so keenly sought.

Adira didn't respond, scanning their path. Ashni looked around, too, wanting to see if anything reacted to her show of power. The shadows might be able to watch them, but that was probably all, unless there was more than Caligo around. By all accounts, he was the only inhabitant of this gods-forsaken place. He couldn't be powerful enough to control shadows so far from his citadel. There was no way he was master of this stolen art.

But, still, something was off. It felt like the air rippled, like the magic shifted. There was something different. Ashni could feel it, much worse than bugs under her skin. It left a thick, bitter taste on the roof of her mouth.

"Hold on." Ashni put her hand up as they came to a patch of freshly turned dirt on the road as well as off to both sides. It was fine and dry, almost like black sand, and set a frown across her face. *If this keeps me from my hellcat, there will be hell to pay.*

"A trap?" Adira guessed.

The rumble answered that question. Crumbled, discolored hands and rusted weapons erupted from the ground. Ashni sneered and turned to her soldiers.

"Prepare for dragon teeth!" Ashni called, resisting the urge to look to the sky for answers of why something irksome had been placed in her path. The gods had done this on purpose, either as part of the test she wasn't sure about or because she was being punished. *This would never stop me, but I still have to be quick about it.* Every second counted for Nakia.

Adira groaned, dipping her head. "I hate dragon teeth. They're such a waste of time."

Ashni unsheathed her swords from her back just as dozens of undead warriors ripped themselves free of the shaded earth. Grey flesh hung from discolored bones covered in dented, fractured, rusted armor. They didn't smell of death or dirt, but more of collected trash. It wasn't right for dragon teeth soldiers, but that didn't matter. Midnight Thunder neighed and charged forward as Ashni cut down the undead soldiers. Her troops followed suit as more and more undead foes sprang from the ground.

"Well, at least now we know what he had that was so tempting to Dorian," Ashni called over her shoulder.

"It just had to be dragon teeth." Adira scowled, drawing her sword.

Ashni slipped off Midnight Thunder, finding it easier to fight standing on her own legs. She cut through the undead as easily as she cut through the living. Adira stayed on her horse and watched with a bored expression, only cutting down any warriors that dared stumble too close to her. Ashni gave her a look, silently ordering her to get them out of this.

"What?" Adira said.

"I know you have it," Ashni replied. Adira hated when they ran into dragon teeth warriors and never left for combat without a lure.

"Oh, you want me to save the day?"

Ashni grunted and put her foot through a warrior whose armor had rusted away. The warrior fell apart before she had a chance to take her sword to it. Several turned to dust from one strike. These were subpar dragon teeth warriors. The soil was too poor to raise them properly. "I want you to shut up and help move us along."

"Maybe you should be prepared."

Ashni's expression darkened. "I couldn't hate you more right now."

Adira snickered and went into her saddlebag. She pulled out a stone, burning bright orange with an enchantment, and pitched it into the crowd. A dull ding rang out as the stone hit one of the dragon teeth warriors, who immediately turned on its undead brethren. One swipe lead to another, and soon, the dragon-teeth troops were fighting each other, and Ashni's group slipped by.

Ashni remounted her horse and gave Adira a scathing look. "Stop being insufferable."

"Oh, I'm sorry, you mean you'd be able to get back your kitten without me?" Adira asked, a smile spreading across her face.

Ashni snarled and urged Midnight Thunder onward. She did need Adira, but her frustration boiled over all the same. She'd be more than enough. She had to be more than enough. *I won't even let the gods stop me from freeing Nakia.*

Chapter Six

LAYLA AND NAREN ARRIVED SEVERAL miles from Phyllida after departing Ashni and splitting with the queen. They had almost the whole Roshan army with them as well as siege machines for what they expected to be a standoff. Of course, they would overrun the Western vermin and take their city before Ashni got back. With them was Hafiz Vivek, his mighty alphyn standing by his side.

Layla stared down on the city from a cliff top, rubbing her chin. Ashni mapped out every detail of the battle, but Layla wanted to be certain the conditions were right. If they couldn't go with the plan, they needed a backup.

"They know we're here," Hafiz said.

"It's not possible for us to hide an army our size," Layla replied.

Hafiz nodded. "Those are thick city walls."

Layla couldn't call him a liar. Fifteen feet thick and twenty feet high, not counting the towers, which stood almost thirty feet. They planned for the walls, but a plan wasn't the action. *It's too long and too much standing around.* Neither she nor Ashni had the patience for walls, not the patience to go through or over them really. She tilted her head, taking in what she could. Wanting a faster way.

"What do you want to do?" Naren asked, standing at her side. His presence gave her strength and confidence. If something went wrong, he'd help her put it right.

"I'm going to let our people inside know we're here. We'll start the attack on the outside and they can go from within," Layla answered.

"That is what the general and the queen want," Hafiz replied.

"You want me to get into position?" Naren asked.

Layla tapped her chin. "Wait for nightfall, regardless of whether I'm back or not. The cover should hide you setting up. I'll move the troops into formation in front. Hopefully, they'll pay me all the attention and Hafiz can show them what we're made of."

Naren nodded and rushed off. Hafiz stuck around, eyeing her. Layla didn't say anything as he stroked Yata with all the care one would a dedicated warhorse.

"Will your shadow beasts be able to handle this without you?" Hafiz asked.

Layla winced. This seemed like a mistake, not the casual hatred he was known for and maybe that was the thing. It wasn't so much he hated outsiders, but didn't know anything about them and didn't want to know about them. "We are called Shadow *Walkers*." And he should know that, but didn't.

Hafiz's dark brown eyes rolled. "Yes, yes, yes. But will they be effective without you?"

"My people can handle themselves regardless of my presence, which is why the Queen can use me in so many different ways." She made sure her tone had bite, so he didn't think he could talk down to her. He needed to remember that Ashni picked her. "I've got my part. You make sure you do yours."

He stared her right in the eyes. "I will. I always do."

"With Adira by your side. Make sure you don't disappoint her."

"I would never. I also would never vault over a wall without knowing what's on the other side." He snorted and walked away, like he got the better of her in their little exchange.

Yes, she was known for leaping before she looked, but she was also known for getting hard things done on her own. That was more than he could ever claim.

Layla's eyes wandered to the horizon, waiting for the sun to disappear. She let Hafiz drift from her mind and thought of the task at hand instead. King Dorian's gall didn't surprise her, not after meeting him once. She was surprised he could rope others into his arrogance. It was like they missed what her sister wrought their first time on the shores of the West. Resistance was futile.

"And I know that better than anyone," Layla said to the warm air, scratching her cheek in memory. Sometimes she could still feel the sting of Ashni's punch from years ago as she halted Layla's run on the Roshan's army. She had been a girl then, wondering why her people were so frightened of the Roshan as she downed warrior after warrior. A teen Ashni floored her with one punch and she understood. "Time to get to work."

Layla leapt from the cliff, wiggled a finger as a chill ran through her hand, opening a shadow. It swallowed her, transporting her into Phyllida. She should only be in the city for a few minutes, alerting any free high-ranking soldiers as to what was about to happen. It was up to them to rally their troops. If that went to pieces, it was more on Adira than on her, but she doubted it would fall apart. *Well, unless the gods truly are displeased with Ashni to the point they'd even stop us to spite her.* Hopefully, that wouldn't be the case.

Slipping into the city was easy, as slipping into most places were for a Shadow Walker such as herself. As long as there was a shadow, she could go there. Teleporting was basic shadow magic learned at a young age. She learned it younger than most. It was a good way to annoy Ashni. She stepped out of a shadow into a villa, finding Captain Varaza Sur reclined on a couch, being fed grapes by barely covered slave men.

"Princess!" Varaza jumped to her feet, towering over Layla. Her deep brown eyes focused on Layla at attention.

"Enjoying the hospitality?" Layla asked with a smirk as she made a show of gawking at the men.

The captain shrugged broad, muscular shoulders. "I'm on house arrest. I have to do something to entertain myself." Months of sitting around hadn't diminished her physical presence and she gained a relaxed glow to her bronze skin.

"I assume you've sharpened all your knives then."

Varaza grinned, as easygoing as always. "Knives, spears, swords. Oh, and my words." She motioned to the four men with her thumb. "Every single slave they left in my service will be with us. They look forward to the freedom of the Roshan military."

Layla nodded. "Good work. Then, you can spread the word. We're ready. How long have you been on house arrest?" The room was lush, cushions to lounge on, a variety of food, and plenty of slaves.

"A few weeks. Back when we sent word Dorian had a scheme brewing. Oddly enough, he only arrested the male officials. Me, he left in this sweet house and servants. You'd think he'd learn to respect women after what our queen did." Varaza shrugged again.

"Some people learn the hard way. The officials he arrested, you have a way to get them out?" If not, Layla would have to pop into the dungeon before returning to the army.

Varaza scoffed, throwing her head back in her usual over the top fashion. "Yes, sir. We've bribed half the city. You wouldn't believe how these guys treat most of their slaves."

"Says the woman who has them in nothing while eating grapes from their hands."

"You can kill a slave here with no recourse."

Layla's mouth dropped open. "And they call us barbarians?"

The Roshan could do a lot to slaves, especially war prisoners, but no one in the Empire had the right to kill anyone, not even the royal family outside of battle or outside of the arena. Even in the arena, there were rules, guidelines, and judgments that needed to be made before a warrior had the right to kill someone. Killing in combat seemed to be excused because the Roshan believed in any and all of their conquests, but once the conquest was over, no one had the right to another person's life in the sense they could end it without consequence. "We'll bring them rule of law."

"They have laws. Murdering a slave just isn't one of them."

"Still, they're the barbarians."

Varaza shrugged once more. "Their library's more extensive than anyone I've seen."

"Then, it'll be ours soon and we'll have the more extensive library." She might even read something to see what these barbarians thought they had on the Roshan. "Do you know what he was planning with allying himself to this Caligo Mor cur?"

Varaza shook her head. "No, sir. He played that one close to the chest. We haven't gotten word on how that man can help Dorian. But he left with the Princess, so I don't see how he factors in."

Layla squinted and looked off to the left, storing the information away. "He had to leave something behind, unless he's double-crossing Dorian, which I wouldn't put past anyone."

"It's possible. You see what Dorian did to us." Varaza motioned around them.

"Yes, you have to endure such great hardship." Layla snorted.

"Anyway, let's get this show on the road. I want this prick to feel us." Varaza punched her fist into her palm.

"You're not the only one." Layla would never forgive him for hurting her sister. Beyond that, she didn't like how he treated his daughter, even though she couldn't stand Nakia. It was time to get the army into position. Summoning a shadow, she vanished into the void.

***

Nightfall in Nex should've been terrifying and probably was to lesser souls. Ashni could hardly stand still, so she didn't have time to be afraid. They stopped to make camp, even though Caligo's citadel was in sight, trying to loom over them like some vengeful god. She would've set fire to it, but somewhere in there was her precious hellcat.

"You should eat," Adira said, calling from their tent.

"I fail to see what eating will do for me," Ashni said, eyes locked on the place that dared hold what was hers. It seemed to glare back at her and part of her wondered if the eyes of the gods were on her. *Would they side with this beast of a man Caligo?* She refused to believe the gods could hold such contempt for Nakia. Maybe for her, but not Nakia.

Adira came out of the tent. "It'll put you at full strength. He might attack tonight since he controls shadows."

Ashni sucked her teeth. "Controls shadows. No, Princess controls shadows and she does so from years of training and divine talent. We both know he's weak, so don't give him more credit than he deserves."

"You want him to be weak, so you can snatch Nakia from his grasp. Don't underestimate him. This isn't our mission. We still have a whole lot of places to conquer. Don't let your pride be your downfall. This might be the reason the gods are pissed at you now."

Ashni twisted her mouth up to the side. "You think? I always thought my confidence was one of my better points."

"There's a difference between confidence and hubris. Perhaps you've drifted toward the latter. You don't want to drown in it."

Ashni tilted her head. "Do you think that's it?" She never thought herself better than the gods, above the gods. *Not until things stopped going your way and you suddenly didn't need the gods. Perhaps it is hubris.* She'd make it a point to pray the second she got a free moment.

"The gods may see it that way. You can turn it around. Now, come eat." Adira pointed into the tent.

Ashni curled her lip, but did as Adira ordered. She needed to eat and get her mind off of the fact that Nakia was so close. There was a plan, and they needed to stick to it. Throwing herself onto the nearest pillow, Adira handed her a bowl of stew. They didn't bring any servants with them, but they all knew how to take care of themselves. She smelled it and sneered before taking a bite.

"Your stew tastes like vomit," Ashni said. It was a lie, but she couldn't let Adira be right and let her think the food was good. It wasn't in Ashni's nature.

"Excuse me your Highness, but I recall the last stew you made gave our entire unit food poisoning."

"I was fifteen."

"That's not an excuse and was that really the last time you cooked?" Adira arched her eyebrow.

"Yeah, it kinda stays with you that you poisoned several dozen people the last time you touched a pot." She could stomach her own cooking, but she didn't think it was safe for her to cook for anyone else.

"You're pouting."

"You're an asshole." It was unnecessary, but she itched and burned and wanted to come out of her skin. *Is this feeling part of my punishment?* She needed to do something to keep herself sane and picking on Adira came naturally.

Adira sat down on her own pillow and sipped at the stew. There was silence for a long moment. Ashni fidgeted, something she hadn't done since she was younger. Riding with her father had cured her of childish nervousness, but now anxiety filled her belly to the point where food wouldn't fit.

Adira sighed. "I can't imagine what you're going through, Ashni. I'm sure Saniyah would be able to relate more to this, but I know if someone took Saniyah from me, I wouldn't rest until I had their spine in my hands. But, I also know, you'd be by my side, making sure I stayed focused, so I didn't lose myself to the madness of not having her."

Ashni nodded. "I know you're here for me. I know you're trying to keep me in check, but she's right there. She's right fucking there." She pointed to the front of the tent, to the building just beyond them. She could almost feel Nakia.

"And we'll get her. But, we have to be smart about it. You never rush in," Adira replied.

That was true, but it was hard to do with Nakia so near. "I'm weak for her." Maybe that was the punishment. She didn't understand what her crime was, so it was hard to figure out what the penalty was.

Adira scowled. "No, you're strong for her. This is why you never understood what made your parents' story so amazing. You thought them falling for each other somehow made them both weak. They made each other stronger, stronger than they ever could've been apart. These soul bonds always make you stronger."

Ashni's stomach twisted. *Is it that?* She never considered it. Yes, she felt deeply for Nakia, held affection for her—*but is it something so connecting?* "What if it's not a soul bond?" *And what if it is?* Both were equally off-putting considering how her stomach rebelled against itself. She definitely wouldn't be able to eat more.

A little crease settled in between Adira's eyebrows. "What do you think it is?"

Ashni licked her lips. "What if...what if she's the punishment from the gods?" Her life had sort of gone off course since meeting Nakia.

A frown cut onto Adira's face. "Is that why you think she makes you weak?"

"I was ready to send us to ruin for her." *How was that not weak?* It was selfish well beyond anything Ashni had ever done.

The frown became a tiny smile. "Yes, I know, I was there. But, again, that's the nature of the soul bond. I don't blame you."

Ashni sighed, not feeling better for it. "But, what if it's not a soul bond?" Adira didn't assure her Nakia wasn't a punishment from the gods, sent to drive her out of her mind, pull her from her path, and destroy everything she worked for. "What if she's a punishment?"

Adira ate some of her stew. "We'll find that out when you get her back. For now, you have to free her. We know she doesn't want to be with him, and you owe her a choice. After all, she honored her end of the deal."

Ashni nodded. Bashira was still traumatized from watching Nakia give herself to Dorian's troops after they instigated a fight in the middle of the Khenshu marketplace. For a while, Nakia would've been the only one between them to honor the deal. Her father probably planned to break it the moment he made it, and Ashni had been ready to throw her word away for Nakia. *Who am I without my word?*

"She's worth this, right?" Ashni asked.

"I can't answer that for you. I have to assume if you're willing to go through all of this, she is. If you would go through the same lengths for her that I would for Saniyah, then yeah, she's worth it. You're worried about if, at the end of this, will she walk with you again."

Ashni rubbered her palms together, letting sparks pop between her fingertips. "Times are different now. She's not obligated to be with me."

"She was never obligated to be with you. You were obligated to keep her alive while we waited for gold. You did what you were supposed to do and benefited from it. She benefited from it as well. Don't worry. See it through."

Ashni nodded. *Adira is an expert on things like this.* A commotion outside the tent caught their attention, and they both went to see. The troops, up and armed, eyed a beast that had been long dead who stood just outside their camp. It was possible the beast was once a yeti, or something like a yeti if the height and what was left of the shoulders meant anything. Decaying, grey flesh sagged and white bone peeked through the rotting skin. Again, absent was the scent of death. It smelled like garbage, even though it should've held some aroma of magic. This spoke of Caligo's talent, or lack thereof. The creature held a scroll in its grip, jagged bones for fingers seemed to barely hold on.

"Oh, great, he controls the dead, too." Adira deadpanned as she pulled her sword.

"All your favorite things in one trip, huh?" Ashni said. Adira hated all things dealing with the undead. Ashni wasn't affected by it anymore, having seen and dealt with it several times in life, even though she felt it was disrespectful to commandeer someone's body in such a way.

"If you're dead, you're supposed to stay dead. Your soul doesn't come back, so it's just a sacrilege to use someone's body for your own gain," Adira replied with a huff.

"For the queen," the creature spoke in a gravely tone, holding out a trembling arm. Fur slid from its wrist, becoming dust before it hit the ground, as it offered the scroll.

Ashni took the scroll and one of her soldiers put a spear through the creature. The creature disintegrated right before their eyes. Not surprising considering the weak dragon tooth warriors did the same. Ashni broke the scroll's seal and squinted as she tried to read it. Adira stepped closer.

"Is that Roshani?"

"I think it is. It looks like a child's writing." Ashni tilted her head, trying to make out what the message was. Calling it scribble would've been kind, and the surrounding darkness didn't help against the dark ink.

"Let's go into the tent and use some light." Adira led the way.

"Carry on." Ashni waved her soldiers off. They rushed to their defenses, reinforcing them.

Back in the tent, Ashni moved her food and spread the scroll out, studying it. She felt like she got the gist of what Caligo wanted. *How does he know about these books? Some of them I haven't even seen.* She'd have to send word to her mother. There were spies or traitors in the capital.

"How does he even know the Roshan written language?" Adira inquired. Of course, he barely knew it, but he shouldn't have known it at all. The West wasn't invited into the Empire to learn their ways, even their language.

"How does he know about these books?" Ashni replied, much more interested in that. Many of the texts he demanded were locked away, deep in the capital, and only a few select individuals knew about them.

"Something's wrong here." Adira pressed her hands together and rested her chin on her knuckles. "Who is this man?"

"We'll find out soon enough. Does he think we walk around with the Royal Archives strapped to our backs?" Ashni rolled her eyes.

"Even if we did, why the hell does he think we'd give it to him?" Ashni snorted. "He's full of himself and other things."

"Well, he does have your princess, as he puts it. Surely, you'll give him the world to have her back," Adira replied.

Ashni shrugged. "Not a bad assumption, except for the part where I'd rather put my hand through his chest."

"Then, we're going ahead with our plan?"

Ashni gave Adira a sidelong glance. "Of course. Do you honestly think I'd give someone openly hostile to us secrets of the Roshan Empire?"

Adira ground her teeth together, as if chewing on some words. "Of course not."

"You'd do it for Saniyah?" Ashni had no doubt Adira would do everything in her power for Saniyah, including betray the Empire. She wouldn't hold it against Adira either, not if her emotions felt anything like Ashni's did.

"I'd want to hold his heart in my hand and watch the light fade from his eyes as I crushed it. But, it's different for me."

"I know." The Roshan Empire and its secrets were Ashni's responsibility. And despite how much she knew Adira identified as Roshan, underneath it all, the connection for her wasn't as deep as it was for Ashni. *It doesn't matter.* Adira's connection with Ashni was deep enough, infinite as far as Ashni could tell.

Adira gave her a grin. "Then go put your hand through his chest, hold his heart in your hand, and watch the life drain from his eyes as you crush it. How dare he try to use your hellcat like this? She's not a pawn."

"No, she's not." Ashni took the scroll into her hand, a charge shot down her arm, and the scroll caught fire. Outside, a thunderclap echoed through the air.

***

"You can't just change our strategy like that!" Hafiz glared daggers at Layla as they stood in camp with the other generals. Layla wanted to start things earlier than intended.

Layla arched an eyebrow. "I can just change it like that. I did, actually." She motioned to the nodding generals and Naren at her side.

"That isn't the way we do things. You can't just change things without my permission." Hafiz patted himself in the chest.

"Why can't I? Am I not the queen?" Layla wasn't sure if this was Hafiz throwing a tantrum because he couldn't fathom straying from the formula or if he couldn't stand the fact that she, technically an outsider, was changing the well-crafted scheme of his mentor and his queen. Maybe, it even bothered him that she was the queen. Ashni always let them know Layla was merely an extension of herself. They were one and the same.

"The Queen made this plan," he replied.

Layla smirked. "Yeah, and I improved it. It's been known to happen."

"This plan doesn't need improving." Hafiz folded his arms across his chest.

Layla's smirk dissolved into a frown. *Does he really think I'll back down?* Her frown then turned into a rough laugh. "You think you're in charge, don't you? I thought we worked this out. I'm here for Ashni. You're here for Adira."

"Yes, and we all know General Gyan steps in when Queen Ashni's about to do something unnecessary," Hafiz replied.

Layla scoffed. *General Gyan. No one calls her that.* But, it was thoughts of Adira that kept Layla civil. Adira saw something in Hafiz, and because of that she stayed her cutting remark. She couldn't see it herself, but she knew from experience that happened. Ashni was the first person in the Roshan to see something in Layla beyond her gods-given talent as a Shadow Walker.

"Hafiz, you and I are supposed to complement each other, as my sister and the general do. Yes, Adira stops Ashni from doing ridiculous things every now and then, but she also steps aside when she recognizes Ashni has made a good change to things. Moving early gives us more of advantage because we can play to the darkness. They can't. They don't have the man who does dark magic with them. We won't get this chance again, and we don't know what that man might've left behind to help them once they do realize we're here," she said, staying as calm as she could.

Hafiz bristled. "We already have the element of surprise."

"We have it more so now. The darkness can protect us."

"It didn't protect you before."

Layla flinched. It was one thing when he brought up her premature charge over the wall while they were alone, but to allude to it in front of those she commanded was a bad call. He overstepped, even though they were probably all there when she rushed through a wall and almost ran right into a sword as well as poison powder. Her nerves twitched as she weighed her options in hitting him.

The generals seemed to shift, probably contemplating if they should or could stop her if she did move on Hafiz. She wanted to kill him, but again, she couldn't take this man's potential away from Adira. But, it was time to stop playing nice.

"I am the stand-in for the queen. We're doing this," Layla said. Once Ashni made a serious decree, even Adira was subject to it. He either had to respect her word now or he was questioning the judgment of their queen, in front of the whole army.

"It's an unnecessary risk," he replied in a measured tone, trying to be respectful, but failing. He didn't seem to understand the argument hurt him more than her on several levels. The troops would do what she wanted, but they might hesitate with him because of this. It would get back to Adira and she might look at him differently. It didn't seem to occur to him that they weren't equal.

"But, it's my decision. Everyone prepare. I expect us to be set up within the hour. Dismissed." Layla stared Hafiz down.

Hafiz kept her gaze for a long moment while everyone else moved around them. He didn't say anything and after heavy seconds, he went to prepare like everyone else. She sucked her teeth, not sure if the siege would go well if Hafiz continued to think he was her equal. She loved and respected Adira, but she wasn't Ashni. Layla was Ashni.

"Highness, you should move as well," Hafiz's mother, one of Ashni's generals, murmured. "Give him time. He'll figure this out."

Layla nodded. She was right on the first part. The second part, she'd take his mother's word on it. He came from great stock, parents and ancestry. Adira wanted him to take her place eventually. Maybe she'd see his potential while they did this siege.

Layla moved her troops into position while Naren marched off with his portion of their forces, along with their heavy artillery. Hafiz was already in position, so they would hit Phyllida from three sides, four counting the troops inside the city. Dorian wasn't even aware the Roshan were at the gates yet. *He had all of this crap planned out, and we still outplayed him.* Layla smirked and her excitement danced down her nerves.

They were about to be under heavy fire and if Phyllida's troops made it out of the city, they'd be heading right for her. She loved it.

Coolness seeped through her, her talent begging to be used, to carry them to their goals. She took a deep breath to stay calm, not wanting to get ahead of herself. She didn't need another story about her recklessness.

"We'll make our sacrifices to the Moon tonight. I'm sure the Sun and his son will understand," Layla said to her group.

No one objected. She was more devoted to the Moon than the Sun, for obvious reasons, but the god she had been taught to honor as a child wasn't among the Roshan's pantheon. She'd love to sacrifice to the Darkness, but Darkness had lost back when she was a child, defeated by Khurshid and Tami. She'd give this victory to Tami instead. Tami loomed in the sky, about to witness their greatness. *Is the Moon not in the sky as the Sun, giving life and safety to those under it?* The Moon could bring them victory just as well as Khurshid.

Layla called for a bull and spilled its blood in the name of Tami. "For you, we'll claim this land, great goddess Tami, our kind and conquering Moon. Ignite!"

Their archers ignited their arrows and the catapults ignited their load, both firing at Phyllida. The night sky was ablaze with their wrath raining down on the city, also a signal to their people inside to start their attack. The night attack gave Naren more cover for his forces at the rear of the city. They'd be able to get over the walls while Phyllida scrambled to deal with the frontal assault. It would also give Hafiz more time at the gates closest to the river. They might have a harder time breaking through, as the river gave them limited space to work with, but they were well-equipped for the job. With luck, they wouldn't need Hafiz to think of something outside of the plan. He had better be over his little tantrum, too.

"Everything appears to be calibrated well. The next attack is without flames," Layla said. She didn't want to give Dorian or his soldiers a chance to see what was happening. They'd have to wait for the sun and by then, it would be too late.

Putting her hand up, she signaled for the next volley. Shots and arrows whizzed through the air. She listened for the damage, smiling at the sound of destruction.

"I'll teach you to betray the Empire, but more than that, I'll teach you what happens when you hurt my sister." Layla growled and raised her hand, signaling for a reload. She wanted to leave a crater where Phyllida once stood, and she wanted Dorian groveling at her feet with tears burning his eyes.

***

Nakia flinched as thunder rumbled through the air. *What's going on? Is Caligo doing something?* The room felt like it was breathing. Shadows swirled and hissed around her. At times it felt like they moved in closer to her, taunting her. She wrapped her arms around herself, wishing she had a weapon. She wasn't sure what she'd be able to do against shadows, but she couldn't just sit there and die.

She searched the room. A straw mattress and tattered blanket wouldn't do her much good. As another thunderclap tore through the air and the shadows thrashed in the room, she shoved the bed instead, skin tingling as the base scratched against the floor. The room gave a groan, stone seeming to shake. She managed to get the bed against where she had seen the door last. *At least that'll stop someone from getting inside.*

Sweat ran down her cheek and she wasn't sure if it was from pushing the bed or the cold fear coiled in her belly. The shadows on the wall rippled and she braced herself, thinking they might shoot out and grab her. After a long, quiet moment, nothing happened.

"I'm not going to let anything happen," Nakia said under her breath. She went to the desk in the corner. Dismay flittered through her as she realized how solid the desk was, and the legs were probably really hard to break off. Still, it never hurt to try. *I'm sure Ashni never thinks she can't do something.*

She flipped the desk over and kicked a leg with all her might. Her leg shook more than the wood, but she wasn't about to give up. She wasn't going to wait to see why the room was upset or why it sounded like there was a thunderstorm outside. She wasn't going with the flow anymore.

"I have to try to figure out what the hell Caligo's next move is," Nakia said aloud to remind herself she wasn't helpless. She wasn't useless because she was a woman. She wasn't bait because someone cared about her.

She kicked the leg several times before the wood splintered. With a grunt, she took hold of the leg and wiggled it. It moved more than she expected and elation energized her to continue working while pride strengthened her grip. Growling, she yanked and pulled, listening to the wood crack. Sweat rolled down her forehead, at the small of her back, and under her arms. *Is this how Ashni and Layla feel when they fight against each other?*

The wooden leg cracked all the way through just as the thunder outside sounded more like an explosion than a storm, like the gods themselves were angry. With a final yank, the leg came loose and she almost crowed in victory, but held it in. She tucked herself into a corner of her room. Her heart pounded, and she tried to take calming breaths. Her body trembled, despite her attempt to remain calm. Still, if an angry god came into the room after her, she at least had a makeshift club, the same for any shadows or Caligo.

What the hell am I even doing? I don't even know how to wield...well, anything! It didn't matter. She wouldn't go down without a fight. Outside, the thunder boomed and the wind howled, but inside the room seemed to growl as the shadows whipped around, sharp movements coming too close to her for her liking. She gripped the desk leg so tight, she felt like it might cut her palms. There was a cracking sound, like a glass shattering, and the far wall exploded, throwing debris in her face. Shielding her eyes, she clutched the table leg, ready for whatever happened next.

Chapter Seven

LAYLA STOOD IN FRONT of her group as she watched the sky for fireworks, a signal from Naren or Hafiz to let her know their troops achieved their goal, breaching the walls of Phyllida. Breaching the walls would allow her and her forces to move to the next phase. For now, they inched their way forward, bombarding Phyllida with some of their most powerful artillery, flaming arrows, bolts, and stones along with pottery filled with poisonous powders, not deadly, but sickening and it took the fight out of many people. She wanted to get in there, dig into Dorian before he had a chance to realize he should retreat, and own his whole being.

"They're firing back!" It had taken them long enough.

Her forces didn't flinch as stones whistled through the air and landed in their ranks. Not everyone saw through the dark like she did, so they were at risk. There were some screams when a soldier was struck, gurgling or groaning as the pain or death set in. The crunch of broken bones and the hollow ping of armor being punctured echoed among them, but her group maintained their composure. They pushed forward and the darkness afforded them a little more time before their enemy figured out the new range.

Layla itched to take the walls. *Come on, Naren. You've had enough time. Hell, Hafiz should be over and through.* Her fingers twitched at her side, and she bit her lip.

What if Hafiz got in and didn't signal? He might want her glory in payback for her changing the plan. She shook that away. *He has honor, at the very least.* She had to wait. She couldn't blow this. Ashni trusted her. Adira trusted her. She had their dreams in her hands. She couldn't rush in, no matter how much her muscles ached to do so.

"Give 'em more of the same!" Layla motioned for her archers and catapults to fire again. From what she could see, the city had large bonfires blazing in it. She could smell the burning and smoke. The scent of winning.

"Princess!"

Layla looked back. Several soldiers pointed to the sky. The sun was climbing slowly into the air, but beyond that, fireworks popped blue, gold, and red. Layla grinned and rubbed her palms together as a charge shot through her and somehow she was even more excited. Hafiz had done it. He had punctured the wall, made a path and a distraction for them.

"Forward!" Layla pointed her sword. Time to get engulf the city and take what was theirs.

Her soldiers gave a bellowing battle cry. Layla was right with them as they moved, making sure everything was as it was supposed to be. They pushed their few siege towers close to the wall, planning to use those and ladders to get over. Layla was tempted to go through the wall with a shadow, but the rest of her unit was with Naren. She wouldn't be able to get enough people through the wall with her shadows alone.

The wall was still protected, but there was a massive hole in it on the other side. Enemy troops rushed to protect the hole, so there were gaps in the defense.

"Go!" Layla ordered as arrows rained down on them. Shields went up while Layla continued running forward. They flooded the walls, met with more arrows, large stones, and boiling oil. Screams filled the air. She kept running. Yes, they lost a few, but they were on the wall, they were pressing on. Some of them went through small holes caused by their catapults, others went over the top, and some even went through broken gates. They were inside, but it was far from over.

Most of Phyllida's warriors waited for them inside, but Dorian took a gamble. Enemy troops hid outside the city, too, and as Layla rushed inside, they came up behind Layla's forces. A good move, she'd give him credit. In theory, he could've routed her, sandwiching her forces between his.

You think you're good, but we're better. Or so she hoped. She couldn't turn around to battle those behind her. Her mission was forward, not back. The rear troops would go at Dorian's warriors and cut them down as they were meant to do. Layla snorted. *Can't believe he thought that would work.* Still, she breathed a sigh of relief anyway.

His backup was over in the north country, she reminded herself, holding a hellcat hostage and about to meet a pissed off demigod. She wished she could see it, wished she could be there when her sister brought down the full might of her power. But Layla had her own things to do, like taking a city and capturing one disrespectful king. She wouldn't be the one to stop the show.

"Gods, I will honor you with great sacrifices if you bring me victory," she muttered, cutting down the enemy soldier who dared to stand in front of her. Dust, ash, and smoke were everywhere, blackening the beige breastplates of her foes. Some tried to loom over her, intimidate her with size as their numbers dwindled, but she went through them just the same.

***

Nakia gripped her desk leg even tighter than she thought possible as debris cut through her, making her wince as pain jolted down her nerves. Light from outside poured in and it sounded like the room hissed and shrieked. There was movement and then a figure came to the hole in the wall. Nakia's guts shook, but she felt steady, more so than she had ever in her life. With a grunt, Nakia swung the desk leg with all of her might. A hollow thud echoed through the room and Nakia found herself unable to pull the desk leg back.

"Shit, you're dangerous," General Adira said.

Nakia blinked and her heart rate increased in the pause. Surely she was seeing things, hallucinating under major stress. But then the general pushed back, making her take a step back.

"I already knew why Ashni was so taken with you, but this definitely adds to it," the general said. Her one eye glinting with amusement in the darkness.

"Is Ashni with you?" Nadia's heart jumped in her chest and her stomach twisted with a good sort of anxiety.

"She went to have a chat with your husband. We think he might have stolen some secrets from the Empire."

"He knows magic." Her mouth moved, but nothing came out beyond that as she tried to let the general know everything she had seen so far. She was overwhelmed and her mind flooded with relief and happiness and safety. She couldn't order her thoughts enough to pass on relevant information.

"Oh, believe me, we know. We had to deal with his damned dragon teeth warriors more times than I like, not that I like to deal with them at all. If I never see another dragon tooth, it'll be too soon." She shook her head. "Anyway, I've been charged with making sure you're out of here in case Ashni forgets herself, which she's likely to do. He's added insult to injury, taking you was more than enough, but also showing he's robbing our culture." She blew out a breath.

Robbing their culture? "What do you mean?"

"Can I tell you after we get the hell out of here? The only reason this room isn't trying to eat us is because Ashni has that bastard distracted."

Nakia wasn't in the mood to be eaten by a room, so she nodded. Tossing away the desk leg, she went over to the general, who took her around the shoulders. Nakia looked out of the hole in the wall and gasped.

"How did you get up here?" Nakia could hardly see the ground. They were on the top floor of the manor, but also seemed to be at the highest point of the hill the manor was on. Below them, she could make out some of the sharp, angled trees this place seemed to breed or kill.

The general scoffed. "That was the easy part. Getting down with you intact and back to camp while probably having to deal with more undead is going to be the thing to drive me mad."

"Undead?" Nakia gulped.

"I'm assuming the support he meant to offer your father consisted of huge amounts of animated corpses. I suspect he killed all his subjects and whatever animals crossed his path at some point. This whole land's dead, or undead." The general shuddered.

Nakia swallowed. The land was dead. The whole land. She knew he had no intention of freeing her, but that drove it home. He killed everything. *Why would I be any different?* "He did say he liked the quiet."

"Yes, well, I could do without. I hate death magic. Things die for a reason."

Nakia knew there was a story there, but she didn't want to hear it until they were far away from this place. "Can we go now, please?" Hope made her anxious and her heart still pounded in her chest, even though her salvation stood before her.

"Well, you did ask nicely. Hold on tight. While Caligo might be occupied with Ashni, some of his magic might still work and he doesn't need to control anything if we run into more undead warriors." The general clutched Nakia tight and then dived right out of the hole.

"Are you insane?" Nakia screamed as the wind whipped past her and the ground sped closer. She felt the urge to vomit as her lungs burned to the point where she couldn't breathe. Tears stung her eyes and she wouldn't be surprised if she broke a finger from how she latched on to the general.

"Probably, but it has little to do with this," the general yelled.

They came to an abrupt halt and were yanked up a bit. Nakia's heart felt like it stopped in shock and her fingers dug into the general's shoulders, which she hadn't thought possible. She gulped in air, but her chest hurt from the fright of that jump. For a second, she expected them to die, but that second didn't come. *How are we still alive?*

"You didn't notice I'm holding a wire." The general grinned.

The general held a thin rope in her hand and being aware of that made her breathing a little easier. It was good, too, as they had fallen more than halfway down. Her heartbeat quickened once more. *How will we get down?* If they died, they'd have to be buried together because Nakia felt like her hands had fused to the general to make sure she didn't fall.

"Now what?" Nakia asked.

"We take it slow, so I don't drop you and ruin all of the world," the general replied, sliding down the rope.

"What do you mean?"

"You honestly don't think Ashni could be right if I lost you, do you? You think this was on our list? The only reason we're this far north in this piece of shit country is for you," the general explained. "Now, hold on tight, so I can get us out of here quick."

"I am holding—" Nakia's words turned into a scream as the general loosened her grip on the rope.

***

Ashni stepped through the gate of the citadel after taking down yet another squad of dragon teeth warriors. She sheathed her swords on her back. *How many dragon teeth does this bastard have?* She hadn't seen a proper dragon in her entire adventurous life, but it seemed like this bastard killed a pack of them for their teeth and then wasted them since the soil of Nex grew terrible fighters. And, of course, there were the scores of regular undead people and beasts he used as soldiers well. His necromancy needed work, as he could raise waves of dead things, but couldn't maintain their movement for long.

"Come out, thief!" Ashni snarled, walking deeper into the belly of the beast. Her forces lagged behind her, dealing with the undead.

"Who are you calling a thief, barbarian?" A low voice hissed, the owner unseen. "I am the Lord of this land. I am the Lord of the Dead, and you're less than a worm beneath my feet."

"Yeah, except worms eat the dead," Ashni smirked.

89

"Worms grovel properly at my feet."

"Step out of the shadows and say it to my face." Ashni rubbed her fingertips together, wanting to unsheathe her swords and slice through the darkness. She didn't want to overplay her hand, though. She didn't want to be overconfident, brought down by hubris. She had prayed to the gods, promised to do better. She couldn't be seen as a liar and couldn't afford a misstep, not knowing if Adira rescued Nakia or not. She needed to give them time to get away. *So, take your time. Control yourself.* Besides, maybe if she got him talking, he'd tell her how he learned of those Roshan texts.

"Place my books down and we can talk."

Ashni laughed. "You're a fool if you truly think I brought the books you want. First off, how the hell would I get them so quickly? Second, you think after stealing my kitten I'm going to give you anything? Third, you think after stealing my Empire's secrets I'll give you anything? Calling you a fool was giving you too much credit."

"You'll watch your mouth, savage!"

A shadow shot out from the wall.

Ashni curled her lip and slapped away the dark limb, feeling the cold of the darkness and slickness of the void. "Is that the best you've got?" *Pathetic. How did this ass kill a dragon? He probably stole the teeth.*

"You think you can beat me?"

"I can teach you what it means to mess with the Roshan. You don't steal from us. We're always too happy to give, so you never take." Ashni felt like one of the reasons the Empire thrived was because they shared the wealth with those they conquered. This bastard wouldn't share in anything. Ever.

A pale man dressed in all black stepped into view. "I'm above your level." His eyes, colder than this gods-forsaken land, said more than his words did about what he thought of her.

She snickered. She had stood before scarier foes. There were warriors out there that brought her to her knees, but she always got back up. He found a different way to cripple her, but it was only for a moment. She'd go through him like she went through everything put in her path.

"You want texts from my people, but you think you're above me? Too rich. How do you even know of our texts? No Roshan would share this information with a bottom feeder like you." *That wasn't very subtle.* But, he seemed so into himself, he might tell her.

"Give me the texts and I might tell you while I show you my power."

I should've known it wouldn't be so easy. "Give me back Nakia and I might not kill you." Of course, she trusted Adira rescued Nakia.

He scoffed. "You want to degrade my wife like some rutting animal?"

"Have you degraded her?" Ashni wouldn't show any mercy if he dared to touch Nakia. She wouldn't even leave enough of him for the afterlife. She'd devour his soul.

He smirked. "She liked it."

Liar. He might have touched Nakia and she might have even felt obligated to let him. But, there was no way she liked it. He signed his death warrant with that.

"You know what's going to be the worst thing about killing you?" Ashni asked, rubbing her fingertips together and feeling sparks of the divine pop between them. *You know, you really should find out how he knows about those books first, though. The gods might even approve of that and it could help you pass this test or get back in their good graces.*

He rolled his eyes. "What?"

"I can't even make a Bloody Orchard for the gods or for a warning. You've already killed everything here." She would've made a glorious Orchard with his blood, earning back at least two gods' support.

"You'll be included in that." He made a fist and more shadows shot toward her.

Drawing her sword, the Golden Feather, she sliced through his meager magic. *Adira had better have my kitten somewhere safe by now.* "You think you can control the Darkness? I fight against this every day. And, the Light always wins." Well, that might have been an exaggeration, but she beat Layla, a master of Darkness, enough times to laugh in his face.

"You don't know anything about Darkness." Caligo drew his own sword, a double-sided straight blade. His body turned to smoke and he floated back and took a fighting stand in his solid form.

Ashni was done talking. She unsheathed the Ivory Claw. Outside, a thunderclap boomed and the wind howled, unleashed like the fury inside of her. She couldn't help it. Caligo glanced behind her, eyeing the darkening outdoors.

"You don't even know, do you?" Ashni asked. For all of his stolen knowledge, he had no clue who or what she was.

"Know what?" he asked, his voice oozing with arrogance.

"Do you know they call me the Sky Cutter?"

He twirled his sword. "A ridiculous name for even you."

No, he had absolutely no clue. She'd enjoy letting him see what the name was for. It was more than an honor. Ashni shook her head. "These techniques you've stolen come from the Tariq tribe, not originally Roshan. They were conquered seven years ago. Masters of Darkness and yet they bow to me now. Think about that."

She had seen the Tariq do some horrifying things with shadows and Darkness, terrors he'd never imagine. Bodies went into shadows and came out as ice or dust or nothing but bone or didn't come out at all. Shadows used living people as puppets or could be used to make the poor souls explode. She had seen them walk through people and all breathing halted. The people turned blue as they convulsed and died in misery without being able to make a sound. The worst she had seen had come from a spritely eleven-year-old who taught her to embrace the Darkness, but she'd never forget her divine light. Dark magic wasn't something she was talented with like Layla, but she knew many ways to fight against it thanks to Layla.

"I'm not afraid of you." Caligo sank into the darkness, disappearing.

Ashni slid her swords against each other and sparks jumped from them, illuminating the hall, revealing him to her for a brief moment. He gasped as she leaped toward him, planning to cut his head off. He reacted just in time, turning to smoke as the Ivory Claw sailed through his neck. She snarled. He wouldn't get away so easily. With a flick of her wrist, lightning danced through her hand into her sword and jumped into the smoke.

Caligo yelped, blasted back. He crashed to the ground with a thud, his body twitching.

"You better not be dead already." She wanted to feel his blood on her fingertips.

He made a noise, probably trying to say something smart. She wouldn't mind as long as he stood up. She'd punish him the way the gods wanted to punish her. At least his crimes were real. *Did they punish you? Yes, they let him take Nakia from me.*

"Get up, rotter. We have so much more to do." Ashni stepped over to him.

Caligo leapt to his feet and came at her with his sword, which she stopped with the Ivory Claw. The clang echoed through the room and the force pinged down her arm, rattling her bones. There was some power in his hit and might have actually broken a weaker blade. She saw an easy opening in his defense and swiped at him with the Golden Feather. The sword floated through him. She brought the sword back, charged with her lightning this time, and he was blown back again. He landed with a cough.

"What the hell are you?" he demanded with a wince.

"Pissed off. Who the hell do you think you are to steal from me? Not just Nakia, but culture from my people. I am a fucking god!" He was nothing more than an insignificant flea, and he thought to challenge her. Hubris didn't even begin to cover it. *I am nothing like this tick.*

"You're nothing!" Caligo staggered to his feet. "I am Death itself and you're a savage!" He stomped on the ground and hands erupted through the wooden floor, splinters flying through the air. Corpses clawed their way to the surface.

"It doesn't surprise me your whole house is built on a graveyard," Ashni said. "Killing people doesn't make you Death, but taking me on makes you dead."

Tentacles of darkness shot out of the wall for her, but she sliced through them with her blades, causing them to fade like black mist. The animated corpses charged and mobbed her. Pushing them back wasn't a problem, but she needed to keep track of Caligo. Through the undead, he came at her as a waft of smoke. A glint of his blade caught her attention as she fought off the darkness and undead. She blocked his sword, but was yanked down to the ground by a shadow. Her chin smashed into the wood, clicking her teeth together, and making her head throb. A shadow sliced her across her face, cutting a thin sliver of pain across her cheek.

Shadows clutched her body, holding her to the floor. The bonds were so tight, the shadows sawed into her flesh and Ashni heard her bones crack. White-hot agony shot through her, bolting through her body as the shadows dug in deeper. His shadows clawed into her wounds. It was like having sand and salt ground into her flesh. But, she had felt this pain before. Felt the pain worse than this could ever be. She coughed, blood flying from her mouth.

She snickered. "You think you have me? You're so weak."

"I know after I let the Darkness suck the flesh from your bones, I'll let it do something similar to my wife and then I have my way with her." He chuckled.

Anger flashed through her and burned every single nerve in her system. She banged her sword hilts on the ground and lightning covered the whole hall, reducing the undead to dust. Small fires ignited the wood as she climbed to her feet, glaring at Caligo.

No more playing around. No more letting him think he had a chance. *I've stalled long enough.* He tried to send a shadow for her, but she rolled out of the way. She sheathed her swords and lightning shot through the hall again. Caligo thought turning to smoke would save him, but nothing would. With a snarl, she amped up the lightning and blew him out of his fancy boots. He hit the floor hard, but she hit him again, striking him with lightning. He crumbled, body smoking without his permission. She grabbed him by the collar.

"You are nothing." She bashed his head into the floor. "Now, you face justice."

***

Layla made a mad dash for the palace. The sun was up and both Hafiz and Naren had breached the walls. There was no word that Dorian had been captured, so it was up to her. She wouldn't let her sister down. Beyond that, she wanted to see Dorian's face when he realized he had been defeated by her, a little girl as far as he was concerned.

The palace was chaos. Servants, nobles, and warriors alike ran about, trying to evacuate or put out fires or save crumbling bits of the place. She ignored all of that, scanning for Dorian. Layla figured Dorian had to be in his not-so-secret tunnels. She had to give it to Adira's spies. The intelligence they gathered on the palace made finding the tunnels easy, as well as discovering the tunnel Dorian was likely to use in his escape. It was the closest to his throne, from where he had been commanding the battle. Using a shadow, she entered the tunnel, finding the stone walls pristine, and even well lit. Her shadow was unaffected by the glow and she blocked Dorian's way. He gasped, meeting her eyes with a wide gaze.

"Don't run," she said, unsheathing her sword. His guards charged her, and she wasted no time clashing with them. While the narrow passage prevented them from overwhelming her, it meant she had a longer line to get through and Dorian had time to get away.

Layla cut down the men in front of her and used her other talents on instinct, like blinking, sucking others into the abyss of her shadows, drinking in their screams before the sound was swallowed by Darkness but keeping her eye on Dorian. She tried to reach out for him with her shadows, but more guards stepped in the way. Her muscles jumped as her shadows changed from holding cells to nothingness, just cold space.

She didn't want to have to deal with the guards again and she needed Dorian before he got to the mouth of the tunnel, which wasn't too far. She'd lose him in the open space of the city.

"Get out of my way!" Layla shoved through several men, their bodies crunching against the walls on impact. *How many of them are there?* It felt like the more she took down, the more came. She sucked guards into the void, but she could see the light at the end of the corridor and feel the air of outside. "No!" she roared, throwing her free hand out.

But, Dorian was out of sight, swarmed by the rest of his guards. Layla made a fist, pulling anyone in the front of the tunnel into her abyss. She could see the purple of Dorian's robes as his troops dropped out of sight, but then he was gone, through the opening of the tunnel.

"No!" Layla screamed, and the whole tunnel went black.

Chapter Eight

AS THE SUN TRIED to filter through the broken trees of Nex, the general led Nakia to a small camp. A handful of people stayed there, wounded or tending to the wounded. The general sucked her teeth.

"Gods-damned dragon teeth," the general hissed. She shook her head, as if trying to rid herself of unwanted thoughts or memories.

Why does the general keep cursing dragon teeth? Nakia heard tales the teeth could be planted and grown into deadly zombie warriors. Before seeing more of the world and what people were like, she would've thought that was made up to scare children. It made sense for someone like Caligo, a master of death and destruction, to use undead soldiers. She couldn't fathom where he got dragon teeth, though. *How many dragon teeth did he need to badly injure at least the dozen people in this camp? How did he get those dragon teeth? Had he killed a dragon or more? How would Ashni defeat someone who defeated dragons?*

The general glanced around. "I need two able bodies doing the least!"

Two youthful warriors clambered over. The general eyed them before nodding. She then turned to Nakia. "They'll see to cleaning you up and making sure you're properly fed. I have to go check on the remaining troops."

"See to me? Where's Ashni?" Nakia didn't want servants. She wanted Ashni. She wanted to see Ashni, see her alive, and there.

The general looked over her, beyond her, to the citadel. Nakia still couldn't believe they jumped from the top, but beyond that, she couldn't believe Ashni was in there, especially since the place appeared to be on fire, thick smoke billowed from several areas.

The general put her hand on Nakia's shoulder. "Don't worry over her. She'll be here soon. She needed to see to your husband."

Fury cut through her, deeper than the cold dawn air. Nakia scowled. "Don't call him that! I didn't have a say in marrying him."

The general didn't even flinch at her outburst. "That's understood. Now, I need to go make sure she doesn't go overboard. She wasn't happy about losing you."

Nakia's heart leaped. She didn't get a chance to ask anything further as the general took off. The two young warriors—one with neat, braided, black hair and the other with wild, light brown curls in his face, both dressed in the Roshan armor—stepped beside her.

"How may we serve you?"

Nakia didn't know what to tell them, but they didn't wait for a response anyway, leading her away to what they promised would be a nice bath. She couldn't pass that up. It had been far too long since she was clean. The bath wasn't as nice as promised—the water, lukewarm and the tub, practically a bowl—but it felt good to be washed and dressed in Roshan garments again. The gentle teal against her skin brought her comfort, letting her know things would be all right. The pair walked her to a tent, identical to the many other tents.

"This is Queen Ashni's tent. You should wait here. We'll bring you some food. She should be along soon."

Nakia nodded and stepped inside. It wasn't the opulence Nakia had come to expect when she was with Ashni, drab and small, but it didn't matter. She was safe and Ashni would be back. Or so she hoped. Caligo had to be a powerful enemy if he killed everyone in his country. He also had to be insane. She had seen Ashni overcome many opponents. *But, can she beat someone so hell-bent on destruction?*

"Have faith. You've made it this far and so has she," Nakia told herself.

Nakia scouted a few pillows in the tent and could tell they were Ashni's pillows by scent. She curled onto the pillow and inhaled, filling herself with the comfort of the queen, and fell asleep before food could make it to her.

***

Ashni wiped blood from her forehead as Adira rushed in, sword in hand. Ashni rolled her eyes. *Does Adira really think I need help defeating this rotter?*

"I didn't know what to expect." Adira curled her lip and sheathed her weapon.

"He's not dead," Ashni replied, kicking Caligo in the side. He was unconscious, though. Broken and pathetic, too, but Adira wouldn't care about those. "He needs to be questioned. And this place needs to be searched for any stolen Roshan artifacts."

Adira nodded. "She's waiting for you."

Ashni tried to control herself, but the best she did was to stay standing there for a few seconds longer. She trusted Adira to clean up after her. Even though camp was right outside the citadel, it felt like it was miles away, years away. Through the crooked trees and blackened earth, she rushed and rushed and rushed and still couldn't get to her tent fast enough. As she burst in, wanting to do nothing but fill her hands with Nakia and inhale her perfect scent, she found Nakia buried her pillow, knocked out with a bowl of stew by her head. Ashni smiled and felt something inside of her melt and settle. She felt whole. With a sigh, she went to get cleaned up and check on the soldiers. She needed to do those things, anyway. When Nakia awoke, she'd give her kitten her full attention for as long as she could.

She got the scratches on her face cleaned and bandaged. Her wrists needed the same, along with a few stitches. Her limbs were covered in shallow cuts and bruises. She flexed her fingers and found everything still in working order. She had Darkness seep into her before and remembered how it felt like her veins had tried to crawl out of her skin. Caligo hadn't done that, proving once again he wasn't a master of anything, just a thief and a wannabe.

After the medical attention, she washed and changed her clothes, simple pants and shirt without her armor. She munched on an apple, happy to be able to stomach them once more, as she checked on her troops. Most of those who needed medical attention had already received it, resting or eating or relaxing after a grueling fight with the undead. They had done well, and she made sure they knew that.

When she knew everything was in order, she returned to her tent. Nakia was still asleep, but she couldn't bear to be without her any longer. Settling down on the pillow, she collected Nakia in her arms and held her close. Nakia tucked in to her, still sleeping. Ashni kissed Nakia's forehead, causing jade eyes to flutter open. A tiny moan escaped Nakia, and Ashni felt it shoot across every inch of her skin. Nakia was here, with her, solid. She could breathe easy, at least for a little while.

"Ashni?" Nakia asked, her voice low and groggy.

Ashni couldn't help smiling. "Hey, kitten."

Nakia gasped. "By the gods!" She threw her arms around Ashni and peppered her cheek with kisses.

Ashni held in a wince, as Nakia's lips landed on several of her cuts. Nakia noticed, pulling back and putting her hand on one of the bandages. They stared at each other for a long time.

"He hurt you," Nakia said.

"I was careless. What about you?" Ashni put her hand to Nakia's cheek and stroked a soft spot with her thumb. "Did he...did he...?" Ashni couldn't even get the question out. If that damned rotter hurt her in any manner, she'd slit his throat right now. She'd then cut his body into pieces and feed some to fish while others would go to birds and he'd never find any hope of peace, knowing his remains were scattered to the four winds.

Nakia shook her head. "I'm fine. Well, as fine as I can be for someone who's been passed along from person to person in the past few months."

Ashni pressed her forehead to Nakia's, at ease for the first time in too long. *Does my presence do the same for Nakia?* "You never have to feel that way again." She wasn't sure what she meant, but she'd do everything in her power to get Nakia some semblance of autonomy.

Nakia leaned in closer, nuzzled Ashni's neck and held onto her like a lifeline. "I missed you."

"I missed you, too. Will you stay?"

"Where else would I go?"

Ashni scoffed at that answer. "Insult me a little more why don't you? If you don't want to stay with me, I'll send you off to wherever you want with everything you could possibly need. Just say the word." It would pain her, haunt her, but she couldn't stand for Nakia to be unhappy.

Nakia blinked and pulled back a little, staring at her with wide eyes. "You would?" The skepticism in her voice cut Ashni to the bone.

"I want only for your happiness, kitten. You have to know that." She caressed Nakia's cheek with a softness she never would've guessed she possessed.

"Then, I can stay with you?" Nakia asked, eyes full of hope.

"If that's your desire." Ashni smiled. Her insides felt like they might float away. Nakia wanted to stay with her. "But, I'm sort of on a conquest right now."

Nakia ran her hand up Ashni's bicep and shoulder. The simple contact made Ashni want to purr. *How in the hell have I survived these past few weeks without her?* She felt grounded and secure in herself, like she knew who she was again.

"Am I not allowed on your conquest?" Nakia asked, her lip poked out in a little pout.

"You would ride with me as I take over your homeland?" The

thought hit her deep in her chest. Adira and Layla had been conquered by the Roshan and now rode with her, and were the closest to her. Adira had even ridden with her father. The Empire gave them chances they never had with their own people, Adira especially. For Nakia, a princess, she had everything. *Except a choice. You can give her that.*

"My homeland? The same homeland which gave me to you in the first place, only to snatch me away and give me to a beast without any regard to my desires?" Nakia arched an eyebrow.

Ashni nodded. She understood that. She kissed Nakia's cheek and down to her neck. Nakia's eyes fluttered shut for a long moment. Ashni would love nothing more than to pay Nakia all the attention she wanted and needed, especially if Nakia honored her and stayed with her.

"I need you to understand, I'm not going to stop conquering the West. This isn't only my father's dream, not only my dream, but everyone in my military. This is the dream of my people. I can't have you objecting when I take cities or towns or worse." While she'd do anything for Nakia, she couldn't ask others to do the same. So, if Nakia was going to be upset as they took over new lands, Ashni wouldn't be able to do anything about that.

A soft smile lit up Nakia's features. "I know who you are, even if I haven't seen you in that context. I know who you are." She cupped Ashni's face. "I know you and I want to stay with you."

Ashni inhaled, feeling full to bursting. She couldn't help herself, going in for a kiss on Nakia's sweet lips. The touch of Nakia's skin felt more powerful than her lightning. It was hot, burning, calming. She felt like she could explode, but also ooze into a puddle. It was sinking into a warm bath after a good sparring match, comforting and easing. *Who gave Nakia this ability to make me feel this way?*

It was in this moment Ashni knew Nakia couldn't possibly be a punishment from the gods. She was the greatest gift and the gods had to test Ashni to make sure she was worthy. She'd go to the ends of the planet for Nakia and still didn't feel worthy. She was beyond blessed and would have to sacrifice so much to the gods. *Thank you. Thank you. Thank you.*

Nakia returned the show of affection, pulling Ashni closer. *She wants me.* Ashni had never felt a greater peace than she did at that moment. This beautiful gift from the gods wanted her, deemed her worthy. She'd live her life in devotion to Nakia for this blessing. All too soon, Nakia eased away.

"Are you sure?" Ashni asked because this seemed too good, too great.

"Do you not want me?" Nakia countered, her voice a whisper again. There was a notable tremble, like she was afraid Ashni wouldn't take her along.

"Of course I want you! You think I came to this burnt out hellhole for the fun of it? I wanted you. I want you. I'll always want you." Ashni was willing to compromise too much of herself for Nakia.

Nakia gave her a hard look. "Then stop asking if I'm sure. I wouldn't say this if I wasn't. Now, was your marriage proposal true or just a ploy to try to outmaneuver my father?"

Ashni sighed and pressed her forehead to Nakia's again. While she couldn't hear Nakia's thoughts, like the tales she had been told as a child claimed, she felt comforted with the contact. In children's stories, it was said people who loved each other and shared a soul bond could hear each other's thoughts. They were that close. It didn't involve them touching foreheads, but supposedly people on their way to a bond like that could hear thoughts from the simple contact. Nakia didn't understand the gesture yet, but she'd tell her in due time.

"I'd be honored to have you as my spouse right after I'm done with this business," Ashni replied with a smile.

"How long do you think that'll take?" Nakia asked with a huff.

"I'm not sure." Ashni liked to think conquering the West would be quick, but there was a lot of West and she knew conquest never went as planned.

The look in those darling green eyes could've killed a lesser soul on the spot. "And I'm meant to wait? Am I not good enough for you to just pause your precious dream?"

Ashni chuckled and caressed from Nakia's neck to her forehead. "I'd definitely pause it for you, but we're already moving and there's a lot of ritual that goes into a Roshan wedding, especially that of a royal." She groaned. "My mother will have to be there." She didn't even want to imagine her mother's reaction just to hearing Ashni wanted to get married, let alone what she'd do on the day of the wedding.

"I look forward to meeting her."

Ashni shook her head. "No, you don't. I'll get word to her and we'll work from there."

"It doesn't mean anything to you that I'm already married?"

Ashni scoffed. "To a man we'll never see again and I don't respect a marriage where one person going in didn't have a say in the matter." There were arranged marriages in the Roshan Empire, much more often than love matches, but both parties had a say. No individual was more equal than another in many aspects of the Empire.

"You don't...you don't care?" Nakia squinted.

Ashni ran a hand through Nakia's hair. It was oily, needing more maintenance than they could provide in the basic camp, but she didn't care. Once they got settled, Nakia would be able to properly freshen up. She kissed Nakia again, just for the hell of it, just because she could.

"Originally, the Roshan were nomads in a harsh environment. You lost family, spouses, and children easily. You learned to treasure the bonds you had, regardless of what a person went through. You're not sullied for marrying him, especially if you didn't want to. You're also not sullied if he touched you, especially if you didn't want him to."

Nakia sat up. "He didn't!" She glared at Ashni as if insulted.

"Of course not. You'd have slain him if he had. Adira told me how you came at her with that desk leg." Ashni wished she witnessed that.

Nakia pouted. "I didn't know it was her. And how did she ever climb such a great height? Is she part bird?"

"You'll find Adira and many closest to me have unique abilities or just wills made of iron. The gods like to shine upon us. But, you are the greatest light they could ever give me." Ashni meant it. Yes, she might conquer the West, but that was something for all of them. Nakia was just for her and no matter how upset the gods might be, they had already given her this gift. She'd never let anyone, even the gods themselves, take Nakia from her.

Nakia arched an eyebrow. "You mean that?"

"Of course I mean that, kitten." Ashni gave her a squeeze. "I had to leave my crazy sister in charge of the actual army while I came out here for you. I shudder to think what Layla might be doing, but it's okay because I'm here with you."

Nakia leaned into her and that was enough. Well, that and Nakia would stay by her side. In fact, Nakia seemed fine with the idea of marrying her. *If I have actually fallen out of favor with the gods and it's not with Nakia, then where?* She'd worry over it later, but she still would make sacrifices and prayers and everything else necessary to thank the gods for Nakia.

***

Nakia couldn't believe Ashni not only came for her, but wanted to marry her, even though she was technically already married. The idea flooded her thoughts, pushing out the trauma of the past few weeks. The desire to kiss Ashni flashed through her, and she didn't fight the urge.

As soon as their lips touched, Nakia was taken back to their first kiss in the tent so many months ago. There was a rush of heat and desire, but a mellowing sensation underneath it. A pool of warmth filling her. It was like spaces inside of her were made whole through Ashni. *Is this the soul bonding thing Bashira told me about?*

Ashni accepted her affection with the same enthusiasm as she had in Khenshu, back before all of this happened, like she meant it when she said it didn't matter Nakia was married. Tears burned her eyes as it felt like happiness floated in her blood. This was what it was like to be accepted. More than accepted. This was what it was like to be loved unconditionally. This was what it meant to be precious.

Nakia couldn't keep her hands to herself as she deepened the kiss. Feeling the caress of Ashni's tongue sent jolts through her. She pawed at Ashni, not sure what she touched, but needed to touch everywhere. Nakia pulled away, finding it harder to breathe as she itched for Ashni.

"Will you...will you..." Nakia had to take a deep breath. She couldn't say it, even though they had done it countless times. From the way her heart pounded, she feared Ashni would laugh, refuse to touch her ever again, and leave her to this accursed land, even though Ashni already said she could go with her.

Ashni grinned. "Whenever you like, wherever you like, and however you like."

The response made Nakia's heart thump even heavier and her throat closed, making breathing even harder. "On top of me." Saying those words at any other point would've made her cheeks burn with embarrassment, but right now, she needed that. She needed Ashni's weight to anchor her to the world, and that Ashni was there, wanting her.

Ashni didn't reply, just moved on top of her. Nakia groaned, feeling Ashni's body push her into the pillow underneath them. Ashni kissed her, full of passion and something else, something gentle and kind, something she wanted more of, now and forever. She clutched Ashni shoulders, gripping her like she might never let go.

"I've got you, kitten. I'll always have you," Ashni promised, pulling a breath away.

Nakia could only nod, breathless. She believed Ashni, and the words filled her heart. Ashni's lips floated across her neck, hands easing underneath her shirt. The feel of Ashni's fingertips on her skin set her on fire and she whined long and loud.

"Are you okay?" Ashni asked.

"Yes, please, continue."

"Then, let's get you out of these clothes, even though you look damn good like this. Remind me to shower you with beautiful royal robes and jewels."

"Later." Nakia would happily take whatever gifts Ashni wanted to bestow upon her, but right now, she needed to feel Ashni, to know this was real, to know they were together.

Ashni sat up on her knees to help Nakia out of her clothes. Ashni stripped just as quickly and came back to kiss her before she could fully appreciate the sight of Ashni's nude form. She got to appreciate the warmth of Ashni's skin against her own. She felt safe and secure under Ashni, like nothing could ever harm her again.

They kissed again, tongues caressing each other and settling Nakia's soul. Ashni's fingers brushed against her ribs and then to the swell of her breast, touching her softly, like she was adored.

"Can I taste you?"

"Yes, please." Nakia wanted nothing more than that, nothing more than this closeness, this intimacy.

Ashni's lips drifted from Nakia's mouth to her cheek to her neck. Each press of her lips made a mark on Nakia's heart. This queen wanted her. This demigod wanted her. Not because of what Ashni could get in exchange for her, but just for her.

Nakia cried out as Ashni latched onto her nipple. It had been weeks since the last time she felt this pleasure and it completely took her by surprise. Ashni changed pressure as soon as the sound escaped Nakia. Her mouth so tender, treating Nakia like she might break. It made Nakia want to melt into the bedding.

She purred as Ashni's hand came to her neglected breast and kneaded it. Her body hummed, and she mewed a little louder. Ashni responded to the noise, flicking her thumb across one nipple and suckling harder on the other. Nakia's hands found themselves lost in Ashni's thick hair, pulling out some braids. She cried out as Ashni's teeth grazed her sensitive flesh.

Ashni looked up at her with wide eyes. "Too much?"

"No, no, no. Please, keep going. Let me feel you."

Ashni dipped her head and went back to giving Nakia her full attention. Nakia's hands went from Ashni's hair to her shoulders. She could feel the lines of hard muscles in Ashni's back, and she groaned from the thought of those muscles protecting her. Soon, Ashni's mouth vanished from her breast, down to her stomach, which flipped in anticipation of what was to come. Ashni paused just below her bellybutton.

"May I?"

"Yes!" Nakia appreciated Ashni checking in, worrying over her, especially considering what could've happened, but right now she just needed Ashni to reaffirm their connection.

Her fingers gripped Ashni's hair just before Ashni's tongue lapped at her. She cried out so loud the whole camp probably heard, but she didn't care. Ashni didn't let up, taking slow, long strokes with her tongue. Her body shook and shivered in bliss, legs falling open wider on their own to invite Ashni in for more. Ashni's lips wrapped around her clit and that was it. Pleasure shot through her, stars danced behind her eyelids, and her body tensed.

Nakia could hardly catch her breath as Ashni loved her. When Ashni slid a finger inside her, passion poured from her. Moans filled the air, not all hers. It sounded like Ashni was delighted to give her pleasure, to let her drown in bliss. Each simple move of Ashni's finger and flick of her tongue was like touching the heavens themselves. Nakia sank into the feeling, crying out as it became harder and harder to breathe, in a good way. Her body trembled and shuddered as she rode out the wave of love crashing through her. Before she even realized it, Ashni had her wrapped in a tight embrace.

"I've got you, kitten. I've got you," Ashni said, her voice low and tickling Nakia's ear.

"You do." Nakia sighed. Her body felt like it was made of liquid.

"I will always have you." She kissed the side of Nakia's head. Somehow, this relaxed Nakia more, and she fell asleep in Ashni's loving embrace.

***

Ashni watched Nakia sleep and felt at peace with Nakia's weight pressed to her chest. Ashni would shower Nakia with all the gifts in the world and never stop letting Nakia know how special she was. She ran her fingers through Nakia's hair.

"You won't have to worry about anything else. I've got you," she promised to not just Nakia, but to the gods as well.

Chapter Nine

SITTING ASTRIDE MIDNIGHT THUNDER with Ashni at her back, Nakia wasn't prepared for the sight of a ruined Phyllida, even though she thought she was. It was a punch to the gut to see the walls of the city broken, but it faded. She wasn't sure what to make of the reaction. Maybe it was growing up with the idea that the city was impregnable and to find out how wrong that was. Just another childhood lie destroyed. Ashni leaned down, nuzzling her.

"You okay?" Ashni asked.

"Yes. I suppose I didn't expect it to look like this."

"You still with me?"

"Yes." The word was as solid as they were. The moment of shock was over. Yes, the city conquered, but this wasn't her home. It had never accepted her.

Ashni took her hand. "The palace isn't as bad."

Nakia doubted that, but nodded. By the time they got to the palace, Nakia adjusted and it didn't faze her to see the palace crumbled in many places. Ashni gave her a little squeeze around the middle.

"It's okay," Nakia said.

"Are you sure?"

"This was just another prison to me not too long ago. I'm fine."

Ashni kissed her cheek, maybe to comfort her or to remind her that she wasn't in prison anymore. She didn't need the reminder, not with Ashni pressed against her. They quietly made their way into the palace, leaving Midnight Thunder with a stable hand.

"Are we sure it's not you who lost the gods' favor?" Ashni asked her sister as she and Nakia entered what used to be her father's throne room. Her father was nowhere to be found, but according to Ashni, Layla managed to conquer the city. Apparently, that wasn't enough.

Layla snarled and kicked the throne, knocking it over onto its side. It landed with a crash, some intricate stonework cracking off in the process. "How could he have so many damn guards? I had him!"

Layla's husband, Naren, seemed to come out of nowhere and

wrapped his arms around her shoulders. His lean arms clutched her and she calmed her down enough to keep her from going off on more of the furniture. Layla growled, but didn't try to break free.

"It's okay," Naren said.

"It's not okay. He's seen our army size and got a taste of our tactics." Layla stomped her foot. "Now, he can go on to warn others about us."

General Adira waved her words off. "No use living in the past. We simply have to press forward and come up with new tactics. You whining isn't going to get Dorian back."

"Do we know where he went?" Ashni asked, looping an arm around Nakia's elbow.

"I've put people on it," General Adira replied.

"He probably ran to Valen," Nakia said without thinking. The whole space seemed to pause and all eyes were suddenly on her.

"Uh...Valen?" Ashni asked.

"It's a city northwest of here. My father married my eldest sister to the prince as soon as he possibly could. Their riches are legendary in the region, as is their army," Nakia replied. Thia had gotten the best of the deal, but she was sold as much as Nakia was.

"Does sound vaguely familiar," General Adira said.

"We need to know everything about it," Ashni said.

"Try asking your spouse." General Adira motioned to Nakia.

Nakia blinked. "Excuse me?"

Layla scoffed. "Oh, please. Don't act shocked now. She went off course for you and you're standing here in the rubble of your home with her. You're married in all but name at this point."

Nakia turned to Ashni, who shrugged. Nakia wasn't sure if this was teasing or some Roshan cultural point she missed. It didn't matter at the moment.

"Let's do it over supper. Nakia hasn't had a decent meal in too long. We could all use a moment to get refreshed anyway," Ashni said.

Layla snorted. "Yeah, refreshed. Whatever."

"Go somewhere and relax. We'll meet..." Ashni turned to Nakia. "Where's a small room for just us to talk things over?"

"There's a small sitting room. I can talk to the servants about setting up in there." Nakia wasn't sure how the servants would look at her, as she aided the enemy. It didn't matter. She'd make them listen to her if necessary.

"Let's make it happen." Ashni clapped.

Layla and Naren vanished into the shadows. General Adira marched off without a word. Nakia scanned for a familiar face, someone she knew to be a servant. Instead, she saw a lot of Roshan warriors.

"Order about the soldiers if you need to. Just don't treat them like slaves. It's disrespectful," Ashni told her.

Nakia nodded and went to test this out. The soldiers listened to her, fetching servants. She ordered food and a bath for her and Ashni. To her surprise, the servants listened, too. No one grumbled about her being a traitor. She returned to Ashni's side and took her hand.

"The bath will be in my rooms. Care to join me?" Nakia smirked.

Ashni grinned, a good enough answer. Nakia's rooms had survived the battle fairly untouched. The familiar rooms didn't move her in the way she thought it would. She had grown up in these rooms, but if they had burned to the ground, she wouldn't have cared. The lack of emotion cemented the fact that this wasn't home.

They were scrubbed and then bathed, the water treated with the flowers and herbs. She cuddled into Ashni, not caring how the servants looked on. Ashni kissed her every few seconds. Servants milling about paused, eyes went wide, some flinched, and brows furrowed. Each reaction barely lasted a second before they went back to work. No one said anything. Once the water developed a chill, they got out, dressed, and went to have supper with the others.

"You have a status report, Adira?" Ashni asked as she shoved a couch away from the table. A Roshan servant came in with pillows for everyone, but then the tables were too high. For a quick fix, servants brought rugs in and placed the food on those. It was a mix of Roshan and Western style food.

All attention went to Adira. Nakia couldn't help gazing at her with admiration. She hadn't expected to feel in awe of Adira for rescuing her, but there it was. There was also something wonderful about knowing those closest to Ashni approved of her as a spouse. She tucked herself under Ashni's arm, even though it would make it hard for Ashni to eat. The smile on Ashni's face let her know it was all right.

"Right now, we're calming the city down. Despite not capturing Dorian, Layla did a good job. There's little resistance to our people outside." Adira reached for a piece of fluffy bread. She didn't hesitate to spread olive oil on it and take a huge bite out of it, like she knew that was how they ate in Phyllida.

"You say that like you expected me to screw this up," Layla said.

"I say this like I expected you to capture the king and, to my great disappointment, you didn't." Adira gave her a hard look.

"Hey, she took this whole city, though," Naren said. Shock dripped through Nakia at the sight of Naren actually coming to his wife's defense. He was always overpowered by the women in his company.

"With your help and with Hafiz. Let's not act like Layla brought the city to its knees on her own," Adira said.

"You're in an especially pissy mood. I thought Hafiz kissing your feet would've made you feel good." Layla's hand hovered close to the roasted, stuffed mice, but she never picked one up. Instead, the octopus tentacles were her first choice. Nakia wasn't a fan.

"We had to deal with a lot of undead up north. I think it's still bothering her," Ashni said. She went for the desserts, a bowl of apples, honey, and roasted nuts. She offered Nakia a spoonful before taking a bite of her own. Nakia decided it was her turn to expand Ashni's world and offered her a stuffed mouse. Ashni took a bite and Nakia smiled.

Layla arched an eyebrow and leaned forward. "Undead? Dragon teeth?" It didn't seem to bother her in the same ways in bothered Adira.

"Among other things. I think the ass stole texts from your people as well as the original Roshan tribe," Ashni said.

Layla's eyes went wide. "How?"

That was a question Nakia had as well. Caligo never explained how he knew anything about these Eastern cultures or how he managed to get ahold of anything from them. This seemed like a big deal to everyone, beyond her confusion. It might have been better if Caligo stole money from them or even kidnapped someone.

"I'm getting answers from him as we speak. A lot of it sounds like he was able to buy these texts from dealers, who probably stole them. Beyond that, Nakia, perhaps you'd like to enlighten us about Valen and why your father would flee there." Adira used a spoon to gather some bits of lamb with flatbread.

Nakia leaned back a little in shock. She wasn't used to the group personally addressing her, unless they were mocking her. Now, they all looked at her expectantly. A tender hand on her knee jolted her enough to speak.

"Valen is a massive city ruled by King Timon. His only son, Wicus, is married to my older sister, Thia. After your first invasion, I know my father exchanged correspondence with Timon about shoring up his army. One of the things he liked was Valen could field an army twice the size of ours if properly prepared."

Adira chewed on both her food and her words. "I think the winter was more than enough time to properly prepare."

"Suddenly, this sounds like it'll be fun," Ashni smirked.

"You don't mind hunting down your father-in-law?" Naren asked, mouth full of a mix of food.

Ashni turned to Nakia. "I promise you I won't kill him."

Nakia opened her mouth to respond, but found she didn't have a reply. She wanted to say she didn't care, but she suspected she did. No matter what, he was her father. No, he wasn't the best, but she doubted he was the worst either. Still, it meant a lot to know Ashni wouldn't kill her enemy if they were related to Nakia.

"Does this mean I get to kill him?" Layla pepped up.

"Why the hell would I let you kill her father? You won't even let me wound this idiot." Ashni motioned to Naren. Naren clutched his chest and glared at her, but couldn't say anything with his face stuffed as it was.

"Can we focus on strategy, unless we're just going to run in there on blind luck like you three enjoy?" Adira said.

Surprised rippled through Nakia as they spoke about their battle plans right in front of her. At times, they even looked to her for input, wanting to know more about Valen or the men in charge. She felt comfortable among them, not just by Ashni's side, but in general.

***

The night had come and Ashni needed to check on her troops, but she didn't want to leave Nakia. She didn't want to bore Nakia either or subject Nakia to all of the teasing Ashni would have to deal with over going up north to rescue her. She wasn't sure if Nakia would be able to stand people making light of their relationship, even if the words were harmless.

"I've got one more thing to do and then I'm yours for the night," Ashni said as they walked to Nakia's room.

"What do you have to do?"

"I like to personally check on my people after we accomplish a mission. I don't mind you coming with me, but you should be aware that if you accompany me, almost everyone we run into will make a comment about our relationship." *What is our relationship? Well, you offered to marry her and she seemed to accept.*

Nakia's eyes went a little wide. "You personally check on all of your soldiers?"

Ashni grinned. "Not all in one night, but most, especially anyone wounded or injured. I also like to thank anyone who did anything that stood out. I bear gifts sometimes."

"My father never visited his soldiers."

Ashni shrugged. "I like to think he and I are different when it comes to ruling. My father always made sure he was close to his troops and I like to do the same. It helps get them in the mood to follow you into Hell if necessary."

"Would it help for them to see me with you?"

"Yes." While she didn't think it was wise to let on how important Nakia was to her so soon, her trip did that. Everyone knew. "They should see and understand you are me."

Nakia's forehead wrinkled. "I am you?"

Ashni nodded. "I know you've heard me say this about Layla and now it's true of you. You are me. You are to be obeyed as if I'm the one who said it." Pausing in both speech and step, she cupped Nakia's face with one hand. "You are me."

Nakia blinked several times. "You...you would give me so much power?"

"I haven't given you anything. You have it." Ashni would never be able to deny Nakia, so no one under her rule could have the privilege either.

Nakia blushed, rose pink coloring her fair cheeks. "Are you sure you want to trust me so quickly?"

"So quickly? It's been months. You're burned under my skin, tattooed on my soul. I need you to understand that. Maybe it's not the same for you—"

Nakia flinched and put a hand to her heart. "Not the same for me?" Green eyes glistened briefly, flashing hurt before Nakia glared at her as if she committed some horrible crime. "Do you honestly think I'd be standing here with you in the rubble of my homeland helping you plot the takeover of another city if I didn't feel something deeper?"

Ashni straightened up and scratched the back of her neck. "Uh...just want to remind you, kitten, I'm new at this and will make a few screw-ups." They had gone through that before. She might mess up with Nakia over and over again. *You have no idea what to do to make your lover happy, but you promised her and the gods you would, so you have to shape up. The gods gave you a gift. You are to honor her.* In fact, she'd make another sacrifice to the gods and pray after seeing her troops.

"Well, try not insulting me to my face to start. Come, I'll see your troops with you. I'm flattered you want me to go." Nakia's features softened and she took Ashni's hand.

Ashni smiled, insides melting at the touch of Nakia's hand. "I want you always with me, if that's what you want. I only want to please you."

Nakia beamed and held her hand as they walked. Ashni worried about what Nakia would think of her ruined city. When they entered Phyllida, she had been content to cuddle into Ashni, not taking in too much of the place, but now they would walk among the damage. But, as they did so, Nakia held her head high, never released Ashni's hand, and didn't flinch. Ashni would be proud to marry Nakia in front of witnesses.

"Captain Varaza, you're still out here coordinating the cleanup? I thought the generals ordered everyone to call it a night," Ashni said as she approached one of her more competent captains. She'd have to remember to promote Varaza soon.

Varaza turned away from directing people on the street who were securing a building damaged by one of the many fires. She grinned. "I'm not too good at following orders, Highness. You hear General Adira complain about it all the time."

Ashni chuckled. "You mean I hear Adira complain all the time."

"Somebody's gotta keep us honest, right?" Varaza's eyes drifted to Nakia. "Oh, this must be your spouse." Varaza bowed. "Highness."

"You're going with manners for once," Ashni said. She was impressed Varaza decided to be professional as the captain tended to be informal with everyone. It didn't bother Ashni since Varaza did her job.

"I'll talk about you behind your back like all the smart captains do." Varaza wiggled her eyebrows.

"Just when I thought you matured. Where's the rest of your unit?"

"This block suffered a lot of damage." Varaza motioned down the street. "We're shoring up whatever we can and destroying what needs to come down so no one else gets hurt. I told them we're working until the area's at least clear."

Ashni nodded. "Good. Don't put yourselves in danger, though. Be sure to go back to your villa and enjoy the victory."

Varaza saluted with a fist to the heart and then rushed off to carry out those orders. Ashni moved on with Nakia by her side. The teasing wasn't too bad from the officers. She didn't have to say anything to them. They showed Nakia respect, understood who she was without a word. When she noticed Nakia leaning heavy on her and her eyelids closing, Ashni cut her rounds short. *Guess I'll sacrifice to the gods tomorrow.*

They returned to the palace, settling in Nakia's rooms. There were servants waiting with their nightclothes and Ashni helped get Nakia into hers. She lifted Nakia into her arms, earning a yelp from the tired princess.

"What are you doing?" Nakia asked.

"Just carrying you to bed." Ashni wouldn't mind doing it every night.

Nakia sighed as she was eased onto the bed. Ashni took off her clothes and joined her, wanting to feel Nakia against her skin. She gathered Nakia in her arms and surprise rippled through her when Nakia pressed a soft kiss to her chin. *Still awake, eh?*

"Are you all right with everything so far?" Ashni asked. Nakia was so strong to walk around the ruins of Phyllida.

"Did we get married and I missed it? Why does everyone keep calling me your spouse?"

"They're mostly joking, but it's an acknowledgement of what you mean to me. It's their way of acknowledging our relationship. When we are married, I promise you won't miss it." Ashni pulled Nakia a little closer. "But, are you all right about what's happening? The Roshan have taken Phyllida."

"Maybe you haven't noticed but the Roshan queen has taken me."

Ashni chuckled. "So she has."

"I might not know how to be part of your empire, but I know you're here for me in ways no one has ever been before. I'm with you. I trust you with Phyllida."

Ashni's heart swelled. "I'll care for it as I do for you." She'd make Phyllida a shining beacon of the West and then give it to Nakia as a gift.

Nakia nodded against her collarbones. "And this is why I'm fine with it." She wrapped an arm around Ashni's waist, her thumb caressing Ashni's side. The small movement made Ashni's eyes droop. Maybe she was sleepier than she thought.

Ashni kissed the top of Nakia's head. "I will honor you."

"I know." Nakia relaxed against her and it settled Ashni's soul again. This woman, this hellcat was her soul and she wouldn't have it any other way.

***

Nakia found herself accepted at another strategy meeting with Ashni and her closest. They sat on mats instead of pillows with papers and maps littering the floor. Breakfast lay waiting for them, too.

"This is a lot of military," Layla said, pointing to one document as she grabbed a hard-boiled egg. Naren was next to her, squinting at a paper while getting biscuit crumbs on it.

"There are still numbers coming in. I've got Hafiz and his mother going through logistics. Added to that, we've got reports on a place called Tyra." Adira turned to Nakia and she straightened. This was something she might never get used to, someone looking to her for her opinion and listening to her.

"My other sister, Saffi, is married to the…I feel like calling him 'king' is a little much. Imagine if a monkey could talk and grew to human size and was in charge of a country. That's him. My father married her to him to prove a point to her." Nakia paused for a moment, a sudden rush of sympathy bubbling in her stomach. "The marriage was a punishment for her daring to voice her thoughts. She once called him out in front of all the nobles. She was married to this brute less than a month later."

"Do we have a name to look into or do we already have reports on him?" Layla scanned the documents, but Ashni passed her several more items from her pile.

"He's called Ferox," Nakia replied.

"You have any other sisters we should know about?" Naren asked.

"Just the two. I'm assuming my father enlisted the Tyrans to help fight you?" Nakia asked.

"Fight us." Ashni pulled Nakia close. "You're with us, are you not?"

"I am," Nakia answered.

"Then, they're fighting us. Apparently, these folks have superior chariots and what some fool labeled 'wild magic.' I don't even know what the hell that is," Ashni said.

Layla shoved her entire hard-boiled egg in her mouth. "So what? I can swallow a chariot just as well as I can a human body. Darkness is the only true magic."

"You can't engulf an army of chariots," Adira replied.

"Especially when they're drawn by Black Dogs," Ashni added.

Nakia shuddered in learning Black Dogs were real. She heard stories, but had never seen them. Demon dogs, the color of coal with fiery red eyes, and the size of a small horse. Their jaws supposedly could bite through metal and their claws could cut a human in half. It made sense to her that the Tyrans would use such monsters.

115

"Yeah, but we have me and several other Shadow Walkers. In fact, we even have the man who taught me much of what I know. And Black Dogs? Please. When I summon my demons, Black Dogs will be the least of our concerns." Layla picked up another egg. Black mist swirled around the egg and then it fell into pieces. Nakia blinked and her stomach twisted, but she didn't say anything, as no one else seemed bothered by the display.

"Do you...do you control shadows?" Nakia asked. She didn't mean for a tremble to enter her voice, but she couldn't help thinking of Caligo and how frigid his home was, how his home seemed to breathe.

Nakia shivered as the world fell away and she felt like she was lost in darkness. A freezing cold overcame her, as if it was winter in her body. Reminding her of the shadows touching her, she flinched and jumped, slamming into something solid.

Ashni gave her shoulder a squeeze, bring Nakia back to the now. "Caligo didn't know what he was doing. Layla's a master." The words were meant to comfort, but the chill in Nakia's blood remained.

Layla scowled. "You mean the bastard who took her was a Shadow Walker?"

A Shadow Walker? Is that what they're called? In all of Nakia's time seeing Layla fight Ashni, she never saw either of them use their powers. Knowing Layla did what Caligo did made Nakia's throat burn. She eyed Layla, waiting for her to turn into a monster like Caligo had been.

"No, he taught himself from stolen texts, but he did it poorly. Honestly, fighting him was like fighting you when you were eleven," Ashni replied, reaching for apples covered in honey. She used a skewer to pick the fruit up, eating them by the mouthful. She looked at Nakia. "Caligo's a liar and a thief. He didn't even know what he was doing with the knowledge he stole."

Nakia hated that she must have looked terrified because Layla turned to her with concerned dark eyes. "He wasn't a true student of Darkness. The night's part of a natural cycle and should be in balance with the world around it. He clearly used it wrong."

It was jarring for Layla to be comforting to her, but Nakia accepted it. Maybe it was because it was easy to see that was the truth. Caligo flaunted his power, used it for terror, and boasted of it. Layla only used her powers in combat and the power came from Layla's people, so obviously Layla knew what she was talking about. Nakia gave her a small nod.

Ashni finished off her apples and focused on Layla. "Your powers

116

aren't infinite. This is why we make battle plans rather just let you Shadow Walkers suck everything into the void and why we don't let you just summon demons whenever the hell you want to. Now, we need to focus. Adira, do we have reports on the terrain?"

Adira nodded. "We have plenty on the surrounding area. But, what do you want to do, choose a battlefield that the enemy won't dare venture into?" She pulled bits of bread off a loaf.

"Why won't they?" Nakia asked. All eyes were on her and she expected venom because this information was obvious to them and she was stalling the meeting.

Ashni shrugged. "It's easy for them to be defensive. Stay in the city walls and hope we go away. That's the nature of warfare."

"What are you going to do?" Nakia asked.

"We've got siege machines. Hell, we just used them," Naren said.

"We don't have time for that. You had the element of surprise, which is definitely gone for us now. Those siege machines wouldn't help us to take the city in a day like you did here. I mostly bring them for show, if you haven't noticed," Ashni replied.

Adira shook her head. "No, you bring them because we'll need them one day. You can't win every battle by hitting it sometime. You have to be patient."

Ashni nuzzled Nakia and kissed her neck. "Adira thinks she's the only smart one among us. You'll never get used to the nagging."

Adira scoffed. "Oh, please. I expect her help now. Someone else to keep you from being reckless." She leaned over, fist posed in front of Nakia, who arched an eyebrow.

"You have to hit her fist with yours or you embarrass us all," Ashni said.

Nakia softly tapped her fist against Adira's knuckles. The simple touch of skin felt like it cemented her in the group as her own person. She wasn't Ashni's lover, but Nakia. She was worthwhile on her own and a standalone member of this tightknit crew rather than an addition because of Ashni.

"This is going to take some getting used to," Naren said.

Adira scoffed. "Please, if we can fit you in, we can fit in anyone. Speaking of that, from now on, I'm bringing Hafiz."

"Please, don't," Layla said.

"I know he's reckless with his words, but you all proved you deserve more responsibility. My hope is that the more he interacts with you, the more he realizes he's putting his foot in his mouth. I mean, he doesn't say those things when I'm around," Adira replied. "Now, we have to figure out how to bring the fight to us and how to fight against mobile units with chariots being pulled by Black Dogs. We haven't done that since I was riding with the Amir."

"You used chariots in the desert?" Nakia asked.

"Not every place we conquered is a desert. The Amir just saw fit to give Ashni the desert part of the Empire," Adira replied.

Nakia squinted as she tried to put this together. *Why would a caring father give his beloved daughter the desert part of the Empire?* Surely there were better bits of land. "Why?"

Adira shrugged. "It was closest to the water and closest to the West. He knew his daughter, knew her heart. Hell, he even knew us." She pointed to herself and Layla. "Knew we'd follow her crazy ass across the sea to do to others what had been done to us."

"Made you richer than you could've imagined? Gave you a beautiful spouse and status beyond your wildest dreams?" Ashni inquired.

"I'm not saying I wouldn't do it again in a second if I had to. But, that doesn't mean I wouldn't fight with tooth and nail when the Roshan showed up in my village again. Just as I'm sure Layla would still fight the Roshan when they showed up for her people," Adira said.

"It's the only way to meet this one." Layla pointed to Ashni, who was busy studying a map and sipping a bowl of oats.

"Don't you regret being conquered?" Nakia asked. It seemed strange to her that conquered people would be Ashni's closest and fiercest friends. "You lost your homes." She glanced at Ashni, who didn't look up from the map. She wasn't sure what to make of that, like Ashni didn't mind that she was testing the waters to find out about being conquered by the Roshan. It was like Ashni was confident nothing they said would change Nakia's mind.

"The place me and my family live now compared to where we lived in Tariq, well, there isn't a comparison. My people were outcasts, condemned for generations for embracing the Dark. The Empire didn't care about that. Hell, it celebrates us. Without the Empire, I wouldn't have met Naren. Or found my sister." Layla grinned at Ashni.

"But, what about the other people?" Nakia asked, shifting back a little on her pillow. "It worked out for you. But, there were hundreds of people who were conquered, I'm sure. Maybe thousands? What happened to them? Or what happens to them?" They made conquest sound so nice and easy and while she would be comfortable with it now, would that last? *What of other people?*

Adira took a breath and glanced at Ashni, whose eyes went to another document. "To be honest, I've seen Ashni do it the best, and I know she gets it from her father, who had to get it from her mother. They respect all new cultures they come across. It's different with her brothers. They were with the Amir when he came into my village. Superior attitudes and entitlement. You'll find it in the Roshan. I still hear it from some, disrespect from them for thinking I'm lower than they are."

"I still hear it from damn Hafiz," Layla said through gritted teeth.

"And how does that help them?" Nakia asked.

Ashni grinned and hugged her tight. "Thinking of your people. Nice. I mostly collect taxes and impose Roshan law on places. Other than that, I'm not interested in changing people. Most cultures under my domain remain intact."

Nakia tilted her head. "So, you don't make things better?"

Ashni gave her a smile. "Well, yes, the Roshan has a lot of social mobility for people. If we didn't, Naren would've died a slave years ago."

Naren shook his fist. "I'll show you slave."

Nakia's eyes went wide and shot to Naren. "You were a slave?" A slave was able to marry the queen's sister? That was well beyond social mobility.

Naren waved his hands around. "No, no, no. She's trying to say I'd have been taken as a slave after the Roshan conquered my people, but I'm capable, even if she wants to act otherwise."

"Anyway, I can't pretend to have all the answers, kitten. What I do have are the values my parents raised me with, for better for worse. My dad always made sure I understood that individuals, regardless of status, can have purpose, value. The shifting you/I thing again. So, I give everyone a chance." Ashni shrugged and put down her empty breakfast bowl.

"Really? So, not gonna give your mother any credit there? Like she isn't the reason your father thought that?" Layla asked.

Ashni sneered at her sister. "You can guess which parent my sister favors."

"Can we get back on track? This is a battle strategy meeting. We can leave all the other nonsense for when we're done," Adira said. "Now, how would you like to do this?"

"We have to give them a reason to come to us," Nakia said.

Ashni kissed her cheek, leaving behind tiny remnants of her breakfast. "You are learning fast. What do you have for me, General?"

Adira scoffed. "I need to learn the weaknesses of these people. What would get them to leave the city?"

"Well, the Tyran love their chariots. I remember when my father married my sister off, he wouldn't stop talking about them. They did a little display at the chariot races to show off. In fact, I think my father got four of them as a wedding present," Nakia said.

"Your dad got wedding presents? We're doing it wrong," Naren said.

Ashni cocked an eyebrow at him. "So, we pick a place where they can show off their chariots and frighten us with their mighty Black Dogs. They'll itch for it."

"Yes, and how are we to stop the chariots?" Adira asked.

Ashni's mouth dropped open. "You're a terrible general and spouse. Why hasn't Saniyah divorced you yet?"

"You're not thinking of using that black tar stuff, are you?" Adira frowned.

"Why wouldn't I? Saniyah developed it. It could be perfect for this," Ashni replied. "How could you be married to our best war engineer and this not cross your mind?" Her brow furrowed as she stared at Adira.

"What if we pretend to ransom your kitten?" Layla said.

"Excuse you!" Nakia glared at Layla with all the intensity she could muster. There was an explosion of anger in her gut, even if the suggestion wasn't serious. She wouldn't be anyone else's pawn. She also wouldn't be talked down to anymore. She found where she belonged, and she wasn't going to be cast aside or pushed around now. She was here to stay.

"I said pretend," Layla replied.

"You will not address me as 'kitten.' That is not yours," Nakia replied. She didn't care that Ashni called her that, but no one else should. She wouldn't be mocked by a genuine term of endearment.

Layla growled and glowered at her sister. "Fine, whatever." Ashni's grin was downright diabolical and Layla looked ready to punch her. "I can't stand you."

Nakia's mouth fell open. *I won that battle without a back and forth from Layla? How often will that happen?* She doubted it would be a regular thing, but it was good to know Layla respected her enough to back down when something was important to her. *I'll have to remember this.*

"Back to the battle at hand." Layla shuffled some of the documents before them, but didn't bother with grabbing any of them. "You know what we could do?"

"No, which is why we're having this stupid meeting," Ashni replied.

"Instead of using the Shadow Walkers to pull chariots into the void, let us into the city. We start trouble, visibly. They realize we're like vermin and the only way to get rid of us is to fight you," Layla said.

Ashni nodded. "Why do I need you, Adira? Princess comes up with gems like this and takes cities while tweaking plans to make them work even better."

"Princess also falls into traps often, bolts off impulsively, and comes with Naren." Adira rubbed her hands together.

"Point taken. All right. We've got two vague ideas." Ashni moved a map between them. Nakia was about to witness an actual battle planned out and she couldn't wait to see.

S.L. Kassidy

Chapter Ten

ASHNI STOOD ATOP A hill with the setting sun at her back, looking at Valen, a city that would've been a target regardless. The population was large, but the economy more so. It had roads cutting through the grasslands of the countryside going out to other cities, but was also by a major river, giving them bountiful farmland, and easy access to sea. She wouldn't be able to bring the Kairon area to heel without Valen. She wouldn't be able to finance her march without it either, but this was sooner than she wanted to take it.

She couldn't give them a chance to rally more support from other nearby cities. The Tyrans had already showed up. While Dorian didn't have any more daughters married to kings, he could've managed some allies without them. Aid could be on their way now. Worry churned in her gut. None of this was planned. Typically, she could go with the flow, but that was when she was in control of the flow.

It didn't help that Ashni still felt her position with the gods was precarious. Yes, she had prayed, lit incenses, made small and grand sacrifices to the gods since getting Nakia back, but there was no way to know it made up for her hubris. It was possible the gods would like to see her fail this day. She'd be humiliated in front of her troops, her little sister, and her beloved.

But, maybe you've been redeemed. The gods hadn't stood in her way when she went after Nakia, after all. They could've had Caligo take Nakia from her, turning her into one of his undead puppets. They could've kept Layla from seizing Phyllida. They could've done many things to ruin her. *But, now, they have a chance to truly destroy me and through a man who thinks he's better than me by virtue of being a man*. She needed to tread carefully, even if the gods were with her. One false move and her army could end up fodder for Black Dogs.

She couldn't see the Black Dogs, knowing the Tyrans were off on the other side of the plain setting up for the battle, but reports had come in. The hounds were larger than they expected, the size of workhorses. Teeth that could go through metal with long claws that could do the same and fire spewed from their jaws. *That's a first.* Their hides were tough, almost like dragon scales, impenetrable. They were fed human flesh for good measure. The Tyrans had bred these beasts specifically for war and had done a fantastic job.

"You all right?" Nakia asked as she came up behind Ashni.

Ashni didn't turn around. "Didn't I tell you to stay at camp? It's bad enough you didn't want to stay in Phyllida. I don't want anything to happen to you."

"Nothing will happen. I want to be close to you." Nakia tucked herself in close, wrapping her arms around Ashni's waist, and Ashni relaxed. She leaned down to kiss Nakia's forehead.

"I want you close, too, but this isn't safe."

"Yet you're out here with no protection."

"I am my own protection. I'm unstoppable in the open air. Actually, I'm unstoppable in an enclosed space, too." *And yet, I can't shake this quiver in my stomach. It's this attitude that probably has the gods looking down on me with anger. I can't keep being this way until I'm sure they're with me again.*

Nakia tightened her grip around Ashni's waist. "You sound like your sister now. Humble isn't something you two do well, hmm?"

"Layla's a master of complicated magic, but I'm the daughter of a god. Maybe two gods. I'm not sure about my mother sometimes. She's weird." Ashni didn't want to think about her mother right now. *She's going to tease the hell out of me when she meets Nakia and remind us all how I'm so much like my father and how even gods can be defeated with the right talent.*

"What are you doing out here?"

"I always like to have a good look at a place before I take it."

Nakia's brow furrowed. "Why?"

"I like to appreciate the view, the scenery before it's altered and to remind myself why I'm here."

"Why are you here? Why the conquest? Just because of your father?"

Ashni was quiet for a long moment, but Nakia didn't press her for an answer. She had been asked many times throughout her life why she conquered and she gave many different answers. Nakia deserved more than what she told others. She deserved everything, like Layla, like Adira.

"Of course, there's a bit of wanting to be like my father, of wanting to continue his legacy. I was reared on stories of his adventures and always wanted my own. But, my mother, she never let me forget I was destined for greatness. I think one of the things I'm looking for out here is what type of greatness. I used to think it was like my father, but not long after he died, my mother told me that's not what she meant, but she never explained it. She just said I'd change the world and I'd do it well. I don't think I've changed the world, though. I've only seen it." The land was beautiful, and she wanted to make her mark on it. "This is possibly the only way for people to know me." She didn't know any other way to change the world than by making herself known throughout the whole of it.

Nakia's brow furrowed. "Is it?"

Ashni looked at her. "What do you mean?"

"You seem to bring out things in people. Your sister. The general. Me. Perhaps, we're better for knowing you and maybe it's like that for many others."

Ashni chuckled. "Those things were already there long before me. Maybe I provide an outlet, but you're all who you are, regardless of me being here."

Nakia smiled at her and Ashni could melt under her gaze. Nakia looked at her like she hung the stars. *Am I the same?* Everyone knew her feelings for Nakia before she did. She feared she did look at Nakia like she was the most precious thing to walk the planet. Of course, she was. She'd have to learn to school her features, though, because she didn't want all the world to know how valuable Nakia was, as it was dangerous.

"What are your goals?" Ashni asked as they started down the hill. She made sure to steer Nakia clear of the stones hidden in the short grass as the sun disappeared beneath the horizon.

"My what?"

"Your goals. What do you want from this life?"

Nakia blew out a long breath. "I've never had a chance to think about it."

Ashni ran her fingers through Nakia's hair before her hand settled on the small of Nakia's back. "You should. Think about it, I mean. Think about it and get it done."

Nakia pursed her lips. "What if my goal takes me from you?"

"Just come back to me whenever you can. The best relationships I've ever seen involve two independent partners who always find their way back to each other after a while. I'll miss you, but I wouldn't mind. Your life should be fulfilling for you. I've always believed that." Maybe she was taught that. She wasn't sure, but she meant the words.

Nakia's face scrunched up. "What life did you live growing up? I've never been told my life should be fulfilling for me, rather that I should fit into my role and be happy with that. Did no one ever tell you that you had to be a certain way because you were born into something?"

Ashni rubbed her forehead. "No. I've never been told that, and you shouldn't listen to that either. Inside of you, there's something crying out for you to do...well, something. Listen to whatever that is and you'll figure it out. Hell, it led a poor fisherwoman to become a general."

Nakia's mouth dropped open. "She was a fisherwoman?"

"Lowest of the low. A bastard child of a poor fisherman. This is how I know society can't tell you what you are. Because society told one of the most brilliant military minds I've ever met that she was a damn fisherwoman. I'll tell you this, though, you put a spear in her hand and she's a monster thanks to fishing."

"But, she doesn't use a spear."

"No, a sword is a weapon of high status, regardless of what society you're in. My father used to talk about when he went into her village how Adira laid waste to a row of soldiers with just her spear. When she agreed to march with him, he had a spear specially made for her and she cherished it, but felt like she earned a sword after a while. Beyond that, she doesn't want to give people more fuel to talk about her behind her back. I'm sure you remember dear Amal."

Nakia frowned at the mention of his name. "He talks about her?"

"All the time. Our father preferred her company to Amal's, but then, who wouldn't?" Ashni would rather be tortured than spend time with Amal, and more often felt like it was one and the same.

Nakia's scowl deepened. "Are your other brothers like him?"

"They all have their pros and cons. I'm more partial to the younger ones. But, the younger ones might respect me more, making them easier to deal with. You should think of what you want in life. I've got a battle to win." Ashni smiled. One step closer to her goal. *Stay with me, Father. I never know when the gods might decide it's time to show me why I've displeased them.*

Nakia nodded. "I have to think about it, but I'll tell you after the battle. This way you have to win to know what I want in this life."

Ashni's smile grew. "Well, if that isn't incentive to win, I don't know what is. I'd come back from the dead to find out what you want in life and to help you make it happen." This statement earned her a kiss. "I'd do even more to have another one of those."

Nakia winked. "More, after you win."

"Then I better win." Not that she planned to do anything else.

***

Ashni had gone to sleep wrapped around Nakia and she was reluctant to leave, but it was time for the battle. The worry was still in her stomach, but small and easy to put away. It was overpowered by the buzz of battle in her blood. She could feel a charge all around her, making her nerves twitch. Time to go win.

She planted a kiss to Nakia's cheek. Nakia mewled in her sleep and then turned, eyes still closed. Ashni gave into temptation and kissed her again. Nakia angled her face so the kiss landed on her lips, and she threw her arms around Ashni's neck, pulling Ashni closer, deeper. Ashni didn't resist, but she was the one who eventually pulled back.

"I have to go."

"Now?" Nakia glanced at the tent flap. "The sun isn't even up yet."

"I know, but we have to set the battlefield. If this goes wrong…" Ashni didn't finish. Most of the time, she wouldn't even think about something going wrong. There was nothing to fear when the gods had favored her. She knew her father was always with her, but even he wasn't always victorious in his endeavors.

"Nothing will go wrong." Nakia reached up, caressing Ashni's cheek. "You'll do as you have been. You'll come back to me, and we'll pick this up from there."

Ashni smiled, even though on the inside she lit up beyond any expression her face could pull off. Nakia had faith in her to do this, to defeat Nakia's own father. The charge in her intensified and jolted down her spine, blazing across her nerves. Ashni felt like she could take on the gods themselves right now. *And I might need to if they heard that little bit of blasphemy or sided with the Westerners.*

"Wait here for me?" It was meant to be a command, but it came out as a request. She wasn't meant to command Nakia any more than she was meant to command the sun.

Nakia gave her a sleepy smile. "This is where you'll find me."

Ashni's shoulders straightened and she was so tempted to stay, but she couldn't. There was too much to do, this battle too tricky to not handle on her own. *Besides, what would my troops think of me staying behind to lie close to Nakia? When they were about to face down at least two armies, one with demon dogs and master chariots? I can't believe I even considered it.* With a final glance at Nakia, smiling softly at her with droopy green eyes, yes, she could believe she considered.

Layla and Adira waited for her. The night was like the camp, quiet and dark. The soldiers had been ordered to keep their fires and lights low, not wanting to give away how many people were in the army. The enemy's spies wouldn't get an accurate estimation of their numbers until it was too late.

"Are we ready?" Ashni asked.

Layla shrugged. "The Shadow Walkers did what we do, caused a panic inside the walls. It should be enough to lure them out, especially since they should think they have the advantage."

"They do have the advantage. They have the high ground. They have the sun at their backs. They have chariots, which are pulled by freaking demon dogs," Adira said, as it wouldn't be a good meeting without her pointing out all of the faults in their strategy.

"We have a good plan. Has our path been paved?" Ashni asked.

"I took care of that," Naren said as he walked over.

"Ah, so not completely useless. Gather the troops. Get into position and then show them what we're made of." Ashni clapped and marched off, the others following.

***

Ashni sat astride Midnight Thunder, eyes locked on a hill with the rays of the sun peaking over the ridge. Her army was at her back, waiting for her word. At the top of the hill, Dorian and his allies had come out, waiting to push the Roshan back, thanks to Layla and her band of Shadow Walkers causing chaos behind the walls of Valen. The enemy needed to move on the Roshan or risk having Layla in their city. She had yet to meet an enemy who would accept the Shadow Walkers terrorizing their citizens on a nightly basis.

Thanks to their best scouts, Ashni knew Dorian commanded whomever he salvaged from his military. There was also the Prince of Valen, Wicus, commanding a large portion of the Valen's military. Then, there were the chariots and King Ferox of Tyra.

Nakia briefed them on all she knew about King Ferox and his chariots. Like the Roshan, Ferox was considered a barbarian, even though he was of the Kairon region. His people were wild and fierce. They tattooed themselves everywhere on their bodies, including their faces, for various reasons, battle glory, to praise to the gods, show connections to groups or family, and as declarations to brag. But, that was where the similarities ended. The Tyran wore no armor, coming from a climate that was too humid for it to be comfortable and believing their gods would protect them. Even on the best of days, Ashni never held that much confidence in her gods, even her father. There were too many times she was sure he blinked, or laughed, knowing him.

This battlefield was perfect for the Tyran chariots and Nakia assured her Ferox was more than cocky enough to assume that meant he'd win the battle. She hoped that was true. Nakia hadn't seemed quite sure when she delivered the information.

"We'll do right by you, Dad," Ashni promised. Beyond that, she'd do right for Nakia. Dorian deserved another personal loss for the way he gave Nakia away, like she was some parcel. That would never happen again.

Ashni doubted she'd ever understand how some people could look down on others as if they were nothing based on simply circumstances of their birth. It was bad enough to know of it with Adira, but to see it firsthand with Nakia and for it to be her own father, it was disgusting. Maybe the other daughters were just as special as Nakia and the world would never know their gifts thanks to him. *Now, isn't the time. Focus.*

Ashni glanced around, looking for confirmation everyone was in position. They were. She took a deep breath and stroked Midnight Thunder's neck. He snorted and leaned into her hand, his way of telling her he was ready for the fight. So was she.

"Midnight Thunder, we have to be careful of the Black Dogs. You've seen demons before, so don't let them get to you. You're more of a monster than they could ever be," Ashni whispered into his ear.

Midnight Thunder had been with her through tough times and had possibly seen more than she had. He should be fine, but Black Dogs were new to him. She trusted his reactions would be appropriate.

"Time to get this done." Ashni drew her weapon and pointed forward. "Onward to glory!"

Her troops roared behind her and Midnight Thunder charged forward. The hill was steep, and Midnight Thunder struggled at first, but galloped toward the enemy without fear. Ashni's army followed. They'd follow her to Hell, she knew, without question. Right now, this plan might be close enough.

Before they were halfway up the mound, a rain of arrows came down on them, thudding into their shields. Behind her, Ashni could hear the clang of arrowheads on bronze shields and the faint screams whenever some unlucky soul was pierced. In the shower of arrows, thin beams of sunlight flickered through as the sun ascended into the sky. Soon, they would need to shield their eyes as well as their bodies. Above, she could hear the enemy soldiers crowing with a victory they thought was in the bag. *We better not make it so.*

"Come on!" Ashni pushed Midnight Thunder forward, the incline almost too much for him. He snorted and panted, but pressed on, even with the arrows raining down on them. She hated to think how tired her foot soldiers were and they were barely halfway up the hill.

A soldier carrying the Roshan banner came up right behind Ashni, trying to keep pace with Midnight Thunder. The soldier's face was covered in sweat and determination, but his grip never wavered on the flag. Ashni grinned and couldn't help the pride that swelled within her. These were her warriors. They never stopped. They grabbed their dreams with both hands, never letting go. So, they moved. They climbed. They stood as death came from above and they stared death in the face with a smirk. They were never defeated.

"Keep it up!" Ashni waved her warriors onward. She'd clash swords with the front lines in a moment as long as Midnight Thunder didn't lose his footing.

Ahead of her, the shouts of the enemy got louder and the growls of the Black Dogs rose above all else, easy to scare any lesser beings in her lines. Stones rained down on them now, too, pinging against the shields. The music of war, and her side seemed to be getting drowned out by it. The madness of this plan was on full display now. Part of her worried the gods laughed at her, at her foolishness, at her inevitable fail.

Spears rose to greet them, but Midnight Thunder moved forward still, like the blades meant nothing. Ashni unsheathed her other sword, cutting through the spears to keep Midnight Thunder safe. Her army was right with her despite the losses they suffered in what had to seem like a suicide mission now.

The enemy was rows deep; there was no way they'd make headway. The chariots were right there, behind a wall of foot soldiers, pike men and spearmen. The Black Dogs, two to a chariot, the size of bears more than horses, flames bursting a few inches from their maws, eager to tear into her people. Crimson eyes with flashes of yellow burned, set in shadowed faces, and fur crackled like fire pits.

Everything was right there, as they expected. The only problem was, there were too many. Two and a half armies stared her in the face and declared this the end of her journey. Her army seemed like they wanted to counter that statement, but they could barely stand behind her. The pushback even sent her back to the edge of the hill, Midnight Thunder's hooves sliding in mud created by spilled blood. It was time for the next phase.

"Retreat!" Ashni called over the din of the battle. "Retreat!"

Midnight Thunder reared back, retreat not in his vocabulary. But, Ashni loved her stubborn stead too much to let him stand in the middle of a suicide mission. She gave the reins a yank. Midnight Thunder snorted and tried to pull away. Ashni snarled and clicked her tongue.

"Believe in me," Ashni told her horse. "You know me. Believe in me."

Midnight Thunder huffed, difficult like everyone else in her life, but he backed up. She called out the retreat once more as her horse slid down the mound. Horns and flags repeated her message. Her soldiers followed, still clashing with their foes as they tried to get to safety. The steep hill grew slippery with the blood from her fallen troops. Midnight Thunder almost lost his footing, jarring Ashni in her saddle. She nearly took a spear to the neck, thanks to the stumble.

"Shit, this might be too much of a risk," Ashni mumbled. When they worked out this strategy, she knew it was dangerous, but they seemed to be losing more soldiers than they anticipated. Midnight Thunder's back legs went out, an arrow in his thigh. Ashni tipped back as his flank slipped into the mud and gore. "Damn it!"

"The queen!" Several of her soldiers called.

"Fall back!" Ashni ordered. The first warrior to try to help her would rue the day. "Fall back!" As the words left her mouth, she felt a burning sting in her arm. Hissing, she turned to see an arrow in her bicep. "Fuck. Fall back!"

Her people could only retreat so quick. Ashni gave Midnight Thunder's reins another tug, encouraging him to get back on his hooves. She clicked her tongue, close to his ear and patted his neck with her free hand.

"Come on, Midnight. We have to stick to the plan as much as everyone else. Come on," she whispered. "We'll get them when the time's right. We'll get them." Midnight Thunder was in this just as much as she was, just as much as her troops were, so he needed to know the glory was waiting.

Midnight Thunder gave a whinny and finally did the right thing, getting up to go back down the hill. He marched down the mound, dragging her hardheaded troops down with them. They stumbled by bodies of their fallen comrades, warriors who wouldn't see their dreams now. She took a look back up, their enemy hadn't moved from their vantage point. *Damn.*

"Come on, Ferox. Be as impulsive as they say you are," Ashni said as she hit the bottom of the hill, soldiers running by her. There were no movements at the top of the hill, though "Come on."

Her army continued to do the smart thing and retreat, projectiles still raining down on them. She needed at least one enemy to do the dumb thing. An arrow whizzed by her face, scratching her cheek. *Come on.*

"Ashni!" Adira's shout could be heard through the noise.

"I know!" Her general wanted her to keep moving, especially if this plan was a failure. But, if this plan was a failure, she wouldn't be able to move for a while. They'd have to dig in for a siege and who knew how long that would take. "Damn it!" *Please, gods, you know I will honor you. Just be with me.*

Without waiting for her order, Midnight Thunder spun and rushed away. *Traitor.* The horse trudged through a thin layer of black mud as he charged into the open field where most of her army was spread out. Just as her heart was about to sink, she heard an unfamiliar battle cry mixed in with howls. She turned and a smirk spread onto her face. The chariots had pushed their way to the front lines, in sight at the top of the hill.

A mountain of a man atop a large horse stood at the front of the chariots. He held his straight sword aloft. "Charge!"

Ashni grinned. "Yes!"

The Tyrans were as impulsive as Nakia promised. They charged down the hill on their chariots, thinking they were chasing a fleeing, defeated Roshan. Foot soldiers even came behind them, waving Phyllida's banner. Dorian seemed to be following his foolhardy son-in-law. He could probably taste the revenge on the tip of his tongue. She wouldn't mind seeing the look on his face when she snatched another victory from him.

"Positions! Positions!" Ashni waved the Ivory Claw in a circle, the adrenaline pumping through her numbed the pain in her arm from her wound. Her troops darted into their new formations. She looked around for Adira, catching sight of her back as she rushed to set the next phase of their plan in motion.

The chariots hit the bottom of the field and then suddenly slowed to a crawl, the black mud her people had spread out did as promised so far. Roshan flaming arrows covered the sky, landing in the specially designed mud. Flames shot up from the patch of mud like an erupting volcano, blazing up to the charioteers' shoulders, flashing bright orange with flickers of blue. The Black Dogs snarled and then whimpered as the inferno lapped at their phantom forms. Demons they might be, but they still felt pain.

Ashni grinned. "I have to remember to reward Saniyah for all her amazing work." Now, she needed to get out of range. She had more than arrows coming soon enough.

The lake of fire was enough to stop the chariots in the mud pit. The enemy foot soldiers paused at the flames, but troops still barreled down the hill, pushing them forward. Some chariots managed to make it out of the mire, dragged by their massive canines back onto the meadow ground. They charged forward again, but new projectiles came from her side and landed between her army and their foes. Seconds later, the Dogs howled and several dropped, whimpering like pups as the barbed caltrops did their jobs. *Good to know they work just as well on demon dogs as they do with horses*. Ashni threw out a fist and lightning shot from the sky, hitting several Black Dogs, stunning them.

"Come on, Adira, you have to move faster than that," Ashni muttered, seeing the siege machines in the distance. The siege towers would narrow the battlefield and block in whatever chariots made it through. They could pick the chariots off one by one, and the soldiers too. The Black Dogs wouldn't be able to rip through the towers without much effort and by that time, she'd have taken care of most of them with the help of a few expert Shadow Walkers, who already summoned their own demons.

More enemy troops cascaded down the hill and Ashni assumed Layla was doing her part. She took a small band to the side, terrorizing the edges of their foes, meant only to push more of them forward. Ashni held in a laugh. Once the stragglers had arrived on the base of the hill, the siege towers barricaded them in.

"Ready the catapults!" Ashni raised a hand. Ropes snapped into place. She dropped her hand and watched the projectiles fly. Sharpened bolts took down the middle ranks, and when her Shadow Walkers called forth their demons, barely shaped creatures of smoke with gaping maws, whose roars were more than enough to pause the Black Dogs. The creatures tore through the enemy ranks, cutting in at all angles, rotting away all things they touched, armor, weapons, and foe. Chaos erupted from their enemies.

For the opponents who made it through the fire and the caltrops, Ashni and her forces waited. A small wave of people came at her. The more she swung the Ivory Claw, the more her arrow wound throbbed and bled. She unsheathed the Golden Feather and used that sword to beat back the masses.

The flames crackled ahead with burning soldiers falling from it. People still came from down the hill, driven by Layla and her sort. The chariots found themselves without space to maneuver thanks to the siege towers boxing everyone in and their Black Dogs were confounded when confronted by larger creatures of the night. And just like that Ashni's side began to crush their foes until the enemy figured out how to properly retreat. Ashni's victory came swiftly after that.

I can't believe this crazy idea worked. The plan came together as Ashni, Adira, and Layla envisioned it. While they had done the false retreat plan a few times, they had never done it with so many moving parts where the opponent had the clear tactical advantage and didn't have to chase them in order to win. They gambled here and won big.

She blew out a breath. *I'll never doubt having the gods' favor ever again.* There was no way the gods were upset with her. Not with this victory.

Chapter Eleven

NAKIA WRUNG HER HANDS together as she waited for word of the battle. She paced outside of the tent she shared with Ashni, feeling useless and out of place. Looking around, she wondered if others left behind felt the same way. *How could they? Their...*Her thoughts stopped. *What's Ashni to me?* She didn't have the words for their relationship.

Would she be my fiancée? Her mind had trouble wrapping around the idea of being engaged to a woman, even though she understood the concept well enough. *She asked to marry me, and I am more than willing and the Roshan allow it. Is this a normal betrothal?*

"I'll have to ask when they return," she mumbled. *If they return.* Dread bubbled and burned in her stomach. It was quite possible when she saw Ashni that morning, it could've been the last time. She should've paid more attention, drank Ashni in, showered her in kisses. *Why didn't I do that?*

Bile rose in her throat and she swallowed it down to avoid vomiting in camp. She didn't want the people left behind to think she couldn't handle herself. *How does Adira's wife cope?* Nakia hated to think she might have to ask. She didn't have any real relationship with Adira's wife. Maybe she could use Bashira as an intermediary.

"Is there anything I can get you?" a slender woman asked, making Nakia pause in her constant pacing. She didn't have on a uniform, so she wasn't a soldier. She was dressed in light colors, trousers, and sandals, even though most of the camp seemed to be in boots. Nakia wasn't sure what to make of her.

"Who are you?" Nakia inquired with an arched eyebrow, annoyed. She had worrying to do and pacing helped her.

The woman bowed her head, feathers braided into her curly, dark hair shifted to one side. "I am one of the general's assistants."

Nakia frowned. "She has assistants?" She felt like Adira was a woman who did it all on her own.

The woman shrugged. "Yes, in a way. Since her spouse doesn't travel with her, a couple of people go on campaign to make sure she uses the tech Saniyah develops properly. We also get a chance to witness what the army might need and develop things in camp or send word back to Saniyah, so she can create things."

Nakia nodded. An army probably had more than soldiers in it anyway. The camp looked like a small city, even without the army there. There were probably all sorts of things that went into making it run properly.

"Is there anything I can get you?" the woman repeated, her brown eyes warm. Her expression made her copper face glow like freshly glazed pottery. She was older than Nakia, probably older than Adira, and gave off an almost motherly presence.

Nakia shook her head. "No. I'm just adjusting."

"To life in camp or to life waiting for a warrior to return?"

"Both," Nakia said before she realized it. Living in the camp wasn't even that difficult. Everyone, especially Ashni, was ready to move heaven and earth for her comfort.

The woman gave her a soft smile. "You'll get the hang out of it, living in the camp anyway. My spouse is a warrior. The wait is always going to be hard until your loved one is back in your arms. In fact, I choose to come with the army just to keep track of my wild woman."

"You're married to a woman? Are any of the women around here married to men?" Layla seemed like the only one. No one treated her as if it was odd, but it seemed like every other woman she met was in a relationship with another woman.

The woman laughed. "There are plenty, if that's your thing. There are also plenty of men married to men."

Nakia shook her head. At this point, she could understand the concept of a same sex relationship thanks to her feelings for Ashni, but a relationship and marriage were two different things. Hell, marriage and feelings were two different things. Yet her feelings for Ashni made her want to marry Ashni and that seemed to be mutual. She shook those thoughts away. Now wasn't the time to have a philosophical crisis.

"How do you handle waiting for your spouse to come back from a battle?"

"One, I have friends and we all distract each other. Two, I work if I have any ideas. Three, I walk around until something catches my eye," the woman replied, ticking off each of her ideas on her fingers.

"And I caught your eye." Nakia wasn't sure how she felt about that. She didn't want to be pitied. She just wanted Ashni back safe. *Is that too much to ask? Is the anxiety threatening to gnaw a hole in my chest, the gods saying, yes, it was too much to ask?* She'd pray for peace if only she didn't already know her peace was Ashni. Ashni's return was the only thing that would make things right.

She shrugged. "Friends have gotten drunk and inspiration hasn't hit me."

"You could get drunk as well."

"I don't like to drink when we're on campaign. I definitely don't want to be drunk when my spouse comes back or if my spouse doesn't."

"Wouldn't the latter be the best time to be drunk?"

She shook her head. "No, because then you can fool yourself into believing the news isn't real and you have to deal with it again when you sober up. I've seen it happen. I don't want that." She gave Nakia a hard look, as if telling her she didn't want that either.

Nakia took a breath as thoughts of waiting for Ashni after countless battles drifted through her head. *What would I do if Ashni didn't come back from one of them? Hell, if Ashni didn't come back from this one? What would my life be like without Ashni?* She couldn't imagine her life, with or without Ashni. She couldn't figure out what her life was right now. *Stop with the deep thinking already. It's not making this any easier.* She'd save the questions for when Ashni was back. *She will be back.*

To distract herself from negative thoughts, Nakia nodded and then looked around the camp, if only to figure out why the woman came to her of all people. There was little movement in the camp. Barely anyone was outside of their tents and those who were, sat calmly, doing something quiet to occupy their time. She probably looked like a nervous wreck, pacing outside of the tent.

"You must think I'm pathetic." It made her throat burn to admit it.

"Of course not. We've all been where you are. The first wait. Perhaps we could take each other's minds off of it."

Nakia shrugged. "What do you suggest?"

"Do you play chess?"

Nakia almost said no, but she did. Ashni taught her and told her she was good. Maybe she could improve enough to one day play Ashni. It would be a great way to take her mind off of a great many things as well.

"Do you have a set?" Nakia had no idea where Ashni kept anything.

The woman nodded. "I'll get it and be right back. I'm Farzana, by the way."

Nakia nodded and then Farzana was gone, coming back in a few moments with a chessboard in hand and a bag of pieces dangling from one finger. Nakia was a little out of practice. She took long moments to make moves, but Farzana didn't seem bothered by it, waiting patiently each time it was Nakia's go. Farzana won the first three games, but it was harder and harder each time.

"Cheating on me already?" The question caused Nakia to gasp and look up. Ashni was hardly a foot away, looking worse for wear. Her skin, generally the color of dark sand, was covered in mud and soot. Much of her honey brown hair was out of her braids, going off in all directions.

Nakia was out of her seat before she realized it, her heart racing with both relief and concern. *She's alive!* "You're hurt." Ashni had an arrow sticking out of her arm, blood oozing down the limb to drip from her fingertips.

Ashni glanced down at her arm, as if she had no idea there was an arrow through her flesh. She had the nerve to scoff. "Oh, this. It's nothing."

"It's not 'nothing.' You're bleeding!" Nakia wanted to run her fingers over the wound, but she didn't want to risk making things worse.

"This is the part where you order her to the medic to get fixed before the wound festers and she dies," Adira said, standing behind Ashni with an almost delighted glimmer in her eye and amused smirk.

Nakia straightened as she stared Ashni down. "She's right! You need medical attention. Come on. I'll go with you." She took Ashni by the hand.

Adira snickered, but Nakia ignored the sound, along with Ashni's protests. Nakia didn't know where she was going, didn't know who might be a doctor in the camp, but eventually one found them. She suspected Adira sent him their way. *Next time I have spare time, I have to get to know who is who around the camp, so I'm not completely useless if Ashni needs me again.* They went to the Queen's tent but didn't go in. The doctor needed the daylight to get a proper look at the wound.

"It's fine," Ashni said through gritted teeth, hand on the arrow shaft as if she had plans to yank it out.

"Can you let the doctor work, please?" Nakia huffed and swatted Ashni's hand away from the missile buried in her flesh.

The doctor, a rather young looking man, gave her a small smile as he unwrapped tools from a leather satchel. Nakia swallowed as she took in the sight of the tools. She hadn't seen a doctor operate before. She wasn't sure what to expect while Ashni seemed more put out than anything else.

"Get on with it, so you can tend to troops who actually need it," Ashni said with her nose turned up.

"Highness, you do realize if I don't tend to this, you could lose your arm," the doctor replied.

Ashni frowned. "You must be new if you don't know I can tend to my own minor wounds."

Nakia glanced at Ashni. *She knows how to mend wounds?* Nakia wouldn't know what to do if she had an arrow in her arm. She wouldn't know how to take care of minor wounds, either. *I have so much to learn if I'm going to keep up with anyone around here.*

"I know you can, Highness, but maybe let others do their jobs as well," the doctor replied.

Nakia gave Ashni's healthy hand a squeeze to get her to leave the poor doctor alone. It worked to the point where Ashni looked at her and smiled. Nakia smiled back and then noticed the doctor holding up a pair of shears, snapping off much of the shaft of the arrow. She gasped and he gave her a look with a tilt of his head. She suspected she was pale, and they hadn't even got to the gruesome part yet.

"Perhaps you'd rather wait in the tent as I tend to the queen?" He nodded toward the open flap of the tent.

Ashni gave her a soft look. "It's fine. You don't have to stay and watch."

Nakia didn't want to, but felt like she had to. Standing with Ashni through this seemed like she was offering support, even if Ashni didn't seem to think it was a big deal. But, she didn't want to see Ashni hurt any further, even if it was to fix her. Taking a breath, she squeezed Ashni's hand. Ashni smiled at her. Even with the beautiful distraction of Ashni's smile, she still noticed the doctor cutting into Ashni's bicep out of the corner of her eye.

"What are you doing?" Nakia's voice sounded hysterical, even to her. She could feel the blood drain from her face, and she dipped to the side a little as if about to pass out. Ashni gave her hand a tug, helping her regain some awareness of what was going on. Nakia gritted her teeth and forced herself to remain standing. She'd have to get used to the sight of blood.

Ashni kissed the side of her head. "Calm down. He's not hurting me. Well, he is, but not in the way you think. He needed to cut the wound and make it wider to pull the arrow out. If he just pulled it out, it would take a lot of flesh with it. It'd be like a skewer."

Nakia winced at the image of a chunk of meat being torn out of Ashni's arm. Ashni gave her hand another squeeze. Taking a breath, she tried to steel herself. She should support Ashni. She was with a warrior queen. Surely this wasn't the last time Ashni would show up wounded, and she'd want to be with Ashni those times as well.

"Did you get more sleep after I left earlier?" Ashni asked.

Nakia had to swallow to find her voice, turning her gaze from the gaping wound to her love's eyes. "I tried. It was cold without you."

"I was tempted to stay. You're better company than Adira any day."

"From the way you call her a nag all the time, I feel like that's not much of a compliment."

Ashni chuckled and her amber eyes danced with amusement. "You're learning. I see you were dusting off your chess skills as well."

Nakia nodded. "I tried. I was going to lose, though, and I already lost three games before you showed up."

"Well, at least you saw that much. I'll practice with you after I get cleaned up. There'll be a little downtime as we wait to see what your father does next. I'll enjoy helping you grow, so the next time you see Amal you can pounce on him like a hungry lion on a gazelle." There was an evil twinkle in her eyes, like Ashni couldn't wait to see that and watch her brother throw a tantrum.

"So, the battle was in your favor?"

"I suppose you could say that. No one won, but we didn't lose. Your information on Ferox made the whole thing possible. I hope to thank you later for it." The look in Ashni's eyes told her how she wished to show her gratitude, and it made Nakia squirm. Yet the look didn't betray the fact that she had a wound cut open and an arrow yanked out of it. *Amazing.*

"You're injured. You should be thinking about that. I know I am," Nakia said. She wanted to take care of Ashni, help her heal, and whatever else a caretaker was supposed to do for someone who was hurt.

Ashni rolled her eyes. "It's not serious."

Nakia might have believed that, but then Ashni winced. Nakia glanced at the wound to see the doctor holding the bloody arrowhead in brass prongs. Ashni glared at him, silently scolding him. The doctor ignored her.

"That's a beauty," the doctor said, twisting the arrowhead in his grip.

Nakia wasn't sure what he meant, all she could see was blood and gore dripping from the weapon. Then it was out of sight, placed in a little pan by the doctor's feet. She made the mistake of looking at the wound. Blood poured from it now. Her stomach twisted and bubbled. Her eyes went back to Ashni's face as she resisted the urge to gag. She searched Ashni's face for some sign of agony.

"I'm all right." Ashni placed a soft kiss to Nakia's forehead.

Nakia nodded for lack of a better thing to do and felt foolish for even doing that. But, she didn't move from where she was. She wasn't sure how much time passed, but she remained there, holding Ashni's hand. Ashni tried to make conversation, but Nakia couldn't muster the proper responses for more than a few sentences. Eventually, Ashni waved her free hand and flexed her fingers.

"Good job, doc, especially on the stitches," Ashni said.

"Change the bandage at least every two days," the doctor replied as he packed up. He handed Nakia a small jar. "Put this on the wound before rewrapping until it's fully healed."

Nakia nodded, her chest swelling. She was given responsibility, not just any responsibility either. She was set to look after the queen, the person in charge of the doctor's dream, the army's dream, and the soon to be conqueror of the West.

"Let's get you cleaned up and get some food in you," Nakia said and she was off before Ashni could say anything.

Nakia went from not knowing her way around camp to making sure Ashni got what she needed. Ashni spurted objections, but she did as she was told. She was washed and changed into more comfortable clothes. Nakia even managed a servant to take Ashni's hair out of the now half-done braids she wore for battle, letting her scalp breath under wild, long curls. The way Ashni sighed and her eyes fluttered shut as the braids came loose let Nakia know she had done the right thing. It wasn't until Ashni sat down for a meal that Nakia paused long enough to enjoy Ashni's return. She curled up into Ashni's side, away from her injured arm.

"Thank you," Ashni said before eating a spoonful of baked apples with cinnamon.

"For what?" Nakia didn't think she did anything that required thanks. "I want to take care of you like you do with me. I want you to let me take care of you."

Ashni nodded, her hair tickling Nakia's cheek. "It'll take some getting used to. Bear with me. I don't want to treat you like a servant."

"No, but there'll be times I want to serve you, as you do with me. Please, let me," Nakia replied.

"I'll do my best, especially if you show up with these apples. I usually eat them with honey. What made you get cinnamon?"

Nakia shrugged. "I thought you'd like it. Make sure you eat the stew, too, though. You need the energy."

Ashni pouted but ate the stew after she finished what was supposed to be the dessert. She shared some of the food and Nakia accepted the offer. She had spent much of the day worrying over Ashni, so she hadn't remembered to eat and probably wouldn't have been able to hold anything down if she did.

"How did the battle go?" Nakia asked. Maybe if she knew more about battles, it would save her some concern in the future.

Ashni reached for bread from a nearby tray. "Better than expected."

"But you said you didn't win." Nakia squinted and shook her head. "Isn't the point of having a battle to win?" *Isn't winning the point of everything?*

"Not always. I'm sure they would've liked to win, hoping to keep Princess from taking her people into the city and causing havoc, but we weren't looking for that. We wanted to see what we were dealing with in real time and also give them something to think about. We got to see that Ferox is as impulsive as you described him. We got to see that even with their Black Dogs, we can keep up with the enemy as long as we have a good plan. We got to see much of the army isn't as disciplined, which we suspect is the Tyrans, but also your father's troops."

Nakia tensed. "Was my father there?"

"I believe he was, but I didn't see him myself. There were definitely men flying his banner. The only ones to stay put were the Valen troops. They'll be the ones we worry about. They understood they had the advantage and didn't move. They're well trained, professional. We might be able to challenge them to a champion match. It's been a year since we were here before, so that might work."

Nakia nodded, not sure if she was supposed to give input there. She didn't know how warfare worked but Ashni didn't seem to be waiting for a response. She reached for a bit of melon from the food tray and offered Nakia a morsel. Nakia accepted, eating right from

Ashni's hand without a second thought.

"So, what are you going to do?" Nakia asked.

"For the moment, finish this meal, hold you close, and get some sleep. We'll figure things out in the morning. Adira's waiting for word from some spies and Layla's going to cause a little more trouble at nightfall. We can't do much else."

Nakia took Ashni's word for it. With the meal done, Ashni went to lie down, taking Nakia with her. Nakia cuddled in close while being mindful of Ashni's injury. Ashni gave her several soft kisses on her lips.

"I worried about you while you were out," Nakia said.

Ashni's face lit up a little. "I know how you feel. I was worried the whole time you were gone."

"Will it get easier?"

Ashni's expression fell. "No, it doesn't. I was always confident my father would return, but that was when I was a child. As I got older, I'd remind myself my father's the son of a god and even then I worried, at least a little at the back of my mind. My mother tried to hide her concern, but there were times she never slept. She'd say it's hard to sleep without him snoring next to her."

Nakia frowned. Ashni would be in dangerous situations for her conquest, however long that would be. She'd accept that, as that was Ashni's dream long before Nakia got into the picture. *But then, where do I fit into Ashni's life?*

"Ashni." Nakia licked her lips, still getting used to the queen's name on her tongue.

"Yes?"

"You plan to marry me, yes?"

"Damn right I do." Ashni nodded. "Oh…"

Nakia arched an eyebrow. "Oh?"

"I need to get you a promise bracelet. My promise to you, to honor you." Ashni got up, moving about the tent.

Nakia sat up. "What are you doing?"

"You need a bracelet."

"Not right this moment. You need to rest. You're injured and exhausted."

Ashni went on like she hadn't heard a word Nakia said, going to a chest she had in the corner of the tent. She knelt by it, digging for something. "I have plenty of bracelets. I don't know if any of them fit you, though. I'll have to get you one made."

"Ashni." Nakia got up and fell to Ashni's side. "Come back to bed.

You don't need to do this right now."

Ashni looked her in the eyes and it felt like those amber pools could see down into her soul. "I need you to know regardless of what happens, I'll always try to come back to you and I want only for your happiness."

"I know."

"And I will damn sure marry you."

Nakia nodded, feeling the certainty in her bones. She led Ashni back to bed, and they fell asleep in each other's arms.

***

Ashni awoke and stroked Nakia's hair. Her eyes fell to her bandaged arm. It wasn't the first time she was wounded and it wouldn't be the last. But, the wound burned and she knew it wasn't from the possibility the arrow tip had been poisoned. It was from the concern and terror she had witnessed in Nakia's eyes. She never wanted to see that look in Nakia's beautiful green eyes ever again. But at the same time, she couldn't stop her dream, either.

If you don't stop, how will you be able to enjoy your hellcat? She frowned. Well, she might not be able to enjoy her time with Nakia right away, but her parents managed. Her father was a conqueror until the day he died. Their marriage was long and happy. *Why can't mine be the same? Isn't this something to worry about later? Like when you're not in the middle of a conquest?*

There was a list of other things to do, but Ashni couldn't bring herself to care about them just yet. For the moment, she held Nakia a little tighter, reminding herself she was there. Nakia was there and wanted to marry her, despite coming from a culture that thought such a thing was laughable. Nakia wanted to stay with her, even as she conquered Nakia's homeland. Surely she was allowed a minute to enjoy that. When she finally got up, she'd make the appropriate sacrifices to the gods and beg for forgiveness for daring to question their wisdom.

Chapter Twelve

ASHNI SAT WITH ADIRA and Layla in her tent, Nakia at her side. According to Adira's spies, Timon, King of Valen, had no plans to release his army again. It was a smart move. He had the advantage unless she wanted to do an outright siege and sit there for months, which didn't appeal to her, ever. She rubbed her palms together in thought.

"They've got sacred lanterns to cut off shadow magic. It probably took a while to set up, but they're all over the place now," Layla reported with a scowl. She sat with her legs folded and pulled on her knees in frustration.

"Your poor ego," Ashni replied. Even though she teased, this was bad news. She couldn't send Layla or any other Shadow Walkers in through their shadows.

"More like my poor fingertips. They damn near got seared off in the light of the lantern. I didn't even know that much sacred oil could be used." Layla flexed her fingers on her right hand, which was bandaged. She probably had blisters from the blessed light.

Ashni frowned. "No one was seriously injured, right?"

"No. Mostly bruised egos, like you said." Layla's frown deepened.

Adira rubbed her chin. "You ready to dig in or do you want to negotiate with Timon?"

"Do you think he's willing to talk? Right now, he's got the better position," Ashni answered.

Adira shook her head. "He's got the advantage now. We could shock everyone, especially our troops, by actually digging in and waiting it out."

Ashni grimaced. "What in my entire existence says to you I'm willing to sit and wait?"

"Nothing, which is why I said we could shock everyone. If you want to see if he'll deal, you can send in the princess. Layla, not Nakia obviously," Adira said.

It was worth a shot. Anything to avoid a month's long, drawn out siege. "Princess, you got this?"

Layla sighed, shoulders dropping as if she now carried some great burden. "Why do I have to be the messenger? We have messengers."

"And we have you. Teach someone to go in the same way you do and you won't have to do this anymore," Ashni said.

"Also, that person would have to be of your status, so they'll be taken as seriously as you," Adira said.

Ashni nodded. "True. It probably wouldn't hurt if they were my sister, too."

Layla sucked her teeth. "I hate you both."

"Now, we just have to figure out what to offer and ask for from Timon. According to my reports, he's not a man to be taken lightly in any manner. He knows he's got us. He's not fielding his army again. He wasn't happy with the battle the other day either," Adira said.

"What went wrong?" Nakia asked, eyes on the documents spread out between them.

"According to the spies, Ferox broke rank, ignoring their battle plan and orders from Wicus to stand their ground. Wicus recognized they had the advantage and our feigned retreat. Ferox is the one who chased after us and then Dorian's troops followed. Valen is ruled by good military minds, who have trained their soldiers well. The fact that they keep a standing army shows they're more prepared than their neighbors for battle. So, how do we want to negotiate this?" Adira asked.

Ashni pressed her palms together. "We could let them know we won't raze their city to the ground if they agree to pay tribute. Eventually, we'll just absorb them into our empire." It wasn't nearly as glorious as conquering the city, but it worked.

"They might not go for that. We don't know how much supplies they have to dig in. We don't want to be sitting around here for months, do we?" Layla said.

"Well, we don't." Ashni glanced at Adira, who was all too willing to do the patient thing, which was probably the right thing. Unless they could plan out a proper battle, they wouldn't fight the Valen forces any time soon.

"Fine. We'll send Layla in with a message about paying us tribute and we'll worry about this problem later." Adira's face pinched like she had something sour.

Ashni arched an eyebrow. "When you put it that way, it sounds like the wrong thing to do."

"Because it is. We can't just leave a city and say we'll come back for

146

it later. What happens if the next city is as well managed as this one? This isn't the easy conquest you thought it was and now you're trying to take an easy way out." Adira threw up her hands.

"I never thought this would be easy!" Fury flared inside of her, and Ashni glared at her general. She'd never treat this journey with anything less than the seriousness and respect it deserved. "Do you honestly think I'm not prepared?" Ashni's fingers twitched as her talent burned down her nerves. She wasn't angry enough for lightning, but it sounded like Adira wanted to fight.

"I never said you weren't prepared. You're not patient, though. Not everything's smash-and-grab. Let's sit down and discuss tactics," Adira replied, her voice calm, and she pointed to the floor.

Adira was right, even though Ashni loathed admitting it. She was restless now, and it felt like she might come out of her skin if she didn't keep moving. *When did I start feeling this way?* That wasn't the way things were. Nakia grabbed her hand and held it with both of hers, shaking her from her thoughts. Her restlessness settled as she eyed her hand in Nakia's, olive tone engulfed her darker hand. It calmed her down enough to see the wisdom in her general.

"You should think of options, in case they don't take the message well," Nakia said. "Or even if they do take the message well. Remember, my father made it seem like he took the deal."

Sighing, Ashni nodded. Yes, she did have to practice some patience, so she put her other hand over Nakia's and brushed Nakia's knuckles with her thumb, her mind calming with the simple gesture. "We have the means for a siege."

"We do, as always," Adira replied.

"We'll send Princess in with our message, but also set up for the siege. We have more forces than they do, even with this battle. We have brilliant technology, probably things they've never seen. We have good supply lines. We can dig in. If we have to wait, we can at least send some people to find out if we have more enemies like this ahead of the conquest," Ashni said.

Adira puffed out her chest. "Look at you, making long term plans. I'm so proud of you."

Ashni snorted. "Shut up." She could make plans, but she wanted things immediately, especially before something went wrong. But, she was lax before and things crumbled. She needed to be cautious right now, and yet it would seem Timon beat her to the punch. A royal messenger showed up with a note. From the seal, it was from Dorian, not Timon.

"What do you think he wants?" Layla's lip curled, eyeing the seal.

"One way to find out." Ashni broke the seal and opened the scroll. She tilted it to Nakia, wanting Nakia to get the idea whatever was hers was also Nakia's, including correspondences from enemies. No one objected. Layla didn't even look at her funny.

Nakia scoffed. "My father must be desperate if he thinks we're going to fall for this."

Adira arched an eyebrow. "What does it say?"

"Dorian was wounded in the battle and the wound can't be healed and has festered. He's not long for this world," Ashni said. It was probably a lie, but the way her stomach rolled, she worried. *What if I've killed my kitten's father?*

Layla rolled her eyes. "Can't say I'm sad."

Ashni shoved her sister. "Show some respect!"

"Respect for who? The guy who married off your spouse to a monster who stole from my people?" Layla countered.

Nakia stared at Ashni. "You're not actually buying this, are you?"

"There's a possibility your father was critically injured. I got shot with an arrow. Why not him?" Ashni asked.

"You know who didn't get shot with arrows, people with good sense." Layla pointed to herself and Adira. "We're not listening to a known liar."

"Exactly," Nakia said.

Ashni looked at Nakia. "Hellcat, you don't mean that. This is your father." *You only get one father.*

"My father has lied to us before. All of us." Nakia made a circle with her index finger.

Ashni shook her head. She couldn't believe what she was hearing. "You don't know that. Your father's dying."

"According to a letter from my father, who we just determined is a liar." Nakia turned to fully face Ashni and cupped her face with smooth hands. "You can't be seriously considering this to be the truth."

Ashni put her hands on Nakia's wrists. "You never know when it'll be the last time you see your father." *But, you never forget the last time you saw him.* Her throat stung as she remembered her father's bright smile as he told her he was sneaking out of a boring meeting and she better not tell her mother.

Nakia leaned back. "You think I want to see him? He's an ass."

"You say that now, but things might change if he dies." Ashni's heart grew heavy in her chest as she thought about all the fights she got into with her father, screaming about how he didn't take her seriously, barking at him for leaving her behind because he didn't want to get shown up by her, and tearing into him for not taking her sooner as she learned to command her lightning. Yes, she and her father got along most of the time, but she still wished she could take back the moments they didn't and just revel in their time together.

Nakia's brow furrowed. "Ashni, my father made me believe I was useless because I was born female and then used me, time and time again so he could sway a situation to his advantage, like he's probably trying to do with you now."

Ashni moved her hand from Nakia's wrist to her neck, stroking up and down. Out of the corner of her eye, she noticed Layla and Adira making their escape. She couldn't understand why at first, but then she stared at Nakia. This was a private matter, something to do with their relationship, not with their military.

"He could be dying," Ashni said.

"Why do you think I should care?" Nakia stared at her and then her jade eyes widened. "You think my father is like your father? You're so wrong."

"You only get one father." She had the best of the best and it hurt to not have him around. She didn't want Nakia to have that along with the regret of not seeing him one last time.

"Good!" Nakia stood up. "I don't need another father using me or my sisters like currency. I was sold to a demon for an alliance that didn't even come through. We knew Ferox was a pig of a man and my father gave my sister to him anyway in exchange for fucking chariots!"

Ashni blinked at the swear word. *Okay, she's worked up. I have to make sure I don't screw this up.* She stood and held her hands up in surrender. "I get it. I'm only saying your father could be dying and you might not get any more time with him."

Nakia's eyes hardened. "You don't seem to understand that I don't care."

"You say that now."

Nakia glared at her. "I say that always! I've already lived through one parent dying, so I know how I'll feel if this one does, too. You don't have a monopoly on the situation."

Ashni flinched. Nakia had lost her mother. Ashni didn't know Nakia's feelings toward that until this moment. She couldn't imagine how she'd feel if her mother died. Probably similar to the way she felt when her father died, even though she'd pretend otherwise.

"You didn't feel anything when your mother died?"

"Do you feel anything when you get news that a stranger died?" Nakia countered.

Ashni squinted as she took in Nakia. *How is it possible to feel nothing when one's mother died?* She needed a moment to consider that, so she turned and left her tent.

***

Nakia couldn't believe Ashni left the tent. *Am I about to lose Ashni over my damn father?* She wouldn't have that. But, she wouldn't stand for anything that might get her back in her father's clutches. *I don't want to end up like my sisters.* Her insides churned at the thought, being a pawn again and being without a choice.

"Wait, Ashni!" Nakia rushed out of the tent. "I'll go see him!" If she had to endure a moment with her father to stay with Ashni, she would. "I'll go!" She reached out, grabbing Ashni's hand, yanking her to a halt. "I'll go." Her voice lowered, and she clutched Ashni's hand, feeling so much like a child.

Ashni ran her hand through Nakia's hair. It felt good, almost loving. Nakia didn't want to lose that feeling, didn't want to lose Ashni. So, if she had to go into the belly of the beast, she would. She trusted Ashni would come after her if necessary, just like before, even if Valen seemed to be way more secure than Nex.

"Are you sure?" Ashni asked.

"Yes. After all, he might be telling the truth." Nakia could understand why Ashni wanted her to see her father. Ashni probably couldn't fathom having an inattentive father and probably thought Nakia was being a spoiled brat.

"I won't send you in there alone. I'll get Layla to go with you."

Nakia offered her a small smile, warmed by the offer, knowing what it meant for Ashni to make Layla accompany her. "She should stay with you, in case you need her. If this was a trick of some sort, I need you to have your best warrior by your side."

"I'm not sending you in there alone. I'm not stupid."

"Just sentimental," Nakia muttered, which was something worse right now.

Ashni caressed her cheek. "I'm trying to look out for you."

Nakia bit back a frown. Ashni thought she was trying to look after

150

Nakia, but in turn, she was putting Nakia in a position that made her uncomfortable, like so many others. But, this time, Nakia was willing to endure it.

"If my father's dying, then I shouldn't need protection." Of course, if he was lying, he'd have her right where he wanted her. *There's no-win in this situation for me.*

"I'm not sending you in there alone. If not Layla, Naren is going with you."

Nakia almost scoffed, but giving it a moment of thought, Naren had to be more capable than Ashni usually made him sound. He was able to keep up with Layla, after all. He hung out with the elite, even if Ashni made fun of him most of the time. She had seen him eat from Ashni's table. He had to have earned that.

"Then, who watches out for your sister?"

"Me and Layla look after each other and Adira's always there to tell us we're doing it wrong. You need someone with you. For now, it'll be Naren." Ashni leaned in for a soft kiss. "Remember, you're precious to me."

That helped fortify her. She was precious to someone. She mattered. She could do this for Ashni because she mattered, just as Ashni could march into the darkness to rescue her from a husband she never wanted. But, still, she felt unsettled.

"What does it mean to be precious to you?" Nakia found herself asking. She needed something that would help her deal with her father, whether he was dying or not.

Ashni smiled, but it wasn't bright or carefree, as she had seen the queen smile. There was a sorrow in her eyes, and it stabbed Nakia in the heart. It took her back to harsh words she heard her entire childhood, how she wasn't worth it. She was already a burden to Ashni, like she had been to her father, like she had been to her mother. The gods had created her to be a stone around someone's neck. *And that's why people always wish to be rid of you.* Her throat tightened as she imagined one day Ashni would be one of those people, trying to toss her aside.

"It means I'd give you the whole damn world, kitten. I'd stand before all the gods to protect you. But, it also means, if you needed to be away from me, I'd accept that," Ashni said in a low voice.

Nakia swallowed, not expecting that. "Would you trust me, then?" Ashni seemed ready to give her everything, even freedom, but didn't seem to think she knew best. She was used to being patronized, but she didn't expect it from Ashni. *But, I have to tread carefully as I don't want to misstep and lose everything when I've only just gained it.*

"With my life," Ashni replied.

"Then send me to my father with the thought that my father's going to betray us."

Ashni frowned. "I don't understand."

"Not every father is your father. I need you to understand that. Would your father have given you up as a goodwill hostage or married you off to the first eligible bastard?"

Ashni licked her lips. "Of course not."

"Mine did. His scheming doesn't stop with me because I'm his child. Send me to him as if he's lying." Nakia wasn't surprised Ashni's blind spot was fathers. Even when accepting Nakia as a hostage, she probably thought Dorian valued Nakia more than he did.

"Then take Layla with you. Your father will underestimate her."

Nakia knew that was the truth. "But, you need her."

"I have Adira, who's almost like Layla, but more annoying. I'd rather you have Layla. We'll work out a plan of attack from there."

Nakia nodded. "Okay."

They went back into the tent. Layla and Adira were called back in with Naren. They got the news Nakia was willing to go in.

"So, what's the new plan?" Naren asked. He sported a bandage on his forearm, probably burned like his wife, not that Nakia understood how light could burn anyone.

"I'd stick to the siege idea, but we're sending in the princesses." Adira motioned to Nakia and Layla.

"Hey!" Layla folded her arms.

"Don't talk about us as if we're a team or something," Nakia said.

"I say we set up like we're preparing for a siege anyway. Let's see their response," Ashni said.

"But, what're we going to do if the princesses get behind enemy lines and the enemy doesn't want to give them back?" Adira asked.

"Couldn't you just take down a section of the wall?" Naren asked, eyes on Ashni.

"That's a thick wall," Ashni answered. Nakia looked at her in surprise. It was weird to hear Ashni admit to not being able to do something.

"But, you could, right?" Naren stared at Ashni, as if he knew something she didn't.

Ashni gathered Nakia in her arms, caressing Nakia's hip. "Have your

152

spies found any tunnels?"

Adira rubbed her forehead. "Some. They're well-guarded, though. No way for us to use them in an invasion. Timon isn't to be taken lightly."

"There has to be something." Ashni's eyes wandered the tent. "Any weapons Saniyah left us with that could work?"

"I'm sure we have some. We just need to think about it," Adira replied.

"What would the Amir do?" Ashni asked, eyes glued to Adira.

Adira smiled a little. "He wasn't as creative as you are. But, I'll tell you what he did in the few situations I witnessed where he had to dig in his heels. Like you, he lacked the true patience for a siege, but he never let that stop him."

Nakia was pleased to see things back to normal and happy to note how much they were willing to work to make sure she came back, but still unease crept through her. She didn't want to do this, especially when they found out neither Layla or Naren would be able to accompany her. Reports came in that the magic that kept them out and burned them was all over the city, especially in the palace. Nakia would have to make do with warriors who didn't command dark magic. At least Ashni would have the couple by her side. *I can do this, for them. To stay.*

***

After some back and forth, with Dorian explaining he wanted Nakia to come alone in case of assassins, Ashni agreed to send Nakia in with a pair of guards Dorian hadn't seen. They were to be Nakia's servants. She felt less and less confident about this, but still felt Nakia should see her father if he was dying.

"You're tense." Nakia curled against Ashni in their tent as they settled in for sleep. In the morning, she'd be leaving for the city of Valen and to see her father.

Ashni's fingers were splayed against Nakia's bare back. The skin contact should've relaxed her, but anxiety like never before scratched just below the surface. It was worse than when Nakia was gone. Maybe it was because she was sending Nakia into this. "This is dangerous."

"It'll work out. You have a plan."

"You have such faith in me." It should've instilled her with confidence, but it made her worry more. *What if I let Nakia down?* If this went sideways, it could derail so many dreams, but she found she cared more that it could ruin Nakia. She had promised to protect Nakia, and she could fail with this scheme.

Nakia leaned in, kissing her chin. "You're the only person who hasn't let me down."

"I'll do my best not to." Even though she already felt like that wasn't true. She had wronged Nakia before. Yes, she apologized for it, regretted it, but it happened. "Are you sure you want to do this?" Thinking back, Ashni wasn't sure what changed Nakia's mind. She went from not caring about her father to caring within seconds. "You're not doing this for me, are you?"

"What other choice do I have?"

Ashni frowned and sat up, staring at Nakia. "You always have a choice with me. Never think otherwise. You can always tell me no."

Nakia scowled right back, a defiant glare in her gaze. "You judged me for not wanting to see him. You walked away from me."

Ashni sucked her teeth. She had done that. *I'm such a damn idiot.* "I'm sorry. I didn't know what else to do right then. I needed to get my thoughts together." She caressed Nakia's back. "Tell me when I hurt you. I need to get better. I don't ever want a repeat like before. I don't want to chase you off."

Nakia sighed. "And I don't want to leave your side."

Ashni enjoyed hearing that, but she wasn't sure it would work. She knew her future held things she wouldn't want Nakia to be around for, too dangerous. "We'll discuss this when you get back from Valen." She'd do everything in her power to make sure Nakia returned to her. *But, from now on, I need her to know she has choices.*

Chapter Thirteen

NAKIA WOULD'VE FELT SAFER entering Valen with Layla by her side, but they couldn't risk Layla being harmed by the sacred lanterns. She had been promised her two guards were experts in warfare. They had just entered the lavish palace and greeted her father when the trap sprung. The men by her father's side, reached as if to extend their hands in friendship, but blades came from up their sleeves. They acted within a blink of an eye, gutting her guards.

Nakia screamed as blood splattered across her face. "What are you doing?" She stood face to face with her father, a wicked grin spread across his face.

"Welcome home, my dear," Dorian said.

She didn't even have the presence of mind to point out that this wasn't home. They were in someone else's city. Her mind stalled on the fact that her father murdered two people right in front of her and their blood was on her cheek. She had barely learned their names.

"Why did you kill my servants?" Nakia glared at him. He couldn't even pretend for two minutes this wasn't a betrayal.

Dorian scoffed. "You think we can trust anyone who comes in here?"

"Yet, you trust me." Nakia would find some way to turn that on him as soon as she could.

"I'm not that stupid," Dorian said.

"That remains to be seen." An old man stepped forward, the tap of his cane echoing through the grand palace. He had a thin crown on his grey head with sharp brown eyes on his aged visage. This had to be King Timon. "After all, it's your foolish charge that led to this shameful plan in the first place."

Dorian scowled. "The charge was a good idea. We could've overtaken the savages if it wasn't for their demon magic."

"Demon magic or superior science and tactics?" Timon didn't seem to want a response, eyes on Nakia. His gaze softened. "You're as beautiful as your older sister. I'm sorry for this."

Nakia nerves calmed a little. He didn't seem to want to slay her right away as they had done with her guards. "Sorry for what?" Although, she could guess.

"You're staying with us until those barbarians pack up and leave." Dorian squared his shoulders, curling his lip at her. "I already know that savage queen went to dispatch Caligo to get her hands on you."

"She saw fit not to leave me with a true savage. She's not willing to sell me off," Nakia said.

"Then why are you here?" Dorian spread his hands wide.

"Because you said you were dying!" Nakia stomped her foot. "She sent me here because you said you were dying and it turns out it's just a trap to use me, which we suspected, but she sent me anyway in case you were actually dying. How dare you call her the savage?"

Dorian grunted, folding his arms. "You're defending her rather hard."

Indignation tensed her shoulders. The gall of this man to act like she was wrong. "Yes, I am, because she didn't leave me to rot with an insane man who killed pretty much every living thing in his kingdom." She looked her father up and down. "Well, before now anyway."

Dorian flinched and fury like she'd never seen before flashed in his eyes. He stepped forward and for the first time in her life, she wasn't sure she'd escape his presence unscathed. Timon might've recognized this as well, stepping closer to her. The simple move made Dorian relax, just enough where Nakia didn't think he might punch her.

"How about you let my servants show you to your rooms?" Timon motioned for her with one hand as the other motioned further into the palace. His hands looked strong, sturdier than she expected of an old man.

Nakia shook her head. "No, I think we should talk." She needed to salvage this, even with the blood of her guards on her face. She refused to be a pawn, a prisoner used against Ashni. They had underestimated Timon and his honor, but she wasn't going to let that stop her.

"Please, relax first." Timon made another sweeping motion with his hand.

Nakia scowled. "I don't see how that's possible." But she could use the time to strategize, try to see the next move and counter it.

"I understand, but I insist. You've already had a shock. You should get a chance to settle your nerves before you talk about anything. You should at least clean the blood off."

She sighed as if this was some great burden. Best to let them think they were in charge and she was helpless female. *Aren't you?* Not anymore. "Fine."

Let him see what Ashni was up to outside their famed walls while she cleaned up. After that, Nakia would make her own move. She glowered at her father as she walked off. Timon offered her a soft smile, like she imagined a grandfather would, as the servants led her away.

Strolling through the palace she got a chance to see were grander than anything they had in Phyllida. Rich frescos hung everywhere showing ocean scenes, sporting events, and stories of the gods. They crossed a large courtyard with gardens and black marble columns decorated with white pearls and turquoise that seemed to touch the sky. It was beautiful and not too long ago she would've been impressed. Now, she only had one thought. *Khenshu is better.*

"Make use of this room as you see fit," the servant said as he opened the door.

The room was nice, as expected. Everything she needed was on hand. The furniture was made of dark wood and lush pillows, but she barely had time to settle in before her eldest sister appeared. Tall and regal with flowing brown hair like liquid cinnamon. Her skin had a lovely glow to it, like an aura of happiness surrounded her, but her dark brown eyes had worry lines under them. She stood with her shoulders squared, somehow similar to how Adira's spouse stood, proud and noble. Her robes were rich, yellow and orange, the material shimmering in the morning light.

"Thia, you didn't need to come." Nakia didn't want to see her sister, didn't need to see her sister. They hadn't been around each other for years and seemed to be better for it.

"I wanted to make sure you were all right. I know Timon said he'd take care of you, but after Father's dishonorable decision to do this, I'm not sure what to expect."

Nakia squinted. "You trust Timon?" From what she recalled, Thia hadn't been pleased to be given to Wicus or join his family.

Thia gave her a small smile and stepped closer. "I do. He's an honorable man. His son's a little weak compared to him, but Timon's a good man."

"You like your father-in-law more than your husband?"

"My father-in-law respects me and I respect him. I happen to love my husband, though."

"You do?" Nakia had been quite young when Thia was carted away, married off to Wicus. She hadn't seemed happy about it, but then again, she hadn't seemed sad either. More resigned than anything else. Nakia understood that now.

A soft chuckle escaped Thia and her eyes sparkled. "Shocking, I know. I think Father accidentally married me off to decent people. He wasn't thinking about that, though. He was thinking about their military might and wealth."

Nakia smiled a little. "You got lucky then."

"So did you if I hear it right. This barbarian queen cares for you enough to steal you away from the horror that was Lord Caligo."

"You know of him?"

Thia nodded. "He contacted Wicus for advice when Father promised you to him. Wicus told him if you were anything like me, he got the better end of the deal."

Nakia wasn't sure what to do with that information. She wasn't close to her sister. There was so much time between them, she barely understood what was going on when Thia left. Thia had always been somewhat mean to her, too. Well, both of her sisters had been, angry at their circumstances and taking it out on her. As a child she could tell Saffi didn't fit in and she could understand that anger now. *Was Thia the same? Hell, was I the same?*

"What's wrong?" Thia asked.

"You're being nice to me. I don't recall that being part of our dynamic." Nakia kept her guard up. She wouldn't let Thia trick her to gain favor with their father or with Timon.

"Yes, well, you were a child when I left. My own children are almost as old as you were when we last saw each other."

That much was true. Nakia had been ten when her sister left and now she was almost nineteen. The world looked much different now. The same might be true for Thia. *How much did I miss as a child?* "You're happy here?"

Thia nodded and a small smile settled on her face. "Very. Wicus is a delight to be married to, even if there are times, he drives me crazy. He and his father have been very open with me. As I said, Timon respects me, which is why he allowed me to enter your room and interact with you. Father wanted to bombard you immediately with questions and demands. Timon's already upset with this idea of using you, but he won't let Father bully you."

"He sounds like a good man." It was possible. After all, Ashni turned out to be better than she expected.

"He is, which is why he's honoring his agreement with Father and housing him after Father lost Phyllida and why he's against this plan of holding you hostage. But, like any king, he doesn't want to be taken over by barbarians."

"He doesn't have to be," Nakia replied. Time to plant a seed. "He can negotiate with Ashni."

Thia arched an eyebrow. "Ashni, huh?"

Folding her arms, Nakia frowned. "She saved me from Caligo. Would you rather I have stayed with him?" *Don't act too familiar with Ashni. They could use that against her, like Caligo.*

"No. No one deserves him. The tales Wicus heard of him still make my skin crawl. Father marrying you to that beast was worse than him marrying poor Saffi to that brute Ferox. At least Ferox's somewhat human."

"But, also an idiot from what I hear."

"He's definitely that. I doubt our sister's getting much conversation from him, not that she'd want to. I had the misfortune of being in the same room with him and felt my brain melting." Thia frowned. "So, what do you think will happen?"

"You tell me. What's Father's plan?"

"He's confident the barbarian..." Thia flinched at Nakia's glare. "He's confident the queen will surrender to us to get you back. Timon isn't as confident, even though Father explained the queen offered to marry you to get you back before."

"Timon's right not be confident. Perhaps the queen just dislikes seeing women treated like property."

Thia shrugged. "Well, she'll dislike this as well then."

"But, will she dislike it enough to surrender her plans? She's passionate about her quest."

"You mean her conquest."

"Either way, she's passionate about it." Nakia needed to change the conversation. She'd already given away quite a bit and knew her sister picked up on it. "How are your children? Will I get to see them?"

"You'll get to see them at lunch. Too bad Saffi couldn't be here. We could've at least all been together."

"I'm sure she's happy to be free of Ferox, even for a short time."

Thia nodded. "I'm almost certain there are rats nesting in that man's head. If you only heard the excuses he offered for why he chased a retreating army."

"I can only imagine. Let me guess, he thought because the Roshan army is led by a woman, they'd be easily conquered."

Thia nodded. "Timon and Wicus aren't so easily swayed, which is why Wicus' men didn't move."

"Wicus is a wise man, then." Wiser than she believed their father was at this point. Once upon a time, she thought her father was the smartest man ever. But, clearly when he wasn't in control, he was sloppy and easily led astray.

Thia gave her a grin. "You'll see when you meet him. Wise isn't a word I'd use to describe him, but he's quite a bit to be around."

Nakia nodded, and she did see when she met Wicus at lunch after cleaning up a bit. Thia had been lucky in husbands, it would seem. Wicus was tall and handsome, matching her sister perfectly in physical form. He looked at Thia with love in his hazel eyes and held their youngest child, a girl toddler, without prompting. The little girl looked much like him and he smiled at her, kissed her cheek, and paraded her around in a way that Nakia knew her father never did with his daughters. Maybe that was how Ashni's father had been.

Nakia smiled, imagining a tiny Ashni being held on a faceless man. He probably carried her around on his broad shoulders and tossed her in the air to hear her giggles. *Is that why Ashni pushed me to see Dorian?*

Thia introduced Nakia to the children, four of them, all healthy and happy. Worry started to gnaw Nakia's stomach. *What will happen to them if Ashni takes this city?* They could get hurt if there was a siege. Ashni wielded lightning that could bring a manor house down, as she saw with Caligo. *What if she did that here?* Nakia doubted her father cared, but if Timon and Wicus were as great as her sister insisted, surely they thought about this.

"Why haven't you evacuated the city if you knew the Roshan were coming?" Nakia asked as they all settled on their couches around tables stacked with food.

"How's that any of your business?" Dorian snapped, glaring her from across the way.

Nakia winced. "I'm curious. You knew they had taken Phyllida. Why not get out who you could and then dig in for a defense?"

Timon smiled. "You remind me of this one already." He motioned to Thia. "Thinking of the people. A good trait for someone who rules over others."

Dorian scowled and Nakia fought the urge to sit up taller. It would've been hard to do and rude while reclining on the couch. Timon's praise didn't mean much to her, but his acknowledgment that she was allowed to think was huge.

"So, why didn't you evacuate?" Nakia asked.

"We can protect our denizens. They're safer behind our walls than anywhere else," Timon replied.

"How can that still be true after losing forces in the battle a few days ago?" Nakia asked. They might not have lost on the same level as Ferox or her father, but they didn't have the forces to stand against Ashni. The Roshan had the largest army anyone in this region had ever seen. They had to know that.

"Numbers aren't always everything," Wicus replied. "Strategy's always better. As long as we have a superior strategy and we stick to it, we'll win."

Nakia nodded. She learned the same from the Roshan. "I suppose that much is true. You managed to keep out her magic users, after all."

Wicus tilted his head, his dark curls falling to the side. "You know about that?"

"I am aware of some things with the Roshan," Nakia said.

Dorian snorted. "Yes, their demon queen's practically in love with you."

Wicus smiled. "Well, if she's anything like her older sister, it was probably impossible for the queen not to fall in love." He winked at Nakia, and a blush flared to her cheeks. Charmer.

"Perhaps you have insight as to what she's up to outside," Timon said.

What could Ashni have gotten up to within in the seven hours we've been separated? Probably a lot. Idle hands and all. "She's waiting for me to be returned to her. If not, she's preparing for a siege."

Timon scowled, as did her father. They obviously didn't want a siege. The Roshan had them beat there, more men, more supplies, and who knew what else. Besides, no one wanted to be trapped in the city for weeks or months, hoping the Roshan eventually got bored.

"If she doesn't stand down, she'll never see you again." Dorian thrust his chin in the air.

"So, you're going to hold me hostage?" Nakia shook her head. Timon and Wicus glanced away. So, they did find this as distasteful as Thia stated. "She's willing to negotiate, you know?" Timon's and Wicus' heads snapped at attention to her. Servants leaned in closer.

"We won't negotiate with that barbarian and her insatiable desire for gold," Dorian replied. "We have you."

"From what we know, is the queen the type to surrender for what she wants?" Nakia asked. Silence was her only answer.

***

Ashni rode Midnight Thunder along the lines, checking to see how her wall was coming along. She and Adira decided the first bit of their siege would involve trapping Valen with a wall of their own. Yes, it would be made of wood rather than stone and not thick, but it would serve its purpose. The soldiers could handle it fairly easy, along with building traps and pitfalls between their wall and the city wall. That was phase one. As long as materials held up, the wall should be finished within a couple of weeks. By then, Valen would be thinking about their rations and how long they'd be able to hold out. It wouldn't matter by then either way.

"I've gotten word back from some of towns and villages around here," Adira said as she trotted up with a satchel of scrolls.

"They're with us?" Ashni knew the answer because everyone had a price. If she couldn't find Timon's, then there were other rulers in the area, rulers who weren't partial to Timon or Wicus.

"Well, they didn't like that Wicus used them to help train himself and the Valenian army some years ago, so yes. Turns out, we'll want less tribute than Timon if we're in charge anyway."

Ashni shook her head. "This is why you don't keep people under your thumb like that. They're always ready to betray you."

This was something she learned from her father, who probably learned it from her mother. Take the territory, but win the hearts and minds, which was how she ended up with an outsider as a sister...and an outsider as a lover now that she thought about it. Building an empire was about uniting people.

Adira shrugged. "They're expected to deliver items to Valen all the time. So, we can get more people inside to create chaos."

Ashni rubbed her palms together, faint sparks passing through her hands. "I'm not sure what I want to do inside right now. We need to get Nakia out first."

"Speaking of that, I have bad news in regards to your kitten."

Ashni wasn't expecting good news until Nakia was back in her arms. "Let me guess, they assassinated the guards."

Adira curled her lip. "You knew what to expect from that man, but sent her in anyway?"

Ashni scowled. "He could've actually been dying. I couldn't take that chance. Besides, all your reports said Timon was honorable."

"But, Dorian isn't. What do you want to do about this?"

Ashni scratched her chin. She wanted to take her lightning and burn the city to the ground. That wouldn't help her cause, though.

"It's been a day. Send word we expect her back and see what the response is," Ashni said.

"By the Sun! You're being rational. I don't even know what to make of this," Adira replied.

Ashni glared. "I'm trying to do right by us and right by my hellcat. I don't want to act impulsively and have her hurt."

Adira leaned back a little. "Wow. Marriage has changed you for the better."

Ashni growled. "I can't stand you."

"I bet this is how it happened with your father, too, after he met your mother."

Ashni punched Adira in the arm. "Cut it out. If push comes to shove, I'll go in after her."

"Oh, and I get to be in charge of this madness you're putting together?" Adira motioned around them.

"You cosigned this. It's your bit of madness as well. Besides, we've seen this work." Well, they heard about it working. Her father had once laid siege to a city, trapping it within a wall. It took some months to work, but it did. "And I'd only be gone for a little while." Ashni doubted it would take more than a couple of hours to go in, steal Nakia back, and return.

Adira shook her head. "You could send me in. You'll send a message she's more important than the mission if you keep ducking out to rescue her. Once is a darling love story. Twice is you losing sight of what we're doing."

Ashni sucked her teeth, mostly because she knew that was the truth. She turned her attention to the city. Hopefully, Nakia was all right. She was resourceful and could handle herself. She needed to trust Nakia, as Nakia trusted her.

"Let's make sure we get this wall up and get everything in place in case we actually need to stay here for a while," Ashni said, moving Midnight Thunder forward. He seemed antsy. He was a warhorse and being used for parading around right now rather than actual war. She could feel his pain, feel the itch.

"This city better be worth it," Adira mumbled under her breath. Of course, it really was if the reports were to be believed. Beyond that,

Ashni needed to get Nakia back.

***

Nakia was in her room, trying to entertain herself with some reading. She didn't see the words, though. It had been a few days. She felt like pacing, but she didn't want to show any signs of crumbling, knowing her father had people watching her, whether she saw them or not. So, whenever she found herself alone, she pretended to read. Sometimes, she even wrote poetry, like she had been taught as a child was proper for a young lady.

"Nakia, you need to come with me!" Thia burst into the room and grabbed her by the hand.

"What? Why?" Nakia struggled to keep up as her sister yanked her out of the room.

"Just come!" Thia's sandals slapped hard against the floor, heavy without her usual grace. Nakia had to jog to keep up as they hurried down a dark corridor. They came to a small room where Timon and Wicus waited.

"What's going on?" Nakia asked as Thia fell to Wicus' side and his hand fell to her waist.

"Queen Ashni continues to devise a wall to trap us within our own city, but we've also gotten word she's enlisted the aid of surrounding villages, adding to her already swelling numbers. If we were to negotiate, what would she be willing to give?" Timon inquired, wringing his hands together.

Nakia arched an eyebrow. "You're willing to talk?"

"Your father would have us hold you until she backs down. Her actions are not that of a warrior planning to back down," Wicus replied.

"Father will always insist on doing things his way, which is how you got into this mess. But Ashni will have her way in the end. If you haven't reached out to her, you should immediately. I think Ashni would be willing to talk with you. I'm sure the right tribute will get her to stop," Nakia said. *It was what Ashni wanted with Phyllida, so why not Valen?*

"And she'll be open to talking?" Timon asked.

Nakia nodded. "She will. Open a dialogue with her. Assure her you'll send me out and I suggest you keep your word."

After a quick glance toward each other, Timon and Wicus nodded. Thia patted Wicus hand on her waist. It would seem her father was out-voted now.

Chapter Fourteen

ASHNI SAT IN HER tent and tried to eat breakfast. Holding down food got harder each day Nakia wasn't by her side. She wasn't sure which was more unbearable, being alone or her sister and Adira encouraging her to eat. She wanted to be miserable in the one place she was allowed, out of view of everyone she was in charge of.

According to their spies, Nakia was fine. She was being treated well. As well as someone confined to her room unless her sister was with her. Ashni was all right with that. Thia seemed trustworthy, according to the reports, and Nakia seemed to be enjoying their time together. Ashni was glad for that since Nakia didn't seem to think her family cared much for her. It was good Thia proved Nakia wrong.

To stay focused, Ashni reminded herself Nakia was fine as she went about her days setting up for the siege. She even tried to goad Valen's military outside yesterday. They didn't take the bait.

"Layla will think that's why my mood has been soured." Ashni wasn't looking forward to that or even the proper guess of her missing Nakia. A thunderclap echoing through the air let her know she wasn't as in control of her emotions as she thought.

"I think you might want to stop broadcasting your mood. The troops think we're about to go to battle," Adira said, stepping into the tent. She had a scroll in her hand. "The sky is dark with thick, grey clouds."

Ashni scowled. "Maybe it's actually about to rain." It was possible.

Adira gave her a deadpan look. "And maybe it's because of you."

"I don't make it rain." *Most of the time.*

"You say that as if I haven't known you for years."

Ashni's frown deepened. "You say that as if you don't know me at all."

"I know you well enough to know I might have something to lighten your mood." Adira waved the scroll.

Ashni arched an eyebrow. "Is that from Dorian?"

"Timon."

Ashni grunted her acknowledgment. The more she learned about Timon, the more she expected him to make the right decision. But, the more she learned about Wicus, the more she expected him to challenge her, despite her gaining more of an advantage with each moment that passed. Wicus was a warrior and he'd want to test himself against her, prove himself against her military. Dorian would challenge her no matter what. Ferox wouldn't be an issue since most of his chariots were destroyed and his Black Dogs torn to pieces by proper Dark demons. With the wall they were constructing, his remaining chariots were useless.

"Do you want me to read it to you?" Adira asked.

"Have you read it already?" Ashni wouldn't mind a brief summary, so she could get back to not eating properly.

"I'll tell you all about it if you at least eat the yogurt with some berries." Adira nodded to her breakfast tray.

Ashni groaned. "I've had some already." *What will it take to get Adira to stop mothering me when we're out on campaign?*

"Yeah, like you've had some apples and honey." They both knew it was bad if she hadn't eaten her favorites. The thought of sweets turned her stomach, though, and the apples reminded her of when Nakia shared baked apples sprinkled with cinnamon with her.

Ashni frowned. "Just tell me. If not, Princess will tell me when she gets here."

Adira rolled her eyes. "Princess doesn't know about it. This came directly to me. Now, do you want to talk about this or do you want to pout?"

Another thunderclap shook the air. Adira didn't flinch and Ashni sucked her teeth. She took a breath to master herself, and then motioned for Adira to sit with her. Adira eyed her, so she made a move for some of the yogurt, grabbing some nuts too. After a couple of spoonfuls, her stomach relaxed. Layla showed up before she was finished.

"Oh, apples!" Naren was right behind his wife and went for the untouched sweets.

"Don't eat everything. Our fearless leader needs something inside of her to keep her going," Adira said.

Ashni scoffed. "I've got this."

Layla nodded. "That explains the thunder."

Ashni gnashed her teeth in Layla's direction, but didn't say anything. Layla rolled her eyes and helped herself to some berries. Adira made a show of unrolling the scroll, clearing her throat. Ashni almost bit her tongue to keep from saying anything. The glint in Adira's eye made it clear she knew what she was doing.

"They're open to discussing terms of partnership," Adira said.

"It's the smart move since they've let us get so far on the wall and we talked to the people under their thumb," Ashni replied.

"They probably couldn't figure out what we were doing with the wall until it was too late. Bless your grandfather for having the foresight of making sure everyone in the army is also capable of basic construction." Adira chuckled.

Ashni waved that off, not in the mood to give her grandfather credit. The war machine that marched with her was due to her father's hard work. Her grandfather did his best job getting sores from sitting on an expanding throne gained from her father's conquests.

"To show they're well meaning, they've agreed to deliver Nakia back to you," Adira said.

Ashni smiled and felt her body untie itself, relaxing. "This is her doing."

"You think?" Layla twisted her mouth up to the side.

"She knew I'd rather negotiate than dig in for a long siege." Ashni's soul rejoiced. She had chosen well.

Layla blew out a breath. "Wouldn't we all?"

"All right." Ashni rubbed her palms together, missing the time when they could grasp Nakia instead. "What would we want with this partnership? Tribute and military assistance in the conquest."

"You want to give them a chance to claim victory with us?" Naren asked.

"Of course. If you can have some of my victory, you're much more likely to accept we're in charge," Ashni replied.

"Because it'll take you too long to realize we're in charge," Adira added.

"What else do we want? We can make them trading partners with the Empire, which is a given as they'll eventually be part of the Empire," Ashni said.

"Tell them to give us Dorian," Layla said.

Ashni snickered. "You want him because he slipped through your fingers, eh?"

Layla scowled. "He's an outlaw, fleeing from Empire justice."

"How do you figure that?" Adira asked.

"He's still proclaiming himself a leader of a city under the Roshan banner. He's a fraud."

Ashni nodded. "You're right. We'll ask for him, but we follow the law once we have him. And, most importantly, I'll tell them to receive us, as a gesture of friendship."

"So, how much tribute would you like to ask for?" Adira asked. This Ashni could handle, especially since it meant Nakia would be back in her arms soon.

***

Nakia watched her father pace the room. A vein in his neck popped out and seemed to get bigger with every passing second. She had seen him mad on several occasions, but not before he had all the facts. She didn't think her father would take the news that his allies were willing to negotiate with Ashni well, but she hadn't expected this eruption of violence.

"This is your doing!" Dorian flung the nearest object across the room.

A bowl of hot aromatic oil hit Nakia in the forehead. Pain spiked in her head as she dropped to the floor. The oil burned her skin, dripping down over her eyes, and she wiped the oil away. Her hand came back bloody.

"Father!" Thia fell to Nakia's side and clutched her close.

Blood poured down Nakia's face, forcing her to close her eyes. The wound throbbed, the oil adding an unwelcome sting. Her entire head hurt, all the way down to her teeth. Liquid fell on her face, washing away the oil. As it slid to her mouth, she could tell it was water. Her vision was fuzzy, but she could dimly see Thai dabbed the water and blood from her face.

"We can't make a deal with that demon whore! She's already corrupted Nakia. She's devoured my city. You're supposed to be my allies. This is outright betrayal." Dorian was a hazy image to Nakia, but she was certain he was pointing at Timon. Wicus stepped in front of her and Thia. The more she got to know Wicus, the more she could see why Thia loved him.

"We have to do what's best for our city. Your city's gone, lost to you. We have people who are still here and counting on us," Timon said. Nakia hoped he meant that and would fight her father on his stance. If not, this could get messy, especially if Ashni found out her father assaulted her.

"We have an agreement, and I'm counting on you to return to me what is mine!" Dorian pounded his fist against an object Nakia couldn't see, but heard it shatter from the force. The sound echoed and it pounded in Nakia's already agonized head.

"We have a responsibility to our people. Are we supposed to stay in here and wait for her to starve us out?" Timon asked.

Wicus backed his father. "Or wait for her to break through our wall and we have nowhere to go thanks to her wall."

"We have the thing she wants most in the world." Dorian pointed to Nakia as Thia helped her to her feet.

Nakia leaned heavily on Thia, unable to stand without her support. With each thump of her heart, her head beat in time and it felt like her skull might break apart. *How did Ashni just take an arrow like it was nothing?* Nakia couldn't figure out how she wasn't dead from the agony. Agony caused by her father, who didn't seem to think anything of the assault.

"Are you planning to kill your daughter to get the queen to do what you want?" Wicus put his hand on a sword on his hip.

"What I do with my daughter is my business," Dorian replied, his voice like ice.

"Not when she's under our protection." Wicus stepped forward.

"I'm going to take Nakia to our healer," Thia said, her arm around Nakia's waist.

It felt a little weird, but Thia's arm around her reminded her a bit like having Ashni's arm around her. There was a protective feel that she never experienced before with her sister. Dorian might snarl, but Thia wouldn't allow him to hurt Nakia further.

"You leave her there and let her suffer for her foul ways. She's betrayed us all," Dorian said.

"How can I betray someone who has never been loyal to me?" Nakia tried to stand up tall as she issued the question, but her head swam and she tilted. Her sister caught her. "You gave me away to someone who was barely a man if only to keep your precious kingdom, which you lost to Ashni's little sister. And now, you're hoping King Timon will throw away his good sense for your pride and a city you'll never see again!" Spots floated before her eyes and Nakia was certain she'd fall, but she refused to do so in front of her father. She wouldn't look weak in front of him ever again.

"You think this bitch will save you? She'll discard you soon enough." Dorian spat in her direction, adding true insult to her injury.

He couldn't possibly respect her, spitting at her feet, as if she weren't a noblewoman, as if she weren't his child. It was beyond not seeing her as an equal, or even seeing her as inferior.

"He has gone mad," Wicus said. "Father, we owe this man nothing. He's been disrespectful to us since arriving. He's insulted Thia multiple times, insisting she's not part of any discussion we have when it's our custom to include her in all matters of Court. And now he injures his daughter while she's under our protection. I say we give Queen Ashni what she wants." Wicus glanced at Dorian.

Why put it that way? It was already agreed she'd go back to Ashni, long before the other demands came in. "What do you mean?" Nakia asked and then closed her eyes for a long moment, wanting to block out the light. Her head throbbed and she just wanted to sit down, but she had to know.

"Queen Ashni wants Dorian. She'll get him," Timon replied. His tone was final and Nakia took that as a good thing, like this was done. She felt relieved.

Nakia cheered on the inside, victorious over her father. He hadn't beaten her; he hadn't used her until the very end. This assault was his swan song, even though she doubted Ashni planned to kill him.

Dorian turned blue and purple. "What?" His voice seemed to shake the room. "You're my allies. You can't just hand me over to our enemy!"

"You haven't acted like an ally. You're only here for your own selfish reasons and don't care how you could bring about our ruin," Timon said.

"We have an agreement!"

"We have lived up to our end. We promised to defend you against your enemies. You squandered it. The decision has been made. And it was my decision to deal with the barbarian. She has betrayed no one," Timon said, making a slicing motion with his hand before he leaned against his cane.

"You can't do this!" Dorian seemed to puff up, like an angry cat. His breathing was heavy and his face was so purple it looked unnatural, but he didn't move.

"Stay there." Wicus unsheathed his weapon and guards came from every inch of the room.

Thia gently urged Nakia toward the exit. She returned Nakia to her room, settling her down onto a couch. A doctor came in moments later. The doctor sat next to her, wiping any remaining blood and oil from her face. Part of her knew she should wince, but the area was numb.

"I have to clean it. It'll sting."

Nakia shook her head. Part of her doubted she'd feel it, as she could barely feel anything beyond her terrible headache right now. But, when he put a cool cloth to the injury, she hissed as more pain shot through her body. It felt like her head was on fire and it burned down every inch of her body. Her hair hurt.

"I can't believe he did that," Thia said.

Nakia wished she could say the same thing. The blow was a surprise, but she could see Dorian doing anything at this point, going out of his mind with the thirst for revenge. Ever since she arrived, all she could see was rage in his eyes. She hardly recognized the man and after this moment, she was certain he was a stranger to her now.

"It's a shame this'll probably scar," the doctor said, examining her wound.

Nakia heard the words he didn't say. Her beauty was marred. In Phyllida, this would be considered the end of her. She doubted Ashni would care she was scarred. Ashni was covered in scars and tattoos. Roshan culture had different standards of beauty.

"It's mostly split your eyebrow. It'll need stitches," the doctor continued and that made her tense.

"Will...will they hurt?" She disliked the tremble in her voice. Ashni's voice wouldn't waver over stitches. Layla's voice wouldn't quaver as hers had.

The doctor only sighed and offered her wine to help relax her. She was about to decline, but caught sight of the needle he'd use to stitch her. She took a gulp, barely tasting it. He rubbed something on her wound, which made the area tingle, and then began stitching. It didn't hurt as much as she thought, more pressure and a sting than anything else. She suspected something in the wine or the salve made it so.

"It's done," he said after a few minutes. He leaned in, studying his work. He handed her a small jar. "Put this ointment on the wound for the next week and you should be fine."

"Can I lie down now?" She'd love nothing more than to sleep this whole nightmare away.

"I think it'd be best for you to stay awake for the moment." He glanced at Thia and she nodded, a signal for Thia to stay with her. The doctor left.

"How do you feel?" Thia asked.

"I've got a bad headache."

Thia nodded. "I'm sure you do. I wish I could say I'm surprised by this level of violence, but he's been frothing at the mouth since he arrived. Losing Phyllida seems to have unhinged him."

"Is that supposed to be a good reason?" Nakia went to touch her wound, but changed her mind. She didn't want to risk opening the stitches or troubling the injury. She didn't want to see the doctor again.

Thia scowled. "Of course not. There's absolutely no reason for him to hurt his child. He's so used to getting his way that he doesn't know how to act. His behavior won't get by here. I told you, Timon and Wicus are good men. They're not going to allow this."

Nakia nodded from lack of a better thing to do. Well, she thought she nodded. It was hard to tell with the throbbing in her head. She couldn't resist touching her head now, feeling a rising lump and the rough string of the stitches. The little brush of her fingertips sent bolts of pain through her head, down into her neck.

"Nakia, this queen...she's true to her word, yes?" Thia asked, her voice low.

"Her word is everything. If she claims you as an ally, you're an ally. She won't use you and disregard all your concerns. This is better than fighting against her because she won't stop until she's won."

Thia nodded. "Is my family going to be safe?"

"I'll make sure of it."

Thia had been nothing but good to her since she had come to the palace. Gone was the mean big sister she recalled, and she was replaced with a mature, wise, and kind future-queen. Well, she wouldn't be a queen now, but she'd be allowed to continue ruling by Wicus' side when Timon was gone. She wasn't sure how this would end, but she'd see what she could do.

"She really cares for you?"

"She does."

Thia gave her a tight smile. "I'm happy for you. This is odd, but I'm happy for you after seeing how Father treats you. He was never quite kind to me, but I can't imagine him assaulting me. I can't even imagine him assaulting Saffi and we know how he felt about her."

"This was the first time he hit me." But, Thia made a point. Saying their father hated Saffi was far from an understatement and he had never hit her. Nakia had pushed him far beyond his breaking point and she couldn't bring herself to care.

"It shouldn't be any times. His bellows, barks, and bites aren't the only way. I learned that here."

Nakia could understand that. She learned there were other ways when she left home as well. *Have I changed like Thia had?*

"Are they really going to give him to Ashni?" The possibility of not having to deal with him anymore filled her with relief.

"She's not asking for much, not at all what we expected anyway. Him, tribute, and men if they wish to join her campaign. The amount of tribute is decent. We get more from nearby towns. Well, we used to get more, but she's called forth those men to stand against us. It's not a huge burden to us."

Nakia could see why they took the deal. Ashni was asking for nothing in comparison to what she asked from Dorian not too long ago. *Why, though, when Valen had much more to give?* She'd have to ask Ashni.

***

"Armor or robes?" Ashni asked as she prepared for her invitation into Valen. She'd pick up Nakia and Dorian. Soldiers, who acted as servants with the hope it would get them some sort of recognition or reward, held up different outfits to help her decide. She needed to make a statement with everything possible, including her clothing.

"Robes. I'll be in armor. It says what you want it to say," Adira replied.

Ashni nodded. She could show up as an elegant queen rather than a warrior queen. Besides, they were aware she was a warrior. She'd march into Valen as she'd march into Khenshu after victory on campaign. She put on her best robes, teal and gold with golden thread, but attached her swords to her back. She even had a diadem on her head, made of gold in the shape of eagle's wings in honor of Khurshid, dotted with the emerald of her kingdom and the pearls of the Empire. Adira nodded her approval.

"You look regal," Adira said, as she buckled her armor in place.

"As opposed to the mess you're used to seeing me in?" Ashni smirked.

"You can't deny you're a mess when your spouse is gone and you don't know what's going on with her."

Ashni didn't say anything. Layla swept in, dressed in a mix of her armor and robes. Naren was behind her, dressed in a similar fashion and eating. Ashni wanted to slap the bread out of his hand but knew it helped keep him calm.

"Let's get going." Ashni wanted to get this over with, get Nakia back, and continue on with their conquest. There was so much West still left to take and she wanted to do it with Nakia at her side.

She rode Midnight Thunder into the city. People cowered in his shadow. Right behind her were Adira on her mighty steed and Layla, who rode a beast she claimed was a horse. Demon was probably closer to the truth, but she could never prove it. There was just something about it, like there was nothing but smoke and darkness inside of it. The creature had been with Layla longer than Ashni had and Ashni wasn't about to question it, as it served Layla as well as Midnight Thunder served her. Adira had Hafiz join them, for the experience and also for people to see him riding his alphyn. People would be left in awe to see him control Yata, as alphyns were believed to once fight with dragons and win.

Music accompanied them through the crowds as they made their way through the gates to the palace, their drums sounding off, keeping the attention of the Valen citizens. As they went down the clean, paved main street, they passed tall buildings of polished white stone, glinting in the sunlight. Some were shops with apartments above, people in the windows staring down at them. At a point, they passed by rows of villas with people at the gates, watching them go.

Many pushed and shoved to see them. Ashni was certain it was morbid curiosity. These people were told horror stories about the Roshan, frightened their children with tales of terrible barbarians, and spread rumors of the savage Roshan doing inhumane things. How different must they look, covered in colored robes decked out with jewels and gold.

Once they got to the palace, they dismounted and swept into the throne room, met by Timon and his family standing in front of the thrones. To the side of them, Dorian, but with them, Nakia. Nakia stood proud and beautiful. But, something was off. As Ashni got closer, she saw Nakia's head had a knot on it and there were stitches going through her eyebrow. A thunderclap echoed outside.

"Calm down," Adira said, hissing in her ear.

Ashni grunted, as it was the best advice for the moment. Timon stepped forward to receive her. They shook hands and even introduced each other to their families. Nakia was escorted to Ashni's side and she went right along with their formalities. This was a meeting of partners, friends even, and Ashni was glad for it. Dorian seemed to seethe, glaring at them the whole time.

"We've prepared a meal," Timon said.

They sat down for the feast. Nakia was at Ashni's side and she couldn't help caressing Nakia's cheek. Dorian scowled. Others watched, including Nakia's sister, but there was curiosity in their gaze instead of disgust.

"What happened to your face, kitten?" Ashni asked, her voice a civil tone, but the fact that she inquired was enough for everyone to understand her emotions.

Nakia glanced at her father. "Nothing. I was on the right side of an argument."

Ashni left it at that for now, as it was a happy time. They had taken Valen without digging in for months. They had a powerful ally. And most of all, she'd walk out of here with Dorian, to punish him for harming Nakia in so many ways.

"It's good that we can put this idea of war behind us," Timon said.

Ashni nodded. "Agreed. I have no desire to be at perpetual war with a neighbor." She already controlled half of the region and there were more than enough nearby towns, villages, and tribes willing to align with her just to get from under the thumb of Valen. Beyond that, linking them to her family gave her a chance to do something else with them in the future. One day, the city could be a gift for her future spouse or she could influence Thia's children. She'd build bonds with them and go from there.

"Then we shall be friends," Wicus said.

"Family." Ashni motioned to Nakia and then to Thia. "And I always do what's best for family. After all, I haven't killed my own little sister, despite how annoying she is."

Layla chuckled. "Perhaps you shouldn't say that while I'm holding a knife." She twirled a dinner knife in her hand. She hadn't eaten much, even though the food wasn't poisoned from what they could tell. Ashni knew Layla was anxious to get back to their quest.

"But, my family doesn't shut me out with gates and walls," Ashni said.

"You want us to remove our walls?" Thia asked with an arched eyebrow.

Ashni laughed and shook her head. "You misunderstand me." She liked that Thia was free to speak. This wasn't what she expected from allies of Dorian. Perhaps they were a little more enlightened than him. "I understand cities need walls—You're allowed your space...but we needn't be locked out."

The feast went well into the night, which was expected. If Ashni had the time, the celebration probably could've lasted all week, but there were things to do and miles ahead of them. It was then she turned her attention to Dorian.

"You'll be my guest for a while. We'll have such fun." Ashni grinned.

Dorian glared at her. "You don't scare me."

"Oh, but I will soon enough."

Ashni felt pretty good. She had everything she wanted, Nakia, a foothold in the West, and everyone's dreams practically in her hand. The gods hadn't abandoned her. She hadn't fallen out of favor. They heard her prayers and blessed her. She decided to show off as they went through Valen's gate, crowds still watching them.

"We don't need to be locked out." Ashni held up her fist and lightning popped from her hand. Feeling the power charge within her, she made a sweeping motion and tore through the wooden door of the city's main gate. People gasped as the wood burned. She smirked.

"Was that necessary?" Nakia asked, sitting in front of her on Midnight Thunder.

"Just for them to understand my power should they think to betray us," Ashni replied.

"They won't." Nakia's jade eyes seemed certain.

Ashni smiled. "I'm glad you're confident. I'll trust you."

As soon as they entered their camp, a soldier ran up to her with a note in hand. She read it quickly, her grin melting into a scowl. Amal had taken her throne in Khenshu, proclaiming himself regent in her absence.

Chapter Fifteen

NAKIA GASPED AS ASHNI turned a note in her hands to ashes. *What happened?* Ashni's entire demeanor changed, her face hardened, and she seemed tense, her high spirits gone. Nakia reached for Ashni's hand, hoping to keep her calm, and followed her as she rushed to her tent. Adira, Layla, and Naren followed, too.

"What's wrong?" Nakia asked.

"That disgusting rotter! He thinks he can steal my throne from me?" Ashni slapped herself in the chest with both hands. Lightning flashed in the distance, followed by smoke far off. Nakia hoped that was a tree and not someone's home.

"Who dares?" Layla's hand went to her sword.

"Amal has betrayed me. Us." Ashni's hand swept out across the tent.

Layla's expression fell into a deadpan look. "Does that even count as a betrayal? How many times has he tried to take your territory?"

"I'm surprised it took him so long to realize he should do it while we're out on conquest," Adira said.

Ashni frowned. "He did it now because he suspected we wouldn't be returning."

Nakia winced. That probably was the best way to stage a coup and avoid Ashni's wrath, so Amal wasn't completely stupid. But, then again, he couldn't be intelligent either to think Ashni would let him get away with this. Nakia couldn't believe the gall of Amal.

"How didn't we know about this?" Naren asked, an unusual frown on his face.

While Nakia would never describe him as cheerful, she had never seen him frown before and it looked strange on his copper features. It was in that moment she realized he actually seemed warm and friendly until now. His face always had a child-like quality to it, but now the light in his eyes had completely vanished. He looked like the seasoned warrior he was.

"I suspect he's intercepted any news that might reach us, because

Saniyah would've warned us otherwise. This could've been a stroke of luck on our part. Unless, of course, he only just managed this, but I doubt it," Ashni said.

"If he harmed her..." Adira snarled like a wild animal, color draining from her face.

"You'll have him if he hurt her. Even my mother wouldn't be able to stop me." Ashni clapped Adira on the back, which straightened her shoulders and brought back the color to her cheeks.

"So, Amal's commanding your city now?" Nakia asked, wanting to be sure she understood.

"Yes, he has taken over Khenshu," Ashni replied.

"Why?" Nakia didn't understand Amal's fascination with his sister's domain. Ashni told her of the area Amal had inherited from the great Amir Khalid. A lush, green area with farms and woods that put Ashni's desert to shame. Neither was the crown of the Roshan Empire, but she made it seem like Amal got the better end of the deal.

"Khenshu is much like it's mistress," Adira said, through gritted teeth.

Nakia arched an eyebrow. "How so?"

"Rough looking exterior, but a diamond in the rough. Or more an emerald and ruby," Adira said.

"There are mines there for those gems. We've got tons of the stuff," Layla added.

"So, this is for money?" Nakia asked. That seemed too easy, not like Amal at all.

"And to expand his influence," Ashni said. "He seems to think I won't come back for my city, and he can add to his territory and possibly make a bid for Emperor when our mother dies."

It sounded like a scheme worthy of Amal from what Nakia knew of him. He did try to kill Ashni, after all, and use her to do it. She could only wonder how he managed to take Khenshu. Surely everyone in the palace knew Ashni wouldn't want him there. Nakia's heart sank as she considered what Amal might have done to those closest to Ashni to get control of her territory. Adira was probably right to worry over her wife.

"So, what are we going to do? If we go back now, we'll lose the whole campaign season and maybe even the territory we've gained," Naren said.

"Princess, you and Naren will stay." Ashni pointed to the pair.

"What? No!" Layla threw her hands up. "You already did that."

"Yes, and it worked, which is why we're doing it again. Or would you rather we turn the whole damn army around?" Ashni gave her sister a hard stare.

Layla ground her teeth together. "Well, obviously we can't do that. But, there are others you could leave in charge. Hell, Adira has a whole fucking protégé."

Ashni frowned. "Who's in no way good enough to be in the inner circle yet, which is why he's not around. He's younger than you are."

"Not by much and that's not a good measure for anything. Your spouse is younger than I am," Layla said.

"I am not!" Nakia was certain she was older than Layla. It felt like a win to be older than Layla for whatever reason. "I'll soon be nineteen."

Layla stuck her chin in the air. "As will I."

"That's unimportant right now," Ashni said.

"Especially if Amal has Saniyah and kept her from communicating with me, except the expected love letter and household update," Adira said.

Ashni nodded. "This is true."

Adira sucked her teeth. "Why the hell didn't I suspect something?"

"It's not your fault. We had a lot going on and he's most likely been planning this for a while, probably since we thwarted his last assassination attempt. He hasn't beaten us, though. Remember, he never beats us at chess, ever. This time won't be any different," Ashni said, looking between Adira and Layla.

"Well, what about my family? My mother should've said something. Hell, my father. He writes constantly to let me know about his pupils and new techniques he thinks I should try and new philosophies he's written about the Darkness. Neither of them said anything to me. What has Amal done to them?" Layla said.

Ashni was silent, and Nakia worried all the more. Amal could've done something to the families of anyone close to Ashni's core group. Ashni put her arm around Nakia and pulled her close. She rubbed Nakia's hip. Nakia understood when Ashni held her, it helped keep her calm and helped her think. She was flattered she could assist in that way.

"Okay, this is a problem. Adira, do you think Hafiz is ready for this? We'll work specific instructions for him to follow. I want to put Captain Varaza Sur with him. I think she's ready for serious command. We'll make sure all of the captains and lieutenants understand what needs to be done. We'll have the advance slow down, but we can't stop. This is a mess." Ashni sighed.

"No kidding, but we've figured things out before. We can figure something out here," Layla said.

Ashni nodded and Nakia watched them work. She didn't have anything to add, didn't know how this situation would work. The best she could do was quietly support Ashni, so she stayed close and caressed Ashni whenever the opportunity presented itself.

Nakia couldn't believe Amal would do something like this. Not because she thought he was such an honorable man, but because it seemed like Ashni and her siblings should be close. They had a good father and probably a good mother from what she could gather. They should've been a close family, but instead there was an older brother trying to kill his sister and steal her land. It hit even harder after reuniting with her own sister and seeing how Thia had matured over the years. *If members of my dysfunctional family can get it together, how is it that a loving family can't?*

***

Ashni had never been so happy her warriors wanted nothing more than to please her. She and Adira left them with specific instructions. They left the lieutenants with tasks, the captains with orders, the generals with plans, and Adira's precious protégé in charge. All Hafiz needed to do was gather troops and tribute from small towns. They could take towns and villages if they found it necessary. If Hafiz came to a major city, he should set up for a siege. If the siege was necessary, they should return in time for it. She didn't plan to spend much time in Khenshu after she knocked Amal from his pedestal. She had dreams to achieve, after all.

"Are you all right?" Nakia sat in front of Ashni, astride Midnight Thunder, riding back to the sea.

They had left the camp at night. She didn't want anyone in Valen to know her core group headed back to the East. She wasn't surprised by Midnight Thunder's willingness to carry Nakia, even though he tended to be tense with most. Her horse was always ready to help Ashni and seemed taken with Nakia, just as she was.

"I'll be better when I see Amal," Ashni replied. She'd be even better when she got to put her fist in Amal's face.

"Why does he hold such contempt toward you?"

Ashni shook her head, even though Nakia wasn't looking at her. "My relationship with my older brothers has always been strange. Amal

180

takes it to a different level since he's the only one to actively seek what's mine."

"But, why?" Nakia turned, trying to look at her. Ashni gave her a little squeeze, wanting her to stay focused. Traveling at this speed, falling from a horse the size of Midnight Thunder could mean death. Nakia took the hint and focused ahead of her. "Does it go back to this whole thing of you not being your father's child?"

Ashni's mouth twitched. "Even you've heard the rumor?"

"Bashira was trying to tell me about your culture and history. She mentioned it to help me understand this notion of bonds and how your father loved you most of all, even if you weren't his child by blood. Is that why Amal does these things to you?"

Ashni smiled and kissed the top of Nakia's head. "You're trying to learn about Roshan culture." Her heart managed to swell at this bit of news, even with the heavy situation ahead of them.

"That doesn't answer my question. Why's Amal like this with you? You're his little sister. Why isn't he like you are with Layla?"

Ashni chuckled. "Because he doesn't have that in him."

"Because he thinks you're not your father's child?"

"I'm sure that's a ready excuse. I think it's a mixture of jealousy and envy with my older brothers. They're jealous of the fact that a lot of people think I'm our father's legacy and they're envious over the fact that it's clear Dad was aware I was the one who'd carry on after him. They could easily try to do the same. Instead, they get pissed at me."

Nakia shifted enough for Ashni to see her arch an eyebrow. "Could they really do what you do?"

"Well, no. Nothing about this is easy, but they could try. Our parents gave us all the same tools. My brothers seem to expect it all to fall out of the sky for them. Well, the older ones anyway. The younger crew, they might make names for themselves, but I don't think it'll be this way."

"You have a better relationship with the younger ones?" Nakia asked.

"The one right after me, Fahim, rode with me a couple of times, but he's more of a scholar than a warrior. He's married to a similarly minded woman and they spend their days having intellectual arguments and coming up with progressive programs for his territory. He's possibly my favorite brother." Thinking of him made her feel a little light. Her relationship with him was different than her relationship with Layla, even though they were both younger siblings. He was quieter, but sometimes, talking to him, Ashni felt like she was talking to someone so much older than she was, someone ancient, someone who would save mankind...or watch the world burn and record it for the next incarnation.

Nakia smiled. "More so than your youngest brothers?"

"They're adorable little bits, Kek and Kiran. Mom's other set of twins. They're a little younger than you and Princess. They're goofy, but she keeps them out of trouble. They were the most open to learning witchcraft from her. I think they'll have their own adventures. I'm not sure what they're going to do or how they're going to do it, but it'll be epic." Thinking about them added to the piece of pleasantness wedged in the middle of her fury.

"Has Amal been the only one to try this?"

"Yes, it might be just be because everyone else's territory is too far or they're content with what they have." Ashni doubted it was the latter. None of them had ever been content with what they had. They always wanted more, an ailment from their father, their mother always groused. Ashni didn't view it as an ailment, except when it came to Amal. He was definitely sick.

Nakia didn't ask any other questions. Ashni tried to remain calm but found herself growing increasingly agitated, as though a growing swarm of hornets buzzed under her skin. If Amal harmed Saniyah, she'd rip his head off his shoulders. Saniyah headed many of her battle weapons. Without her, they'd lose a great advantage in warfare.

Beyond Saniyah, there were families Amal might've gone after, families which would oppose his rule. At the top of the list would be Layla's family, who was basically her family, and Naren's family, along with any family connected to them. Every noble in her Court could be in danger, if not from Amal then later from her if they didn't oppose her brother.

And then, when she was done with Amal, she had to do something with Dorian. He was coming along, tied up and thrown over Naren's horse. Naren was the only one she could trust not to kill Dorian should he do something stupid. Adira was too tense and Layla already itched to taste his blood. Ashni planned to exile him onto a small island in the sea around Khenshu. A nice little barren rock where desolation covered every corner. She'd give him supplies every month to make sure he lived a nice, long time, knowing he crossed the wrong woman. At least she'd be able to do that sooner rather than later.

***

The wind howled, pushing the ship, and salt filled Nakia's lungs with each breath. She wasn't sure what she should say to Ashni as they made their way back across the sea. The others were quiet, too, standing, watching the waves roil. This business with Amal was something she might not be able to comprehend. It seemed like this action was more than him trying to usurp Ashni, even more than him trying to kill Ashni. The grim nature behind their eyes made it seem like Amal had the power to end the world.

It felt off to her that they chose to do this alone. They left the whole army in the West. Yes, the army knew what happened in Khenshu, but they didn't insist on coming. There had been some rousing, but Ashni quickly shut it down. They seemed to trust Ashni to put the world in order. Much like she did. *Maybe Ashni is touched by the gods. Perhaps even divine herself.*

If Ashni was divine, then Nakia pitied Amal for going against the gods. Yes, he might be the son of a god, too, but the rumor had it that Ashni's father was a god while the Amir was possibly one half-god, if that. Amal was tempting fate. *Why? Does he think he could defy, defeat, and conquer the divine?* Except, Ashni didn't seem quite as confident as Nakia had seen her in the past.

"Are you afraid you might hurt your brother?" Nakia asked as they settled onto a corner of the ship taking them back to Khenshu. They sat on the wooden deck, not even on a pillow. She didn't mind as she was pressed against Ashni, who shielded her from the damp sea air as best she could.

"I want to destroy him for daring to try this, but I can't," Ashni said, voice rough and rumbling in her throat, making her chest vibrate against Nakia's back.

"Why can't you?"

"Our mother would never forgive me. This is why he still wanders about free after trying to kill me on several different occasions. I need proof positive of his actions or my mother won't do anything."

"Surely this is enough to do something." *What more could their mother possibly want?*

"I'm sure he has an excuse worked out for why he's done this."

Nakia shook her head. *What excuse would their mother believe?* Surely she knew her son better than that. "Why doesn't he take this energy to just go conquer his own land?"

"I'm sure he thinks this is easier. I'm also not sure he wants to conquer territory outside of the Empire. None of my brothers seem interested in expanding the Empire. They felt like expansion's what killed our father."

"It's possible."

Ashni gave a light shrug. "Yes, but he died doing what he loved. Conquest isn't just about taking over territory. It's about seeing the world, experiencing new things, and meeting interesting people. If he didn't expand the Empire, I never would've known I had a spirit sister out there."

"Layla's your spirit sister?" Having seen the two interact, Nakia would never doubt their sisterhood.

"We bonded at the soul." Ashni shifted Nakia a bit and tapped the center of her chest. "There's an energy to us all. Layla and my energy is almost the same. She is me."

"And the same with Adira?" Nakia's curiosity spiked.

"We bonded at the head."

Nakia's brow furrowed, even though she felt she understood what the bond meant anyway. Ashni and Adira thought alike. "Is that why she's not your sister?"

Ashni rubbed the bridge of her nose with her index finger. "It's complicated. Adira's family, no doubt about it, but if she needed a title, she'd probably be more of an aunt. But, I wouldn't be able to acknowledge that."

Nakia chuckled. Giving Adira a title like that would make her seem like an authority figure to Ashni and while Ashni clearly respected Adira's opinion, she didn't defer to her. And, yes, Ashni and Adira were close, but not close like she was with Layla. A question settled in Nakia's mind.

"How are we bonded? At the heart?" Nakia asked.

Ashni was silent for longer than Nakia expected, and her stomach twisted. *Was that too far? Did I misunderstand?* Ashni kissed her cheek and nuzzled her neck for a moment, letting out a content sigh. It helped settle Nakia, but she was still curious. *How are we bonded?* She never knew bonds like this existed until Ashni. It helped to see Thia with her husband, but she felt like she and Ashni were more than that. Yes, there was love, but it felt like it something deeper, more vast than she thought possible.

Ashni held her a little tighter. "I'm not sure how we're bonded. Maybe it's all of those. I can feel you in my soul, my head, and my heart.

It's intense and almost tangible to me sometimes. If I was asked to describe you, there aren't enough words in all of creation for me to do it. I've never experienced it before. I'd do anything for you. I'd give you anything you want. If you asked me for the moon right now, I promise I'd figure out a way to bring it to you."

Nakia grinned. "That's how I feel, too. I've never felt it either. I wouldn't have believed it was real if someone told me about it. I don't feel quite as capable as you, though. If you asked me for the moon, I'd ponder, but I don't think I'd come up with a way to get it to you."

Ashni scoffed. "You, who delivered Valen to me, would easily grant me the moon."

Nakia turned around, studying Ashni's face. "I delivered Valen to you?"

"Did someone else talk them into negotiating? You saved us a siege and a lot of deaths. Although, a Bloody Orchard might've served us well."

Nakia flinched. "How could something so grotesque serve us well?" While she didn't want to change Ashni, she'd like to talk about the morbid practice one day.

"The god Mar loves a garden, for it attracts Life."

Nakia turned fully around, needing to see Ashni as she enlightened her about these Bloody Orchards. "Mar?"

"A god of the dead. It's his job to collect souls. He's enamored with Life. So, whenever one makes a garden for him, he's always grateful for he'll see his love."

Nakia squinted as she followed along. "Life?" *Death loves life.* Stranger things were true.

"Oh, yes. Mar loves Myesha. She's the one who brings us all the spark of Life. She's busy, making sure all living things have the spark. So, when Mar comes to collect the dead in the Bloody Orchard, he's able to meet with Myesha, who'll also come to the Orchard to give the spark of Life to tiny creatures, like maggots, who'll feast on the flesh. Mar is always grateful to anyone who leaves him the garden for him to meet with his love. It's in a Bloody Orchard where Life and Death meet."

Nakia frowned. That was oddly romantic. "Is Mar's blessing potent?"

"Quite. It'll keep him from visiting us for quite a while. After all, should he do away with the ones who make the Orchards, who'll make the Orchards? How'd he meet with Myesha then?"

Nakia wasn't sure how she felt about it. The gods were beyond her much of the time, but the Roshan gods even more so. But, then again, the gods were a mystery to everyone. If Ashni could find a positive thing from the bloodshed of war, Nakia figured that was better than countless lives lost for nothing. Of course, Ashni didn't look at it as lives lost for nothing and Nakia knew better than to ever say something like that to her.

"What do you think will happen when we get to Khenshu?"

"I suspect Amal has the port, which is why he can control the flow of information to me. We'll clear that and then getting into Khenshu won't be a problem. I don't care what warriors Amal has at my city. I'll destroy them and march into my kingdom as I always do."

The grit in Ashni's voice made Nakia pity Amal. While Ashni might not outright slay her own brother, he wouldn't like it when Ashni stood before him. *Can Amal actually stand against Ashni?* Nakia felt like it was impossible, but surely Amal knew a standoff was coming.

"Do you know what Amal might have planned for you?" Nakia asked.

"He thinks he can stand as my equal. He'll learn otherwise. I don't care who's with him, and I don't care if the gods have suddenly seen fit to cast me from their light. I'll not let him have what's mine."

"Why do you think the gods no longer favor you?" Nakia felt like that until Ashni showed up to rescue her from Caligo. Ever since that moment, she felt like every god in existence smiled upon her and that was why Ashni was in her life.

"I've had you stolen from me, the dreams of everyone who follows me put on hold, and now Amal puffing himself up. There are walls before me, but I'll tear them down. I'll tear everything down if necessary, even the Heavens themselves if the gods wish to test me," Ashni replied and Nakia believed her.

When they pulled into port, Ashni was proved correct. Armed soldiers met their ship and questioned the captain and crew of the vessel. Ashni didn't even bother to hide. She stepped into view as thunder echoed through the sky and clouds gathered overhead. The soldiers, almost twenty in all, seemed to shiver.

"If you think you can stand my power, come," Ashni said, holding up a hand. Lightning popped from her fingertips.

The soldier at the head of the group aimed his sword at Ashni. Ashni snapped her finger and lightning shot down from the sky to the tip of his sword. There was a bright flash and when the light cleared, his body lay smoking on the ground.

"Who else wants to try me?" Ashni's voice dark like the sky. No one moved. "Wise decision."

Ashni waved her group on. Nakia wasn't surprised with that display of power. Surely Ashni was a god. *Does that mean her father was a god? If so, which father? Does Amal also have such talent?*

***

Amal's men moved quickly from her path, and Ashni smirked. At this point, she felt like she could go through an army on her own. Her blood buzzed with lightning, and she wasn't sure how she contained herself. It was more than Amal trying to take her position. It was about him ruining so much for selfish reasons. As much as she rode for herself, she rode for their people, their nation, and their father's legacy. *How dare he think he's worthy of my throne if he couldn't think of any of those things?*

"I'm going to peel him like a grape if Saniyah is hurt." Adira spoke through her teeth as they rode on horses taken from Amal's cowards. Their own steeds, loyal and true, deserved a rest.

As they arrived at the city gates, Ashni thought it was possible Adira might end up peeling Amal like a grape. The gate crawled with his people. If he had the gate, then the guards she had there were probably dead. Inside the city was probably worse.

"Halt!" A guard with a wolf's head symbol on his chest plate stood before them.

Ashni struck him down with her lightning. His comrades made a path for her and her group, opening the gates to reveal the usually bustling streets of her fair capital to be devoid of life. Pockets of destruction and ashes waited for her instead, places where blood was clearly left as a message, and the still smoldering remains of a temple.

"Should I go to my parents' villa?" Layla asked.

"You should check on them. Adira, you do the same," Ashni replied. Amal might have used them to make examples to the rest of her people.

Adira scowled. "So you can have Amal all to yourself?"

"It's not like I can kill him." No matter how much she liked to at the moment. Adira might actually get away with it if Saniyah was harmed.

Layla and Adira agreed, breaking off with Naren going along. Ashni continued on with Nakia sitting behind her. As they made their way to the palace, people flowed out of their homes, their faces flashing with delight. *How long has Amal oppressed my people?* She pushed the horse onward, up to the palace. No one tried to stop her.

"Is this a trap?" Nakia asked.

"It's an invitation. One I'll gladly take." Ashni pushed the horse right into the throne room.

Amal sat atop her throne, in his finest robes with a servant feeding him dates. Officials, nobles, and priests lingered along the side walls. *Confident fool.* He had her people there to witness her downfall.

"Welcome, dear sister. You're just in time to tell everyone you gave me Khenshu as a gift." Amal grinned as he took a goblet of wine from a tray.

"I'll give you something all right." Lightning crackled from her hands. She'd give him everything owed to him and more.

Chapter Sixteen

ASHNI CRACKED HER KNUCKLES to the tune of roaring thunder outsider as she dismounted the horse, eyes locked on Amal. He had the nerve to smirk and sip wine, like she wouldn't rip his ass off of her throne. In fact, that seemed like the best course of action. She marched toward the dais, lightning flashing from her hands. Thunder boomed outside with a howling wind. She'd unleash everything on him and rebuild whatever was necessary when it was done.

"Sounds like you're having a temper tantrum," Amal said.

Lightning crackled at her fingertips. "I could say the same for you. Isn't that what all this bullshit's about? You need my attention so badly you try to take what's mine." Maybe that was really Amal's problem. He wanted her to notice him, and he didn't know how to go about it. Not that she cared.

His intense glare could rival the heat of the desert. "I don't need anything from you."

"Yet you're trying to take the territory our father specifically willed me. Get off my throne right now, Amal, and I won't embarrass you in front of this crowd you've gathered." Ashni glanced around at the faces of her subjects. Everyone looked exhausted, wan, and ashen. No one was dressed as finely as expected to be in the presence of royalty. They wore the rags of prisoners. Amal probably confiscated their finery.

His own people were easy to spot in the crowd, wearing dazzling colors and jewels. They had color in their faces and didn't look beaten down. She'd change that.

Amal shook his head. "You can't have land willed to you. The great Amir wasn't your father." He said the words deliberately, trying to get a raise from her.

Ashni arched an eyebrow. "Even if he wasn't my father, he can will whatever the hell he sees fit to me. Didn't he claim me as I claim my own family? Call me his child? Who are you to decide?" *Honestly, who the hell does Amal think he is to try to change our father's decisions? Our mother's decisions?* Joint decisions made by the greatest people the

Empire had ever known, joint decisions made by demigods. *So, who the hell is Amal to decide anything?*

Amal slammed his fist against the throne, a thud echoing through the quiet room. "I am his son, by blood and birth!"

"I am his child by birth and choice. Is that what bothers you the most? The rumors have been going on since my birth, but Dad still chose me. And maybe he accepted me because of the rumors. After all, was it not said our father was born when lightning struck a rock?" Well, that was one of the many stories. Their father never seemed to actually believe that, even though he was certain he was part god.

"You are not his child!" Amal roared and his golden eyes burned with fury that could've put the sun to shame, sparking with flames. The people around them flinched. "Children of a storm are no match for a descendent of Khurshid."

Ashni inclined her chin. "Is Rami not the child of Khurshid and Dima? Do you think Rami inferior as if his parents aren't the Sun and Sky? I'm sure Dima would be impressed with you mocking her own god child."

The rumors said that she was the child of Rami, one of the storm gods, through a union of the Great Eagle and Dami, the Sky, the life giver, ruler of Rain. Depending on who told the story, Rami had a taste for human women and disguised himself to roam the globe, mate with women, and abandon them soon after the affair bored him. No matter how great she believed the storm god to be, she couldn't see him doing that to her mother. First off, her mother was never boring. Second off, there was no way her mother was with any man other than her father. Her mother would sooner kill Rami than sleep with him.

Amal rose, glaring down at Ashni, orange sparks bursting from his fingertips. "You think you're even worthy of being Rami's child?"

"Oh, so our mother slept with some random man claiming to be a god and then had me?" His opinion of her seemed to get worse and worse and seeped over to a mother they all were certain he loved so much until now.

"Mom isn't infallible."

Ashni was surprised at how far her lightning jumped, blowing a hole in the high ceiling. Their mother who was the only reason he lived. *Who the fuck does he think he is?*

"Is our mother not the daughter of a god as well?" They had seen more than enough proof of that.

"She has never said."

"Neither has Dad. So, let me see if I have this correct, I'm not worthy of my throne and don't even have a proper claim to it because I'm the product of an adulterous relationship between our human mother and some random human man who tricked her into believing he was a god?" It was a good thing Layla wasn't around. She'd have beat Amal to within an inch of his life for disrespecting Empress Chandra like this.

Amal tilted his head, eyes dancing. "Isn't that what happened?"

"I wasn't there. I simply respect our parents enough to take them at their word, but apparently, you know better than the gods themselves. Now, to add injury to that insult, how about you outright challenge me for what's mine and we'll see who's superior." That was what this whole thing was about. He wanted everyone to witness how she was inferior to him.

Amal scoffed. "It's beneath me to challenge you."

Ashni smirked. "You've already done so. Coming after what's mine is a challenge. Besides, don't act like you're above me because even if everything you said is true, I'm still Mom's child, which means I am still royal."

Amal tensed. "Mom's nothing more than the wild daughter of feral mountain people. Her blood's as common as mud."

People gasped around the room. Amal spoke blasphemy now. Perhaps, this would be enough for their mother to stop protecting him. Ashni had more than enough witnesses to comment on the level of disrespect. She'd enjoy every second of shutting him up.

"She was good enough for the Amir."

"She was never good enough for the first Emperor. The Amir's father knew what she was."

"We didn't even know him." This was way beyond her. *How could our grandfather be the one to poison Amal's mind when the man was dead before we were born?*

"I knew him well enough through those who knew him."

"I see." Her brothers had always attracted the wrong sort of people when they lived in Helli. Their parents tried to shield them from the snakes, but not even Khalid and Chandra could be everywhere all the time. Ashni rolled her shoulders and thunder clapped outside. "Well, I guess there's only one course of action left."

"You're not worth it." Amal tried to dismiss her.

"Neither are you, but my kingdom and Mom's honor seem like better things to fight for than sibling rivalry." Ashni threw out her fist, lightning directed at Amal's head. He had more than enough time to dodge and the lightning cracked beside his head. It blew a hole in the wall behind him. This was a warning, a reminder. She wielded power beyond his, even if he didn't want to believe it.

Amal snarled and his eyes glowed bright with fury. "You can't beat me."

"History has proven otherwise."

"I was taking it easy on you. Mom wouldn't like it if her darling baby girl got hurt."

Ashni smirked. "Oh, is that why I always got reprimanded when I took you down?"

People snickered and that made Amal snap. Small flames danced on the edges of his fingertips. He charged down the dais toward her, raising his hand, ready to cut her down without a blade. But, then one of his people tossed him his sword and he caught the long, curved blade just in time to try to cut her in half. She sidestepped the swipe, losing some loose hair to his weapon, and unsheathed her swords.

"Are you sure this is what you want to do?" Ashni inquired, eyes on her brother. She knew the answer, but she wanted to give him a moment to be smart.

He took another slash at her. Ashni blocked it with the Golden Feather. Amal's blade flashed orange, his fire trying to strengthen his weapon, as it clanged against her sword. He pushed forward, coming at her again, trying to back her up. She didn't give an inch. He growled, glaring at her with hatred in his burning gaze.

Amal shrugged out of his long, teal outer robe. Gems and jewels rang out as the robe hit the floor, leaving him in a short-sleeved shirt with gold stitching. She planned to physically strip him of all his adornment. Even watching him take off his outer robe was satisfying. He needed to treat her like the serious threat she was.

"Sure you don't want to take anything else off?" Ashni asked, knowing he was weighed down by other wealth.

"I won't need to in order to deal with you."

Ashni shrugged. "Suit yourself. Just know by the time I'm done with you, you might be standing here naked."

He twirled his sword. Ashni tightened her grip on her blades and made sure her footing was true. He ran at her again, trying to take her head off. She blocked and moved, ducking every blow, listening as his sword whizzed by her.

While making sure she avoided her brother's attacks, Ashni kept tabs on any movement in the room. Most of the people there were her subjects, but there was no telling who might have betrayed her for Amal while she was gone. She wanted to make sure no one got close to Nakia. The second she thought Nakia was in danger, this dual be damned, as would the threat to her love.

***

Nakia watched with bated breath as Amal and Ashni battled. *Is this to the death?* Ashni made it seem like it wouldn't be a good idea for her to kill her brother. She had a feeling Amal wouldn't lament cutting his sister down. Not after all the horrible things he said.

Nakia wasn't sure Ashni could defeat Amal, even though she had seen how capable Ashni was. It was hard for her to overcome years of teaching—men were stronger, smarter, better than women. Her logical mind knew that was bunk. She had seen Ashni take down multiple men in battle. She had seen Ashni defeat Amal every single time in chess, which according to her father was a great mark of intellect. Ashni was smart enough to coach her in chess so she could defeat Amal. *So, she should win this.* Never mind the fact that Ashni controlled lightning.

But, Ashni didn't use her lightning. She clashed swords with Amal. As Nakia studied it, she realized Ashni wasn't even attacking. She was defending. *Is she even trying to beat Amal or just hold him off?*

Someone started in her direction. She tensed and checked for her dagger, a gift from Ashni, she now kept tucked in her sleeve. Layla had given her strange, magic pellets in case of something serious, explaining she only needed to throw one to the ground and run right after. She wasn't going to be the reason Ashni yielded the contest, but then Ashni roared, kicked Amal in the chest, and sent lightning at the person inching toward Nakia. The guy fell back on his ass and the smell of fire wafted into the air.

"Stay away from her!" Ashni pointed one sword at the man on the floor.

"You should worry about me!" Amal came back at her and she slashed, just missing him. It might have been on purpose, but it seemed more like he stopped just in time.

"I would never worry about you." Ashni cut him across the arm and blood oozed from the laceration.

Amal hollered like a wounded animal. The continued fight was enough of a distraction for Nakia to move further away from the crowd.

She wasn't sure who among them were for Ashni and who were for Amal.

Amal hissed. "You little bitch."

Amal came in swinging again and Ashni blocked or dodged every one of his strikes—until she didn't. He cut her across the cheek. Nakia's heart jumped and she flinched, but then shook that off. She'd seen worse happen to Ashni. Many people in the room gasped while a few applauded. Nakia was actually happy for that. This gave her a chance to figure out who was against Ashni, who she had to watch out for. Well, she knew a few anyway.

"That was almost your eye," Amal said. "Yield, or next time it'll be."

Ashni scoffed. "You're kidding, right? You barely drew blood." The wound on her cheek dripped.

Maybe she was trying to toy with him. Nakia recalled her teasing Layla when they sparred, and while the principle was similar, it wasn't the same. Ashni needed to be careful.

Nakia took her eyes off the fight, noticing a man who clapped for Amal coming toward her. The movement stopped as Amal cried out. Blood dripped onto the floor, a tear down Amal's sleeve, and his knuckles were stained crimson.

"Your goons are going to run at my hellcat. I'll take a piece out of you every time one of them moves," Ashni promised.

Nakia felt something stir in her. Ashni wasn't trying to hurt Amal, but all of that went out of the window for her. *I am precious to her.* Pride filled her to the brim.

Amal shot toward Ashni again, but Ashni had no problem getting out of the way of his sword, especially since his arm was injured. But then Amal feinted a sword attack and put his free hand up in Ashni's face instead. Flames shot from his hand into her face. Ashni roared in pain, pulling back. She thrashed her head from side to side to get rid of the fire.

"Ashni!" Nakia wanted to run to her. Of course he would have powers like Ashni did. He was the son of a demigod, even if he was an ass.

Amal brought his sword down on her, but Ashni still managed to block with one sword and slashed at him with the other. She sliced him across the chest. He hissed and backed away. She blinked as if testing her eyes. *How is she not blind?*

"Don't think I won't take your damn head off, Amal," Ashni said, squinting at him.

"You couldn't." But, he didn't move.

Ashni's nostrils flared as her eyes remained locked on her brother. Amal scanned the room like he was searching for a way out. Nakia doubted he'd find an exit.

"The girl!" Amal barked as he ran at Ashni.

Nakia didn't have to wonder who he meant. Two men rushed her. She backed away, digging for her dagger. She didn't have a chance to pull it. Lightning flashed and the two men stopped. One had a sword sticking out of his chest, and the other got a chest full of lightning. Others, who Nakia hadn't even noticed, halted. Nakia glanced at Ashni to thank her only to see Amal throwing both palms at Ashni and columns of flames leapt from his hands. She backed out of reach of the fire and then slashed at him. He sidestepped. A knife came up out of his sleeve and he tried to stab her.

"You think you could ever be the Amir's daughter? You don't even carry his Fire!" Amal blew a pillar of flames from his mouth, backing Ashni up several steps.

Ashni punched the air, lightning flying from her fist. Amal dodged it, but the wall at the far side of the room felt Ashni's wrath. It crumbled. Quite a few people had to get out of the way of the debris.

"Fire?" Ashni scoffed. "Didn't our father come from a bolt of lightning?"

"The Amir wielded Fire, as do all of his sons. You're nothing but a lie."

Nakia wondered if these were the sort of things Ashni had to deal with growing up. *Were there whispers of her not being her father's child when she was a little girl?* Maybe her brothers believed and spouted those rumors back to her. *Whenever her lightning manifested itself, did her brothers use it as proof against her?* Maybe their families weren't so different.

Ashni chuckled. "Your confidence is a lie."

"Is it?" Amal's body glowed and flames danced up his arms. The fire swirled around a knife lashed to his other arm.

Nakia's stomach twisted. She had never seen such a display of power, and it didn't seem like Ashni could match it. She had only seen Ashni throw lightning from her hands.

Amal went at Ashni again and she dodged his blade attack, but the fire ate at her, burning away much of her shirt. She had on another underneath, but no armor. Nakia wanted to do something. *I'm helpless and she's worried about me so she can't focus completely on him.*

Nakia hated being such a liability. She was the reason Ashni had to split her army when going back into the West, giving her father a chance to escape and get help, making her conquest even more difficult. She distracted Ashni enough for Amal to take her kingdom. Ashni hadn't noticed something amiss in her messages, too focused on having Nakia back with her. And now, her presence might cost Ashni her life as she tried to divide her attention to protect both of them. *Maybe Ashni did lose favor with the gods and they sent me to be a curse onto her.*

"Don't worry." Adira came up behind her. "Ashni's got this."

Nakia jumped. "Where did you come from?"

"Saniyah's safe, so now I have to honor my place with Ashni."

"Is Bashira with her?" Bashira was her first friend and she wouldn't forgive Amal if he hurt her.

"Bashira's a little shaken up, but safe. You can talk to her later. Watch your beloved work." Adira nodded toward Ashni.

***

Ashni panted as Amal's fire licked at the scarred flesh of her arms. Bubbles pulsed and popped on her skin. Her lightning refused to come through such injured vessels. If someone came up to Nakia, she'd have to throw her daggers. She only had a limited number of those. When Adira stepped behind Nakia, Ashni wanted to make sacrifices to *her*. Hell, she'd do just that when this was all over. Grant Adira honors and celebrations and whatever the hell else she desired.

The great Amir wasn't your father. Amal's taunts rang through Ashni's mind. Ashni might not ever know if she was the biological child of Amir Khalid Akshay, but she felt that in the same way, no one could ever truly know if they were the biological child of their father. Her birth could've easily been a way for people to discredit her mother, and her idiot brother obviously bought into it. She didn't think anyone could poison her brothers against her mother. Jay turned down the whole damn Empire out of reverence for her, yet Amal talked about her like she was some whore from the hills.

Ashni took a deep breath and focused. She wasn't going to give Amal a chance to walk away from this. He was a danger to Nakia. He mocked their mother. He thought he knew better than their father. He was of the belief he could stand in the way of Fate, in the way of the gods.

For all Amal's talk, when he heard the wind howl, he paled. Ashni could feel a charge building in her, could feel a current like never before under her charred skin. She pointed the Golden Feather at Amal and lightning powered down her shoulder through the sword toward him. He moved out of the way in time. Ashni blew a giant hole in the wall and the only problem she had with that was that she missed her damned brother. Amal's eyes went wide and a bead of sweat ran down his cheek.

"Stand down before you insult the gods further with your foul mouth," Ashni said, voice hard. *Do I have it in me to muster another bolt like that?* Wind would be easier, but she couldn't hit him alone with a gush of wind, not in her current state. It would take out the whole room.

Amal snickered, but it sounded like his teeth chattering. "You're such a failure you can't even control that power." He nodded toward her arm.

Ashni didn't look, but she could feel what he meant. Her skin had split, burning lesions down her arms. Her blood painted the floor of her throne room. She didn't flinch, didn't want him to know her body wasn't ready for that sort of power, not after taking so much damage from his flames. It didn't matter. His body wouldn't know what hit it either.

"Just surrender, Ashni. You're inferior to me."

"A god can't be inferior to an insect, especially one who's also favored by the gods." Ashni knew she had fallen out of favor long ago, but he didn't know that. Before this mess of falling in love, her being a favorite was undeniable. The heavens parted for her, for crying out loud.

"Then you should know you're done for."

Ashni barely had time to get out of the way as he threw wave after wave of fire at her. He hoped to catch her in a massive wall of fire and be rid of her, maybe rid of every semblance of her, but she'd never make it that easy. In fact, she had to remind Amal why he never beat her at anything. He made horrible decisions.

"I'll drown you in Fire like the beast you are! Give you up to the gods in the purity of my divine light!" Amal unleashed a tsunami of fire in her direction. He couldn't control his fire any more than she could with her lightning right now, but he was reckless with his. She could hear the people behind her panic, scrambling for cover as the flames could engulf not only her but everything at that end of the room.

Ashni took another breath, making sure everything inside of her calmed. *Merciful gods, forgive me for any disrespect I've given you, but grant me the strength to show him I'm not only my father's daughter, but my mother's defender, my hellcat's protector, and the keeper of all my people's dreams.* She drew in everything she could, feeling in tune with the Sky and well beyond that. She always thought she could reach the stars, but this was the first time she actually felt it.

Lightning broke through the ceiling, hitting Ashni. She roared as power like nothing she'd ever imagined poured into her and directed the lightning at her brother's flame wall. Wind howled as it blew from her, like a monsoon broke free from her body. The lightning cut right through the flaming wave and into Amal. When it hit him, thunder shook the room, the palace, the world maybe. She wouldn't be able to name the sound he made, but she was certain she could hear his bones splinter through it all. Amal was blown back, body flying like a doll before he dropped to the floor, body smoking. Her wind cut his fire into slivers.

Shaking, Ashni wanted to fall to her knees, but she refused. A god would never fall.

Chapter Seventeen

"ASHNI!" NAKIA CRIED OUT, breaking away from Adira when she saw the massive wave of fire headed toward her beloved. When Ashni let loose her counterattack, a lightning bolt that might have had the power to destroy the whole city, Nakia stopped, too shocked to move. The bolt was accompanied by a powerful wind that somehow only blew in a tight tunnel around Amal. She could see the terror in Amal's eyes right before it hit him and he let out an unholy sound. Then, he dropped, nothing more than a smoldering pile in the ruined throne room.

Nakia ran toward Ashni, somehow still on her feet. Adira chased after her, shouting her name, but Nakia couldn't be caught, not until she was holding Ashni. Ashni collapsed against her, burying her head in the crook of Nakia's neck and wrapping her arms weakly around Nakia's waist. The smell of burnt flesh invaded Nakia's nose, twisted her stomach, but she held Ashni steady. Adira stood behind them, silent and watchful.

"Kitten." Ashni's voice came out as a scratchy croak.

Before Nakia could figure out what Ashni wanted to tell her, she heard the lightning strike. She turned in time to see Amal fall for a second time. A small gasp escaped her before she realized it. *How could he still be alive, let alone able to climb to his feet?* Regardless of how she felt about him, he probably was the son of god, so it sort of made sense. Maybe. It didn't matter as long as he didn't get back up. Nakia turned back to Ashni, who gave her a weak smile before passing out.

"Ashni?" Nakia hoped she wasn't holding onto Ashni's dead body.

"We need healers!" Adira waved people over to Nakia and Ashni. The masses in the room moved in a mad rush, but Nakia suspected many of them weren't getting healers. Adira stood between Ashni and Amal, hand on the hilt of her sword.

People tried to take Ashni from Nakia, but she clung to Ashni, refusing to let go. Ashni stirred awake and held onto a fistful of Nakia's shirt.

"They're doctors. They have me, kitten," Ashni whispered.

Nakia let the doctors have Ashni, but she followed them off to wherever the hell they were taking her lover. She didn't trust any of them. *What if one of them is secretly with Amal?* It would be all too easy to kill Ashni in her exhausted state.

Ashni was rushed to her apartments in the palace with Nakia hot on their heels. She stood back, questions on the tip of her tongue. Ashni kept eye contact with her, as if letting her know it was all right, but then the doctors blocked her view. Nakia moved, ready to bark at the doctors, when a hand grabbed hers. She turned to see Layla next to her.

"It's okay," Layla said. "Ashni's awake and if she suspects any one of these healers, I'll cut them down."

She knew Layla wouldn't gamble with Ashni's life. She wasn't sure how long they stood there, but eventually servants brought them sitting pillows. Soon, the scent of charred skin was replaced with herbs and blood, and bandages littered the floor. Food was brought, but Nakia couldn't imagine eating.

"She's going to be fine, you know?" Layla said around a mouthful of bread and honey.

Nakia didn't have that confidence. "That fire…" Nakia would've doubted she saw it if only Ashni wasn't suffering because of it. "Was that divine power?"

Layla scoffed. "All her brothers throw fire. Fire and tantrums. Well, except the younger twins. They throw fire and madness. They're fun."

Nakia's forehead wrinkled. "But, Ashni has lightning." Maybe she wasn't the child of Khalid Akshay.

Layla shrugged. "Some kids have brown eyes and then one has green."

Nakia nodded. "I'm one of those kids."

"Right. Do you ever doubt your parents are your parents because your eyes don't match the color scheme?"

"No." It never occurred to her.

"We all know lightning is only commanded by the Heavens. So, her commanding lightning must mean something. Besides, it makes sense if her father really was born from lightning striking the rock or whatever the hell the story is."

Nakia didn't have an argument against that. "Have any of her other brothers used their powers against her?"

Layla ate some more bread. "Only when sparring. Amal has always been the most openly hostile. She knew something like this would happen eventually."

"So, her other brothers won't do this?"

"I didn't say all that. I've spent a lot of time around her family and while she can consider my family her family and they'd do the same, her brothers have never looked at me as such. Her mother is kind to me and treats me like a daughter, but her brothers, even the younger ones, look at me like I'm beneath them."

Nakia nodded. "Ashni made it sound like she liked them."

"She does. I think they respect her in a way the older ones don't. But, I also think they haven't been molded by intrigue like the older ones have. Amal seemed to buy into it the most. He thought he was deserving of the crown for whatever reason. I'm sure he'll be wanting a refund on those beliefs once his mother finds out about this."

"Will she do something about him now?" Nakia was nervous of this the most. *What if Amal's allowed to roam free?*

"Well, provided he doesn't die of his wounds—and I'm sure he won't because no god is ever that good—we'll see. I have to think Chandra will do something now. I mean, he almost succeeded in killing Ashni with his own hand in front of almost a hundred people."

"I hope you're right."

Layla didn't say anything, but Nakia could tell from the haunted look in her eyes, Layla hoped she was right as well. She sat with Layla until the doctors began to disperse. Ashni was covered in bandages, including her face. Nakia wanted to fall to her side and take her hand, but both were bandaged as well. She sat by her, instead, finding Ashni awake.

"Hey, hellcat," Ashni said, her voice low, groggy, like there were pebbles in her throat.

Nakia didn't feel like a hellcat right now. More like a helpless kitten. "How do you feel?"

Ashni chuckled and it sounded smoky, like the fire had burned her vocal cords. "Good."

"You feel good?"

There was an amused glint in her uncovered eye. "Do you know how long I've wanted to put a bolt of lightning in Amal's ass?"

Nakia forced out a smile. "I can imagine."

"Yeah, that second bolt was for you, from the time he tried to hurt you because you won at chess."

Nakia let out a weak giggle, bordering on hysterical. She wasn't sure how she hadn't come apart at the seams yet. "Well, thank you for that, but I'm sure there were people more deserving of the second bolt honor."

Ashni smiled. "No one will ever deserve more than you."

Nakia sniffled and her eyes stung with tears. She wasn't sure if she was about to cry out of happiness or frustration. *I've never felt like such a mess. A good mess since she's alive, but still a mess.* "You're such a romantic."

Ashni sighed. "This is a big fucking mess he's gotten us into. I hate to think about how I need to fix Khenshu. What if I can't get back to the West?"

"Silly girl. You're the daughter of Amir Khalid Akshay. How could you not get back to the West? We'll root out the problems here, and then strengthen anything that needs to be fixed and you'll get back to the West. I know you can do it." She meant that. Ashni would rise again and fulfill her dreams. Someone like Amal couldn't stop a force of nature like Ashni.

Ashni smiled. "Stay with me while I sleep?"

"I'll stay with you always." She'd also pray to every god she knew to make sure Ashni pulled through.

***

When Ashni woke up the next day from a dreamless sleep, she struggled to her feet, determined to walk to her throne. Pain beyond her understanding stalked through her with every breath she took. It took all of her willpower to stay standing.

Nakia quietly watched Ashni, standing close in case she needed support, but she managed on her own. Ashni wouldn't give Amal or his followers the satisfaction in seeing her incapacitated for even a full day.

Beyond that, she thought she'd need to stay on her feet to make sure Nakia didn't think she was weak, but she already knew that wasn't true. It was like being around Layla or Adira after being injured, except Nakia hadn't teased her. *It must be love.* The thought made her chuckle inside.

In the throne room, Ashni discovered her throne had been destroyed in the fight, but there was a makeshift throne in its place—a table with a fancy sitting pillow atop it. She sat on it like it was made of priceless gems and inched over for Nakia to have space.

"Are you comfortable sitting?" Nakia asked in a low voice.

Ashni nodded. She had to be careful of all the bandaging, but sitting was fine. *Better than walking.* She could feel her skin pull as she sat, but it wasn't bad considering the herbs she drank before making the journey from her bed to her throne. Her medicine kicked in, numbing the agony enough for her to function.

"Where is Adira?" Ashni tried to call out, but getting her voice to cooperate was like raising the dead—annoying, unnecessary, and disrespectful. Servants rushed out in all directions to get her needs met, so she knew she'd see Adira soon.

"What do you think they did with your brother?" Nakia asked.

"He's probably still unconscious from wounds suffered at my hands, but I'm sure Adira secured him somewhere. I need to get word to my mother, even though I'm sure she knows this happened."

"And she allowed it?"

Ashni sucked her teeth. "She's always telling us to work it out amongst ourselves." Her mother didn't like to take sides, 'loving them all equally,' which Ashni was sure was true. Still, it was irksome.

Nakia tilted her head. "Work out an attempted coup and assassination?"

"I think my mother feels like the techniques she used on us as kids should still work now. It doesn't help that she's an only child, so she doesn't know how irksome an older brother can be. I think she also hopes one day we'll all get along." That was a dream inside a dream as far as she was concerned. Her older brothers had no desire to get along with her.

Nakia nodded and ordered some breakfast for Ashni while a servant delivered documents for her to look over. These were updates from the army in the West. Since they had been gone, the army still held its territory and took over a few small towns to advance. That was good enough for now. Hafiz had his sights set on a city, but Varaza talked him into waiting, which Ashni was thankful for. Yes, Hafiz was a good leader, but he wasn't great yet.

"I've had things in hand since you went down," Adira announced as she marched into the room.

Ashni glared at Adira, wishing she could disintegrate the general with her gaze. "I did not go down." She stayed on her feet until the doctors worked on her.

Adira shrugged. "However you want to look at it. Layla's investigating how Amal gained control. I suspect he poisoned your regent and appointed himself to the position."

"And no one challenged that?"

Adira scoffed. "The only reason I didn't get here sooner to make sure someone protected your princess is because he had most of the nobles locked down on my property with men who were threatening to burn down one of the storage spaces that had everyone's children in it. When Layla showed up, I trusted her to handle it since I knew you'd need me. That coward took everyone's children to keep them in line. Kidnapped them from their beds, like the worm he is. He couldn't face anyone in this."

Ashni sucked her teeth. "And he calls me a bastard. How's it possible he's my father's child?"

Adira blew out a breath. "Damned if I know. To take a child from his bed is one thing, but to threaten to burn them to death is beyond me."

"The children are all right, yes?"

"Some have cuts and bruises, beaten for being unruly, but they're alive."

Ashni scowled. "He beat children?" *Really, how was Amal related to me in any way?*

"If Layla was here, she'd remind you that you beat her."

Ashni scoffed. "She was on the battlefield when that happened. She was a soldier, not asleep in her bed, minding her own damned business. Amal has managed to top being the scum I always thought he was."

"Yeah, he's definitely worse than we ever gave him credit for." Adira rubbed her forehead. "But, getting things in order won't be too hard now that the trustworthy members of the Court are able to make some moves."

"Have you contacted my mother?" It needed to be done sooner rather than later and it wasn't something Ashni desired to do. She wouldn't know how to put it into words without letting her emotions get in the way and how Amal deserved nothing less than death for what happened here.

Adira sneered. "I did. If something doesn't come of this, your mom needs some serious help. I understand you're all her kids and she loves the hell out of you to the point where it makes me want to throw up, but come on. How many times does this little fucker need to try to kill you? He's a fucking worm."

"I agree with you completely. Have you made an assessment of how long this might take to fix?"

Adira rocked her head from side to side. "I think it shouldn't take too long. I just want to make sure we gather up his men and any traitors among us. But, the trustworthy courtiers will handle most of it. Layla's parents were hot over this, so I think we best leave her mother in charge and laugh when someone tries to poison her for the regency."

Ashni chuckled. "Could you imagine? I should've done that from the beginning." She had planned to leave Layla's grandmother in charge as only a suicidal person would try to take anything from her, but she had students to train. The regent she left was trustworthy, but unfortunately mortal. Not that Layla's family was immortal, but people tended to think twice about poisoning Shadow Walkers because sometimes it didn't work.

"I'll keep you involved, but you should heal up. No reason to return to the West too injured to get anything done beyond barking out orders. You know you want to do more than that."

Ashni couldn't argue. She wanted to charge back into the West and take part in battle just like her army. So, she let Adira handle the heavy lifting and ate breakfast to help her convalescence. She enjoyed Nakia feeding her, but it was nothing like she dreamed. It didn't help that Nakia was quiet.

"Hellcat, you okay?" *Is Nakia disappointed in me for getting injured?* Nakia heard her bragging way too often to not think something was up for her getting hurt, especially by Amal. She was surprised at how he got the better of her. It was time to humble herself. *No more hubris.* She couldn't take risks, like angering the gods or almost losing an eye now that she had Nakia in her life.

Nakia gave her a small, sad smile. "I am."

"You look troubled."

"Of course I'm troubled. You're all bandaged up. Your brother tried to steal your kingdom and kill you. You don't think your mother's going to do anything about it. And to top it all off, you wouldn't stay in bed to heal because you don't want anyone to think Amal gained even an inch from you."

Ashni nodded. "Is it too much?"

Nakia stared at her with a furrowed brow. "Is what too much? What do you mean?"

"Are you...would you...should I prepare to send you somewhere?" Ashni's stomach dropped at the thought, and she feared the little she managed to eat would come back up.

Nakia squinted. "Why would you need to send me somewhere?"

Ashni shook her head. She was being paranoid. Nakia wanted to be with her. "In case you were worried about Amal and his people."

"No. I don't even know why I'd think to be worried. I'm with you. I'm staying by your side, just like I promised."

Despite the fact that she was on a makeshift throne, Ashni felt like she was on a cloud reigning over the Heavens. She could settle this mess and go back to the West. She would also shower Nakia with every gift a woman could possibly want, because Nakia gave her the strength for everything she wanted.

Nakia stayed by her side as Ashni handled light work in regards to getting Khenshu back in working order. Nakia made sure she ate lunch and pulled her away from work to change her bandages. Well, Nakia watched someone change her bandages with the expressed desire to learn how to do it herself. She also learned how to apply different medicines to Ashni's wounds. Ashni felt blessed once again. *Nakia is definitely the best gift from the gods.*

Ashni had Nakia and her closest friends with her. Everything seemed possible through them, which reminded her, she needed to make a sacrifice in Adira's name sometime soon. The gods would have to understand her reasoning, after all Adira saved their greatest gift to her. Adira deserved honors.

***

Ashni could barely keep her eyes open. It had only been a few days of righting the wrongs Amal subjected her dear capital city to, but it felt like an eternity. Nakia reached out, caressing her bandaged cheek.

"We should go to bed."

Ashni had already learned this was code *for you look tired. Time to stop working.* "In a moment. I'm still waiting for Layla's mother to show up." Layla's mother typically was punctual, but she had shouldered a lot of burden with this Amal mess. One of the most pressing matters for her was making sure all of the children Amal kidnapped were all right. Layla's mother had gone around to check on them. The last report said most were healing well physically and a little shaken mentally, but fine.

Nakia sighed. "If she's not here in an hour, we're going to bed. I'm exhausted."

Again, Ashni knew that was code for *your exhausted.* Nakia wasn't wrong, but Ashni would never say so.

Samar, Layla's mother, showed up a few minutes later. Nakia tensed beside her and she realized Nakia never had the chance to meet Samar. She probably didn't know what to make of the plainly dressed

206

woman with nearly black eyes that always seemed to study the whole universe while scrutinizing those in front of her. Her skin glowed like polished ebony, sweat from a hard day's work.

"Highness." Samar bowed her head as she stood before the makeshift throne. Adira had tried to replace it almost as soon as Ashni was up, but Ashni waved it off. The state of the throne wasn't important. She was on the throne and that was all that mattered.

"Lady Samar, I trust all your business has been handled," Ashni said.

"For the most part. I don't take you summoning me lightly, especially on this matter. But, we let our guard down while you were on campaign and we can't let that happen again, not after what he did. So, for as long as you need me, I'm here."

Ashni smiled. "I know if anyone else tries anything, they'll have to wrestle this throne from your cold dead hands after they step over the bodies of your clan."

Samar scoffed. "After what Amal tried, I wouldn't even let something grow into that. Do you know he came to us in peace, sat with us, had tea, talked of when you and Layla first met, and then stole away all the children while we worked? Held our clan's next generation and let us hear their cries."

"He'll pay for his crimes. Adira has made a list and sent it to Empress Chandra."

"There has to be justice." Samar's eyes said what her words didn't. If her mother let them down, Khenshu would be in revolt against the Empire. Hell, Ashni might even back it. Her brother couldn't be left to do this again. He had used his position as her brother, as a prince of the Empire, and as Empress Chandra's son to get in close to people and even used their children against them. He was nothing short of a monster.

"There will be justice." If her mother didn't do the right thing, she would.

Samar gave her a small nod. "Now, you haven't introduced me to the young lady. I've heard so much about her."

"I'm sure you have." Ashni laughed. "Lady Samar, this is my consort, Nakia Lysand, soon to be queen of the West." Ashni held her head up high. Yes, maybe she'd give Nakia the entire West as a wedding gift.

"Consort, hmm?" Samar looked Nakia up and down and for once Nakia wisely kept her mouth shut. Ashni had once made the mistake of sassing Samar. She'd sooner slap her own mother than dare to do that again. "I hear she's a good match for you. I also hear Layla complain day and night about her whenever she has my ear, but who wants to share a sister?"

"She doesn't have a say in the matter." Nakia rested her hand on Ashni's knee.

"No, I don't suppose she does, but now she knows how Ashni felt when she married Naren. I'm a bit disappointed she's never brought you by the manor. Our traditions always have the family meet a mate before the relationship is official."

Ashni could feel her cheeks flare, and she was glad most of her face was covered in bandages. "Things have been busy, Samar."

"They weren't busy when you were here for the winter."

Why Ashni tried to argue, she'd never know. "We didn't really know what this was at the time." It was the truth in a way. She didn't realize what Nakia meant to her until Nakia was gone.

"You still have to make time for tradition. From what I've heard, I approve, but I'd still like to see. I won't approve of an official joining if that doesn't happen." Samar wagged her finger.

"Yes." Ashni glanced at Nakia, who looked a little too amused at the exchange. Soon, Nakia would learn the intensity of Samar and know it was best to do what she said or else.

"Now, you should probably be in bed." Samar gave Ashni a scolding look.

"She was just taking me. Promise." Ashni motioned to Nakia.

"I was."

Samar folded her arms and smiled. "Good." With that Samar was gone, like the whirlwind she was.

Nakia blew out a breath. "I don't know what I thought Layla's mother would be like, but that was both it and not it."

Ashni shrugged. "I still don't know what to make of Samar and I've known her for years. I'm almost certain she's what Layla's people call a night nymph. They're described as creatures of deep wisdom, who have knowledge well beyond the stars, but are relatively harmless as long as you don't cross them. If you piss them off, they literally devour you with teeth sharper than even my own swords."

"Well, to avoid that, I should get you to bed. Come on." Nakia tapped her elbow, which got her to rise.

Ashni knew if she wasn't careful, Nakia would be able to command her without words.

***

Nakia's main goal was taking care of Ashni as she tried to take care of her beloved city. Ashni's team was efficient and effective. They also backed Nakia whenever she suggested Ashni needed to do something for her own good and Ashni wanted to put up a bit of a fight. Nakia got to meet a lot of people who worked in Khenshu. Day by day, Ashni lost bandages, revealing burn marks on her face and arms. She was given salves and ointments and promises they would eventually fade.

Nakia thought of her own cut, going through her eyebrow, caused by her father. That would never fade, but Ashni never mentioned the mark on her face. Nakia wasn't worried over the physical scar, but did fret about the mental ones. *Will Ashni have the same trouble?* Her body was marred by her brother. *Will she be able to get over that?*

"I'm ready to go back West," Ashni said. *Yes, she'll get over it.*

"Then why are we still here?" Nakia asked. Everything was in place for Ashni to return to her army, return to her dream.

"I'm waiting for word from my mother. We still have Amal and shouldn't." Ashni inhaled. "She's studying the evidence Adira sent her. She's the final judge when it comes to treason against the Empire. So, first, judges look at it and then she'll look at it."

"Judges will judge a prince?" Nakia would have to get used to the idea that no one was above the law in the Roshan Empire, except maybe Empress Chandra. She hadn't seen any evidence the empress could be stopped by judges, law, or anything else. Sometimes, she felt like they believed Empress Chandra was infallible.

"No, for this, they're just giving their opinion. My mother has final say."

"Are you confident?" *How many assassination attempts did Ashni put up with and her mother turned a blind eye?*

Ashni sighed. "I don't know. I just know I want to be here when her judgment comes in."

The answer that came later that day didn't lift Ashni's mood. The Empress Chandra as Ashni kept saying with a sneer, decided they should just send Amal to her, going as far as sending an envoy for him. There were too many accounts and circumstances to sort through and she'd rather have Amal with her to 'keep an eye on him.'

"That's such bullshit. She never keeps an eye on him!" Ashni growled as she heaved the parchment across the room.

"Trust in Empress Chandra," Layla said.

"I'll trust in her to mess this up. He's her fucking baby, after all," Ashni said.

Adira arched an eyebrow. "It's so funny to see your colored perception of your mother. Let's send him off to her and get back to our business."

"You're too calm about this." Ashni glared at Adira.

"It's the right thing to do right now," Nakia said. It would be one less thing for Ashni to worry about. One less thing to stress her out. Adira glanced at her and even though her mouth didn't move, there seemed to be a light in her eye, like she was smiling.

Ashni sighed, her shoulders slumped, defeated. Nakia wanted to kiss her until she smiled, but not in the open, not with her closest present. They'd make fun of her and it would undermine her authority. Instead, she took Ashni's hand.

"Let's go take care of your destiny," Nakia said.

"Yeah, don't argue with your consort," Layla said with a grin. Nakia wanted to glare at her, but Layla was helping. Ashni squared her shoulders and climbed to her feet. Onward to destiny.

Chapter Eighteen

ASHNI BREATHED IN THE air of the West. This was the third time she'd graced these shores and now the air tasted different. The sweetness remained, but not to the degree of enchantment it had. It was tinged with a hint of citrus, lightly burning her tongue as she inhaled. Oddly enough, it didn't bother her. The burn felt like it healed tiny cracks in her.

"This is where I belong," Ashni said, digging her feet into the soil.

"With me by your side." Nakia stepped forward and took her hand.

"Of course, my dear queen." *Why not call Nakia a queen?* She already introduced her to Samar and other officials in Khenshu as her consort. The only thing missing was time to have a wedding. When things settled down, maybe when it got too cold to wage war, they'd have their wedding. For now, there were cities and nations to conquer.

Their little group made their way back to the army, finding them several miles away from Valen. Hafiz greeted them, his face bright with victory, and Ashni clapped him on the shoulder to show her appreciation. But, she knew it wasn't her praise he craved. He turned to Adira and grinned, looking much younger than he was.

"You did a good job," Adira said, but her tone was a little clipped. Ashni knew she liked to keep him on his toes, wanting him to reach his true potential without getting full of himself, but also feeding him the acknowledgment he deserved.

But it was an understatement to say he did a good job. "We need to see about getting you your own unit to command." Ashni would have to do the same with Varaza, who according to every piece of correspondence that came her way, handled things with the power and efficiency Ashni had come to expect of her.

Hafiz threw his shoulders back. "Yes, Highness."

"You've earned it."

Hafiz had done everything she wanted and a little more. Now that she was back, it was time to seriously move. They had a strategy already worked out, and they needed to get back to it.

***

Nakia didn't think anything could get her 'barbarians' to leave the West, but there were a number of factors that finally did it. One, they didn't want to do another winter up north in the West. Even the Roshan who weren't from Ashni's desert territory felt like winter was serious business and they didn't want any part of it. Two, Ashni wanted to check on Khenshu and relieve Samar of her regency if only for a little while. Samar had been in charge for over a year and she had a life aside from representing Ashni on her throne. And three, Empress Chandra reached out to Ashni, wanting to meet Nakia. So, now, they made their way back to Khenshu and Nakia knew Ashni was up to something.

"What makes you think Ashni's up to something?" Bashira asked Nakia.

They were in Nakia's apartments in the palace. Even though Nakia had grown used to sharing a bed and space with Ashni, she was quite insistent Nakia needed a space to do her own thing. Nakia agreed, even though she was still trying to figure out what 'her own thing' was. She had filled her year with sitting in on military meetings, learning self-defense from several willing teachers, reading up on Roshan culture and history, and honing her chess skills. When she had spare time, she had taken to writing poems to her beloved, who smiled whenever she read one.

"I haven't seen her for almost three days. Her mother's going to be here in a couple of days and I don't know what to expect and she's not helping me prepare to meet with Empress Chandra." Nakia made a fluttering motion with her hand.

"She could be preparing for her mother's arrival."

Nakia shook her head. "She would've asked for my help." Well, more like she would've helped and Ashni would've watched her work.

From being with Ashni over a year, Nakia learned to work alongside her as best she could. While she wasn't useful in battle, she learned to negotiate with the best of them and Ashni always talked deals with her. It was a talent she didn't know she had. She also learned how to organize events. Whenever Ashni needed a meeting with diplomats or representatives, Nakia was the one who arranged everything, much to Adira's delight. It was a job she was glad to hand off.

"Shopping could get your mind off of it," Bashira said.

Nakia laughed. "You always want to shop."

"Well, the conquest's going well and Aunt Adira got a huge bonus because of how she handled Khenshu while Queen Ashni was injured." Bashira shrugged. As far as she was concerned, the bonus was pretty much hers because her aunts were childless and only spent money on projects.

Nakia grinned. She knew the real reason was because Adira showed up to the battle in time to protect Nakia and gave Ashni a chance to focus only on Amal.

"I can't believe she got a bonus and two festivals in her honor."

Nakia chuckled. She couldn't believe it either. The only reason Ashni hadn't thrown Adira a third festival was because they had to return to Khenshu. For both festivals, Ashni sent for Adira's family, bringing them to wherever the army was in the West at her expense and letting them celebrate. For Nakia, this was wonderful, knowing Ashni would shower someone with honors for protecting her.

"I'm sure when the time comes, Ashni's going to name a city in Adira's honor," Nakia said. Ashni had already thrown the idea around several times. It wasn't something Adira wanted, but that didn't matter to Ashni.

A servant rushed in, delivering a message and cutting their conversation short. They were wanted in the throne room. They looked at each other and shrugged.

"Is this an immediate thing?" Nakia asked.

"Yes. Please, come now." The servant motioned to the door. "The queen requests it, Highness."

Nakia's stomach clinched a little. The servants had taken to calling her by that title, even though she wasn't part of the royal family. Nakia and Bashira climbed to their feet and went to the throne room. Ashni was on the throne, waving Nakia to her, and Bashira found both of her aunts in the crowd of courtiers. No one was dressed to the nines, so she didn't think Empress Chandra had arrived early, but something was certainly going on. Layla stood by the throne.

Nakia knew she had taken a spot Layla used to occupy when she was in the Great Hall. The first time it happened, Layla glared at her and tried to throw her from the seat, but Ashni gave her a stern look. It was established Nakia would sit at Ashni's side from now on, sharing the throne. It was cozy.

"Why are we here?" Nakia asked, eyes on her love. Ashni still bore faint burn marks on her right cheek from her fight with Amal. It wasn't until they removed the bandages so long ago that Nakia realized how close Ashni had been to losing her eye by her brother's hand.

"Wait for it." Ashni rolled her eyes as she put her chin in her hand. Well, this was a guarantee something annoying was about to happen. It explained why the nobility was there in their everyday clothing rather than looking ready for a ceremony. Everyone was probably going to go about their day as soon as they could.

An announcement rang through the hall. "King Jay Akshay and King Asad Akshay!"

Nakia's eyes went wide. "Your brothers?"

"The older ones. One of whom is Amal's twin. Oh, joy." Ashni made a gagging noise.

The mentioning of Amal made Nakia's stomach twist. He was being held in the Empire's capital, Helli. He had been found guilty of a number of crimes, but no one in Khenshu felt he was properly punished for it. From her understanding, he was on house arrest. No one was allowed to see him beyond his family, any servants were deaf-mutes, and they weren't there all the time, so there were days when he was totally alone. The isolation sounded awful, but she felt it was deserved, just like with her father.

Dorian had been placed on a tiny island off the coast of Ashni's desert. A shelter of small rooms had been set up for him. Food was brought every few days, but no one stayed. No one visited. Such was the nature of punishment for the crime of treason in the Empire. Apparently, it counted as treason when Ashni took the city of Phyllida and Dorian raised an army against her in another city. Nakia didn't feel sorry for him.

"Why are your brothers here?" Nakia asked.

Ashni let loose a long sigh from her nose. "Mom's coming to see you, so they have to kiss Mom's ass after Amal's bullshit."

Nakia scowled. "So, this is all a show? They don't even care that Amal tried to kill you." The younger brothers had contacted Ashni throughout the year, checking on her and her adventures, but never the older ones. Ashni shared all of those, hoping Nakia could get to know her brothers through the missives. These two, Nakia wanted to wait to judge them, but it was hard.

"Of course they don't. But, that doesn't matter to me. Asad might want to show he doesn't share his twin's beliefs, but Jay doesn't really have to worry about that. He's turned down the throne enough from scheming nobles for Mom to know he'll wait for her judgment."

Nakia felt like this was more than the throne for the older brothers.

They might not feel the same way about their mother as Amal did, but they probably felt the same way about Ashni. She didn't want to have to deal with people badmouthing Ashni.

When Jay and Asad entered the hall, it was easy to tell Jay was the older one, even if she didn't know. He projected an air of eldest, tall and distinguished. He had the same amber eyes as Ashni, but they weren't as feline. There was something else there, but she couldn't put her finger on it. His wide body seemed to glow and she wondered if it was his fire. He looked like he had been sculpted from terra-cotta and then brought to life. His robes were rich, but not like Amal. Oddly enough, he didn't take advantage of the Roshan's love of colors, only wearing the royal teal and gold. Each step he took made a chiming sound, reminding her of Ashni with all of her bangles.

Asad was easy to pick out as Amal's twin, even though they weren't identical. A small scar marred his face across his nose. It stood out, raised sand across fine cinnamon. He was smaller than Jay, but broad and had a glint in his eyes that reminded her way too much of Amal. The difference was he looked like an experienced predator while Amal merely attempted to be one.

"Brothers, welcome!" Ashni grinned and put her hands up. Nakia was amazed how her lover could fake her enthusiasm where it seemed both genuine and forced at the same time.

"Thank you for hosting us, dear sister." Jay pressed his palms together.

Nakia had to bite her tongue. *If Ashni was so dear to him, why didn't he bother to check on her after Amal pulled what he did?* Instead of asking, Nakia smiled, too. It was the brightest expression she could manage, one she used when she wanted to appear almost vapid when they were in negotiations.

"You know most of the people here, but you haven't met my consort. May I present you, Princess Nakia Lysand." Ashni motioned to her.

Nakia stood and bowed slightly to the brothers, as that was the polite and expected thing for her to do. "It is a pleasure to meet you both."

They bowed back. "The pleasure's ours."

"Forgive our lack of festivities for your arrival, brothers. More attention's being paid to when Empress Chandra arrives. We had short notice with her, and we're working in a hurry. I do have a feast prepared, but nothing extravagant," Ashni said.

Again, Nakia had to bite her tongue to keep from scoffing. She had something beyond extravagant planned, even if Empress Chandra was set to arrive in two days. Ashni wouldn't give them the satisfaction of having something to complain about.

Once all the pomp and ceremony was done, everyone moved over to an entertainment room. There were musicians, dancers, and servants brought in food as everyone found sitting pillows. Ashni took her usual space in a corner and Nakia cuddled into her. Adira and Saniyah were with them as were Layla and Naren. Bashira stuck around, even though royal parties were a bit too fast for her. She dealt with it to be around Nakia. *Damn, who would've thought I have a best friend.*

Jay and Asad came to sit with them, but only to share a drink. Then, they found their own spaces with their attendants and possibly their spouses. Nakia wasn't sure, but Asad shared his large sitting pillow with a young man and woman, both dressed to the nines with fabulous jewelry. Jay had a petite woman with him.

"Are those their spouses?" Nakia asked.

"The two with Asad are. I think the woman with Jay is just his favorite for the moment," Ashni said.

Nakia put her hands on Ashni's cheeks. "I better be your only favorite."

"My only spouse, too. Eventually, right?" Ashni grinned, even as Nakia pressed her cheeks.

"Of course. Whenever you see fit to halt your conquest for me. I mean, you'll stop for your mother, but not me."

Ashni chuckled. "We didn't come back here for my mother."

Nakia's brow wrinkled. "Then why did we?"

"Because it was cold as a bitch where we were. I think we're not going to bother with the North. How the hell is the West so nice until you start going north?" Ashni gave an exaggerated shiver.

"Isn't your mother from the northern part of the Empire?"

"Making the North even more worthless and useless and horrible to me."

Nakia scoffed, but didn't say anything. She couldn't figure out Ashni's relationship with her mother and no one would help her understand it. Ashni made it seem like she disliked her mother, but whenever she talked about what Amal did, one of the things that got her the angriest was how he degraded their mother. And, whenever Ashni made some negative comment about her mother, Layla defended the empress or Adira would act like Ashni was making it up. Nakia

216

couldn't wait to see the relationship play out in front of her, so she could at least figure out how to approach the subject with Ashni.

For now, Nakia would try to understand Ashni's brothers. She studied Jay and Asad, but it was hard to pick up anything at a distance. Jay didn't interact with anyone beyond the woman next to him. Asad indulged in everything the party had to offer, including feeling up one of the dancers, even though he had two spouses with him. Neither of his spouses said anything to him. He downed cup after cup of wine as well.

The party wasn't like Ashni's usual fare. Many nobles seemed to fade from the room much sooner than she expected and they all retired at a reasonable hour. Jay complained the whole set up was "too much," whatever that meant. Asad went the opposite way and said how "there should've been better wine and your dancers need more practice." Of course, that didn't stop either of them from taking two dancers each back to their apartments.

"Your brothers are…" Nakia searched for something kind to say. Ashni always said kind things about her sisters after meeting both of them, but nothing came to mind for her to finish that sentence. They walked through the palace, heading back to her room.

Ashni sucked her teeth. "Pains in the ass."

Nakia shrugged. "I'll wait and see if they throw tantrums during chess."

"Oh, yeah. Play them tomorrow. You think Amal was a baby about it? You haven't seen anything until that big idiot Jay gets hit with a checkmate. He actually breathes fire."

Nakia shuddered. She still had nightmares about the way Amal glared at her when Ashni helped her win the first time she played him. *And to think that could've been worse had he used his fire.*

She grabbed Ashni's hand and held it. "Anyway, are you finally coming to bed with me?"

Ashni arched an eyebrow. "Finally?"

"Come now. You haven't slept beside me in days."

Ashni sighed. "Forgive me, my queen. I'm putting something together. You'll see."

"Is it for your mother's arrival?"

"Yes."

Nakia squeezed Ashni's hand. "Don't run yourself into the ground for one guest, even if she's the empress. You could always let me do it."

"I could, but I won't."

"You let me handle plenty of things." It seemed strange Ashni wouldn't trust her to do this. She had organized so many other things in the last year.

"I know. If I could let you do this, I would. And, it's not me letting you. Have you ever tried to stop you from doing something you want to do? It's a headache. You beat me down every time."

Nakia scoffed. "Liar."

Ashni grinned, eyes sparkling with pure affection, and Nakia let her off the hook. She didn't want to give Ashni a reason not to go to bed with her tonight. She missed their intimacy. Lying next to Ashni gave her a chance to cuddle and caress Ashni in ways she couldn't with people around. They always talked before going to sleep. She missed that.

"I miss you," Nakia said.

"I miss you, too. Let's not have that happen when it's unnecessary. Should we go to your room or mine?" Ashni asked. Nakia's was closer, so that was where they spent the night.

***

"This is crazy, right? I shouldn't have done this. I mean, this is crazy, right?" Ashni paced her small sitting room. *Why did I think this was a good idea?*

"No, this is good," Adira said from her space at a desk, going through a list they had.

Ashni's face scrunched up. "You sure? I mean, do people do this?" She felt like no one did this. This was her own little unique bit of madness.

"People don't do it, but that's what makes it good. You'll see tomorrow when it happens. When are you going to have her outfit delivered?"

"In the morning. I'm going to tell her it's for meeting my mother."

Adira nodded. "Is your mother here yet?"

"She should be within the hour. Layla rode out to meet her."

"Little brothers with her?"

"Last I heard. Think the twins are still cute?"

"Considering what I've seen Layla, Nakia, Naren, and Hafiz do at this age, no. There's no way they're close to cute, especially if your mother taught them witchcraft."

Ashni couldn't argue. "I'm pretty sure she did, but then again, she taught us all a little. Apparently, they just find it more interesting than the rest of us. So, is everything in place?"

"We're good to go whenever you are. Keep her away from the main garden until it's time."

Ashni scrubbed her face with her hands and sighed. Keeping Nakia away from stuff was difficult. "Why couldn't we just get Bashira to take her shopping again?"

"She's not going to keep going shopping. Bashira said she didn't want to do it the other day when your brothers arrived."

Ashni groaned. "Those two. They have such nerve!"

"At least they didn't try to kill you."

"Such a small favor. They're more secure in their positions than damned Amal. It's a lot easier to be first and second than third."

Adira waved the matter off. "Don't worry about it. Let's get this out of the way and then worry about the other things later."

Ashni nodded. She wanted to make sure everything was perfect for tomorrow. So, until her mother arrived, she checked, double-checked, and triple-checked everything. Butterflies flitted around in her stomach. She wanted to vomit them up. Despite Adira assuring her so many times that this was good and romantic and great, she felt like it was the dumbest idea she ever had and that said a lot.

"Adira told me you were pacing."

Ashni gasped and turned at the sound of her mother's voice. Her pacing had traveled from the small room to one of the gardens, but she kept glancing at the main garden. Just the thought made it feel like her guts were going to fall out of her body.

"Mommy, when did you get here?" *Shit! I was supposed to greet her.* She then winced as she realized she said 'mommy' instead of 'mom.' Standing before her mother took her right back to her childhood.

Chandra gave her a small smile with pale, pink lips. Her mother often reminded her of someone who was freezing. She was even cold to the touch, like the northern frost was etched in her bones. But there was also a warmth about her. Ashni sometimes felt like it lived inside of her, too, but she didn't want it to. A warrior wasn't supposed to have the warmth of an embrace inside of her.

"Not too long ago. Adira showed me the space. It's beautiful." Chandra's smile grew and her eyes twinkled.

Ashni frowned and folded her hands across her stomach. "You don't think it's stupid?"

Chandra shrugged, her white and gold robes swishing from the movement. "You know her better than I do."

Ashni sucked her teeth. They had spoken about this so often, but she still wasn't sure if a surprise was the way to go. She wanted something no one had ever done. Adira promised her every single time they had a meeting, no one had ever done this. *Because it's stupid and you're an ass.*

"How are you feeling, Ashni?" Chandra tilted her head. She had to be careful or her crown, a golden eagle design studded with priceless gems, would slide off.

"Stressed," Ashni replied before she could think. She scowled. "Don't work your witchcraft on me."

Chandra rolled her eyes. "Yes, because we both know you'd never admit the truth to me. Would it make you feel better to know I cast bones for you?"

Ashni frowned even deeper. "No. I need you to not do things to draw attention to me. I've been blessed by the gods and I'm good with what I've been given. I don't want them to think I'm dissatisfied in any way, so don't look into my future. It doesn't help that my last few sacrifices have been in Adira's honor rather than theirs, which I'm sure the gods aren't happy about."

"Adira does a great deal for you. I'm sure they'll understand. Why do you fear losing their favor? You told me before you thought they cast you out of their grace. I don't understand why. Life isn't as easy as it used to be? Life isn't meant to be easy when you're destined for greatness, when you're building something that'll outlast all of us."

Ashni ran her hands through her hair. "It used to be."

"It was easy for your father at first as well."

"And then he met you?"

Chandra chuckled. "Indeed. Maybe it's because I was the first thing he couldn't just bowl over, and at first, he questioned why the gods would give him these emotions for me. I did the same. We started out the worst for each other, toxic, poisonous until we learned to navigate each other and found we coexisted better than we ever did floating alone. You couldn't bowl over Nakia, could you?"

Ashni shook her head. "That's none of your business."

Chandra reached out and caressed her cheek. Because her mother ran both hot and cold, it was always strange to experience her touch. There was an initial chill followed by soft flare under the skin. The sensation calmed Ashni and reminded her of happier times, times when she was too small to hug her mother anywhere but around the waist, times when her father was there, and times when she didn't know her older brothers wouldn't be there for her the way she'd been taught a family should be.

"Your father would be so proud of you right now. Well, he'd make fun of you, but he'd be so proud." Chandra chuckled.

Ashni scoffed. "He is in the Heavens right now, laughing and joking with all the gods about this, especially since I can't figure out if it's stupid or not."

"He doesn't have the right to laugh. He knows what happened to him on his own special day."

"I'm not going to the surgeons at the end of the night." At least she could be confident about that.

"I doubt you are." Chandra stepped closer. The long, flowing white robes she wore always made it seem like she hovered. Her pale skin made her seem so much like a ghost. "Your father would be proud of you for everything, but this would be the biggest. You know how he felt about family."

Ashni scratched her eyebrow. "And I count?"

Chandra frowned. "Of course. Don't you dare believe any of that venom Amal spouted. You are the child of the Amir, not just in blood, but in legacy. And, I promise you, even if it wasn't in blood, he'd choose you out of a hundred thousand children and he'd love you just as he did. And trust me, disguised as your father or not, there's no way the storm god could've fooled me."

Ashni shook her head. "I know you'd never be fooled by anyone pretending to be Dad."

Her mother wore all white always as a sign of mourning. White, the color of death, she'd wear it until her own funeral. She respected her mother more than words could express just for honoring her father in such a way. Bonds didn't have to be blood. Amal proved blood meant nothing sometimes. Connections went deeper than blood. *Layla taught me that.*

"You know, it doesn't bother me about the blood. I know Dad chose me and that's all that matters. I am his daughter. No matter what." Ashni knew that, but saying it aloud fortified her in a way she hadn't expected. She was connected to her father in ways her brothers could only dream of.

Chandra gave her a gentle pat on the shoulder. "Blood doesn't mean family all the time. You have bonded to a good family. You're growing that family."

"Dad will be here, won't he?" She needed her father to see this moment, even if it was from the afterlife.

Chandra smiled. "He wouldn't dare miss it. After all, I have to die eventually. If I get to him and find out he missed it, he'll be looking to get reincarnated to escape my wrath."

Ashni finally smiled. Tears pricked her eyes, but she could cry later, when her mother wasn't right there to tease her. Her mother gave her another pat on the shoulder.

"Come. You have a wedding to attend and no princess deserves to be kept waiting."

Chapter Nineteen

NAKIA WAS QUITE NERVOUS about meeting Empress Chandra. Ashni hadn't helped prepare her, too busy in whatever project she had going on, so Nakia didn't know what was expected of her. This was Ashni's mother and ruler of about half the known world as far as Nakia understood. There had to be all types of ceremony and tradition to go with this, like when she formally met Samar and Badar, Layla's parents. The only help Ashni had been was to have a dress delivered to her.

"Highness, please, we must begin to dress you." The servants rushed about, fluttering around the rooms in ways she had never seen.

Nakia turned her eyes to her outfit, more fabric than she was used to. There was so much teal, gold, and red. Servants kept coming in with jewels and gems that went with it. Then there were so many shoes. She couldn't remember a time Ashni even suggested what sort of footwear she should use to meet someone. Empress Chandra had to be even bigger than she thought. *I have to do everything right.*

"Would it be too presumptuous for me to wear pearls?" Nakia had worn them on many occasions, but they were for royalty. Yes, everyone around saw her as Ashni's consort, but that wasn't official and she wasn't sure how Empress Chandra would take it.

"Of course not."

Not expecting an answer, especially not from an unfamiliar voice, Nakia jumped and turned. An unknown woman, dressed all in white, stood before her. She looked almost ethereal with skin so pale, it could rival the most polished pearl. Nakia knew her, even without her saying. She knew those eyes, had seen them in painting, mosaics, and tapestries.

"Empress!" Nakia quickly ducked into a bow.

"Stand, child. You're my daughter's consort. No need to stand on ceremony for me," Chandra said.

Nakia did as ordered. Her heart hammered in her chest. *I'm not ready for this.* She didn't know any of the rituals that went with meeting Empress Chandra. "I don't...I don't..." Her mouth and brain refused to work together. "I'm getting ready to meet you."

Delight danced in the empress' faded green eyes. "Oh, well, we'll pretend we didn't meet to save face, but I wanted to see you as soon as possible. I can help. We'll decide on the best arrangement, and you can impress Ashni that you knew exactly what to wear to meet me. Of course, as soon as I express any praise, she'll act upset. She might think I've tainted you."

Nakia swallowed down a lump in her throat. "Tainted me?"

Chandra chuckled. It was a surprisingly light sound for someone so intense. "Don't worry. She just hates when I approve of anything she does. Or at least, she likes to pretend she does. On the inside, when I tell her how well she's chosen, she'll preen more than the happiest eagle. You are her sun, after all."

A blush burned Nakia's cheeks. The empress seemed to know more about her than she knew about Empress Chandra. It was nice to know she was liked already, but it didn't calm her nerves.

"Samar wrote me after you had dinner with her family. She told me how much she liked the way Ashni acted with you. So, I don't want you to be nervous."

Nakia swallowed again. "A way to make me less nervous is to not bring up Samar again." Every time she went to their villa—compound really, hosting all of the Shadow Walkers of Khenshu—Samar watched her like she could see under Nakia's skin. Of course, she looked at everyone that way, but it was unsettling.

Chandra laughed. "Yes, she can be unnerving, but you call her Samar, so that's a good sign. She and I took a while to warm to each other as well. I always feared she was trying to steal my daughter, but we've learned to share. She thinks highly of you. I'll think highly of you as well. You're my daughter now."

"I am?" Nakia squeaked.

Chandra smiled. "You are. So, first things first, you're to call me Chandra, if not Mom."

Nakia could only nod. She hadn't expected Chandra to take to her so easily. Even though in the year, she had gotten used to the idea of same-sex couples, she still got her fair share of flack, of grumbling, and harsh whispers for being an outsider. She often expected anyone she met from the Empire to do the same, but Chandra was all smiles and softness for her.

"Now, let's get you ready." Chandra touched her shoulder.

An intense cold ran through Nakia at her touch, but the most wonderful relaxing heat followed it. She remembered Chandra practiced witchcraft, so that might have had something to do with it, but she felt like it didn't. From the stories she heard, she knew Chandra had to be special to catch and keep the attention of Amir Khalid and to keep up with him.

Nakia felt it was best to go along with Chandra. Soon, she was caught up in fine fabric and jewels on her head. Chandra didn't pick out any bracelets or bangles, though. *Weird.* Maybe she didn't like that, which might explain why Ashni lived for them when she wasn't in battle. One day Ashni wore bangles halfway up her forearms.

"Hey, kitten, what's the holdup?" Layla's obnoxious voice called out before she came into the room.

Nakia scowled. "I told you not to call me that, Princess!"

"Hey, don't use my title to mock me!" Layla came into view and jumped. "Oh, sorry, Empress." She bowed to Chandra.

Chandra waved the whole thing off. "You don't have to be formal, Layla. Don't make me have a conversation with your parents about how you're calling me empress again."

Layla went stiff. "Can we please leave my parents out of things? My father already has me training students since I'm in the city. My mother has me reading all of these old religious books about the Darkness. I don't need them to give me more chores."

"Then, stop being so formal." Chandra held her arms open and Layla wasted no time giving her a hug.

Nakia didn't expect this, but she liked it. Chandra kissed the side of Layla's head and Nakia wasn't sure she had ever seen Layla smile quite so brightly. "What are you doing here?"

Layla threw her hands up. "I was supposed to come get you, but as usual, Empress Chandra does what she wants. So, I guess I'll just go make sure everything's ready to transport you."

"Transport me? Where are we going? I thought this was all happening here."

Layla shook her head. "Nope. It all has to do with ceremony."

Nakia arched an eyebrow. "Even though I've already technically met her?"

Layla scoffed. "You have to do it in front of the Court, obviously. This doesn't count. You look nice, though."

Nakia glared at Layla. "Why are you being nice?"

Layla blew out a raspberry. "Empress Chandra is here. Respect."

Chandra rolled her eyes. "I've already heard about you two getting on about as much as a pair of rabid dogs, so don't bother to pretend on my account."

"Anyway, everything's all set up, so don't give the servants any guff when they anoint you with oils and put you on the palanquin, okay? Definitely don't give any of the priests and priestesses a hard time when they walk with the palanquin and pray around you, for you, about you. Darkness knows you need it." Layla was gone before Nakia could answer.

Nakia glanced at Chandra. "Is all that necessary to meet you a second time?"

"It's all necessary. Tradition, ritual, and such. It'll be fine." Chandra patted her shoulder as if the simple touch would make it so.

Nakia took a breath. "I think I'm ready."

"That you are. Do you know Ashni's like her father?"

Nakia arched an eyebrow. "In what way?"

"She'll set off to conquer the world for the adventure of it, but she'll give it to you as a gift."

"I know." Nakia smiled. She knew Ashni would pull down the stars for her if she asked.

Chandra grinned. "Then she's taking the best of care of you. Please, continue to support her. Especially when she realizes how much she has conquered and it needs to be maintained. You need to be prepared to govern when she lays the world at your feet and looks at you with panicked eyes, because who knew you actually had to link places you conquered and treat them a certain way to maintain them."

Nakia nodded. "I'm learning."

"Good." Chandra caressed her cheek. The same sensations as before raced through Nakia and she settled. "You might end up being my favorite of my children's spouses. Of course, it's hard to top Najiba. Fahim found the literal other half of his soul with her. It's almost strange and I say this as someone whose spouse was almost like an inverse image of myself."

Nakia nodded. She knew of Fahim. He was the brother right under Ashni. He had a large bit of territory and only seemed interested in governing it and learning about everything. He was an expert in science, math, alchemy, and philosophy, and his spouse, Najiba, was interested in the same. Ashni was certain when they had children, their children would figure out how to dismantle the whole world, but they'd put it back together again when they were done. *What will Ashni and I do about children?*

"Please, be good to my daughter."

"I strive to do my best by her."

Sometimes, Ashni made it hard because she always seemed like she could do everything. But, there were moments, times, instances, when Ashni looked like she had the weight of the world on her shoulders and Nakia was the only one who could lift it off. She'd do that for the rest of their lives.

"Then, my dearest daughter, I'll see you out there." Chandra gave her wink and rushed off.

Nakia felt like that was a little strange to have her dart off so quickly. She stepped out of her room to see the palanquin waiting for her. It was like something out of a royal's dream. Large enough for two, it was gold with silk cloth hanging from the top. She allowed the servants to spray her with different oils and then sat down on the cushion inside the palanquin and was carried off. Priests and priestess followed, chanting prayers Nakia had never heard while ringing bells and waving incense. Admittedly, she wasn't deep into the Roshan religion, but it seemed like a little much to meet Empress Chandra.

***

Ashni kneeled on the platform, trying not to pick at her finest teal and gold robes. Earlier she almost pulled an emerald off of the inner robe, needing something to keep her fingers busy. She wouldn't make that mistake again. Nervous didn't even begin to cover it, but it was an eager nervousness. She should've done this months ago. She looked down the way to the entrance of the palace from the garden and took a deep breath to calm her heart. This was worse than riding into battle in the freezing north.

"Calm down, sweetheart," Chandra said as she came up behind Ashni.

Ashni jumped. "Damn it! Make some noise every now and then, woman." Her mother floated, never walked, she had been convinced of that her entire life.

Chandra smiled. "Why? It's how I used to catch you kids always being where you weren't supposed to be."

Ashni opened her mouth, a brilliant retort on the tip of her tongue, but then Nakia entered and all words and thoughts fled her mind. Her heart skipped a beat, hearing the bells of the palanquin ring out with each step, each second bringing Nakia closer. Ashni stood as servants set the palanquin on the platform. Servants took the top off of the litter and then helped Ashni to sit by Nakia's side.

"Ashni, what's going on?" Nakia whispered.

Ashni licked her lips. "A surprise wedding." Like so many times before, saying it aloud made it seem both idiotic and brilliant. This moment would prove which one it was.

Nakia blinked. "A surprise..." She looked out into the audience. With luck, she spotted her older sister, Thia, quite the supportive ally. The other sister, not so much thanks to Ferox's iron grip. He was still on the run, but if this wedding went well, Ashni planned on her first anniversary gift to be reuniting Nakia with Saffi. Dorian was there, too, but in chains and watched by several guards. Ashni just wanted him to see he couldn't stop her.

"Yes, a surprise wedding." *Please, don't think it's stupid. Please, don't run away.*

"For us?" Nakia's eyes were wide and wet. If she cried, her kohl makeup would run, but Ashni didn't care.

A light, nearly hysterical laugh escaped Ashni. "Of course for us." Nakia bit her lip. "Now?"

"Yes, now. Right now actually if we just turn and face each other and my mother can start the ceremony."

"I really want to kiss you right now." Nakia grinned.

"You could do that all you want after the ceremony," Chandra said.

Nakia jumped, like she hadn't even noticed Chandra there. They turned to each other and Chandra began, calling on the gods to recognize the union between Ashni and Nakia. *The gods never abandoned me,* Ashni realized. She might've lost their favor or maybe they tested her, but they were with her. *How could I not have at least the gods' blessings to be sitting here with my perfect match and being linked in marriage?*

She never heard her mother's voice, lost in Nakia's eyes. Nakia never broke eye contact with her, not until Chandra took their hands with her own and pressed their palms together. Ashni blushed at the mental slip. Chandra tied a teal ribbon around their hands down to their wrists and sprinkled their joined hands and faces with sacred water as she chanted prayers along with several priests and priestesses behind her. When her mother slipped identical golden bangles on their wrists, the ceremony was complete. The audience erupted into cheers.

"Are we married now?" Nakia asked.

Ashni grinned. "We are. You're officially my spouse, my consort, as promised."

Nakia squealed and tossed herself at Ashni. The feeling of holding her spouse, Ashni couldn't describe it with a thousand words. She had conquered so much, could even be considered a liberator by some, but none of that compared to holding Nakia.

"I'll give the world to you," Ashni promised.

Nakia shook her head. "I already have everything I want." She kissed Ashni with love and passion. It was like the sun rising in Ashni's soul, a brand new day, a promise of something great. The audience applauded even louder.

Ashni pulled away. "I'll give you the world anyway." After all, there was always conquest to be had.

Warrior Class – Blood Rain

This is the final book of Warrior Class. Ashni and Nakia work on establishing their kingdom in the West. When Ashni takes ill under mysterious circumstances, Nakia has to go through a trial by fire in leadership to hold their territory together. When it's all said and done, the West (and the world) might escape being called Roshan.

Chapter One

THE SMELL OF THE library never failed to set Nakia Akshay at ease and it was only a recent love she acquired. *How did I not know how amazing books are until a couple of years ago?* Being surrounded by so much knowledge, all at her fingertips made her giddy sometimes. She giggled in a way that was probably inappropriate for the royal consort of the ruler of the largest territory in the Roshan Empire. She could not help herself. Besides, her spouse would love to hear the sound of her happiness and would delight in knowing how much Nakia enjoyed the library.

Sighing, Nakia snuggled into her chaise, which was tucked into a quiet corner of the library. The low lounge was backed with fluffy pillows, giving her optimum comfort. The space was nice and warm thanks to it being a gorgeous day outside. Any other time, she probably would have been outside, but she was in a reading mood. It was a new feeling and she loved it, making sure to nurture the desire whenever it popped up.

She had a stack of tomes and scrolls by her along with the book in her hands. Roshan history was her current craving. She always came back to it, but every now and then strayed to other subjects. Everything was so fascinating.

"Why am I not surprised to find you here?" Saniyah Gyan, her spouse's most brilliant, chief weapons engineer, asked as she moved around a shelf and stepped into view. She regarded Nakia with warm eyes and an amused smile on her lips, but Nakia knew there was a plot behind the kind expression. She stood out in her vibrant colors against all the shades of brown in the library.

Nakia grinned, even though there had to be trouble afoot. "If my spouse has spent the last three years putting together this grand library for me, wouldn't it be rude of me not to spend time here?" The library was a wonderful gift that kept on giving. It grew a little every day. There was no way Nakia would be able to enjoy the whole place in her lifetime, but she would try.

Saniyah's smile deepened and their eyes met. It was a warm, even loving smile, as it often was when she discovered Nakia in the library. Nakia learned over time how much Saniyah respected knowledge and education. She did not suffer fools, but a stupid fool was the worst. She made it a point for Nakia to understand how much and how far simple competence in an area would carry her.

Saniyah's eyes drifted around the library, focusing for a long moment out a window on the back wall. Sunlight from outside poured in as if calling attention to this haven. "Your spouse also gave you a grand city."

Nakia nodded. "Yes, she did, and I enjoy it as much as I do the library." *She's trying to get me out of the library. What book do I have that she wants?* She tried to mentally go through her list, but there were so many. *So, don't let her distract you. Protect your horde like the Roshan would.*

"When you're not locked away in the library."

"Whose fault is that? I do believe both our spouses lay the blame squarely at your feet."

Saniyah chuckled, a light, airy sound that settled Nakia when she first accepted Saniyah as part of her life. "What can I say, I'm a great role model." She flipped her long blond hair over her shoulder.

Nakia did not dispute that, eternally grateful for the moment

Saniyah decided to help her understand what it meant to be the spouse of a powerful figure in the Roshan Empire. The education was necessary, and it was good she did not have to trouble Ashni over it. Ashni had enough to worry about with conquering the west.

Saniyah showed her how to be the spouse of a queen without losing herself or the things Ashni loved about her. Saniyah helped her understand issues she would face being married to Ashni and how she should deal with those matters. One of the most whispered matters to come up had to do with her being an outsider and Saniyah helped her navigate that, with some suggestions from her spouse, General Adira Gyan.

Saniyah also introduced her to her second favorite place on the planet, the library. The only place better than the library was Ashni's arms. Saniyah's estate back in Khenshu had a library beyond imagination and she walked Nakia around it more than once as if it held secrets of the universe. Saniyah moved most of it with her across the sea, but often found herself in Nakia's library where there was a wider variety of knowledge.

"And because I'm a great role model and a great aunt, I'm here to remind you that you're supposed to have lunch with Bashira. She refuses to come searching for you again." Saniyah gave her a stern look.

Nakia winced. "I lost track of time again. I'm still trying to understand the early history of the Roshan nomads. The clans are difficult to pin down and it's still unclear how Ashni's great grandfather was able to rise in his clan and unite the others." She had read so much and still did not understand how Ashni's family ended up in the position they did. Ashni was of little help, even though she was quite the Roshan historian. Ashni just did not have the same questions as Nakia.

Saniyah offered her a small smile for her troubles. "I'm sure you'll figure it out, but not in this one sitting. Go to your lunch. Bashira mentioned your sisters will be there."

Nakia yelped and leaped to her feet. "That's right! Has Ashni received Wicus and Thia yet?" If she missed that, she would never forgive herself. The Court would whisper about it for days as well.

Saniyah waved her hand. "No. Adira told me they're going to formally receive your sisters tomorrow since you have your lunch and they're going to take Wicus to the arena and enjoy a spectacle or two. Apparently, those things are more important than decorum."

Nakia shrugged. "Wicus didn't object." Besides, their spouses were more about decorum when it suited them than any other time.

Wicus was a devoted ally, even though he did not want to concede his territory was pretty much part of Ashni's territory. Wicus' city, Valen, was surrounded on all sides by Ashni's land. He liked to pretend he had autonomy and Ashni allowed the pretense, but Wicus could not make a move without Ashni's say so. It did not matter, though. Ashni treated him as family, something like a brother, so everything was civil. He and Thia visited often, so the relationship only grew as time went on.

Nakia had no choice. She had to leave. Now, it was clear why Saniyah strolled into the library looking like mischief personified. She held up a finger as she stared Saniyah down. "Don't take my books." It was not unheard of Saniyah to let Nakia hunt for works and wait for Nakia to become distracted. Saniyah would walk off with many of them, searching for new weapon ideas or learning of old battles to see what her spouse might come up against in the field.

Saniyah pressed her palms together. "Considering this is your personal library, I can't help but take your books."

Nakia's face fell into a deadpan. "You know what I mean." Yes, it was her personal library, but she left it open to anyone close to her.

Saniyah grinned. "Do I?"

Nakia pointed to her pile of books. "Those specific pieces are off limits. Do not touch them." She wagged her finger to let Saniyah know how serious she was.

Saniyah's eyebrows furrowed up. "Why? You can't possibly read them all at once. Would you even notice if I left with one?"

"No, but I'll notice if you leave with five, which would be if I'm lucky. I found these books." Nakia tapped herself in the chest. Her books would vanish with Saniyah the second she left them unguarded.

Saniyah smiled at Nakia, bright and beautiful, a promise those books would be gone the second she left. She could not do anything about that. She needed to see her sisters and best friend. She gave Saniyah a hard look before walking off, which did nothing to change the smile on Saniyah's face. Before Nakia left the library, she instructed a servant to go to her area and gather her books. If the servant acted fast enough, she would not have to spend tomorrow finding new pieces. With that out of the way, she rushed through the palace, not wanting to be late for her own lunch date.

Hurrying through her partially completed home, Nakia could not help taking in some of the art as she zipped by frescos and tapestries, depicting a multitude of stories, which she had learned to appreciate. There was a mix of religious stories from both Kairon and the Roshan.

Her favorite, like much of the Empire, was the story of Ashni's parents and it was told in several different areas across mediums.

Nakia patronized many different artists to tell her and Ashni's story. Nakia worked hard to normalize their relationship in Kairon, to get Westerners used to seeing two women together, happy like any other couple, and doing things they were often told women could not do. There were plays, stories, and art of all types showing, promoting, and embracing same sex relationships. Beyond her own, Nakia patronized art throughout the territory depicting Roshan same sex couples' love stories and adventures. There were no shortages of such tales and they were growing in popularity among people who did not quite fit in with Kairon's strict society.

Nakia had to dodge many people in her mad dash. The palace was always a hive of activity. It did not help that it was still under construction, as was the city. This was *home*. Their western capital, but it actually used to be home even before it became *home*.

The city was once known as Phyllida, but Ashni changed the name for several reasons once it fell under her control. It was now Nakian, a reminder to the people of why it was still standing after the way their former king behaved toward the Roshan, especially toward Ashni. While Ashni never had plans to destroy the city, she could have, but she would rather give it to Nakia.

The gesture still made Nakia's heart flutter. It reminded her of what Ashni's mother told her when they met; Ashni would conquer the world and give it to Nakia as a gift. Ashni tried to rename all of Kairon after her, tried to gift the whole territory to her, but Nakia objected. That was too much.

"You made it," Bashira said the moment Nakia stepped into the lush eastern garden. The smell of mint and mist greeted her. There were fountains to keep the area cool, but also made the whole place shine when the sunlight hit it properly. It was like walking into a place for the gods or great heroes.

Nakia smiled as she stepped close and greeted her dearest friend with a kiss on her cheek. "Of course I did. You didn't even have to send someone to find me this time."

Bashira scoffed. "Because my aunt was already headed to the library." She looped her arm around Nakia's and walked her to the lunch area.

"Nakia, we feared you forgot us!" Thia climbed to her feet, rising with all the elegance and grace of a queen, and her smile beamed at her younger sister.

"How could I? This is our first lunch with Saffi." Nakia's eyes fell to her other sister. She smiled so hard at Saffi it hurt her face but filled her heart with joy.

Saffi rose to her feet. She was not as graceful as Thia and did not stand with the same posture as Thia and Nakia. Her brown eyes sparkled, but the light was new and helped display age lines on her face. She seemed worn, older than Thia, even though Thia had a couple of years on her. Time with them should remedy that, or so Nakia had been told by others.

Saffi wore Roshan attire, like Nakia, which Nakia delighted in. She wanted her sisters to embrace her and her adopted culture. Saffi adorned herself in Roshan fashion for a similar reason to Nakia. She viewed the Roshan as her saviors. Ashni rescued her from her husband, Ferox, a wild man king who foolishly stood against Ashni and the Roshan.

Ferox put himself in Ashni's line of fire first by aiding Dorian, Nakia's father, and standing against Ashni. Then, he ran after she made a fool of him in battle. He probably thought he got away or she forgot about him as she conquered more of Kairon, but it was really that his kingdom was too far at first. That changed a year ago. Ashni's army made it close enough to his land and also found a purpose for what most of Kairon thought was a wasteland. As it turned out, it was a great place for rice fields. That was enough for Ashni, who conquered it with glee, and was all too happy to defeat Ferox and his prized chariots. When it was all said and done, Ashni brought Saffi to Nakia, reuniting the sisters. It was slow going to build a relationship, more because Saffi had been through so much than anything else.

Saffi bowed her head to Nakia and Nakia grabbed her into a hug. "Please, we're sisters. You have to stop bowing."

"I'm sorry. This is still so incredible. Never in my wildest dreams did I think I'd be able to see you both again," Saffi said, her voice low. It was like that whenever she spoke, like she had been trained to whisper, like her voice did not matter. She glanced back between Nakia and Thia.

Thia smiled as she reached out, stroking Saffi's cheek. "I'm happy for it. I worried over you." She embraced Saffi and then pulled Nakia into the hug. "I worried for you as well. Our father didn't do right by either of you."

None of them could argue that. Saffi got the worst of it, though, which was probably their father's intent. Saffi's time with Ferox had not been kind and it turned out it was not even him. His other wives had tormented and tortured Saffi. Saffi had not opened up much about it, but it was clear she had been at the bottom tier with Ferox's wives because she had not produced a child.

"Let's eat." Nakia motioned to their lunch set up.

Lunch was set up in a Roshan style, pillows for them around food trays on low tables. There was an umbrella shading them from the radiant sun. The spread was a mix of Roshan and Kairon foods, which Nakia always did when she set up for a meal. They settled on their pillows, all close to each other. Bashira sat by Nakia and Saffi sat on the other side of her. Thia was close to Saffi.

"How long will you be here, Thia?" Bashira asked. She was very familiar with Thia after moving to the West with Saniyah two years ago. Saniyah wanted to be close to her spouse and Bashira wanted to be with her aunts.

Thia studied the food for a moment. "I believe we'll be here for the rest of the month. Wicus wants to discuss the trade routes and Ashni had a matter."

"It's probably the tribes across the river," Nakia said. The tribes up north, across the Great River Reve, were giving Ashni, Adira, and Layla fits. Ashni did not even want to expand across the river. It was too cold for her liking, but the northerners did not know that. They raided towns and villages in Roshan territory, making pests of themselves. They needed to be stopped, but they were spread to the point Ashni wanted as many soldiers at her disposal as possible to take them out at roughly the same time.

"So, an invasion?" Thia arched an eyebrow.

Nakia shook her head. An invasion implied plans to stay. "Nothing of the sort. Just getting the tribes to stay on their side of the river."

Thia let loose a delicate snort. "We all know they won't stay on their side. They want all of the new, shiny goods in Kairon."

Bashira waved her hands around. "Can you two save this for when you're sitting in the meeting with your spouses and generals and such?"

Nakia laughed. "Sorry. That was rude." She glanced at Saffi, whose head was down. While this was annoying for Bashira, who simply had no desire to hear about military matters, it was foreign to Saffi, who did not have the type of spouse who shared any information with her as theirs did.

"Very. Forgive us." Thia bowed her head.

"You can sit in on meetings and discuss what the army is doing?"

Saffi asked.

Nakia nodded. "We can bring you too, if you like." She recalled reigning had actually been an interest for Saffi. It was one of the biggest divides between her and their father as she would challenge his decisions and how dare she do such a thing as far as he was concerned. He always wanted Saffi to stay in a woman's place and she never seemed to know what that meant or where it was.

The color left Saffi's already ashen face and Nakia hated to imagine what her life had to be like with the Tyrans. It would seem they broke Saffi. That would not do. She would devote time to Saffi and rebuild her the moment Saffi allowed it.

"We should go shopping," Bashira said. Not the most subtle change of topic, but it was safe.

"Don't you have a show you're doing?" Nakia asked, as that was more interesting than shopping to her now.

Bashira's face lit up and she clapped. "You can all come! It's a wonderful show if I do say so myself."

"I still can't believe you're allowed to be in shows. And dancing of all things," Thia said.

"I still can't believe you refuse to come see me. Nakia will tell you. I'm quite good," Bashira replied.

"She's not lying or boasting." Nakia reached for some dates. They used to be considered a delicacy, but since trade opened up with the East, they were easier to get. "She is quite good. Her friends in her troupe are all nice as well."

Thia scoffed as she finally settled on having ginger cookies. They were also from the East. "They're obligated to be nice to you," she said with a smirk.

Nakia laughed. "I wish that was the case. I've had diplomats sit across from me with Ashni three seconds away from burning their cities to the ground and they'll treat me like I'm lower than dirt."

"And then you still talk them into an impossible deal and save their cities," Thia said.

Nakia did not dispute that. Technically, her sister could be considered the first to fall victim to her. She had done that to Wicus and Thia. No, they did not look down on her, but they had underestimated her early on when Ashni sent her to hammer out the details of their alliance. But, now was not the time for that. She swung the conversation back to Bashira and they enjoyed the good food and warm weather.

***

Ashni typically did not mind relaxing or spending the day watching matches at the arena, but there was so much to do. Sitting in the arena, while she was supposed to be watching rather important matches, all she could think about was half the seats were empty because those sections of the building were not done. Even as she, Adira, and Wicus made their way back to the palace, all Ashni could see were the things in the city that needed to be taken care of. Temples were barely up. In fact, every temple they passed was under construction. There was no theater yet. Shows were put on in tents and some streets were unpaved. They cut through the marketplace, which was small, especially compared to Khenshu.

Ashni wanted Nakian to become Khenshu's sister city. Nakian had a long way to go, not enough temples, the palace was still a work in progress, and the city was a fraction of the size she had planned. It would take time to become what she wanted, but it would take longer if she was out lazing about. A city named for her spouse needed to be as spectacular as her spouse.

"The city has become quite a crossroads. I see so many Roshan influences," Wicus said as they walked through the crowd. He used to complain about walking among the commoners until he realized it was a thing Ashni did and would not stop to accommodate him.

"Things are coming along," Ashni replied. The city was very much Roshan meets Kairon, East meets West, and Ashni wanted it to stay that way. She liked that both she and Wicus blended in, even though she was dressed in Roshan attire while Wicus had on the robes of someone from Kairon. The mix was all around them.

Wicus had to split a wooden pole with Ashni as they walked. "Then we'll be able to get more goods into Valen?"

Ashni sighed. "I thought we were waiting for tomorrow to discuss business. Our spouses would have our heads if we did this without them." Not to mention Layla was not there. She would never hear the end of it if she discussed business without her sister.

Wicus nodded and the matter was dropped. Ashni liked that he respected Thia so much. She had not come across much of that in Kairon. The concept of men being above women was not new to her, but it never failed to set her on edge. Any society that valued appearance over talent did that to her.

They continued on before Wicus cut into the silence again. "That arena was a work of art. What were those matches we watched again?" He liked to make conversation. It gave him ample opportunity to be charming. He could not help himself.

"We got lucky today. Those matches were for joining warrior guilds," Ashni replied. It would only be a matter of time for those who won their matches today would end up in the military, helping her take more of the West when she was ready. For the moment, she needed to shore up her power in conquered territory.

Wicus arched an eyebrow." A warrior guild?"

Ashni took a breath. *How to explain this to someone not from the Empire?* "There are four warrior guilds in the Roshan society. You join one and those are your partners for life. We respect all warriors, of course, but the members of your own guild are special to you."

"So, which are you?" Wicus asked.

Ashni was about to question his eyesight, certain her guild was obvious. But he did not know about the warrior guilds. This was all new to him, even though she had introduced guilds to the West two years ago when she paused her conquest to establish herself and her spouse.

"I'm of the Lion guild, as is Adira," Ashni answered.

Wicus nodded. "So, to become a member of your guild, I would have to kill a lion in the arena?"

Adira snorted. "If only it was so easy."

Ashni touched a lion's tooth around her neck. No, the trial to join a guild was much more ruthless than simply killing a beast in the arena. Despite being proud of her guild, what it took to join would always leave a mark. That was why all big cats were to be respected and treated well in her land. It was the least she could do.

"You don't think I could do it?" Wicus asked, a daring glint in his eye.

Ashni spoke up before Adira insulted the man. "I don't doubt you could. I'm not sure you'd want to. You noticed everyone we saw was a teenager, right?"

"Yes."

"There's a reason for it. You're hungrier to prove yourself. When you're an established warrior and commander, it's a little harder. It takes more of a toll on you." It took a toll no matter what, but if she did it now, after all her experience, it would come across as senseless. "If it's really something you want, I'll arrange it." The guilds helped Ashni's popularity in the West. Social mobility gave her the masses. For a person who had nothing, joining a warrior guild was like suddenly gaining fame and fortune. Joining the military was the same. It gave people who had nothing something and that was worth keeping, worth fighting for. Ashni was worth fighting for. The Empire was worth fighting for.

Wicus nodded and squared his shoulders. "I have to discuss it with Thia."

Ashni and Adira laughed. "This is why you're our ally." Ashni patted him on the shoulder.

"You're definitely one of us," Adira said.

Wicus smiled at this, his eyes twinkling. "Not a bad place to be."

The trio made their way back to the palace. Wicus went to check on his children. Ashni really admired that. Wicus was a good guy.

"Why aren't there more of him around here?" Ashni asked as she and Adira made their way to the throne room.

Adira shrugged. "Would make things too easy?"

"Probably." Ashni had not expected to like Wicus as much as she did, but it was a pleasant surprise. He really was family. Well, the right kind of family. Some of her actual family left a bad taste in her mouth. "Should we try to get some work done before tonight's feast or not?"

Adira squared her shoulders and smiled. "I really like how responsible you've become. There are some reports we could go over since your spouse is with her sisters and my spouse is doing research." That settled it.

***

While the feast last night was amazing, Ashni was glad to get to the business portion of Wicus' visit. If things went well, the rest of the visit could be friendly and calm. For now, a small meeting room held everyone necessary for the matter. Ashni settled on a pillow with Nakia pressed to her. To her right, Layla and Naren sat. To her left, Adira and her now second-in-command Hafiz Vivek. He had matured in the three years he had worked more closely with them. Ashni had to admit Adira picked well when she picked Hafiz.

"So, we want to discuss getting more trade into Valen," Wicus said, sitting across from Ashni and Nakia.

Ashni gave a shrug. "What's the issue? You have merchants coming into the city. You're getting goods from all over the Empire like everyone else."

Thia spoke up. "We get goods well after other cities. It's all leftover goods, if there's anything at all. Our nobles expected better, expected more. Where is the luxury? Where is the beauty? Where is the ease?"

Ashni rubbed her chin. "And I'm supposed to get merchants to you faster?" The fact that their nobles were up in arms because they could not be decadent was a waste of time. "You could easily remind your nobles where they would be without this trade deal."

Nakia patted her thigh. "Not helping."

"So, you want the merchants to come to you first?" Layla asked.

"It would calm down our nobles who think we made a mistake allying ourselves to you. We don't want them to have an excuse to start trouble, as we know we'll be the first to have to deal with any issues they start," Wicus replied.

"We were thinking maybe we could build a direct road from the eastern ports to Valen," Thia said.

Adira smirked. "You mean, you want us to build the road."

Wicus returned the expression. "You do have the money, manpower, and it's through your territory."

"That benefits us in no way," Ashni replied. It would cost them money and manpower that she could use to continue working on Nakian. Why waste it on them?

"What about your canal idea?" Nakia asked.

Ashni looked at her spouse. There was an idea. She had plans to build a canal system. Water was the fastest way to move things and her territory was quite vast now. If she wanted to keep it together and remain connected to the rest of the Empire, she needed to make sure she could move people and goods around quickly. A canal that connected to the rivers running through Kairon would be a good thing and had been a plan long before she took the West.

"A canal would be good if it's going to come to Valen," Thia said.

"In an ideal world, it would touch all major cities," Ashni replied.

"But, when would construction begin?" Wicus asked.

Ashni looked to Adira, who shrugged. "I've had my hands tied with our military. Ask your spouse." Adira pointed to Nakia.

"I've spoken to some engineers, but most of their attention is on the city and the palace," Nakia said.

"So, no canal?" Thia asked.

Ashni took a breath. "We'll start the canal." She needed something to make her start it, or it could end up being something she kept putting off.

"We need more than a start," Wicus said.

Ashni rubbed Nakia's shoulder for her attention. "Find or pull some engineers."

"And people to work on it." Nakia was technically in charge of the canal system anyway, as she handled most of their non-military infrastructure. It was a job she gave herself. Ashni did not argue it.

Ashni gave Wicus a look. "She's on it. It'll get done. Problem solved."

"Now, onto our business," Layla said, pressing her palms together.

"The northern barbarians," Wicus said.

"Yes. They've been coming across the river and terrorizing towns. We're going to march on them. I merely need to know you'll support us, as allies do," Ashni replied.

"That is our agreement. I feel you want more than that," Wicus said.

"For the moment, your support is fine. We'll work out the numbers and such now, if you like," Adira said.

"Proceed." Wicus motioned to Adira.

It was really all that was needed. Wicus would honor their agreement, but now Ashni would let Adira entice him with why he should fully commit to their cause. They would need his full army thanks to the tribes and northern borderland. Beyond that, they had to run strategies by him to find out if he felt he was capable. Fighting the tribes across the river would not be the open warfare he was accustomed to. Her new troops would have problems possibly. They had not done anything beyond open field combat. She frowned. What if she had expanded too far? She could not believe that to be true and she would not be stopped.

Available in 2020

About S. L Kassidy

What is there to know about me? Not much. I was born, bred, and raised in New York and I have no desire to live anywhere else. One day, I would like to travel to a few places, but for now I am content where I am.

I started out writing poetry in junior high and continued to do so for ten years. I wrote short stories, usually fantasy and romance stories, for my own entertainment throughout high school and college. Back then, I wrote strictly for me and those stories remain locked in the back of my closet in little notebooks, written in my almost unreadable, tiny handwriting. In between writing those stories and poetry, I managed to get a college degree in history.

After graduating college, I had a semester off before graduate school and I didn't really have anything to do with my time. So, I took a chance and wrote a fanfic and dared to upload it to the Internet. I was surprised that other people enjoyed my work and I've been posting ever since. I had quite a bit of fun with fan fiction and eventually decided to try my hand in original fiction. I suppose it was sort of like coming back around to what I had been doing in high school and college, except this time the stories were for whoever wanted to read them. I uploaded my first original story a few years ago and haven't looked back. I plan to continue writing as long as I continue getting ideas for stories and it continues to be fun.

Connect with ...

Email: slkassidy@gmail.com
Facebook: S.L. Kassidy

Note to Readers

Thank you for reading a book from Desert Palm Press. We have made every effort to edit this book. However, typos do slip in. If you find an error in the text, please email lee@desertpalmpress.com so the issue can be corrected.

We appreciate you as a reader and want to ensure you enjoy the reading process. We would like you to consider posting a review on your preferred media sites and/or your blog or website.

For more information on upcoming releases, author interviews, contest, giveaways and more, please sign up for our newsletter and visit us as at Desert Palm Press: www.desertpalmpress.com and "Like" us on Facebook: Desert Palm Press.

Bright Blessings

www.ingramcontent.com/pod-product-compliance
Lightning Source LLC
Chambersburg PA
CBHW051636260626
47170CB00004B/1202